THE R DOCUMENT

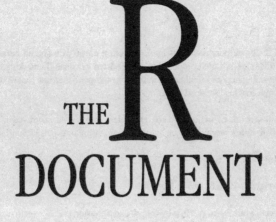

IRVING WALLACE

FORGE®

A TOM DOHERTY ASSOCIATES BOOK
NEW YORK

THE R DOCUMENT

Copyright © 1976 by Irving Wallace

Originally published in 1976 by Simon and Schuster.

A Forge Book
Published by Tom Doherty Associates, LLC
175 Fifth Avenue
New York, NY 10010

www.tor.com

Forge® is a registered trademark of Tom Doherty Associates, LLC.

ISBN 0-765-35447-0
EAN 978-0-765-35447-1

First Forge edition: May 2006

Printed in the United States of America

0 9 8 7 6 5 4 3 2 1

For Sylvia with love

In 1787, after the delegates in Philadelphia signed the new United States Constitution, a woman approached Benjamin Franklin. "Well, Doctor," she asked, "what have we got, a republic or a monarchy?" Franklin replied, "A republic, if you can keep it."

"Those who would give up essential liberty to purchase a little temporary safety deserve neither liberty nor safety."

BENJAMIN FRANKLIN

I

—————

THE VISIT HAD BEEN quite unexpected—he had forgotten that he had made the appointment, had forgotten to cancel it after he'd promised to have dinner with the President—and now he was trying to get it over with as quickly and gracefully as possible.

Yet Christopher Collins didn't want to hurt the man sitting opposite him, because this was apparently a nice man, sensible and sensitive and gentle, and at another time Collins would have enjoyed talking to him. But not now, not tonight, with the heap of papers on his desk still to be read, with the long, tense evening in the White House still before him.

He would have to handle this carefully, Collins decided. Not merely because he didn't want to hurt the man's feelings, but because he didn't want to offend FBI Director Tynan. Obviously, the Director had encouraged this man, or had even told him to interview Collins for the autobiography of Tynan that they were writing together. No one was foolhardy enough to offend Tynan, and Collins, in his new position, least of all.

Collins' eyes went to the portable cassette tape recorder his visitor had placed on the edge of the desk ten minutes ago. It was still recording, although nothing of consequence so far. Collins' eyes rose to take in the older man, perhaps in his mid-fifties, who was studying his list of questions, aware that they were pressed for time and anxiously seeking the most telling and important questions on his list.

Studying his visitor, Collins was suddenly struck by the incongruity of the man's appearance and his name, and he was forced to smile. The man's name didn't fit his person at all. His name was Ishmael Young, and Collins wished there were time to ask him how he'd got such a name. Ishmael Young was a short, pudgy person, probably New England, possibly Presbyterian and Scottish (with a Jewish strain back somewhere), and he bulged out all over through his rumpled gray suit. He had odd tufts of hair along the sides of his head and a balding pate, and he pitifully combed his side hairs over the top of his head so that it looked as if he had sideburns on his scalp. He also had two chins and the makings of a third. His blubbery body filled and seemed to hang over the edges of the chair. He resembled a small beached whale. Collins decided that "Ishmael" might be appropriate after all.

Nor did he look in the least like a writer, Collins thought. Except for the horn-rimmed glasses that needed cleaning, and the charred brown briar pipe, he did not look like a writer at all. But then, right from the start he'd said he was a ghostwriter. And Collins had never met one of those before. Apparently a successful ghostwriter, too—one who had written books for a depraved actress, a black Olympics hero, a military genius. Collins tried to recall whether he had read any of the books. He knew that he hadn't but that Karen probably had, and he would try to remember to ask her about them.

He realized now that Ishmael Young had lifted his head, shyly meeting his gaze, and was already posing his next question.

Listening to the question, Collins at once saw an out, a way to terminate this interview as quickly and gracefully as possible. It simply required honesty.

"What do I think of Vernon T. Tynan?" Collins said, repeating the question.

"Yes. I mean, what's your impression of him?"

Collins immediately thought of the physical Tynan: a blustering, braying Brobdingnagian of a being, and almost as legendary, with small squinting gimlet eyes in a small round head set atop a short thick neck on a brawny expanse of chest, a man almost as tall as himself, with a rasping voice. That picture of him was clear. But of the inner Tynan he knew next to nothing. He need only say so, honestly, and be done with it, and let Ishmael Young look elsewhere.

"Frankly, I don't know Director Tynan very well. I haven't had time to get to know him. I've been on this job just one week."

"You've been Attorney General just one week," said Young, correcting him nicely, "but you've been in the Department of Justice—according to my notes, you've been here almost eighteen months. As I understand it, you were Deputy Attorney General under the last Attorney General, Colonel Noah Baxter, for thirteen of those months."

"That's true," admitted Collins. "But as Deputy Attorney General I saw Director Tynan very little. He'll confirm that, if you ask him. It was Colonel Baxter who saw him, actually quite often. They were friends, after a fashion."

Ishmael Young's eyebrows went up a notch. "I didn't know Director Tynan had any friends. At least that's my feeling, from my talks with him. I thought only his assistant, Harry Adcock, was a close friend. And I sort of regarded that as mainly a business relationship."

"No," Collins insisted, "he was also close to Colonel Baxter, if he was close to anyone. Though I suppose you're right in one way. Director Tynan is actually a loner. If you look back, I think you'll find other FBI Directors have been loners. It's in the nature of the job. Anyway, I never got to see him very much or to know him at all."

The writer would not be put off. He removed the old pipe from his mouth and licked his lips. "But Mr. Collins . . ." He paused. "Is that right, the Mr., or should I call you Attorney General Collins, or maybe drop the Attorney and make it just General—"

Collins smiled. "Mr. Collins will do."

"Very well. What I was going to say was that after Colonel Baxter suffered his stroke—that was five months ago—you were temporarily in charge here, unofficially the head of Justice, until it was made official a week ago. As we all know, the FBI is under you. The Director of the FBI, Tynan, is your subordinate, so you'd have contact—"

Collins was forced to laugh. "Director Tynan my subordinate? Mr. Young, you've got a lot to learn."

"That's really what I'm here for, Mr. Collins," said Young earnestly. "I'm here to learn. I can't ghostwrite an autobiography for the Director of the FBI without knowing his precise relationship with the Attorney General, with the President, with the CIA, with everyone in government. You might think I should ask the Director. I have, believe me. But he's surprisingly vague about the governmental process, and his own place in it. There are certain things I can't get clear from him. Not that he won't tell me. It's just that he's not interested, and rather impatient. What he is interested in is talking about his exploits in the FBI under J. Edgar Hoover, and then his resignation and comeback. Well, I'm interested in those things too. They're the meat of the book. But I'm also interested in where he stands—I mean, in relation to his colleagues—in the whole power structure."

Collins made up his mind to be helpful, clarify this, even if it took a few minutes longer. "All right, Mr. Young, let me level with you. It says in the *Government Manual* that the FBI Director is under the Attorney General. According to the book, that's the way it is. But in fact, it's not that way at all. According to Public Law No. 90-351, title VI, section 1101, the Attorney General doesn't appoint the FBI Director, the President does, with the advice and consent of the Senate. While the FBI Director confers with me, consults with me, works with me, I don't have ultimate authority over him. Again, the President does. The President alone can remove him without Senate approval. So except on paper, Director Tynan is not my subordinate. A man like Tynan, as you know by now, would be nobody's subordinate. I'm sure that Tynan, like all FBI Directors, is aware that he has his job for life if he wants it, and regards all Attorneys General as mere transients. Therefore, to go back to your original question or questions, he hasn't been working for me and I haven't had that much contact with him—

no, not even as Deputy Attorney General, when I was in charge here after Colonel Baxter was taken to Bethesda Naval Medical Center. I'm sorry I can't be more helpful. In fact, I can't imagine why Director Tynan sent you to see me."

Young sat up slightly. "Oh, he didn't. This was something I wanted to do on my own."

Collins also moved his lank body up in his high-backed leather executive swivel chair. "Then that explains it." He felt relieved. He owed nothing to Director Tynan. He could cut the interview short without giving offense to Tynan. Still, as before, he wanted to be decent to Young. He wanted to throw him a bone, no matter how small, and send him off happy. "Anyway, to come to the point, you wanted to hear what I thought of Director Tynan for your book—"

"Not for my book," said Young hastily. "For Tynan's book. It'll be by Tynan. I've been trying to understand the framework around him, from those who work with him. Even if you don't know him well, I was rather hoping—"

"All right, in the little time we have left, let me give you my impression of him," said Collins, searching for something bland and safe. "My impression of the Director—he's plainly a man of action, a doer, a no-nonsense guy. He's probably just right for his job."

"In what way?"

"His job is investigating crime, investigating Federal violations. His job is digging up facts and reporting them. He doesn't draw conclusions from his findings, doesn't even make recommendations. My job is to do the rest, to do the prosecuting based on his findings."

"Then you're the man of action," said Young.

Collins considered his interviewer with even more respect. "Not really," he said. "It may sound that way, but it doesn't work that way. I'm strictly a lawyer among lawyers in Justice. We go the slow, careful route, Tynan and his agents do the direct, dangerous stuff. Now, for your purposes, my only other judgment of him is—well, when he gets into something, something he believes in, he won't stop pushing for it. He's very dogged, in the best way. Like the new 35th Amendment to the

Constitution that's out there for ratification. Once the President originated it, Tynan got right behind it—"

Ishmael Young interrupted. "Mr. Collins, the President didn't originate the 35th Amendment. Director Tynan did."

Startled, Collins stared at the writer. "Where did you get that idea?"

"From the Director himself. He speaks of it as his baby."

"Whatever he thinks, it isn't his. But what you've said makes my point exactly. When he believes in something passionately, he makes it his own. And now, indeed, he's the main force behind the 35th Amendment. He's as responsible as anyone, maybe more than anyone, for putting it over."

"It's not been put over yet," said Young quietly. "Forgive me, but it's not been ratified yet by three-fourths of the states."

"Well, it will be," said Collins, a trifle impatient at the digression. "Only two more states have to approve it."

"And there are only three to go."

"Two of the three are doing their final voting tonight. I think the 35th will be part of the Constitution tonight. However, that's neither here nor there, except for Director Tynan's role in putting it over." He glanced at his watch. "Well, now, I think that's about all—"

"Mr. Collins, just one more thing, if I may . . ."

Collins looked up and observed the intent expression on his visitor's face. He waited.

"I—I know this has nothing to do with the interview," Young continued, "but I'm interested to know the answer." He swallowed, and then said, "Do you like that 35th Amendment, Mr. Collins?"

Blinking, Collins was momentarily silent. The question had been unexpected. Moreover, he had never clearly answered it for anyone—not even for his wife Karen, or for himself. "Do I like it?" he repeated slowly. "Not especially. Not really. In truth, I haven't given it too much thought. I've been busy reorganizing. I've trusted the President and—and the Director—"

"But it has to do with you, with your Department, sir."

Collins frowned. "I'm aware of that. Still, I think the President can handle it very well. Maybe I have some reservations about it. But I can't suggest anything better." He realized that the gentle Mr. Young was appearing less gentle by the moment. He was tempted to ask him, and then did ask him, "Do you like it, Mr. Young? Do you like the 35th Amendment?"

"Strictly between us?"

"Strictly."

"I hate it," said Young, flatly. "I hate anything that wipes out the Bill of Rights."

"Well, that's something of an overstatement, I'd say. The 35th is meant to modify, to supersede the Bill of Rights, but only under certain conditions, only in the event of extreme internal emergency that might paralyze or threaten to destroy the country. Obviously, we're heading in that direction fast, and the 35th will give us something with which we can organize order out of chaos—"

"It'll give us repression. It'll sacrifice liberties as the price for peace."

Collins felt a trace of annoyance, and was determined to end the discussion. It seemed as if everyone knew what to do about everything, about every problem, until he had the chance to try to do it. "Okay, Mr. Young. You know what's going on out there in the streets. The worst crisis of crime and violence in our history. Take that attack on the White House by that organized gang of hoodlums two months ago. Bombing, machine-gunning—killing thirteen guards and Secret Service men, murdering seven helpless tourists, gutting the East Room—nobody's done anything like that to the White House since the British sailors did it in 1814. But the British were our enemies then, and we were at war. This attack two months ago was done by Americans—by *Americans*. Nothing is safe. No one is safe. Did you see the TV news this morning? Or read your papers today?"

Young shook his head.

"Then let me tell you," said Collins. "Peoria, Illinois. The police department. The morning shift finished its briefing and assignments, and the officers started outside to their motorcycles and squad cars, when they were ambushed by a gang lying in wait for them. Just ripped to shreds—a blood-bath. At least one-third of the force dead or injured. How do you handle that? Or the fact—a mathematician came up with this today—that one out of every nine persons born in Atlanta this year, if they stayed on in that city, would wind up dead by murder? I repeat, we've never had a crime crisis like this in our entire history. How would you propose to solve it? What would you do?"

Plainly, this was a subject Ishmael Young had discussed before, because he was ready with his answer. "I'd put our house in order by rebuilding it. From the bottom up. As George Bernard Shaw said, 'The evil to be attacked is not sin, suffering, greed, priestcraft, kingcraft, demagogy, monopoly, ignorance, drink, war, pestilence, nor any of the other consequences of poverty, but just poverty itself.' I'd take drastic measures to get rid of poverty, get rid of economic oppression, inequality, injustice—to get rid of crime—"

"There's no time for the total overhaul now. Look, I don't disagree with you on what must basically be done. That'll all come about in due time."

"It'll never come about once the 35th Amendment is passed."

Collins was in no mood for further debate. "I'm curious, Mr. Young. Do you talk like this when you work with Director Tynan?"

Young shrugged his shoulders. "I wouldn't be here now if I did. I talk like this with you because—because you seem to be a nice guy."

"I am a nice guy."

"And—I hope you don't mind my saying this—I simply can't figure out what you're doing with that crowd."

This hit a nerve. Karen had made the same point, over a month ago, when he had decided to accept the job of Attorney General. He had had some answers for her then, but he was not going to bother to repeat them to a virtual stranger. Instead, he said, "Would you like to see someone else in this job? Someone Director Tynan recommended? Why do you think I took this job? Because I believe nice guys can finish first." He glanced at his wristwatch again, and stood up. "I'm sorry, Mr. Young. We've run out of time. I told you when you came in, I have a stack of cases to review. Then I've got to get over to the White

House. Look, I'll know a good deal more, perhaps be able to help you further, in a few months from now. Why don't you give me a ring then?"

Ishmael Young was on his feet, putting away his notepaper, taking up his tape recorder and shutting it off. "I will call you. If you're still around. I hope you are."

"I'll be around."

"Then I'll be calling. Thanks a lot."

Chris Collins reached over and shook the writer's hand, and then watched him waddle toward the conference room that led to the reception room and the hall elevator.

Suddenly, he was inspired to ask the writer something he had neglected to ask before. "By the way, Mr. Young, how long have you been working with Director Tynan?"

Ishmael Young halted in the doorway. "Almost six months. Once a week for six months."

"Well, you haven't told me—what do *you* think of him?"

Young offered a weak half-smile. "Mr. Collins," he said, "I'll cop the 5th." He grinned. "There still is a 5th, isn't there?" Then he added, "This work is my bread and butter. I never risk that. Besides, I was sort of pressured into taking this assignment. Thanks again."

He was gone.

Collins remained where he had been standing, thinking about their exchange, about the crisis in the country, about the new Amendment that was to stop all that, about Director Tynan himself, assessing in turn what he felt about each of these. Then he realized it was taking too long, and there was too much to do. Finally, he settled down in his chair, rolled it up to his desk, and began to examine the papers lying there.

Soon he had forgotten his visitor completely. He was utterly absorbed by the cases that required his immediate attention—an interstate kidnapping, a violation of the Atomic Energy Act, an Indian Lands claim, an antitrust suit, a tremendous narcotics case, an appointment of a Federal judge, a subversive plot against Congress, a deportation, a number of riot problems, a series of leads on five conspiracies aimed at disrupting or overthrowing the Government.

Absorbed though he was, Collins was acutely sensitive to sound. Now, in the stillness of the huge seventy-foot office, he could hear the brush of her footsteps on the thick Oriental rug. He looked up from his two stacks of papers to see Marion Rice, his secretary, coming hastily toward him from her adjacent office. She was holding up a large manila envelope.

"Just came in—hand-delivered—from across the street," she said.

Across the street meant across Pennsylvania Avenue—the J. Edgar Hoover Building and the FBI and the FBI Director.

"It's marked *Confidential* and *Important*," she added. "It must be from the Director."

"Odd," said Collins. "He usually has everything in before noon."

She handed the manila envelope across the desk to him, and hesitated. "Unless there's something else, Mr. Collins, I'll be leaving now."

He was surprised. "What time is it?"

"Twenty after six."

"My God. I'm not even half through yet. I shouldn't have let that writer fellow take up so much of my time." He thought about it. "Well, maybe it was useful. He was interesting." Ruefully, he looked down at the first stack on his desk. "I guess I'll have to take most of this home. Okay, Marion, you can lock up and go."

"You'll have no more time for work now. Don't forget, you have a dinner date tonight, seven fifteen, the White House."

He grimaced. "That may be work, too."

She still hesitated, and then a reticent smile surfaced on her plain, elongated face. "I—I just want to say, Mr. Collins, congratulations on your first week's anniversary as Attorney General. We're all happy you're here. Good night."

"Good night, Marion. I appreciate that."

After she had gone, and he was quite alone, he considered the large manila envelope that Marion had given him. There was rarely good news from the FBI these days, so it was with reluctance that he unsealed the package.

He withdrew what appeared to be a half dozen pages of

typed statistics. Attached to them was a covering letter, a hand-written note really. From the crabbed hand already familiar to him, from the erratic punctuation (mostly dashes), the impatient abbreviations, he knew that the note had been written by Director Vernon T. Tynan even before the signature confirmed it.

His curiosity aroused, Collins began reading the note.

Dear Chris—

Heres the latest figures on last months nat'l crime statistics—the worst yet by far—the worst in our history—I'm sending a copy to the Pres and one to you so that you get it before we see the Pres tonight. Note the jump in murders, riots, armed robbery, interstate kidnapping. See my addendum on leads to probable conspiracies and organized revolutionaries—we're really in a stew and we'll be cooked, and the only thing that can pull us out is final passage of the 35th Amend—pray for it tonight. I already had these latest statistics phoned in to legislators in Albany, NY, and Columbus, O, so they know the true situation before they vote tonight. Hate to give you this terrible report, but feel its vital you are up to date before seeing the Pres. This is in rough form—will check it out thoroughly before making it public tomorrow—see you at the TV dinner in a few hours.

Best,
Vernon

Folding back Tynan's note, Collins glanced through the Uniform Crime Reports, slowly turning the pages. In the past month, compared with the previous month, violent crimes, including murder, had gone up 18 percent, forcible rape had gone up 15 percent, robbery and aggravated assault up 30 percent, riots up 20 percent.

He laid down Tynan's pages. He went over some other statistics in his own mind. Because of this growing lawlessness, prisons were filled to bursting. Five years earlier, there had been two million persons, at one time or another, in the 250 major prisons and reformatories in a given year. Despite a stepped-up effort to put the lid on lawbreakers, despite the 45,000 lawyers and FBI agents working for the Department of Justice, despite three special divisions of Army troops assigned to domestic control by the Pentagon, despite the 22 billion dollars that would be spent on law enforcement this year (it had been only 3½ billion in 1960), the crime rate continued to spiral upward. The cancer could no longer be kept in remission by force, it seemed. In another year it might be terminal, heralding the death of organized society.

He sat back in his chair, hands and fingertips together on his chest, as if in prayer. It was the darkest period in American history since the Civil War, of this he was certain. Anarchy and terror dominated every new day. When you woke in the morning, you did not know whether you would see the night. When you went to sleep at night, you did not know whether you would wake in the morning. Every day when he kissed Karen goodbye before going to work, he felt the frightening uncertainty that he might not find her (and the child she was carrying) alive when he came home.

He felt the invisible fist of fear grip his stomach. It was not the first time. Momentarily, his thoughts shrank from the chaos in the streets beyond his window to personal pity for himself. Certainly, he—he and Tynan—had the worst, most hopeless, jobs on earth.

Self-pity led to morbid self-fascination. Then why had he, Christopher Collins—thoughtful, self-effacing, withdrawn, sometimes selfish (he could be objective, too)—taken this impossible job as the nation's number one law-enforcement officer and the head of the nation's largest law firm?

Had he come here, without passionate convictions (except, as Ishmael Young had suggested, that democratic society had to be restructured) or solutions, because of a desire for power? Or had it been for ego gratification? Or had it been to fulfill a patriotic duty? Or had it been from a chivalrous feeling that he could do some good? Or had it been that he was the victim of a masochistic, even suicidal, strain in his makeup?

He did not know. At least, not tonight.

And then he heard his telephone ringing. He spun to his left, facing the oak cabinet on which rested the bank of buttons, and saw that his personal button (for Karen, for friends, as distinct from other buttons for the President, the Director, his Deputy, Ed Schrader) was lighting up.

He lifted the receiver. "Collins here."

"Darling. I hope I'm not interrupting something . . ." It was Karen's voice.

"No, no. I was just going through some last-minute things. How are you, honey?"

She didn't answer directly. She said, "I know we're going to dinner tonight. I wanted to check on the time your driver is picking me up. Is it seven?"

"A quarter to seven. You'll be meeting me at seven. We're due at the White House fifteen minutes after that. The President wants us to be on time. We're all watching the TV specials from New York and Ohio. Are you dressed?"

"I'm dressed underneath. And all made up. I just have to slip into something. What's it going to be like? Can I wear the red knit?"

"Wear whatever is casual. His secretary said this was going to be very informal."

"I guess the red knit will do. It's almost the last time I can wear it before my stomach starts showing."

"Any action today?"

"Where? Oh, you mean there. A few tentative kicks."

"Good. The Redskins need a punter. You still haven't told me—how are you otherwise?"

"I'm fine, I guess. All things considered."

"What things considered?" He knew, but he had to ask anyway.

"Well, you know how I feel about those big protocol affairs. I've been to the White House with you only once, that time in the State Dining Room when we went with the Baxters. That was bad enough. But this one—you said this one was a small affair, intimate—that's doubly scary. I won't know what to say."

"You won't have to say a darn thing. We'll all be watching television."

"Why do you have to be there? What's so important about
your being there?"

"Don't you remember? I told you this morning."

"I'm sorry—"

"Never mind. I'll tell you again. First of all, the President
wants me there. That's reason enough. In the second place, I *am*
the Attorney General—and the 35th Amendment is up for a
crucial vote tonight, and that falls in my province. I'm supposed to be very interested. There are special late sessions of
the New York and Ohio lower houses tonight, being televised
live, and since two of the three states that haven't voted yet are
voting tonight—and only two more states are needed to pass the
35th and make it part of the Constitution—this is a big deal. Is
that clear?"

"Yes, I understand. Don't be angry with me, Chris. I just
didn't realize so much was going on tonight." She paused. "Do
we want it to pass? I've read some bad things about it."

"So have I, honey. I don't know. I really don't know what's
right. The Amendment can be good if good people are running
the country. It can be bad if there are bad people. I can only say,
if it passes, it'll make my job easier."

"Then I hope it passes." But her voice carried no conviction.

"Well, as they say in the mysterious Mideast—what is to be,
will be. Let's just eat the President's food and look and listen."
He checked the time. "You'd better get into the red knit. The
driver'll be there any second. Love you. See you soon."

After hanging up, placing one stack of papers in the OUT
tray on his desk, stuffing the rest into his briefcase, he sat thinking of Karen. He was sorry he had been even passingly gruff
with her. She deserved better, his best. He knew the evening
ahead would be an ordeal for her. She had been against the
change from the start, against the job as Deputy Attorney General, against the move from his private practice in Los Angeles
to public office in Washington, and even more vehemently
against the Cabinet post as Attorney General.

While she was not outspoken generally, and pretended to be
apolitical, he knew where Karen stood. It had all come up before he entered the Justice Department. She did not like or trust

the people he would be associated with, from President Wadsworth to Director Tynan. Furthermore, she had tried to tell him, it was a loser's job. For all the importance he would have, in the end he would be a scapegoat. The country was going rapidly downhill, and he'd be at the wheel. Nor did she like the business of his office. Above all, Karen did not want to live in a fishbowl, did not want the forced friendships and socializing and the nakedness before the news media demanded by his position. They were newly married then—the second time for each—only two years married now, and here she was in her fourth month of pregnancy, and she wanted only closeness, privacy, bliss, and she did not want to share him.

He rose from his chair with the resolve to be by her side all evening, no matter how difficult that proved, and to be kind. He stretched to his entire stringy six feet two, until he could hear his bones crack. He briefly considered his cadaverous—but not unhandsome—visage and rumpled dark hair in the mirror, and then he saw that the limousine would arrive in twelve minutes. He started for his private sitting room, beyond his secretary's office, to wash and change, wondering all the while whether it would be a momentous and memorable night.

WHEN THEIR CADILLAC LIMOUSINE drove through the open gate in the black iron fence along Pennsylvania Avenue and entered the curving White House driveway, Collins could see that a great number of news people were on the lawn across from the north façade, with their lighting equipment turned on and waiting.

Mike Hogan, the FBI agent who was his bodyguard, twisted around in the front seat and asked, "Do you want to talk to them, Mr. Collins?"

Collins squeezed Karen's hand and said, "Not if I can help it. Let's go right inside."

Once they had left the car at the North Portico, Collins was affably noncommittal with the press. Taking Karen's arm, he hurried after Hogan toward the White House entrance. He answered only one question before they went inside.

A television newscaster called out to him, "We hear you're going to be watching television tonight. How do you think it'll come out?"

Collins called back, "We'll be watching a rerun of *Gone With the Wind*. I think the North will win."

Inside, two surprises awaited him.

He had expected the gathering to take place in the Red Room, or in one of the smaller entertaining rooms located upstairs, but instead he and Karen were escorted to the Cabinet Room in the West Wing. He had expected thirty or forty people to be on hand, but there proved to be only a dozen or so besides Karen and himself.

Along the wall that faced the green draperies covering the French doors that led to the White House Rose Garden, near the shelves of books, a large color television console had been installed. Several persons were standing watching the picture on the screen, although the audio had been turned down low. Half the black leather-covered chairs around the long, shining dark Cabinet table (which suggested to Collins a coffin lid for the Cardiff Giant) had been turned to face the television set. On the opposite side of the table, beneath the Great Seal set in the east wall and between the United States flag and the Presidential flag, President Andrew Wadsworth was engaged in an animated conversation with the Senate and House majority leaders and their wives.

Although Collins had been in the Cabinet Room a half dozen times before—five times as Deputy Attorney General substituting for ailing Attorney General Baxter, and earlier this week as Attorney General himself—the room seemed suddenly unfamiliar to him. This was because it had been rearranged, with many of the chairs moved away from the Cabinet table to be nearer the television set. At the far end of the table, before the Gilbert Stuart portrait of Washington hanging over the mantelpiece, hors d'oeuvres were being kept warm in gleaming copper chafing dishes set on a green cloth and supervised by a chef in a jaunty white hat. The staid room had been transformed, by informal disarray, into oversized, comfortable play quarters.

As Collins, with Karen clutching his arm, surveyed the

scene, the President's chief aide, McKnight, hurried forward to welcome them. Quickly, they were taken on the rounds of the Cabinet Room, to meet either again or for the first time Vice-President Frank Loomis and his wife; Miss Ledger, the President's personal secretary; Ronald Steedman, the President's private pollster from the University of Chicago; Secretary of the Interior Martin; then the Congressional leaders and their wives, and then President Wadsworth himself.

The President, a slight, dapper man, suave and urbane, almost courtly, with dark hair graying at the temples, a pointed nose, a receding chin, took Karen's hand, shook Collins', and was at once apologetic. "Martha"—he was referring to the First Lady—"is so disappointed she won't be here tonight to get to know you better. She's in bed with a touch of the flu. Oh, she'll be all right. There'll be a next time. . . . Well, Chris, it looks like a happy evening."

"I hope so, Mr. President," said Collins. "What do you hear?"

"As you know, the state Senates in New York and Ohio ratified the 35th early yesterday. Now we're entirely in the hands of the New York Assembly and the Ohio House. Immediately after yesterday's votes, Steedman had his teams of pollsters swarming over Albany and Columbus, buttonholing state legislators. Ohio looks like a cinch. Steedman has the figures, and they're impressive. New York is a little more iffy. It could go either way. Most of the legislators polled were Undecided or No Comment, but among those who did reply, there's been a definite gain over the last poll. It looks favorable. Also, I think Vernon's latest FBI statistics— Hello, Vernon."

Director Vernon T. Tynan had joined them, occupying all empty space, a formidable presence. He was shaking the President's hand, Collins' hand, complimenting Karen on her appearance.

"I was just saying, Vernon," the President resumed in his vibrant voice, "those figures you sent over an hour ago, they should have great impact in Albany. I'm glad you got them in on time."

"It wasn't easy," said Tynan. "It took a lot of hustle. But you're right. They should help. Ronald Steedman seems less certain. I just had a word with him. Based on his projection, Ohio should be in our corner, but he feels New York is up in the air. He doesn't seem too confident there."

"Well, I'm confident," said the President. "Two hours from now we'll have thirty-eight out of fifty states, and a new amendment to the Constitution. After that, we'll have the means of preserving this country, if it ever becomes necessary."

Collins nodded in the direction of the television set across the table. "When does it start, Mr. President?"

"Ten or fifteen minutes. They're just warming up with some background."

"I think we'll have a look," said Collins. "And a drink as well."

As he guided Karen away, he realized that Tynan remained in step beside him. "I think I can use a drink, too," said Tynan.

They went silently toward the end of the Cabinet table where the President's valet, Charles, was supervising the drinks over his rows of glasses and bottles, an ice bucket, and a champagne cooler.

Tynan looked past Collins at Karen. "How do you feel, Mrs. Collins? Are you feeling okay these days?"

Surprised, Karen raised her hand to smooth her short blond hair, then automatically lowered it to touch her loose chain belt. "I've never felt better, thank you."

"Good, good to hear that," said Tynan.

After Collins had got a glass of champagne and some caviar on a wedge of toast for his wife and a Scotch and water for himself, and started her toward two empty chairs in front of the television set, he felt her tug at his sleeve. He inclined his head toward her.

"Did you hear that?" she whispered.

"What?"

"Tynan. His sudden concern about how I feel—if I'm feeling okay. He was practically telling us, in his own way, that he knows I'm pregnant."

Collins seemed confused. "He can't know. No one knows."

"*He* knows," whispered Karen.

"But even if he has found out, what's the point?"

"Just to remind you he's omniscient. To keep you and every-one else in line."

"I think you're overreacting, honey. He's not all that subtle. He was just being social. It was an innocent remark."

"Sure. Like the wolf's in 'Little Red Riding Hood.'"

"Shh. Keep your voice down."

They had reached the chairs almost directly in front of the large television set, and they both sat down.

Sipping his drink, Collins tried to concentrate on the screen. The distinguished network commentator was saying that several minutes would be given over to recapping the procedure of adding a new amendment to the Constitution and, more specifi-cally, to the laborious passage of the 35th Amendment from its inception to this moment when it was on the brink of ratification.

"There are two means by which a new amendment to the United States Constitution can be initiated," the commentator began.

Collins set down his drink, lit Karen's cigarette and then his own, and eased back to listen half-attentively.

"One means of initiating an amendment is to have it pro-posed in Congress. The other is to have it initiated by a national convention called by Congress at the request of the legislatures of two-thirds of the states. No amendment has ever been started by such a convention. All have begun in Congress in Washing-ton, D.C. Once a resolution proposing a new amendment is made, in either the United States Senate or the House of Repre-sentatives, hearings are held on it by the Rules Committees and the Judiciary Committees. After the amendment is approved by these committees, it goes to the floors of the Senate and the House. To be approved, it requires a two-thirds vote of each legislative body. Once approved, it does not need the signature of the President. Instead, copies are sent to the General Ser-vices Administration, which in turn distributes the amendment to the Governors of the fifty states. The Governors merely send the amendment to their state legislatures for debate and vote. If three-fourths of the state legislatures—that means 38 out of 50 states—ratify the amendment, the amendment becomes an offi-cial part of the Constitution."

Collins snuffed out his cigarette in the nearest ashtray and then reached for his drink, still watching the television screen.

The commentator went on. "Since the original ten amendments became part of the Constitution, and since the year 1789, there have been 5,700 resolutions introduced in Congress to amend the Constitution one way or another. There have been suggested amendments of every sort—to replace the Presidency with a three-person ruling council, to get rid of the Vice-Presidency, to change the name of the United States of America to the United States of the Earth, to change the Electoral College vote system, to change the free-enterprise system so that no one individual might possess more than ten million dollars. Of the handful of 5,700 amendments that did not die in Congress, that did get out to the states, only thirty-four have been ratified by the necessary three-fourths of the states. There has usually been no limitation as to the time the states have to ratify or reject. The most quickly approved amendment in our history was the 26th, giving 18-year-olds the vote. Only three months and seven days after it came out of Congress, it was ratified by three-fourths of the fifty states. Which brings us to the latest amendment, the 35th, which we may see killed or made law of the land tonight."

Collins heard the movement of bodies, the scraping of chairs, and observed the guests who were beginning to crowd around the television set on either side. Then he devoted himself to the television screen once more.

"The controversial 35th Amendment, designed to supersede the first ten amendments—or the Bill of Rights—under certain emergency circumstances, grew out of a desire by Congressional leaders and President Wadsworth to forge a weapon to impose law and order on the nation if required."

"Weapon?" interrupted the President, who had just sat down near Collins. "What does he mean, weapon? If ever I heard prejudicial language, that's it. I wish we could pass an amendment to take care of commentators like that."

"We're passing one," Director Tynan boomed from his chair on the opposite side. "The 35th will take care of those trouble-makers."

Collins caught Karen's sharp glance, and squirmed uncomfortably toward the television screen again.

". . . and so after it came out of committee and was introduced as a joint resolution," the commentator was continuing, "it went to the floors of the Senate and the House for final vote. Despite vocal—but limited—opposition from the liberal blocs, both bodies of Congress gave the 35th Amendment overwhelming approval, far exceeding the two-thirds vote required. Then the new Amendment was sent out to the fifty states. That was four months and two days ago. After a relatively easy passage in the first states voting on it, the voyage of the 35th became increasingly stormy, as opposition was organized against it. To date, forty-seven of the fifty states have voted upon it. Eleven have turned it down. Thirty-six have approved it. But since the Amendment needs thirty-eight votes of approval, it is still two states short. As of tonight, there remain three states that have not voted—New York, Ohio, and California. New York and Ohio are concluding their voting this very night—a historic event that will be seen shortly on this network—and California has scheduled its vote a month hence. But will California be needed? If both New York and Ohio turn down the Amendment tonight, it will be dead. If both ratify the Amendment tonight, it will become part of the Constitution immediately, and President Wadsworth will have his arsenal to combat the growing lawlessness and disorder that is slowly strangling the nation. The voting tonight in New York and Ohio may be fateful, may change the course of American history for a century to come. Now, after a brief commercial break, we will take you to the State Assembly in Albany, New York, where the floor debate is just concluding before the final roll-call vote will be taken."

The commercial for an oil conglomerate, which declared that at least one conglomerate was in business only as a public service to make life happier and easier for the people, was quickly drowned out by the rising babble of voices in the room.

Collins came to his feet, ready to refill his drink. Karen had covered the top of her glass with her fingers, indicating she'd had enough champagne, so he left her and pushed between the other guests toward the makeshift bar on the Cabinet table. He saw that the President was in the company of his pollster, Steedman, as well as Tynan and McKnight, and he guessed that they were once more reviewing the pollster's last-minute findings on the sentiment of the New York State Assembly.

When Collins returned to his chair, fresh Scotch in hand, and settled down, he could see that the television coverage had moved to a full shot of the New York Assembly.

"What's happening?" he asked Karen.

"Just about to begin," she said. "The floor debate is coming to an end. The last speaker is winding up his speech in favor of the Amendment."

Collins downed a large portion of his Scotch and watched as the telecast now cut to a close shot of a dignified gentleman, identified as Assemblyman Lyman Smith, concluding his speech. Collins listened.

". . . and while the United States Constitution as written by our forefathers is a noble instrument of law," the speaker was saying, "I once again tell you that it is not sacrosanct. It was not meant to be petrified by time. It was meant to be flexible—that is the reason provision was made for its amendment— sufficiently flexible, changeable to meet the needs of each new generation and the challenge of humanity's progress. Remember this, my friends, this Constitution of ours was written by a group of largely youthful radicals, men who came to its signing in horse-drawn carriages, men who wore wigs, men who used quill pens. These men had never heard of ball-point pens, typewriters, electronic calculators. They never heard of television sets, jet airplanes, atomic bombs, or space satellites. And certainly, they never heard of the Saturday-night special. But they built into their Constitution the instrument for adjusting our Federal laws to whatever the future might bring. Now the future is here, the day for change is at hand, and the time has come to modify our supreme law to suit the needs of our present citizenry. The old Bill of Rights, as set down by those founders in wigs, is too ambiguous, too general, too soft to meet the onrush of events conspiring to destroy the fabric of our society and the structure of our democracy. Only passage of the 35th Amendment can give our leaders a firmer hand. Only the 35th Amendment can save us. Please, dear friends and colleagues, vote for its ratification!"

As the speaker on the screen returned to his seat, the camera roved over the Assembly showing the thunderous applause.

In the Cabinet Room around Collins there was also hearty applause.

"Bravo!" the President exclaimed, setting down his Upmann cigar and clapping. The President searched over his shoulder. "McKnight," he called out to his chief aide, "who's that New York Assemblyman who just spoke? Somebody-or-other Smith? Check him out. We could use a person in the White House who thinks that straight and is eloquent besides." His gaze went back to the screen. "Everybody, attention. The roll call is about to begin."

It was already beginning, and Collins could hear the names of the Assemblymen, and their Yeas and Nays. From inside the room, he could hear Director Tynan predict that it was going to be a horse race. From behind him, he could hear Steedman's clipped voice say it would take a while for the verdict since there were 150 members in the New York State Assembly.

Because it would take a while, because he was tired, Collins allowed his attention to drift from the screen. He fastened on Tynan, who was standing, his bulldog face flushed with anxiety, his eyes hooded, as he followed the voting. He looked over his shoulder at the President, whose countenance was granite, impassive, unmoving, as if he were posing for a carving on Mount Rushmore, as he concentrated on the screen.

Honest, dedicated men, Collins thought. No matter what others said on the outside—carpers like that Ishmael Young, or even doubters like Karen—these men were responsible human beings. At once, he felt comfortable in this circle of power. He felt he belonged. It was a wonderful feeling. He wished he could thank the person who had put him there—Colonel Baxter, who was missing, who was lying in a coma on a hospital bed in Bethesda.

Collins had believed he owed everything to Colonel Baxter, but actually, examining it now, he saw that it was a series of accidents and mistakes that had elevated him to Attorney General.

For one thing, he had been his late father's son, and Colonel Baxter had been his father's college roommate at Stanford and his father's closest friend in their early, struggling years after graduation. Collins' father, who had wanted to practice law, had turned to business instead and had become a wealthy electronic-parts manufacturer. Collins remembered the great pride his father had taken in his son, the lawyer. His father had always kept Colonel Baxter and other friends apprised of his son's advancement and growing legal reputation.

Two distinct events, a few years apart, had further brought him to Colonel Baxter's attention. One was his brief but well-publicized tenure as an American Civil Liberties Union lawyer in San Francisco. He had successfully defended the civil rights of a thoroughly fascist right-wing American organization, because he believed in free expression for all. It had been a matter of highest principle rather than principals. Colonel Baxter, a conservative, had been impressed for the wrong reasons. Shortly after, when serving as the new District Attorney in Oakland, Collins had gained national attention by successfully prosecuting three black killers who had committed particularly horrendous crimes. This had impressed Colonel Baxter even more, showing that he was no bleeding heart meting out more compassionate justice for blacks than for whites. What had never got into print was Collins' true feelings: that these impoverished, ill-raised, ill-used blacks had been the real victims, the victims of society. The law, unfortunately, had no mitigating provision for the lucklessness of possessing the wrong genes.

Yes, it was the headline achievements that had impressed Colonel Baxter. The fact that Collins, in private practice in Los Angeles, had also successfully defended the rights and lives of several organizations of blacks and Chicanos, and saved the necks of dozens of white dissenters had been regarded by Baxter as a youthful aberration or a sop to a rising young attorney's conscience. Thus, backed by these credentials and his father's old friendship, Collins had been summoned to Washington to become, eventually, Colonel Baxter's Deputy Attorney General, and thus by chance, by a flaw in the Colonel's arteries, he had become Attorney General of the United States and a part of this elite company.

The thoughts in his head seemed unnaturally loud, and then he realized this was because the Cabinet Room had become unnaturally hushed. He started to look around, when suddenly he saw the President leap from his chair, and heard a tremendous cheer go up in unison.

Bewildered, he looked at the screen, then at Karen, who was not cheering, and she whispered, "It just passed. The New York State Assembly ratified the 35th Amendment. Can you hear the announcer? He's saying that means only one more state is needed to put the 35th over. They'll be switching to Columbus after a station break and a brief sum-up by the network panel."

Everyone was standing, jubilant, and Collins' view of the screen was momentarily blocked by Steedman, who was addressing the President. "Congratulations, Mr. President!" the pollster was saying. "I will admit that was a definite upset, a surprise. Our percentages allowed for it, but there was no clear indication that it would happen the way it did."

Director Tynan gripped Collins' shoulder until he winced. "Great news, old boy, isn't it? Great news!"

"Vernon—" It was the President addressing Tynan.

"Yes, Mr. President?"

"—you know what did it? You know what swung New York to our side? It was that last speech delivered by that Assemblyman, that Smith fellow. That speech, it was perfect. It was just as if you had written it yourself."

Director Tynan grinned broadly. "Maybe I did write it myself."

All the others, listening, laughed knowingly, as if enjoying a shared secret. Collins laughed, too, because he didn't quite understand and wanted to continue to belong.

A shrill voice interrupted. "Buffet dinner is ready!" It was Miss Ledger, the President's personal secretary, directing the guests to the far end of the Cabinet table. "All prepared specially so you can put your plates on your laps. No knives, just forks. Better get your food before the Ohio vote starts."

Collins took Karen's arm, and they came to their feet. He could see the portion of the Cabinet table that had been converted to a hot buffet. He and Karen were almost the last in line, and before they could reach the food the others were rushing back to find their places. Apparently the Ohio vote was about to begin in living color.

Soon, his plate heaped with chicken linguine, cold poached salmon with cucumber sauce, mixed green salad, and fresh fruits—but devoid of bread—he was following Karen back to the semicircle of guests around the television set. He saw that President Wadsworth had taken his old seat, so he guided Karen to two empty chairs in the rear. He peered between the guests in front of him.

From the podium of the Ohio State House of Representatives, someone was reading the resolution. Collins gave up trying to see, and sat back to listen, as he consumed bites of the chicken linguine.

A voice from the television set was droning:

"Proposing an amendment to the Constitution of the United States providing for domestic security.

"Resolved by the Senate and House of Representatives of the United States of America in Congress assembled, two-thirds of each House concurring therein, that an amendment is hereby proposed to the Constitution of the United States which shall be valid to all intents and purposes as part of the Constitution when ratified by three-fourths of the legislatures of the several states. Said amendment shall be as follows:

"The 1st to 10th Amendments to the Constitution shall be superseded in time of internal national emergency by the following new Amendment.

"Section 1. Number 1. No right or liberty guaranteed by the Constitution shall be construed as license to endanger the national security. Number 2. In the event of clear and present danger, a Committee on National Safety, appointed by the President, shall meet in joint session with the National Security Council. Number 3. Upon determination that national security is at issue, the Committee on National Safety shall declare a state of emergency and assume plenipotentiary power, supplanting Constitutional authority until the established danger has been brought under control and/or eliminated. Number 4. The chairman of the Committee shall be the Director of the Federal Bureau of Investigation. Number 5. The proclamation shall exist only during such time as the emergency is declared to be in effect, and it shall be automatically terminated by formal declaration upon the emergency's resolution.

"Section 2. Number 1. During the suspensory period, the remainder of all rights and privileges guaranteed by the Constitution shall be held inviolable. Number 2. All Committee action shall be taken by unanimous vote."

Collins had read about all this before, several times, but somehow hearing it aloud made it seem harsher, and he sat worried, picking at his food.

"There's the call of the House," he heard the President say. "They're beginning the roll call. Well, this one's a cinch. We're in. The 35th is in the bag. Okay, here they go. The names of the ninety-nine legislators are being called off."

Collins set down his plate, and was again fully attentive. He could see the close-ups of the various representatives on the Ohio State House floor pushing the buttons at their desks. He could see the votes being registered on one of the two huge boards at either end of the chamber. Ayes and Nays, about even, very close.

Except for the occasional interruption of the television newsman's voice repeating the progressive tally, the Cabinet Room was silent. Minutes ticked away. The voting continued relentlessly to its finish. The big board reflected the votes. Aye. Nay. Nay. Nay. Aye. Nay. Aye. Nay. Nay.

The announcer's voice broke in quickly over the voting. "The Nays have just gone ahead. This is a surprise. Ratification seems to be slipping away. Despite the pundits and pollsters, an upset seems in the making."

More minutes. More votes. As suddenly as it had begun, it was over. The 35th Amendment had been voted down, rejected, by the Ohio House of Representatives.

There were audible groans, and outcries of disappointment and disgust, from those in the Cabinet Room. Unaccountably,

Collins felt his heart pounding fast. He cast a sidelong glance at Karen. She was composed as she tried to suppress a smile. Collins frowned and looked away.

Everyone was beginning to rise. Almost everyone appeared crestfallen. Puzzled, most of the guests gathered about the President.

Shrugging, the President looked to his pollster. "I thought it was in the bag, Ronald. What went wrong?"

"We had projected a win by a comfortable margin," said Steedman. "But our last sampling of the House members was thirty-six hours ago. Who knows what variables were not taken into account or what may have happened among the members during the last thirty-six hours?"

The President's aide, McKnight, was waving his arm. "Mr. President, the announcer—he seems to have some kind of answer. . . ."

The President and his guests, Collins included, turned back to the set. The network newsman did, indeed, seem to have some kind of explanation.

". . . and this word has just come up to us here in our booth. We haven't been able to confirm it yet, but several legislators indicated to our floor man that there had been an intensive lobbying campaign last night and throughout this morning here in the state capital—a blitz effort by Anthony Pierce—Tony Pierce, head of DBR, that national group known as Defenders of the Bill of Rights—who only a month ago started a campaign among legislators of the most recent states to vote on the Amendment and who has just had his most resounding success in Ohio. We're told that at the eleventh hour, Pierce met with many fence-sitters, and even backers of the Amendment, and briefed them with documentation to show how the 35th Amendment would do irreparable damage to the country, and apparently he was successful in swaying a sufficient number to help vote down the Amendment, which, an hour ago, appeared unbeatable in Ohio. Tony Pierce, as most viewers will remember, is the onetime FBI agent who turned successful author, lawyer, and civil rights advocate. His record—"

A bellowing voice drowned out the television audio. "We

know his record!" roared Director Tynan, bounding in front of the television set, shaking his fist at the screen. "We know all about that sonofabitch!"

He whirled around, red-faced, staring at the others, and then fixing on the President. "Forgive my language, but we know that bastard Pierce too well. We know he headed a radical activist group at the University of Wisconsin. We know how he got a medal he didn't deserve in Viet Nam. We know how he weaseled his way into the FBI, playing the war hero, even lying to our great Director, Mr. Hoover, who tried to help him. We know he was negligent in his duties—freeing criminals he was supposed to detain, doctoring his reports, trying to take over, being insubordinate. That's why I kicked him out of the Bureau. We know the names of four radical groups his wife belongs to. We know one of his kids has had children out of wedlock. We know at least nine subversive organizations his law firm has represented. We know Tony Pierce inside out, and we knew he was bad medicine before all this started. We should have demolished him the minute he headed up DBR—but we didn't because we didn't want to give a former FBI agent such negative headlines, hurt the image of the Bureau—and besides, we didn't think anyone would take that crackpot joker seriously."

"Never mind, Vernon, that's all water under the bridge," said the President, trying to calm him. "He's done his damage, if indeed he was responsible. We'll just have to see to it that it doesn't happen again."

Observing the scene, Chris Collins found himself embarrassed and upset. He had been taken aback by Tynan's initial outburst. It had been venomous, and had revealed an inquisitor's side of the FBI Director that Collins had never seen before.

Collins had taken Karen's hand, as if to share his upset with her, when he saw the President signaling him.

Releasing his wife's hand, Collins pushed between McKnight and the Senate Majority Leader to reach the President, who had already been joined by Tynan.

For a moment, the President stood rubbing his jaw thoughtfully. "Well, gentlemen, we won one by an upset, and we lost one by an upset. It shows you how volatile the country is. But we can't let it happen again. There's only one state left. All our marbles are on California. In a month." He paused. "I haven't been paying much attention to the polls out on the Coast. I was sure we'd lock it up tonight. Now we'd better pay attention. Ronald tells me we're ahead in the Golden State Poll. That's not enough for me. California is something to worry about. You know how unpredictable they are out there. It's our last shot, and I'm staking everything on it. I want you, Vernon, and you, Chris, to give it everything you've got. We've *got* to win."

Both Collins and Tynan nodded vigorously.

The President clipped a fresh cigar, and waited while Tynan lit it for him. Puffing, the President turned to Collins. "I have one idea, to begin with, Chris. You come from California, don't you?"

"Yes, I do. I'm from the Bay area, but I also practiced in Los Angeles."

"Perfect. I think it might be worthwhile for you to get back out there in the next week or two. You can do some subtle but effective lobbying for the cause."

"Well," said Collins, troubled, "I don't know if I'd have that much influence. The only really popular native son—he's practically an idol in California—is Chief Justice Maynard."

The President shook his head. "No, Maynard wouldn't do. I have it from good sources he's not on our side. Besides, he's just too impractical. Even if this weren't so, it's not at all likely a Justice would speak out on a political issue like this."

"We can thank God for that," interjected Tynan. "I wouldn't trust him on a real law issue like the 35th."

"We don't need Maynard," the President continued, addressing Collins. "But we may need you. After all, Chris, don't underestimate yourself. You are the Attorney General. That counts for something. The right people will listen. Yes, I like the idea of sending you to California. We can arrange a reason for your having to be there. Let me think about it."

Uncomfortable as he was with the idea, Collins knew that he dared not resist. "I'll do whatever you say. If you feel it's important—"

"Damn important," Tynan broke in. "Nothing more important. I've said it a hundred times and I'll say it again. This is the most crucial piece of legislation ever voted on by the states. Without it, we'll have—we'll have no country at all."

"Vernon's right," the President said. "We should have someone in California. Either you or—perhaps someone of stature who's been in the Administration longer." He paused, then added with emphasis, "We're not going to lose this one. I won't allow it. I won't let things go on the way they have. This morning I walked over to the East Room to look at the work being done on it. What a shambles, and what a disgrace. When the President's house isn't safe, we know we're in trouble. And it could happen again. You know those trained German shepherds and Doberman pinschers they made me put out there on the grounds? Security, they said. Last night we lost our sixth one to snipers. Now I'm being advised to allow an electrified barrier to be installed, to surround the White House, to isolate me, to make me a prisoner in my own home, the way most decent citizens of this country have been forced to confine themselves behind dead bolts and alarms. Well, gentlemen, I won't have it. We're going to bring civilization back to this land of ours with the 35th Amendment. And we're going to do it by winning in California."

"Amen," said Tynan.

At that moment, Miss Ledger appeared. "Pardon me, Mr. President. . . . Mr. Collins, your bodyguard is at the door. He has to speak to you. He says it is urgent."

"Thank you," said Collins. He turned back to the President. "I'm prepared to do whatever I can do."

"I'll let you know next week. You'd better go now and attend to your business."

After bringing Karen forward to join him in thanking the President for the evening, Collins said a perfunctory good night to those in his immediate area.

Preceding Karen, Collins hastily crossed the Cabinet Room to the doorway where the sturdy figure of his bodyguard, Agent Mike Hogan, was waiting.

"What's the problem?" Collins asked as he reached his bodyguard.

"It's Colonel Noah Baxter, sir," said Hogan in an undertone. "He's come out of his coma. He's conscious. But he's dying."

"Dammit, that's terrible. Are you sure?"

"Definitely. No question. The word came from Mrs. Baxter herself to the Justice switchboard, and it was relayed to me in the car. Colonel Baxter's first words, when he regained consciousness, were that he wanted to see you. He has to see you. It's about something urgent. He wants to tell you something important. Mrs. Baxter begged me to get you to his bedside before it's too late."

Collins grabbed Karen's arm and headed into the corridor. "Okay, let's get over to Bethesda. We'd better not waste a minute." He looked down at Karen. "I wonder what the devil this is all about."

THE CADILLAC LIMOUSINE HAD gone at breakneck speed north on Wisconsin Avenue, crossed the Maryland line, passed the golf course of the Chevy Chase Country Club, slowed through the business district of Bethesda, taken the curved road into the hospital facility, and braked to a halt before the main entrance of the white tower that was the main building in the Bethesda National Naval Medical Center complex.

Bidding Karen to remain behind in the car with Hogan and Pagano, the driver, Chris Collins hastened into the building. As he entered, a Navy officer wearing two bars on his open-collared shirt quickly intercepted him.

"Attorney General Collins?"

"Yes."

"Follow me, sir. They're on the fifth floor."

As they ascended in the elevator, Collins inquired, "How is Colonel Baxter?"

"When I came down twenty minutes ago, he was hanging on by just a thread, I'm sorry to say."

"I hope I'm in time. Who's with him?"

"The Mrs., of course. And their little grandson, Rick Baxter. He's staying with his grandparents while his parents are in Kenya on some Government business. We tried to reach them tonight. No luck. Then, there are two doctors and a nurse in attendance. And—I almost forgot—Father Dubinski is standing by. He's from Holy Trinity Church in Georgetown, the church the Kennedys used to attend. . . . Here we are, sir."

As they proceeded quickly up the corridor, they passed several uniformed medical officers in consultation. To Collins, Bethesda seemed more a military installation than a hospital.

When they reached a private hospital room with an open door, Collins' guide gestured toward it. "In here, sir. The Colonel has two adjoining rooms, and this one is used as a sitting room. He's in the other."

Entering the temporary sitting room, which was empty, Collins heard a soft sobbing off to one side, turned, and saw that the door to the next room was ajar. He could see only a portion of the bed, but then he made out a tableau in a dim corner of the next room. There was gray-haired, dumpy Hannah Baxter, for whom he had great respect, seated in a chair, a handkerchief to her eyes, weeping inconsolably. There was the boy, the grandson, Rick—he was twelve, Collins recalled—clutching her arm, looking pale, confused, tearful. Standing over them was the black-garbed priest.

"Please wait, sir," said the officer who had escorted Collins. "I'll let them know you're here."

He disappeared into the next room, closing the door behind him.

Collins found a cigarette, brought his lighter to it, and paced nervously around the small, cheerless room. Again, for the dozenth time, he wondered what was so urgent that Colonel Baxter had to tell him on what was to be his last night on earth. Although Collins knew the Colonel and his wife fairly well from occasional social invitations, he had never been close to them, and most of his relationship with the Colonel had definitely been of a business nature. What could the Colonel have to say to him in these fading moments?

Presently the door to the adjoining room opened, and Collins automatically put out his cigarette and stood stock still. The officer, who did not look at him again, emerged, followed by a nurse and little Rick. They went past Collins without recognition and out into the corridor. Seconds later, the doorway from the next room was filled by a black-robed figure. This obviously was Father Dubinski, of Holy Trinity Church.

As the priest carefully but firmly shut the door behind him, he gave Collins a silent nod, then crossed to close the corridor door. Collins watched him: a short, stocky, quiet man, the clergyman, with jet black hair, surprisingly light blue eyes, sunken cheeks, a composed mouth; a man perhaps in his mid-forties.

"Mr. Collins? I'm Father Dubinski." He had reached Collins, and for a moment he stared down at the floor.

"Yes, I know," said Collins. "I was at the White House when I got the message from Hannah—from Mrs. Baxter—that the Colonel was dying, that he urgently wanted to see me, that he had something important to tell me. I came as quickly as I could. Is he conscious? Can I see him now?"

The priest cleared his throat. "I'm afraid not. I'm sorry to say it's too late. Colonel Baxter died no more than ten minutes ago." He paused. "May his soul rest in peace for all eternity."

Collins did not know what to say. "That—that's tragic," he said, finally. "He died ten minutes ago? I—I can't believe it."

"I'm afraid it's true. Noah Baxter was a fine man. I know how you feel, because I know how I feel. But, once again, God's will be done."

"Yes," Collins said.

He did not know whether it was proper, in this immediate period of mourning, to try to find out why the Colonel had summoned him here. But proper or not, he knew he must inquire.

"Uh, Father, was the Colonel lucid before he died? Was he able to speak at all?"

"He spoke a little."

"Did he tell anyone—you or Mrs. Baxter—why he wanted to see me?"

"No, I'm afraid not. He simply informed his wife that it was urgent that he see you, speak to you."

"And he said nothing more?"

The priest fidgeted with his rosary. "Well, after that, he did speak briefly to me. I advised him that I was present to administer the Sacraments of Reconciliation, Anointing of the Sick, and Viaticum if he so wished. He requested that I give him these sacraments, and I was able to do so in time for him to be reconciled with God Almighty as a good Catholic. Almost immediately after, he closed his eyes forever."

Collins was determined to cut through all this spiritual talk. "Father, are you saying he made a deathbed confession?"

"Yes, I heard his final confession."

"Well, was there anything in this confession that could give me a clue—a clue to what he was trying to tell me that was so urgent?"

Father Dubinski pursed his lips. "Mr. Collins," he replied gently, "confession is a confidential matter."

"But if he told you something he wanted me to know—?"

"I cannot permit myself to determine what might be for you and what was meant for the Lord. I repeat, Colonel Baxter's confession must remain confidential. I can reveal no part of it. Now I'd better return to Mrs. Baxter." He paused. "Again, I'm sorry, Mr. Collins."

The priest started for the adjoining room, and Collins walked slowly out into the corridor.

Minutes later, he had left the hospital, and settled into the back seat of the limousine beside an anxious Karen. He ordered the driver to take them home to McLean.

As the car began to move, he turned his head to Karen.

"I was too late. He was dead when I arrived."

"That's terrible. Do you— Did you find out what he wanted to tell you?"

"No, I haven't the faintest idea." He slumped deeper into the seat, worried and wondering. "But I intend to find out—somehow. Why would he waste his last words on me? I wasn't even a close friend."

"But you are the Attorney General. You succeeded him as Attorney General."

"Exactly what I was thinking," Collins said, half to himself. "It must have had something to do with that. With my job. Or with the country's affairs. One or the other. Something that

might be important to all of us. He said it was important when
he sent for me. I can't let this remain unresolved. I don't know
how yet, but I've got to learn what he wanted to tell me."

He felt Karen's hand tighten on his arm. "Don't, Chris, don't
get involved further. I can't explain it. But it scares me. I don't
like living scared."

He stared out the window into the night. "And I don't like living with mysteries," he said.

II
_____

THEY BURIED COLONEL NOAH Baxter, former Attorney General of the United States, on a wet May morning in one of the few available plots left in the 420-acre Arlington National Cemetery across the Potomac from Washington, D.C. Relatives, friends, members of the Cabinet, President Wadsworth himself, were at the graveside as Father Dubinski intoned the final prayer.

It was over now, and the living, filled with sadness and relief, wended their way back to the business of life.

Director Vernon T. Tynan, his shorter sinewy assistant, Associate Deputy Director Harry Adcock, and Attorney General Christopher Collins, who had come to the rites together, were now leaving together. They walked silently in step down Sheridan Avenue, past the gravestones of Pierre Charles L'Enfant and General Philip H. Sheridan, past the eternal flame burning low over the grave of President John F. Kennedy, going steadily toward Tynan's official bulletproof limousine.

The silence was broken only once, by Tynan, as they moved past a cluster of Civil War headstones. "See those Union and Confederate headstones?" said Tynan, pointing. "Know how you can tell the Union ones from the Confederate ones? The Union dead have headstones with rounded tops. The Confederate dead have headstones with pointed tops—pointed, they said, "To keep those goddam Yankees from sitting on them.' Know who told me that? Noah Baxter. Old Noah told me that one day when we were walking like this away from some three-star general's funeral." He snorted. "Guess Noah never imagined how soon he himself would be here." He turned his face toward the sky. "Guess the rain's through for the day. Well, we'd better get back to work."

They had reached Tynan's car, where an FBI agent held the rear door open. Harry Adcock climbed in, followed by Tynan, and then Collins.

In moments they had moved out of the cemetery through Arlington's Memorial Gate, and headed over the Memorial Bridge, going between the gold statues of horses at the far end of the bridge and on into the city.

Tynan was the first to resume talking. "I'll miss old Noah," he said. "You don't know how close we were. I enjoyed the old curmudgeon."

"He was a good guy," agreed Adcock, who in public was usually an echo of his superior.

"I'll miss him, too," said Collins, not to be outdone. "After all, he's the reason I'm here doing what I'm doing today."

"Yeah," said Tynan. "I'm just sorry he didn't hang around long enough to see the fruits of his labor on the 35th Amendment come into being. Everyone gives the President credit for coming up with the 35th. But actually, Noah was responsible for getting it off the ground. He believed in it like a religion that could save us all. We owe it to him to put it over in California."

"We'll try," said Collins.

"We've got to do more than try, Chris. We've got to do it absolutely." He gave Collins an appraising look. "I know old Noah would be counting on you, Chris, to push it over in the last lap as he would have done it himself if he were here. I tell you, Chris, Colonel Noah Baxter considered the passage of that amendment the most urgent priority of all."

Sitting there in the back seat, squeezed against the steel-lined side of the car by Tynan's expansive bulk, Collins caught the word *urgent*. Instantly, his mind went back to the night scene in the hospital when the priest had confirmed that Colonel Baxter had wanted to see him about something *urgent*. Could it have had to do with the 35th Amendment? Later, Collins had told his wife that he didn't like mysteries, that he intended to solve this one. At the time, he had had no idea where to begin. This moment, there seemed to be a place to begin. Maybe Tynan, who had been so close to Colonel Baxter, could offer something helpful, a lead.

"Vernon," Collins said, "apropos of the Colonel's priorities, something possibly relevant to that came up the other night when we were at the White House. It was all very strange. Remember how I had to leave in a hurry? Well, I got a message from Bethesda that Colonel Baxter was dying, and he wanted to see me on an urgent matter, to tell me something of vital importance. I rushed to the hospital, and went up to his suite. It was too late. He'd died just minutes before."

"Oh, yeah?" said Tynan. "That is kind of strange. Did you find out what he thought was so important for him to tell you?"

"That's the point. I didn't. He spoke some last words, just before dying, not to me but to a priest. He made his confession to the priest, the one at Arlington today, Father Dubinski. Well, when I heard that from the priest, I thought maybe in his last moments the Colonel might have got something off his chest that he wanted to speak to me about. But Father Dubinski wouldn't say. He only said there was a confession, and confessions are confidential."

"They are," Adcock chimed in.

"What I'm wondering," Collins continued, "is if you have any idea of the kind of information Colonel Baxter might have wanted to communicate to me—some unfinished business in the Department he might have discussed with you—some program or job or background I should know about. It really puzzles me."

Tynan stared at his chauffeur's back a moment. "I'm afraid it puzzles me, too. I can't imagine what Noah had in mind. I can't think of anything outstanding we discussed before he had his stroke five months ago. I only repeat what had been uppermost in his mind. Of the thousand things he was involved in, one dominated all others. That was getting the 35th Amendment ratified and made into law. Maybe what he had to tell you had to do with that."

"Maybe. But exactly what about the 35th? It had to be something special if he summoned me to his deathbed."

"Of course, he didn't know he was on his deathbed. So maybe it wasn't all that special."

"He said it was urgent," Collins persisted. "You know, I was thinking of going back to that priest and giving him another try."

Adcock leaned across Tynan. His face, blemished by acne, was solemn. "If you knew priests the way I do, you'd know you'd be wasting your time. Only God can get anything out of them."

"Harry's right," Tynan agreed. He bent and peered out the window. "Well, here we are at Justice. Home again."

Collins glanced outside. "Yes. Time to get to work. Thanks for the lift."

He opened the door and stepped down into Pennsylvania Avenue in front of the Department of Justice.

"Chris," Tynan called after him, "better get your bags packed. The President is still considering sending you to California next week. He's just trying to make up his mind."

"If he says Go, I'll be ready."

Tynan and Adcock watched Collins enter the building as their limousine started for the rear of the J. Edgar Hoover Building and the Director's private parking place in the second of three basements beneath ground level.

As the car rounded the block and headed toward E Street, Tynan's eyes met Adcock's. "You heard all that, Harry, didn't you?"

"I sure did, chief."

"What do you think old Noah wanted to say to him that was so goddam urgent he had to say it before he died?"

"I can't imagine, chief," Adcock replied. "Or maybe I can, but don't want to."

"Maybe I can, too. You think maybe Noah Baxter got religion at the last minute and wanted to spill his gut?"

"Could be. Can't say. No way to know. No way ever to know. Anyway, thank God, he didn't have time to babble."

"But he did, Harry. You heard. He babbled something to the priest."

"Hell, chief, that was a holy confession. A dying man making a confession, he doesn't talk—he doesn't talk business."

Tynan screwed up his face. "How do we know? Call it what you want, a confession or whatever, the fact is that Noah talked to someone about what was on his mind before croaking. He *talked*, you hear me? He wanted to talk to someone about something urgent, and he talked to someone after all. I don't like it. I want to know what Noah talked about and how much he talked. I want to know that very much."

The limousine had dipped down the ramp leading beneath the J. Edgar Hoover Building.

Adcock took out a handkerchief, coughed and then expectorated into it. "That's a tough one, chief," he said finally.

"They're all tough ones, Harry. After a while, they're not so tough. Let's be honest, Harry. Tough ones are our meat. The boss, J. Edgar himself, used to say that. Tough ones are our meat. We live by them. They sustain us. The Bureau's profession is making people talk. Especially when they have information that endangers Government security. There's no reason that priest—whatever his name is—"

"Father Dubinski. He's at Holy Trinity in Georgetown. That's where all the Government Catholics go."

"Okay, that's where I want you to go, Harry. The Bureau makes people talk, and I don't see why this Dubinski should be an exception. I think it's time you went to church. Pay the good Father a friendly visit. Find out what old Noah said to him with his last words. Find out how much this Dubinski knows. If he knows what he shouldn't know, we'll find the means to shut him up. Harry, I'd like you to get right on that."

"Chief, you know I'll do anything. But on this one, I don't think we have a chance."

"Oh, no? Well, I say we've got every chance in the world. In fact, I say you can't miss if you handle it right. Harry, for Chrissake, I'm not asking you to go in there unarmed. Have the Department run a thorough check on Father Dubinski first. These God lovers are no different from anybody else. You know our axiom. Everybody's got something to hide. So has this priest. He's human. He must have vices. Or had them. Maybe he boozes on the side. Maybe he laid a choirboy once. Maybe he's banging his eighteen-year-old housekeeper in the closet. Maybe his mother was a Commie. There's always something. You go to that God lover with what *he* hasn't confessed, and you confront him with it. He'll talk all right. You won't be able to shut him up. He'll trade anything for our silence."

The limousine had reached the second underground level and had drawn to a halt in the Director's parking slot.

Tynan stared ahead, motionless for a moment. "I'm damn serious about this, Harry. We're too close to home to have anything go wrong. Clear your slate. This is priority one. Okay, Harry?"

"Okay, chief. It's done."

VERNON T. TYNAN WORKED at his desk for two hours after the funeral, and then, at precisely twelve forty-five, he rose from his desk, went into his private bathroom to spruce up, pulled one of the Official and Confidential file folders out of the top-security cabinet, and walked briskly to the elevator.

Downstairs, in the second-level basement, between the indoor ballistics range and the gym, he found his driver and car still waiting.

"Alexandria," Tynan said to the driver.

"Yes, sir," the driver said automatically, and seconds later they were on their way.

It was Saturday. And every Saturday at this hour, as he had done since he had become Director of the Federal Bureau of Investigation, Tynan observed the sacred ritual of driving out to the Golden Years Senior Citizens Village to have lunch with his mother.

He had learned, some years after the death of J. Edgar Hoover, that the Old Man had lived with his own mother, Anna Marie, until her death in 1938. Hoover had treated his mother with kindness and respect, and it had been an example Tynan had taken seriously. Great men, he knew, always had a big place in their hearts for their mothers. Not only Hoover. Look at Napoleon. The trouble with the country was that not enough young people, and older people, too, had respect for their mothers. There would be less crime in the country if wayward young men began to consider a regular visit to their mothers, instead of their guns, their Saturday-night special.

When they reached the Senior Citizens Village, and pulled up before the building where he had purchased a comfortable four-room apartment for his mother, Tynan reminded the driver, "One hour."

"One hour, sir."

Tynan went into the building and swung left to her apartment door. He had an entrance key as well as an alarm key to her apartment. He pressed the red alarm signal to see if it was on or off. It was off. He would have to remind her again to keep the alarm on, even when she was in. No precaution must be overlooked, especially these days with hooligans and thugs and left-wing Commie terrorists rampant. It would not be beyond some revolutionary conspirators to try to break in on the mother of the FBI Director, and then hold her for some incredible ransom, like demanding the freedom of all the other hundreds of left-wingers now incarcerated in Federal penitentiaries (where they belonged). Yes, he must definitely alert his mother.

He inserted the entrance key into the door, opened it, and went inside. He found her in her usual place, in the padded contour chair before the color television set.

"Hi, Mom," he said.

She waved a veiny hand without looking up, and concentrated fiercely on the antics taking place on the television screen. Despite her absorption in her favorite game show, Tynan went to her and pecked a kiss on her powdered forehead. She acknowledged this with a quick smile, then held a forefinger to her lips. She said, "Lunch is all prepared. This'll be over soon. Take off your jacket." She again riveted her attention on the screen, then held her sides and cackled with laughter.

Tynan laid down his file folder, removed his jacket, and hung it neatly on the back of a chair. He plucked a cigar from the breast pocket, unwrapped it, nipped off the end of the cigar, and held his lighter a half inch from the cigar (as the President always did), inhaling and enjoying the aroma.

Smoking, he stood beside his mother, watching the mindless game show with her, then looked at her with pride.

He had done well by his mother. Had J. Edgar Hoover been able to see him now, this minute, the Old Man would have commended him.

At eighty-four, Rose Tynan was still as healthy as an Abkhasian—no, not that Commie place—as healthy as a Vilcabamban—much better—a Vilcabamban peasant. She was a down-to-earth Irishwoman, big-shouldered, hefty, with the mealy features of an Irish potato. Considering her age, she was in good shape, except for a slight stoop, an arthritic limp, and an occasional lapse of memory.

At last the game show was over. Rose Tynan grunted her way to her feet, snapped off the television set, took her son by the arm, led him into the small dining room, and sat him down at the head of the table.

"Lunch is coming," she said.

"Mom, the alarm was off when I came in. You should keep it on all the time. For my sake."

"I forget sometimes. I'll try to remember next time."

"Be sure you do."

"How are things at the office?"

"As usual. Busy."

"I won't keep you here long."

"Mom, I'm here because I want to be here. I enjoy seeing you."

"So then let's be making it twice a week for lunch."

She disappeared into the kitchen and returned with the platter of corned beef and cabbage. His normal lunch, just as the Old Man's had been, was cream-of-chicken soup and cottage cheese. But this was Saturday.

"Smells great, Mom."

"The bread's on the table. Pumpernickel. Have some. Sure you won't have a bigger slice? Oops, I forgot the beer."

She went into the kitchen again and emerged with a foaming beer stein. Setting the beer before him, she lowered herself noisily into her chair.

"Well, Vern, what was your morning like?"

"Not very happy, I'm afraid. I was a pallbearer at Noah Baxter's funeral."

"The funeral was today? That's right, it was."

"It was this morning."

"Poor Hannah Baxter. Well, at least she has her son, and a grandson also. I'll have to call Hannah."

"You should."

"I'll call her tomorrow. How's the corned beef? Is it too fatty?"

"It's perfect, Mom."

"All right, now tell me what's new."

"You tell me."

They fell into the never-changing Saturday routine.

Rose Tynan first. She recounted the latest gossip about her neighbors in the Senior Citizens Village. Midweek there had been a movie about a man and an orphan and a dog. She gave a lengthy synopsis of the entire scenario. Then she spoke of the letters she had written and the mail she had received.

Vernon T. Tynan's turn. He spoke of Harry Adcock.

"How's Harry?"

"He sends his regards."

"He's a fine young man."

He spoke of Christopher Collins, the new Attorney General.

"He's nice, Vern?"

"I don't know, Mom. We'll see."

He spoke of President Wadsworth. He discussed two murderers on the FBI's Ten Most Wanted Fugitives list who had been apprehended in Minneapolis and Kansas City. He came to the 35th Amendment just as he took the last bite of the stringy corned beef.

"Don't worry, Vern. You'll win it."

"We need one more state, and there's only one left."

"You'll win."

The lunch was over on schedule. There were ten minutes left before the driver was due to return.

"Ready for the OC file, Mom?"

"Always ready," she said with a broad smile.

He left the table, went into the living room, and brought the top-security Official and Confidential file back with him.

This file, for the next ten minutes, was his regular Saturday gift to his mother. This file contained the FBI's weekly input, largely sexual and potentially scandalous, on celebrities of the stage, screen, and sports worlds, with additional juicy tidbits on a variety of well-known politicians, industrialists, and jetsetters. Rose Tynan, who read all the fan magazines and national weekly newspapers, reveled in the gossip.

Again, Tynan felt that had J. Edgar Hoover been here, he would have approved. After all, it had been Hoover who had gathered material on the sex lives and drinking habits of prominent Americans and who had regularly passed this secret material on to President Lyndon B. Johnson for the Chief Executive's more pleasurable bedtime reading.

Tynan opened his folder and took up the OC memorandums one by one.

"For starters, a real treat, Mom. Your favorite movie star." He read off the name of the handsome liberal motion-picture actor his mother adored, and she clucked with anticipation. "He went to a massage parlor in Las Vegas last week, undressed, had two nude girls tie him down to a cot, and then had them whip him."

"That's all?" said the jaded Rose Tynan, a connoisseur of the outrageous, with disappointment.

"Well, some people think that's pretty hot stuff," said Tynan. "But I can do better. You know the Congresswoman who makes all those anti-Pentagon speeches?" He gave his mother the name. "Nobody knows this, but we've found out she's a lesbian. Her press secretary, a Radcliffe girl of twenty-two . . ."

He went on, then on and on, for the remainder of the ten minutes, as Rose Tynan sat enchanted.

When he was done and had closed the folder, his mother

said, "Thank you, Vern. You're a good boy. You're always thoughtful about your mother."

"Thank you, Mom."

At the door, she studied his face.

"You have lots of troubles," she said. "I can see."

"These are bad times in the country, Mom. There's a lot to do. If we don't get the 35th Amendment through, I don't know what will happen."

"You know what's best for everybody," she said. "I was telling Mrs. Grossman the other day—she's in the apartment above me—I was telling her you'd know what to do if you were President. I believe it. You should be President."

He winked at her as he opened the door. "Maybe I'll be better than that one day," he said. "We'll see."

IT HAD BEEN A long day for Chris Collins. Trying to make up for the time he had lost attending Colonel Baxter's funeral in the morning, he had worked straight through without taking off his usual hour for lunch. Now, seated with his wife and two of their closest friends near the white Parian marble hearth in the upstairs dining room of the 1789 Restaurant on 36th Street in Georgetown, he was just beginning to satisfy his hunger.

Two Scotches, a bowl of French onion soup, and the Caesar salad he had shared with Karen had brought him to his first moment of relaxation today. Cutting and eating his roast duck in orange sauce, Collins glanced up to see whether Ruth and Paul Hilliard were enjoying the entrées they had ordered. Obviously, they were.

Collins considered Hilliard—it was hard to think of him as the junior Senator from California—with affection. He had known Hilliard from their beginnings, when Hilliard had been a San Francisco city councilman and he himself had been an ACLU attorney. In those early days, they had played handball together three times a week at the Y, and Collins had been best man at Hilliard's wedding. And here they were, years later, both in Washington, he Attorney General Collins and his friend Senator Hilliard. They both had made it big.

Hilliard was a pleasant man, bespectacled, scholarly, moderate, soft-spoken, the perfect companion for an evening like this. The talk, as usual, had been easy—some gossip about the Kennedys, the prospects for the Washington Redskins football team in the fall, yet another film on the life of Lizzie Borden that everyone was going to see.

Hilliard had finished with his broiled filet mignon, placed his fork and knife neatly on his cleaned plate, and begun to fill his new Danish pipe.

"How'd you like the wine, Paul?" Collins asked. "It's California, you know."

"Just look at my glass." He indicated his empty glass. "The best testimony for our vineyards."

"Want more?"

"I've had enough of California wine," said Hilliard, lighting his pipe. "But not enough of California. I was waiting to discuss it with you. I guess that's where it's all going to be happening from now on."

"Going to be happening? Oh, you mean the 35th."

"Ever since the Ohio vote the other night, I've been getting calls from California. The whole state is buzzing with it."

"What's the word?"

Hilliard blew a smoke ring. "The odds are the bill's going to be ratified, from what I hear. The Governor is going to be announcing his support of it later in the week."

"That'll make the President happy," said Collins.

"Between us, it's a deal," said Hilliard. "The Governor is going to run for the Senate after this term. He wants Wadsworth's backing, and the President's always been lukewarm about him. So they've made a trade. The Governor'll come out for the 35th if the President will come out for him." He paused. "Too bad."

Collins, who had been chewing his last morsel of duck, ceased chewing. "What does that mean, Paul?" He swallowed his food. "What—what's too bad?"

"That the big guns are lining up behind the 35th in California."

"I thought you were for it."

"I wasn't for it or against it. I sort of played the innocent bystander. I just watched and waited to see what would happen. I suspect that's the way you've felt privately. But now that the decision is in our backyard, I'm inclined to act, to get involved."

"On which side? Against it?"

"Against it."

"Don't be hasty, Paul," Ruth Hilliard said nervously. "Why don't you wait and see how people feel about it?"

"We'll never know what people feel until they know how we feel. They're depending on their leaders to tell them what's right. After all—"

"Are you sure what's right, Paul?" Collins interrupted.

"I'm becoming sure," said Hilliard quietly. "Based on what I'm gradually learning of the situation back home, the provisions of the 35th Amendment amount to overkill. That bill is loaded with too heavy an armament aimed at too small an enemy. That's what Tony Pierce thinks, too. He's coming into California to fight the Amendment."

"Pierce isn't to be trusted," said Collins, remembering Director Tynan's tirade against the civil rights advocate in the White House the other night. "Pierce's motives are suspect. He's made the 35th a personal vendetta. He's fighting Tynan as much as the Amendment, because Tynan fired him from the FBI."

"Do you know that for a fact?" said Hilliard.

"Well, that's what I've heard. I haven't checked it."

"Check it, because I've heard different. Pierce became disillusioned by the FBI when he was part of it. He threw his support to some Special Agents Tynan was manhandling. In retaliation, Tynan decided to exile him to somewhere—Montana or Ohio or some such place—and so Pierce resigned to fight for his reforms from the outside. I'm told Tynan spread the story that he was fired."

"No matter," said Collins with a trace of impatience. "What matters is that you say you've decided to side with those opposing the 35th."

"Because that bill troubles me, Chris. I know the underlying purpose of it, but it's too strong, and more and more I feel its provisions could be abused or misused. Frankly, the only thing that makes me feel safe about its passage is that John Maynard is on the high bench as Chief Justice. He'd keep it honest. Still, the possibility of its passage is really beginning to bother me."

"There's a positive side, Paul. It'll keep crime from overwhelming us. Crime in California alone is just becoming too much—"

"Is it?" said Hilliard.

"What do you mean, is it? You read the FBI statistics as well as I do."

"Statistics, figures. Who was it said that figures don't lie, but liars figure?" Hilliard squirmed uneasily in his chair. He put down his pipe and then looked directly at Collins. "Actually, that is something I've been wanting to discuss with you. Statistics, I mean. I've been a little hesitant about bringing it up, because it's your Department and I was afraid you might be touchy."

"What do I have to be touchy about? Hell, we're friends, Paul. Speak your mind."

"All right." Still, he hesitated, then decided to go ahead. "I had a disturbing call yesterday. From Olin Keefe."

The name did not register with Collins.

"He's a newly elected state legislator from San Francisco," Hilliard explained. "He's a good guy. You'd like him. Anyway, he's on some committee that required him to talk to a number of police chiefs in the Bay area. Two of them—the police chiefs—wondered aloud why the FBI was trying to make them look bad. The police chiefs claimed the figures on crime that they submitted to Director Tynan—and which they said were accurate—were nowhere near as high as the figures you put out."

"I don't put out any figures, except technically," said Collins, mildly irritated. "Tynan gathers them from local communities and computes them. Formally, my office releases them, makes them public for him. Anyway, that's not important. What are you telling me, Paul?"

"I'm trying to tell you that young Keefe—State Assemblyman Keefe—suspects Director Tynan is doctoring those national crime statistics, tampering with them, especially the figures delivered to him from California. He's giving us a bigger crime wave than we actually have."

"Why should he do that? It makes no sense."

"It makes plenty of sense. Tynan is doing that—if he is doing it—to scare our legislators into passing the 35th Amendment."

"Look, I know Tynan is gung-ho on getting the Amendment passed. I know the Bureau has always been statistics-happy. But why trouble to do a risky thing like falsifying figures? What does he have to gain?"

"Power."

"He already has power," said Collins flatly.

"Not the kind of power he would have as head of the Committee on National Safety, if the emergency provision of the 35th were ever invoked. Then it would be Vernon T. Tynan *über Alles*."

Collins shook his head. "I don't believe that. Not one bit. Paul, I live in Justice. I've been part of it for eighteen months, in one capacity or another. I know what goes on in the Department. You're removed from it. And that young Assemblyman of yours, Keefe, he's also on the outside. He doesn't know a damn thing."

Hilliard would not be stopped. He pushed his rimless spectacles high on the bridge of his nose and said earnestly, "He seems to know plenty, from our phone conversation. There are some other things he knows, too, and they're not pretty. You don't have to take it from me, Chris. Find out for yourself firsthand. Earlier, you said you might be going to California soon. Fine. Why don't you let me have Olin Keefe look you up? Then, just hear him out." He paused. "Unless for some reason you don't want to."

"Cut it out, Paul. You know me better than that. There'd be no reason I wouldn't want to hear facts—if they are facts. I'm not a company man. I'm as interested in the truth as you are."

"Then you're willing to see Keefe?"

"You set up the meeting and I'll be there."

"With an open mind, I hope. The fate of this whole damn republic can depend on what happens in California. I don't like some of the things going on in California right now. Please listen to everything he has to say, Chris, and then make up your own mind."

"I'll listen," Collins said firmly. He picked up the menu. "That orange sauce with the duck got to be pretty sour. Now, for a change, let's have something sweet."

THE FOLLOWING DAY, EXACTLY at noon, as he had done once every week for six months, Ishmael Young arrived in the basement of the J. Edgar Hoover Building after a drive from his rented bungalow in Fredericksburg, Virginia. Even though it was Sunday, he knew that in these critical times everyone in Justice, in the FBI, was on a seven-day week. Tynan would be expecting him. Young parked in the basement, with effort pushed out of the front seat of his second-hand red sports car, and met Special Agent O'Dea in front of the Director's private-key elevator. Sometimes it was Associate Deputy Director Adcock who met him. Today it was O'Dea, the former track star with the crew cut.

They rode the elevator up to the seventh floor, there parted company, and Young walked alone—carrying his tape recorder and briefcase—down a corridor that separated two rows of offices, and in moments he entered Director Tynan's suite.

Presently, in Tynan's spacious office high above Pennsylvania Avenue, Ishmael Young rolled a heavy easy chair closer to the low-slung circular coffee table, faced it toward the sofa where the Director would soon sit, took out his papers, and made himself ready. By twelve fifteen, Tynan's secretary, Beth, had placed a beer on the coffee table for the Director and a Diet Pepsi-Cola for his writer. Next, she brought in two containers of lunch delivered by a delicatessen nearby on 9th Street. She laid out the cream-of-chicken soup and cottage cheese for the Director, and the potato salad, pickle, and egg salad on an onion roll for his writer. Then she left. Finally, Tynan got up from behind his awesome desk, after telling someone on the phone that no calls were to come in except from the President, and he secured the office, locking both doors from the inside. Next, he went past Young into his dressing room and on to his bathroom. A minute later, rubbing his dried hands together, he emerged refreshed and dropped down on the sofa to gulp his beer.

Vernon T. Tynan enjoyed these autobiographical sessions. Obviously, because they were about himself.

Ishmael Young hated them.

Young loved the FBI, but he hated Director Tynan. He loved the FBI not for its raison d'être, but because it was flawlessly, smoothly efficient, which Young was not. He cherished all great organizations that worked—IBM, the Russian Communist party, the Vatican, the Mafia, the FBI—irrespective of what they stood for. He disliked how these mammoth machines manipulated and exploited people, but he loved how effectively these machines—bigger than life—painlessly got things done. He himself got things done mostly with a pencil, a typewriter, a mess of papers, in fits and starts, with nervous tension, and it was no way for a man to live.

He had loved and respected the FBI as an organization from that time, before his first session with Director Tynan six months ago, when Associate Deputy Director Adcock had taken him on a tour of the Bureau to give him "the feel." There had been the tourist part of the tour. Over a half million tourists came to see the exhibits annually. He didn't blame them. It had been exciting: the criminal Hall of Fame displaying John Dillinger's actual guns and bulletproof vest and his death mask; "The Crime of the Century—The Case of the A-Bomb Spies," featuring Julius and Ethel Rosenberg; the Ten Most Wanted Fugitives list; the Brink's Robbery Case exhibit; "The Sinister Hand of Soviet Espionage," starring Colonel Rudolf Abel; the indoor shooting range where every nine minutes a Special Agent gave a demonstration of deadly marksmanship using a .38-caliber service revolver and then a Thompson .45-caliber submachine gun to riddle a life-sized paper target.

Above all—and here he had been taken backstage, off limits for tourists—Ishmael Young had been enamored of the FBI files. In this clearinghouse for criminal apprehension, there had been fingerprint sets, over 250,000,000 of them. If God had hands, Young had decided, the FBI would have his fingerprints.

Among the other 8,700 gray file cabinets, there had been the Typewriter Standards file, a record of the typeface and make of every typewriter, regular or toy, ever manufactured (he would never again fantasize the typewriting of an anonymous letter). There had been the Watermark file, the Bank Robbery Note file, the National Fraudulent Note file. There had been so much else—the Serology section, where body fluids and blood were tested; the Chemistry department, where human organs were boiled; the Spectrograph room, where particles of paint were examined. He had found it hard to tear himself away from the Hairs and Fibers Unit. "When people get into a fight," Adcock had explained, "the fibers of their garments may adhere to each other. We shave all fibers off the garments, separate them, and test them to learn which belonged to the assailant and which to the victim." Then Adcock had gone on, "Our lab is our silent secret weapon. It is invincible. J. Edgar Hoover established it in 1932. As he once said, 'The minute stain of blood, the altered document, the match folder found at the scene of the burglary, the heelprint or fleck of dust often provide the essential link of evidence needed to link the criminal to his crime or clear the innocent person.' "

When he left, Young's mind had been bursting with a hundred ideas. It had been a writer's heaven. He had wondered, but had not asked Adcock, how any criminal could ever hope to escape the FBI. He had not asked because the nation was teeming with crime, and most of the criminals did get away with it.

And then he had been brought to his first official bookwriting session with Director Vernon T. Tynan.

He had somehow expected that some of his love for the Bureau would rub off on its Director. It hadn't, and then he was not surprised. He had hated Tynan from the start, before ever setting eyes on him. Tynan had wanted an autobiography, and Young had been recommended. Tynan had read two of Young's ghosted books and approved. Young had resisted. From hearsay, he had known Tynan's reputation, his egomania, and had rejected the offer to collaborate. But only briefly. Tynan had, in effect, blackmailed him and forced him to do the book.

He had never forgotten his first meeting with Tynan in this

office. There was the Director—a cat's eyes set in a bulldog's skull—saying, "At last, Mr. Young. Glad to meet you, Mr. Young." He had replied, jocularly, "Call me Ishmael." The Director had looked blank. Then, Young had known that was how he was, and that was the way it was going to be. Incidentally, Tynan had never called him Ishmael, either. The Director had probably thought it a foreigner's name. Thereafter, the Director compromised by calling him "Young" or simply "You."

Now six months of weeks had passed, and once more they were seated across from each other, Ishmael Young drinking his Diet Pepsi and Vernon T. Tynan gulping down the last of his beer. As Tynan put the beer mug aside and reached for his soup, Young knew it was the signal to begin. He leaned over, simultaneously pressed the RECORD and PLAY buttons on his portable tape recorder, nibbled at his egg-salad sandwich, and reviewed the notes in his lap. A week ago, the Director had announced the subject of this session, and Young had done his homework and had come prepared. It was not going to be easy. He reminded himself to show restraint.

"We were going to talk about J. Edgar Hoover," Tynan said, spooning up a portion of his cottage cheese, "and how he broke me in and made me what I am. I owe a lot to him. When he died in 1972, I didn't want to work for Gray or Ruckelshaus or Kelley or any of the others who followed. They were good men, but once you'd worked for the Old Man—that's what we used to call Hoover, the Old Man—once you'd worked for him, you were spoiled for anyone else. That's why I decided to quit after he died, and set up my own investigation agency. Only the President himself could make me give up my private agency to take on the head job. I guess I gave you all that already."

"Yes, sir. I have it all in transcript and edited."

"With things deteriorating the way they were, the President needed the Old Man again. Since they couldn't have him, they—meaning the President—he decided he wanted a real dyed-in-the-wool Hoover man. So he pulled me back. He's never been sorry. In fact, the opposite. I told you—didn't I?—how he took me aside a month ago and said, 'Vernon, not even

J. Edgar Hoover could have accomplished what you've managed to accomplish.' His very words."

"I remember," said Young. "That was quite a tribute."

"Well, Young, I don't want this part of the book to be a tribute to me. I want it to be a tribute to the Old Man, so readers will know why I respected him and what I learned from him."

"Yes, I've been doing a lot of reading on Hoover all week."

"You forget your reading. Those vicious press people were never fair to the Old Man, especially toward the end. You listen to what I have to say and then you'll get it right."

"I'll do that, Director."

"You write down carefully what I'm going to tell you next, just to be sure you get it with no mistakes."

"Well, sir, I have the tape on. There's no need to write it—"

"Oh, yeah, I forgot. Okay. Now, you listen. It was J. Edgar Hoover who introduced professionalism into law enforcement. He got rid of the Keystone Kops image—that's not bad, use that—and he made the public respect us. The FBI was started under Teddy Roosevelt by Attorney General Charles Bonaparte. He was born in the United States, but he was the grandson of Napoleon's youngest brother. There were a bunch of Bureau Directors that followed, and they were all either mediocre or downright bad. The last before the Old Man was William J. Burns, and he was God-awful. According to Harlan Fiske Stone, under Burns the Bureau became a private secret service for corrupt forces inside the Government. So Stone, the year before he went to the Supreme Court, he picked a twenty-nine-year-old kid named J. Edgar Hoover to head the Bureau. Hoover had worked as a library clerk for the Government. He took over the FBI when it had only 657 workers. It had some 20,000 employees when he died. He introduced the crime laboratory, the fingerprint files, the training academy at Quantico, the National Crime Information Center with its computers and almost three million records. The Old Man did that himself. And under him—like under me—no FBI agent has ever committed a criminal or corrupt act. That's something."

"It sure is," Young agreed.

"Just think of what J. Edgar Hoover did," said Tynan, finishing his cottage cheese. "He nailed John Dillinger, Pretty Boy Floyd, Alvin Karpis, Machine Gun Kelly, Baby Face Nelson, Ma Barker, Bruno Hauptmann, the eight Nazi saboteurs who landed from submarines, Julius and Ethel Rosenberg, Klaus Fuchs, the Brinks' robbers, James Earl Ray—the list is a mile long."

Ten miles long, Ishmael Young thought. He thought of the triumphs Tynan had conveniently left out. For most of his career, Hoover had ignored the Mafia, refusing to believe in its existence. Not until 1963, when Valachi decided to talk, did Hoover recognize organized crime. Singed by this evidence of the Mafia, Hoover never referred to it by that name, preferring the euphemism La Cosa Nostra instead. Apologists would claim that the Old Man had ignored the Mafia because he was afraid that the underworld might bribe and corrupt his agents as they had the local police, and thereby ruin his scandal-free record. Cynics would insist he avoided the crime syndicate because investigations would take so long that they might lower his crime-statistics batting average.

Ishmael Young thought of other Hoover triumphs that Tynan had neatly passed over. Hoover had called Dr. Martin Luther King, Jr., a notorious liar, and had wiretapped his telephone to record details of his sex life. Hoover had called former Attorney General Ramsey Clark a jellyfish. Hoover had called Father Berrigan and other Roman Catholic antiwar activists kidnappers and conspirators before their cases had been presented to the grand jury. Hoover had slurred Puerto Ricans and Mexicans, insisting people of those two nationalities couldn't shoot straight. Hoover had bugged Congressmen, as well as nonviolent civil rights and antiwar protestors. He had even investigated a fourteen-year-old Pennsylvania boy who had wanted to go to summer camp in East Germany and an Idaho scoutmaster who had wanted to take his troop camping in Russia.

Ishmael Young recalled a column by Pete Hamill that he had read. "There was no single worse subversive in this country in the past thirty years than J. Edgar Hoover. This man subverted our faith in ourselves, our belief in an open society, our hopes that men and women could live in a country free of secret po-

lice, of hidden surveillance, of persecution for political ideas."
There was all of this to discuss, but Young held his tongue.

"And I'll tell you a little personal thing few people know
about J. Edgar Hoover," Tynan was saying. "You can learn a lot
about a human being by the way he regards his parents, I always say. Well, Hoover lived with his mother, Anna Marie, until he was forty-three years old. A guy who would do that has
got to be a decent guy."

Or at least a case for Freud, Young thought.

"Let me tell you another story that gives you a picture of why
the Old Man was respected and why I especially respected him.
When J. Edgar Hoover was seventy, a lot of pressure was put on
President Lyndon Johnson to have him resign. President Johnson, to his credit, said No, he'd never let him go. Someone
asked him why, and President Johnson said, 'I'd rather have
him inside the tent pissing out than have him outside the tent
pissing in!' How do you like that?" Tynan slapped his thigh and
broke into raucous laughter. "Isn't that something?"

"It sure is," said Young doubtfully.

"I don't know if I should use the story in my book."

"Oh, yes," said Young quickly. "It's an amusing story. We can
use all the anecdotes we can get."

"Maybe you can say President Johnson said it to me," said
Tynan, winking. "No one'll know the difference. Johnson is
dead. Hoover is dead. Who's going to contradict us?"

"LBJ could have said it to you," said Young. "I think we
should put it that way. It makes the anecdote stronger."

"Yeah, you put it in that way, Young. You know how to do it.
And you can put in something else. It's a dream I had about a
week or so ago. I dreamt that J. Edgar up there was jealous as
hell of me. He was jealous because I was getting the final big
solution to crime in America—the 35th Amendment—because
I'd always have that sort of as my monument, and he wished
he'd had that opportunity. And I told him that in a way he was
as responsible as I was for the 35th because without him I
couldn't have been Bureau Director at a time like this." He
grinned at Young. "That was really my actual dream. Now, isn't
that something?"

Before Ishmael Young could say that it was, or say anything, the buzzer sounded from the Director's desk.

Tynan appeared surprised, got quickly to his feet, and tramped toward the desk. "Now, who could that be? I guess Beth must be telling me it's the President."

He picked up the receiver. "Yeah, Beth?" He listened. "Harry Adcock? Well, ask him if it can't wait. What's so important?" He stood by, then listened more intently. "Baxter what? The Holy Trinity matter—Oh, yes, of course, of course, the Collins thing. Okay, tell Harry I'll be ready for him in a minute."

He placed the receiver back on the cradle, lost in some reflection. At last he slowly turned away from the desk, and then he saw Ishmael Young and was genuinely startled. "You—I forgot you were still here. Did you hear that conversation?"

"What?" said Young, pretending bewilderment as he studied his list of questions.

"Nothing," said Tynan, satisfied. "I'm afraid some pressing business has come up. We're still running a country, you know. Sorry to shortchange you this time, Young, but I'll give you an extra half hour next week. Okay?"

"Certainly. Anything you say, sir."

As Young obediently shut off his tape recorder and hastily stuffed his papers into the briefcase, he made a mental note to replay the last of the tape the moment he returned to his bungalow. What was it that the Director had not wanted him to hear? Something about Harry Adcock's having to see him at once concerning Baxter—that would be the former Attorney General who had been buried yesterday—and the Holy Trinity matter— that would be a code name or—or maybe—Holy Trinity Church in Georgetown—and the Collins thing. That would be Christopher Collins. What could be important about all that? He determined to file away carefully these pieces of what might be an interesting jigsaw puzzle. Maybe, with a few more pieces, they'd give him a better picture of Tynan's activities.

How he'd like to get something on Tynan, he thought, as he fastened the catch of his briefcase, something to counterbalance and possibly eradicate what Tynan had on him. Something that would enable him to get out of this rotten project.

With a wheeze, he came to his feet and started across the office just as Tynan finished unlocking the second of the two doors. Tynan waited, holding the door open for his ghostwriter.

"I think this wasn't a bad session," Tynan said cheerfully. "Next week will be even better. We'll go into what I learned from the Old Man, and we'll talk about some of Vernon T. Tynan's own contributions to the Bureau. How's that?"

"That's great," said Ishmael Young. "I can't wait."

But what, he wondered, would a dead Attorney General and a Catholic church in Georgetown and a Collins thing have to do with running a country?

Maybe, if he told Collins, Collins could tell him.

Maybe Collins would then owe him a favor.

Or maybe, Young decided, for the sake of his health he'd better forget he'd heard anything at all.

"HOLD ANY CALLS," TYNAN ordered on the intercom, "unless they're from the White House." He hung up and swiveled to face Harry Adcock, who sat in the pull-up chair across from him. "Okay, Harry, what is it?"

"We ran the check on the priest, on Father Dubinski, of Holy Trinity Church. There wasn't much. Just one item, way back. He was involved in a drug case in Trenton once, but the police dropped it. Still, we—"

Tynan straightened in his swivel chair. "That's more than enough. You go in and spring that on him, and then we'll see—"

"I already have, chief," said Adcock quickly. "I went over to see him late this morning. I've just come back."

"Well, goddammit, what did he say? Did he spill Noah's confession?"

Harry Adcock was orderly and chronological in all his narratives. He never gave answers out of sequence, the way newsmen wrote leads, because he felt it led to distortions, omissions, misunderstandings. Tynan had learned to live with this habit, and he did so now. He drummed the fingers of his right hand on his desk and waited.

"I phoned Father Dubinski early this morning, identified myself, and told him I had to make an inquiry on a matter of Government security," said Adcock. "I saw him in his rectory at exactly five after eleven. I showed him my identification, my badge, and he was satisfied. At my request, we were alone, just the two of us."

"What kind of man is he?" asked Tynan.

"Dark wavy hair, lean face, swarthy, as you know. Five feet seven. Forty-four years old. Has been at Holy Trinity about twelve years. An extremely calm and cool man."

"Go on, Harry."

"I didn't waste any time. I told him it had come to our attention that he had been Colonel Noah Baxter's confessor the night Baxter expired. I said we understood that Baxter had spoken to no one but him—that is, to Father Dubinski—before dying. I asked him if that was true. He said it was true." Adcock fished into his suit-coat pocket and extracted a folded envelope with some jottings on it. "I made notes of our conversation while I was being driven back here." Adcock reviewed them. "Ah, yes, then he—Father Dubinski—he asked if I had obtained this information from Attorney General Christopher Collins. I said No."

"Good."

"Then I said, 'As you must be aware, Father, Colonel Baxter was privy to some of the Government's highest secrets. Anything he had to say to anyone outside Government, when he was ill or not in complete control of his faculties, would be of extreme interest to the Bureau. We've been trying to trace a leak on a matter of utmost security, and it would be useful for us to know if Colonel Baxter spoke to you about it.' Then I said, 'We'd like to know his last words, the words he spoke to you.'" Adcock looked up. "Father Dubinski said, 'I'm sorry. His last words were his confession. The confession is privileged. As Colonel Baxter's confessor, I can reveal his last words to no one.'"

"The bastard," muttered Tynan. "What did you say to that?"

"I said we didn't expect him to reveal the contents of a confession to any individual. This was information desired by the Government. He answered right away that the Church was not beholden to the Government. He reminded me of the separation of church and state. I represented the state, he told me, and he represented the Church. One could not encroach upon the other. I saw I was getting nowhere fast, so I toughened up."

"Good, Harry. That's better."

"I said to him, in effect—I don't remember exactly—I said to him that despite his clerical collar, he wasn't above the law. In fact, I said, it had come to our attention that he had once been very much involved with the law."

"You laid it right in there? Good, good. How did he take that?"

"He didn't say a word at first. Just let me go right on. I reeled off the evidence we had of charges against him for possible drug possession in Trenton fifteen years ago. He didn't deny it, didn't even answer, as a matter of fact. I said while he had no formal arrest record, this information—if made public—would make him look pretty bad today. I could see he was angry, all right. Ice-cold anger. He said only one thing. He said, 'Mr. Adcock, are you threatening me?' I was quick to tell him the FBI doesn't threaten anyone. I told him the FBI merely collects facts. The Justice Department acts on them. I was very careful. I knew we had no real offense to hang on him. We could only cause him trouble with his parishioners."

"All priests are vulnerable in the public relations area," said Tynan sagely.

Adcock went on. "That's what I was counting on. That's all I had to go with. I tried to make it more than it was. I told him that because of his position, he may have inadvertently stumbled upon some vital security information. I told him if he withheld it, then it was inevitable that his name and his past might come up when the security leak was probed. 'But if you cooperate with your Government now,' I said, 'then your past is no issue.' I strongly advised him to cooperate. He flatly refused."

Tynan hit the desk with his fist. "Sonofabitch."

"Chief, when we deal with clergymen, we're not dealing with the normal run of men. They don't react like ordinary human beings. It's because they've got all that God stuff for a backup. Like after he refused to cooperate, he stood up to dismiss me, and he said something to the effect, 'You've heard me. Now you can do what you want, but I must obey my vow to a higher authority than yours, one that considers the confession sacred and inviolable.' That was it, actually. When I left, I thought I'd give him one last warning. I told him to think it over—because if he didn't cooperate for the good of his country, we'd have to speak about him and his behavior and his past to his ecclesiastical superiors."

"And still he didn't crack?"

"Nope."

"Do you think he might yet?"

"I'm afraid not, chief. My evaluation is that nothing will make him talk. Even if we aired his dirty linen, I think he'd prefer minor martyrdom to talking, betraying his vows." Adcock was out of breath. He shoved the folded envelope back into his pocket. "What do we do next, chief?"

Tynan rose, thrust his hands in his trouser pockets, and paced behind his desk for a few moments. He stopped. "Nothing," he said. "We do nothing. My judgment is this. If Father Dubinski wouldn't talk to you, despite what you could have done to him, he won't talk to anyone." Tynan exhaled. "Whatever he knows doesn't matter. We're safe."

"I could still go to one of his superiors, put the screws on him that way, and maybe that'll—"

The buzzer sounded. Tynan started for his telephone. "No, forget it for now, Harry. You've done good work. Just keep tabs on Dubinski from time to time, to keep him in line. That'll be enough. Thanks."

As Adcock left the room, Tynan reached for his telephone. He picked up the receiver. "Yes, Beth? . . . Okay, I'll take it." He waited, then said, "Hello, Miss Ledger." He listened. "Fine, of course. Tell the President I'll be right over."

VERNON T. TYNAN DID not know any foreign languages, and he knew only a few foreign words he had picked up here and there. Two of the foreign words he knew were French, and they were "déjà vu." He knew them because a Special Agent had once used them in a field report, and he'd gotten sore as hell and written the agent that the FBI wrote and spoke English only and to stick to English if he didn't want to wind up in Butte, Montana. But meanwhile, he had a hazy idea of what the words meant.

Well, whenever he visited the Oval Office in the White House, which was more and more often lately, the very minute he walked into that room he had the feeling of déjà vu, of reliving an earlier experience. This was because President Wadsworth, a great admirer of President John F. Kennedy's image if not his politics, had restored the Oval Office to the way it had been when Kennedy was Chief Executive. Director Tynan, as a young FBI agent, had on several occasions accompanied J. Edgar Hoover to the Oval Office when the Director had been summoned by Kennedy to witness the signing of some crime bill. There had been the elaborate Buchanan desk, with a green-shaded lamp holding a fluorescent light. There had been, behind the desk, the green draperies hiding the White House lawn, and the six flags—the American and Presidential flags and the Army, Navy, Air Force, and Marine Corps flags. There had been two square coach lamps on the wall, and on the fireplace mantel, two model ships. The curving walls were painted antique white, and the ceiling with the Presidential seal imprinted upon it looked down on the gray-green rug with the American eagle woven into it. Across the room there had been the fireplace, the facing sofas, and the rocking chair between them. And in the tall black executive swivel chair behind the brown desk there had been President John F. Kennedy.

Now, as Appointments Secretary Nichols ushered him into the Oval Office, Vernon T. Tynan again had that feeling of déjà vu. For a half second, he thought there was President Kennedy behind the desk, speaking to someone, and there was Director Hoover beside him, and here he was a young man once more. But the moment he was announced, the past was dispelled. The man beside him, now backing away and leaving him, was Nichols, not Hoover. The man behind the desk was President Wadsworth, not President Kennedy. And the someone he was speaking to was not a Kennedy aide but Ronald Steedman, the President's personal public-opinion pollster.

"Glad you could make it, Vernon," President Wadsworth said. "Pull up a chair. You can take those newspapers off the chair and—in fact, you can throw them out—they belong in the garbage. Have you read any of them?"

Tynan removed the papers from the chair. He glanced at them—*The New York Times*, the Chicago *Sun-Times*, the Denver *Post*, the San Francisco *Chronicle*—before folding them into the wastebasket.

Without waiting for a reply, the President went on. "Coast to coast, they're ganging up on us. Like a pack of wolves, howling for our blood. We're trying to gag the country, did you know that, Vernon? You should see the editorial page of *The New York Times*. They call their State Assembly a disgrace for ratifying the 35th. They write an Open Letter to California's legislators telling them the fate of freedom is in their hands, imploring them to vote down the 35th. And someone tipped us that the next issues of *Time* and *Newsweek* carry the same defeatist sentiments."

"Self-interest," said Steedman. "The press is worried about its own future."

"They should be," growled Tynan. "The inflammatory crap they run day in and day out, along with the stuff on the tube—that's as responsible for crime and violence as anything else." He moved closer to President Wadsworth. "It's not all that one-sided, from what I've seen, Mr. President. We have as many allies as enemies."

"I don't know," said the President doubtfully.

"The New York *Daily News* and Chicago *Tribune*," cited Tynan. Then he added, "*U.S. News and World Report*, also for the 35th and on our side. Two of the networks have been neutral, but I've heard they'll come out for the 35th before the California vote."

"I hope that's true," said the President. "In the end it'll be up to the people, to the pressure they exert on their representatives. Ronald and I were just discussing that. We're just about through now. In fact, it's because of our talk that I wanted to see you. I need your advice."

"Ready to be of any help I can, Mr. President," said Tynan, dragging up a chair closer to Wadsworth's replica of Kennedy's desk."

The President wheeled toward Steedman. "Those latest figures you have from California, Ronald. How big a sampling was that?"

"Exactly 2,455 people were polled. They were asked only one question in three parts. Were they in favor of having the California Legislature approve the 35th Amendment? Or were they against its ratification? Or were they undecided?"

"Review the results again, so Vernon can hear them."

"Certainly," said Steedman. He held a computerized printout before him and began to read to both the President and Tynan. "The results of our public-opinion poll of 2,455 registered California voters, taken the two days following New York's passage of the Amendment and Ohio's rejection of it, are as follows." His finger underlined the figures on his page. "There were 41 percent in favor of the passage of the 35th. There were 27 percent against its passage. There were 32 percent who were undecided."

"That's a lot of undecideds," said the President. "Now read your poll of the California State Senate and Assembly."

Steedman nodded, shuffling his papers, and held up a new printout. "This one was less satisfactory. The legislators are obviously being cautious, waiting to hear from their constituents. Here we have 40 percent who were undecided or refused to express any opinion at all. Then, of the 60 percent of the legislators who did express an opinion, 52 percent favored passage, 48 percent were against passage."

The President shook his head glumly. "Too many fence-sitters. I don't like that."

Tynan spoke up. "Mr. President, it's our job to get them off that fence and down on the right side."

"That's why I wanted you here, Vernon. I wanted to discuss strategy. . . . Thank you, Ronald. When do I see you again?"

Steedman stood up. "Per your instructions, Mr. President,

we're running a new poll in California every week now. I should have this week's results for you next Monday."

"Call Miss Ledger and make an appointment the minute you have something."

After collecting his papers, Steedman departed, and the President and Tynan were alone in the Oval Office.

"Well, there you have it, Vernon," the President said. "Our fate is entirely in the hands of people who haven't made up their minds. So we know what has to be done. We have to instigate every stratagem, exert every possible pressure, to make them see things our way—for their own good. The life of our one last hope is at stake, Vernon."

"I'm confident it'll work our way, Mr. President."

The President was less confident. "We can't leave it to chance. The future depends upon our actions."

"You're right, of course," agreed Tynan. "I've already undertaken several moves. I'm speeding up the FBI's Uniform Crime Reports. I've notified all local police officials in California to teletype their latest crime statistics every week instead of every month. We'll now be releasing the Reports every Saturday for media coverage on Sundays. We'll saturate California with the rise in its crime rate."

"Excellent," said the President. "The problem there is that people become inured to the repetition of mere figures. Statistics simply do not dramatize the gravity of the situation." He reached across the green blotter to his scratch pad on which he'd scribbled some notes. "Often, a well-worded speech can dramatize the situation far better. And get more coverage. I was thinking of scheduling a number of Administration people— members of the Cabinet, department heads—to speak at conventions or meetings already scheduled in California's major cities. I've been listing some names here. It's difficult, however, to know who would be most effective."

Tynan pushed forward in his chair. "There's only one person who could be really effective." He pointed his finger. "You, Mr. President. You could rally the people around the 35th, and implore them, for their own future security, to put pressure on their state representatives in Sacramento."

President Wadsworth considered this, but only briefly. He shook his head. "No, Vernon, I'm afraid that wouldn't do. In fact, it might have just the opposite effect—a negative effect. You're not a politician, Vernon, so you may not understand. You have no idea how jealously the individual states guard their states' rights. The legislators and citizens alike might look upon an address from me—a speech devoted to a decision that belongs to them—as Federal interference. They could resent a President's telling them what to do. I'm afraid we have to be more subtle than that."

"Well, then," said Tynan, "what about me? I could go to California and scare the bejesus out of them so they'll support the 35th."

"No. You're too obviously a lawman. You would not be regarded as objective and reasonable. Everyone would say you have an ax to grind. Anyone from the FBI would be suspect. As I mentioned before, I've been thinking of Collins. I'd rather send someone like Chris Collins. He doesn't wear a uniform so to speak. An Attorney General would more likely be regarded as a civilian."

"Umm. Collins. . . . I've been thinking about him, too. . . . I'm not sure about him. I don't know if he's strong enough or has the conviction—"

"Exactly. His weaknesses can be assets in this case. Give him more credibility. Actually, Vernon, I have no real doubts about him. He's clearly on our side. He knows where his job is buttered. He understates, which in this situation is good, yet he carries the authority of his office. Last week we discussed sending him to California. But now I think he should play a bigger role."

"What do you have in mind? Scheduling him for a speaking tour up and down the state?"

"No, that would seem too much like programmed propaganda." The President thought about it. "Something less obvious." The President snapped his fingers. "I just remembered. I had a notion yesterday— Yes, if it could be worked out— I asked Miss Ledger to look into it. You see, Vernon, it occurred to me that if Collins *had* to be in California because he had specific business there, then it would all appear more natural. One second."

He buzzed for Miss Ledger.

Almost instantly, the door on the far side of the room opened and she appeared.

"Miss Ledger, do you recall— Yesterday when I was leaving I asked you to look into the conventions that have been set up in California—anything taking place in the next two weeks or so—an event where it might be logical for the Attorney General to speak."

"Yes," she said. "I had an answer to my inquiries an hour ago. I didn't want to disturb you."

"Well, is there anything?"

"You're in luck, Mr. President. The American Bar Association is having its annual national meeting in Los Angeles from Monday through Friday."

The President came to his feet, beaming. "Perfect. Just great. You get right on the phone to the president of the ABA—he's an old friend—and tell him I'd appreciate it very much if he could book Attorney General Collins in as their main guest speaker the last day of the convention."

Miss Ledger looked troubled. "It won't be easy, Mr. President. I learned they already have all their guest speakers set, and the main one appearing on the ABA Presidential Program on Friday at 3 P.M. is Chief Justice John G. Maynard."

"What's the difference?" said the President. "Now they can have two main guest speakers. Attorney General Collins can either precede or follow the Chief Justice. You tell them I'd consider their doing that as a personal favor."

"I'll call immediately, Mr. President."

After Miss Ledger had gone back to her office, President Wadsworth remained standing. "Well, that's taken care of. I'll inform Collins. I'll get him to give a very generalized speech on the changing approach to criminal justice. He can allude to the 35th Amendment as the hope of the future, and speak of the historic role California will play when it ratifies. I think a fair number of the state legislators will be in the audience. Maybe Collins can hold an informal cocktail party for them afterwards, do a little low-key lobbying. Well, I guess that takes care of . . ."

He was looking down at the memorandums spread on his desk. Suddenly, he snatched up one piece of paper.

"I almost forgot, Vernon. There's another matter. The television show. Did I speak to you about it?"

"No, Mr. President."

"There's a national network television show that originates from some locale prominent in the news each week. A Miss—Miss—" He squinted at the memorandum. "—Miss Monica Evans, the producer of this half-hour show, phoned McKnight. Apparently she's an old friend of his. The end of next week they want to tape a debate in Los Angeles on whether or not California should ratify the 35th Amendment. The program is called *Search for Truth*. They have two guests, each giving a different side to some controversial issue. Have you seen it?"

"I'm afraid so," said Tynan with a grimace.

"Well, they want you on this one, Vernon. They want you to present the arguments in favor of the 35th. It would be on the same day Chris is addressing the ABA. You could fly out together. I think this exposure would be important for us."

"Who's taking the other side?" asked Tynan. "Who's the other guest?"

The President consulted the memorandum once more. "Tony Pierce," said the President.

Tynan bolted upright in his chair. "Mr. President, forgive me, but I think it would be a mistake for the Director of the FBI to appear on the same program with a former FBI agent who's been a traitor to the Bureau. I don't think I should dignify the views of a lousy Commie like Pierce by being on the same show with him."

The President shrugged. "If you feel that strongly about it, Vernon, I won't press you. But I do think the exposure of our own views is important—of great importance—on a national television program like this. One of our team should appear."

"Why not Collins?" suggested Tynan. "He's going to be out in Los Angeles at that time anyway. He could do the show as well as make his speech. As Attorney General, he should be welcome on the program."

President Wadsworth seemed pleased. "Good idea," he said. "Very good idea. I'll have McKnight call this Miss Evans and confirm Collins as your substitute." He bobbed his head thoughtfully. "Well, that gives Collins plenty to do out there for our cause. It's got to be a help."

He extended his hand, and Tynan scrambled to his feet to shake it. "I'm sure it will, Mr. President."

"Thanks for everything, Vernon." He grinned. "Well, California, here we come." He reached for his telephone. "And Attorney General Collins, there you go."

IN HIS DEPARTMENT OF Justice office, the phone receiver caught between his ear and shoulder, Chris Collins busily wrote the pertinent parts of the President's instructions on the sheet of paper before him.

Although making the obligatory agreeable sounds to the President's proposals, Collins did not like what he had been hearing. He did not mind going to California. It would be Old Home Week, a chance to see his grown son, catch up with friends, get some sunshine. What he did not like was being forced to defend the 35th Amendment publicly, debate it with someone like Tony Pierce, before a nationwide television audience. He had often watched *Search for Truth*, enjoyed it, but he knew a guest could not equivocate or pussyfoot on that show. The debates often led to terrible wrangles, exaggerated positions, and his seat on the program could be a hot seat.

Collins felt equal distaste at the idea of appearing on the same platform with Chief Justice Maynard, a man whose libertarian beliefs he respected and whose civil rights decisions he admired, and being forced in Maynard's presence to take a definite public stand in favor of the 35th Amendment. Until now, Collins had avoided anything more than a mild commitment to the Administration's policies. Now he would have to put it on the line, play the President's pitchman. Doing so in front of

Chief Justice Maynard would be an embarrassment. Still, he had no choice.

"So that's it, Chris," he heard the President say. "Have you got it all straight?"

"I think so, Mr. President. Next Friday. Los Angeles. One o'clock in the afternoon, *Search for Truth* at the network studios. Three o'clock, American Bar Association, Century Plaza Hotel."

"Really bone up for those two. Don't let Pierce trample all over the 35th. Belt him hard."

Collins swallowed. "I'll do my best, Mr. President."

"As for the ABA, prepare a solid speech, Chris. This will be a different audience from the television one. This will be a houseful of professionals. Don't hit them on the head with the 35th too early. Save it for a strong windup. Lay the nation's destiny on the wisdom of California."

"I'll try."

"We're depending on you. See you before you leave."

After hanging up, Collins stared gloomily out the window for a while. Finally, shoving the sheet with his schedule aside, he resumed his paperwork.

Soon, he was immersed in legal briefs. The telephone rang constantly, but he was not interrupted. Apparently Marion was able to field the calls herself. The next time he lifted his head from his work to stretch, to gaze out the window, he saw that darkness had fallen. He consulted his watch. Day's end for everyone in Justice. If he too left now, it would be the first time in months that he would be home in time for dinner. He made up his mind to surprise Karen and get home at a reasonable hour.

Rising with his briefcase, he began to fill it with what remained of his papers.

The telephone rang. He ignored it. Then he heard the sound of the intercom, and Marion's voice coming through. "Mr. Collins, there's a Father Dubinski on the line. I don't recognize the name. He says you might. He would not give me a message. He says it is important that he speak to you personally."

Collins recognized the name at once, and was immediately curious. "I'll take it. Thanks. See you in the morning."

He sat down, took up the receiver, and punched the blinking button. "Father Dubinski? This is Christopher Collins."

"I didn't know if you'd speak to me." The priest's voice sounded very distant. "I didn't know if you'd remember. We met the night Colonel Noah Baxter died at Bethesda."

"Certainly I remember you, Father. In fact, I had considered getting in touch with you myself. I wanted to talk—"

"That's exactly why I'm calling," said the priest. "I would like to see you. The sooner the better. In fact, if possible, I'd like to see you tonight. It's about a matter that may be of some interest to you. Nothing I'd wish to discuss on the telephone. If you can't make it tonight, then perhaps in the morning—"

Collins was alert, his curiosity now totally aroused. "I can make it tonight. In fact, within the next half hour."

"I'm glad." The priest sounded relieved. "Would it be an imposition to ask that you come to the church to see me? It would be, well—rather awkward for me to call on you."

"Of course I'll come to you. Holy Trinity Church, isn't it?"

"It's on 36th Street, between N and O Streets in Georgetown. Actually, that's the main entrance on 36th Street. I'd rather you not use it. I'd prefer that you come to the rectory where we can speak in privacy. From 35th Street you turn left, or west, on O, and it's the first church building on your left." He paused, as if hesitant to say more. Then he added, "I think you deserve an explanation. The front entrance is being watched. It would be better for both of us if your visit is not observed. You'll understand once we've had a chance to talk. In a half hour, then?"

"Or sooner," said Collins.

ALL THE WAY TO Georgetown, in the back seat of the official Cadillac limousine, Chris Collins continued to speculate about why Father Dubinski wanted to see him as soon as possible. There was no clue. At their last meeting, at Bethesda, the priest had firmly refused to reveal Colonel Baxter's final confession. There was no reason to think that he would ignore his vows of clerical secrecy now. Perhaps he had come across some other information that he felt Collins should know. But information about what? More unsettling had been his remark that the front entrance of Holy Trinity Church was being watched. If this was not paranoia but fact, then watched by whom and for what motive?

It was baffling. Collins was tempted to try out the riddle on the two men in the front seat. There was Pagano, an ex-prizefighter with a bashed face, whom he had imported from California, as his chauffeur. He had once befriended Pagano—successfully defended him in a criminal action in Oakland—and Pagano had been forever grateful. He was thoroughly trustworthy. Beside him in the front seat, there was Special Agent Hogan, his carefully handpicked FBI bodyguard, who was also trustworthy.

But then Collins realized it was no use soliciting anyone's opinion. A priest had sent for him on a matter of importance. There was no hint as to what it was all about. Truly, there was nothing to discuss, except Collins' own inexplicable sense of foreboding.

Collins could see that they were on 35th Street, approaching O Street, and he leaned forward in his seat. "Pagano. Pull up at 35th and O. Drop me off on the corner. I don't want anyone to see this car."

When they reached the corner, Collins hastily opened his door. As he stepped out, he said over his shoulder, "Take the car north on 35th about a block or so, and park wherever you can. I'll find you. No idea how long this will take. Maybe fifteen or twenty minutes."

He closed the door and stepped away, only to find Hogan beside him. Momentarily, they watched the limousine move on up the street. Collins considered his bodyguard. "Okay, you can come with me to the church rectory. I'll go in myself. You can wait outside. But don't be too conspicuous."

They crossed the thoroughfare and proceeded a short distance on O Street. Collins pointed left. "There it is." The rectory was a red brick building trimmed in white. "I'll leave you here."

As Collins neared the door, it was unexpectedly opened by an unseen hand. He heard and recognized the voice. "Come right in, Mr. Collins."

He entered a tiny vestibule, dimly lighted, and found himself confronting the dark-haired, olive-skinned, black-robed priest. After a brief handshake, Father Dubinski motioned for Collins to follow him.

They passed through a doorway into a hall. Midway down the hall, there was a door. The priest opened it. "Our larger rectory parlor," said the priest, adding, "It's soundproof."

In the parlor, Collins quickly got his bearings. Immediately to his right were a desk and two chairs. Straight across the room, against the wall opposite the door, was a credenza, and hanging above it a modern picture of Jesus Christ being removed from the Cross.

Father Dubinski had taken him by the elbow, and now was directing him toward the sofa and coffee table at the left.

"No one saw me come in," said Collins. "Who is it that's watching the front entrance?"

"The FBI."

"The FBI?" Collins repeated incredulously. "Watching you? For what reason?"

"I'll explain," said Father Dubinski. "Do sit down. Would you like coffee or tea?"

Collins declined both, and sat on the edge of the sofa at the end near the small lamplit table.

Briskly, Father Dubinski settled on the sofa a few feet from Collins.

The priest wasted no time. "I had a visitor late this morning. A Mr. Harry Adcock, whose identity card showed he is Assistant Deputy—or is it Associate?—to the Director of the FBI."

"He's Director Tynan's Associate. That's correct. What was he doing here?"

"He wanted to know what Colonel Noah Baxter confessed to me the night the Colonel died. He said it might involve a matter of internal national security. I might have accepted the inquiry as well-meaning, if somewhat ill-advised, except for one thing. When I refused to repeat Colonel Baxter's confession, Mr. Adcock threatened me."

"Threatened you?" Collins repeated with disbelief.

"Yes. But before we go into that, I'm mystified by one thing. How could he have known that Colonel Baxter had time to speak to me—to confess—before dying? Had you told him?"

Collins was silent, trying to remember. Then he remembered exactly. "As a matter of fact, I did speak of it. We were driving away from Baxter's funeral—Tynan, Adcock, and I—and we were discussing the Colonel, his death. Quite innocently— because it was on my mind—I mentioned how I had been summoned to the hospital the night he died. I mentioned that he had wanted to see me urgently, but I arrived at the hospital too late. He was dead. Then I must have spoken—I'm sure I did—of my meeting with you. That Colonel Baxter's last words were his confession to you, but that a priest could not repeat what was told him in what amounted to the confessional." Collins' brow furrowed. "I brought this up with Tynan—and Adcock— because I thought they might have a clue to what Baxter wanted to tell me. I mean, Tynan was fairly close to Baxter. Unfortunately, they knew nothing that would be helpful." He paused. "Tynan actually sent Adcock here—Adcock always does Tynan's dirties—to find out Baxter's confession from you? And when you refused to cooperate, Adcock threatened you? That's incredible."

"Maybe not so incredible. Only you can be the final judge of that."

"How did he threaten you?"

Father Dubinski fixed his gaze on the coffee table. "The threat was neither implied nor indirect. The threat was open and direct—well, blackmail. Apparently, the FBI had run a thorough check on me, on my past—I suppose that's routine these days?"

"Standard operating procedure when the Bureau is investigating someone."

"Or when the Bureau wants to get something on someone, to make him talk? Even someone innocent of any crime?"

Collins squirmed. "That's not part of the procedure. But we both know it happens. There have been abuses."

"I assume this check of my past could have been instigated only by Director Tynan. You've indicated that Adcock is merely his—his flunky?"

"Correct."

"Very well. The FBI unearthed what had long been buried, an unhappy incident in my past. When I was a young priest, on my first assignment—I had a church in a Trenton, New Jersey, ghetto—I started a drug-control program. To stop my crusade, some of the hard-core delinquent youngsters planted a small cache of drugs in my rectory, and then informed the authorities, with the idea of entrapping me. The police came around. They located the cache. They'd been notified I'd been peddling drugs. It could have ended my service. Fortunately, a scandal was averted when my bishop prevailed upon the chief of police to let me testify at a private hearing. Based on my testimony, I was cleared. Since the culprits were never found, the case rested entirely on my word. I can see how, reviewing the incident today, someone might consider my guilt—or lack of guilt—as unresolved. Somehow the whole abortive affair got into the FBI files. This is what Mr. Harry Adcock confronted me with this morning."

Collins was stunned. "I—I can't believe it."

"You had better. You had better believe it. Mr. Adcock threatened to make this information about my past public if I continued to refuse to divulge the details of Colonel Baxter's last confession. It was as blatant as that. I decided that my holy vows were more important than his threat of character assassination. Anyway, if the story does get out, it wouldn't seriously harm my status. It could embarrass me. But little more. I told Adcock to do whatever he chose to do. I would not cooperate with him. I sent him packing. Afterwards—in fact, this entire afternoon—I was quite enraged. What concerned me most—now that it had happened to me—was the strong-arm methods being used by a Government agency against the very citizens it is supposed to protect."

"I still find it incredible. What could possibly have been so important about Baxter's confession to make Tynan go to such lengths?"

"I don't know," said Father Dubinski. "I assumed you might know. That's why I called you."

"I don't know what Colonel Baxter told you. So I have no way—"

"You shall know some of what Colonel Baxter told me. Because I'm going to tell you."

Collins felt a thrill of excitement. Holding his breath, he waited.

Father Dubinski resumed, speaking slowly. "Mr. Adcock's visit had so angered me that I spent several hours today reconsidering my position. I knew I could not cooperate with Mr. Adcock or Director Tynan. But I began to see your own request, made at Bethesda, in a different light. Obviously, Colonel Baxter had trusted you. When he was sinking, it was you alone he sent for. Obviously, then, he was prepared to tell you some of what he told me. I began to see, also, that much of what he told me was probably meant for you. I realized more clearly that my duties were not only spiritual but temporal, and that perhaps I was merely the caretaker of information that Colonel Baxter wished passed on to you. That is how I came to my decision to repeat his last words to you."

Collins felt his heartbeat quicken. "I deeply appreciate that, Father."

"Dying, Colonel Baxter was prepared, in the words of St. Paul, 'to be dissolved and to be with Christ.'" said Father Dubinski. "He was reconciled with God. Once I had given him the Sacraments, and his confession was completed, he made a final effort to address himself to one remaining, lingering earthly matter. His last words, spoken almost in his dying breath . . ." The priest searched inside the folds of his cassock. "I wrote them down after Mr. Adcock left so that I would not misstate anything." He opened a crumpled slip of paper. "Colonel Baxter's last words, which I fully believe were meant for you, were the following. 'Yes, I have sinned, Father—and my greatest sin—I must speak of it—they cannot control me now—I am free, I no longer have to be afraid anymore—it's about the 35th—' "

"The 35th," murmured Collins.

Father Dubinski cast him a sidelong glance, and resumed reading from the slip. " '—it's about the 35th—' He was momentarily incoherent, and then I caught this. '—The R Document—danger—dangerous—must be exposed at all costs at once—The R Document, it's—' He drifted off, then tried again. Very difficult to make out what he was trying to say, but I'm almost sure he said, 'I saw—trick—go see—' There was a dying gasp, and then he was still and, moments later, dead."

Collins sat chilled. He had heard a voice from the grave. Confused and troubled, he said, "The R Document? That's what he spoke of?"

"Twice. Clearly, he wanted to say something about it. He couldn't."

"You're sure he said no more?"

"Those were his only intelligible words. There were more, but I could not make them out."

"Father, do you have the faintest idea of what The R Document might be?"

"I'd hoped you might know."

"I never heard of it before," said Collins. He considered Colonel Baxter's last words, what had likely been his urgent message for the new Attorney General. "He was saying he had sinned by being involved with this—this—whatever it is. He had been forced to be involved. Whatever it was concerned the 35th Amendment and something called The R Document, a trick which was dangerous and had to be exposed. He'd sent for me to tell me that."

"His legacy to the living, a desire to right a wrong."

"His legacy to me, his successor," said Collins, half to himself. "Why not to the President? Or to Tynan? Or even to his wife? Only to me alone. But why to me?"

"Maybe because he trusted you more than he did the President or the Director. Possibly because he felt you would understand where his wife would not."

"But I don't understand," said Collins, desperately. "The R Document." He felt lost, reaching, but getting hold of nothing. "What could it possibly be?"

Father Dubinski was rising to his feet. "Perhaps you had better find out, find out as soon as possible." He handed Collins the slip of paper. "Now you know all I know, and all Noah Baxter meant to tell you in his last agony. The rest is in your hands." He sucked in his breath. "There is danger here. I will pray for your success and your safety. God be with you."

III

HE HAD AWAKENED EARLY the following morning, and showered and dressed, and left their nine-room house in McLean, Virginia, to drive the seven miles to work without having told his wife about his adventure at Holy Trinity Church the night before.

During dinner that night, and throughout the evening, he had intended to relate the entire episode with Father Dubinski to Karen. But some instinct of care and protection toward his loved one had kept him from revealing the meeting. He knew that it would upset and worry her, because it had upset and worried him.

Instead, he had told her about the President's call that made the trip to California definite. His only assignments were to deliver an address to the American Bar Association, appear on a television show, and, if possible, lobby informally with some state legislators. Otherwise, he would be free, and they might have a few days in the California sunshine. He had asked Karen to come along. She had resisted, pleading her pregnancy and general state of exhaustion. She had insisted that he could better use his spare time seeing his son, Josh, and looking up some old friends. After that, he had not pressed her further. He knew that he could use any free time seeing not only young Josh but also

that man Paul Hilliard wanted him to see, State Assemblyman
Olin Keefe, the man who claimed the FBI was doctoring California crime statistics. Since Collins' encounter with the priest
earlier in the evening, he had begun to entertain his first con-
cerns about the FBI.

When he had gone to bed last night, Karen was still awake.
Embracing her to say good night, he knew that she wanted to
make love. He had been so obsessed with the mystery of The R
Document that love was the last thing on his mind. Nevertheless, because he wanted to be considerate, and especially because he would be away from her a number of days, he had
gone along. After several minutes of foreplay, he had forgotten
all about business and was as ready as she to make love. Despite his care not to put pressure on her stomach—he constantly
feared that she would have a miscarriage—their coupling had
been long and frenzied. It had been natural and mutually giving, in a way that he had never enjoyed with Josh's mother—
why did he think of his first wife, Helen, as nothing more than
Josh's mother?—and afterward, he and Karen had gone to
sleep almost instantly.

But when he had awakened this morning, it was no longer
Karen that was on his mind but The R Document.

Driving to the Department of Justice, he reviewed the urgency of Colonel Baxter's request that he learn about it and expose it. Learn about and expose what? Some kind of trick that
Baxter had seen. But how to find it? Where even to begin? He
tried to think about the problem in a logical and orderly fashion. To learn more, the place to begin was with anything or anyone connected in some way with the late Colonel Noah Baxter.

First of all, there were Baxter's private files. These the Colonel had kept separate from his papers as Attorney General,
which were preserved in the regular files in Marion's office.
Collins would have to examine the regular files as well as Colonel Baxter's own personal files.

He speculated on the task. It sounded so simple, but where
did one look? What did one look under? Did one check out R
for The R Document? Or T for 35th and A for Amendment? Or
S for Secret? Or D for Danger? He didn't hold much hope for

the files. The tone of Baxter's message made it clear that any further information would not be readily accessible or found in an obvious place.

So much for Baxter's possessions. This left only those persons close to the Colonel: family, associates, friends—anyone who might have heard him mention, at some time or other, a paper called The R Document. Whom to see first? Director Vernon T. Tynan seemed the best bet. Baxter's last words had not mentioned him or warned against him in any way. In his final message, Baxter surely had meant for Collins to start with someone close at hand. Had Baxter wanted him to start with Tynan or to avoid Tynan?

Warily, Collins weighed Tynan as a prospect. There were two significant points of caution. Why had the Colonel not sent for Tynan instead of Collins to hear his warning? Because he hadn't trusted Tynan? There was no evidence of that. Still, Collins wondered, could Tynan be trusted? The second point of caution came up before him like a red flag. Returning from the cemetery, Collins had made some innocent remarks about Baxter's last confession. Immediately, Tynan had sent an emissary to Father Dubinski to find out by hook or by crook, by blackmail if necessary, what had been in that confession. Had Tynan sought some information he did not have? Or want to know if Baxter had leaked security information they had shared? In either event, there was a likelihood Tynan might know the meaning of The R Document. And might be prepared to explain it to a colleague and Department superior. He was the person to see. But the red flag still fluttered in front of Collins. Proceed with care.

At once, his priority shifted to someone less questionable, more dependable, someone who might be equally knowledgeable about the Colonel's secrets. This was Colonel Baxter's widow, Hannah. The red flag was gone. She was accessible. She would be friendly. Collins had a nice relationship with Hannah, who had always regarded him maternally. How good a prospect was she? After all, she had been married to the Colonel almost forty years. There could be nothing serious the Colonel was engaged in that she would not know about. On the other hand, if this had been their relationship, why hadn't the dying Colonel confided in her instead of sending for Collins to hear his warning? Baxter had used her only as a conduit to reach Collins. Still, there could be an explanation. The Colonel might have been the kind of person who believed men's work was a business between men, especially when it involved a former Attorney General and his successor.

By the time he had entered his office, Chris Collins was thoroughly uncertain which step to take first.

At his desk, ignoring the messages lined up on the blotter, he continued to mull over the matter. When Marion arrived with his cup of strong tea, he had made up his mind where to start. He would begin with a source less complicated than human beings.

"Marion, Colonel Baxter's files," he said. "Where are they?"

"Well, he kept two sets of files—"

"I know."

"The bulk of the files, the main ones, are in my office. Then he kept more personal files—his private correspondence, memorandums—in a fireproof cabinet in his sitting room off my office."

"Is it there now?"

"Oh, no. About a month after he went to the hospital, that file was moved to his home in Georgetown."

"So that's where it is now?"

"Yes. If there's something you want to look up, I could go over there."

"No, not necessary. I can do it myself."

"Do you want me to call Mrs. Baxter?"

Instantly, he knew the person he would interview first on The R Document.

"Yes, call her and ask her if she's up to seeing me for a few minutes this afternoon." As Marion started to leave, he added casually, "By the way, Marion, I've been looking for a memorandum called The R Document. Does that ring a bell?"

She tried to remember. "I'm afraid not. It's nothing I've ever filed."

"It was a memorandum related to the 35th Amendment. Do you want to take a look in our regular files?"

"Right away."

Drinking his tea, Collins disposed of the morning's messages in rapid succession. On the phone he discussed a Government brief with the Solicitor General, then phoned back his Executive Assistant on a personnel matter. He met briefly with the Director of Public Information, who was supervising preparation of his speech in Los Angeles to the American Bar Association. He conferred at greater length with Ed Schrader, the Deputy Attorney General, on a corporate income-tax-evasion case; riot arrests in Kansas City and Denver; the latest findings on the HIL, or Humans for Internal Liberty, conspirators.

By noon he had heard from his secretary on two important matters. First, she had searched the general files. There was no reference, she said, to anything named The R Document. Somehow, he was not surprised. Second, she reported that she had finally contacted Mrs. Hannah Baxter, and Mrs. Baxter would be glad to see him at two o'clock.

After lunching in his private dining room with three United States Attorneys brought in from the field, and answering four more telephone calls, Collins was ready to begin his private investigation of The R Document.

Pagano drove him, and Hogan accompanied him, to Georgetown, and they arrived at the familiar white brick three-storied, early-nineteenth-century house on the tree-shaded street at five minutes to two o'clock. Leaving his chauffeur and bodyguard behind, Collins went up the magnificent ironwork stairway, rang the bell, and was admitted by the cheerful black maid.

"I'll fetch Mrs. Baxter," said the maid. "Would you like to wait in the patio? It's such a lovely day."

Collins agreed that would be fine, followed her to the sliding glass doors, and then went out on the flagstone patio by himself. He watched his reflection in the swimming pool, turned back to settle into a padded wrought-iron chair next to a ceramic-topped table, and lit a cigarette.

"Hi, Mr. Collins," he heard a young voice call out.

He looked over his shoulder and saw Rick Baxter, Hannah Baxter's grandson, on his knees on the flagstone, fiddling with a portable cassette recorder.

"Hello, Rick. How come you're not in school today?"

"The driver was sick. So Grandma let me stay home."

"Are your parents still in Africa?"

"Yup. They couldn't come home in time for Grandpa's funeral, so they're staying there for another month."

"You seem to be having trouble with that contraption. Anything wrong?"

"I can't make it work," said Rick. "I'm trying to fix it for tonight so I can tape the TV special that's going to be on—*The History of Comics in America*—but I can't—"

"Let me see it, Rick. I'm not a mechanic, but maybe I can help."

Rick brought his machine over to Collins. He was a brown-haired boy with alert wide-set eyes and the obligatory braces on his teeth. He was, Collins remembered, bright and mature for a twelve-year-old.

Collins took the tape recorder, checked all the buttons to be sure they were set right, and then opened up the machine. In a moment he saw what was wrong, made a simple adjustment, and tried the machine. It worked.

"Thanks!" exclaimed Rick. "Now I can take down the show tonight. You should see my collection. I tape the best TV and radio shows and interviews. I have the best collection in school. It's my favorite hobby."

"It'll be very valuable one day," said Collins. The Age of the Tape, thought Collins. He wondered if any of these kids, even smart ones like Rick, could write anymore. And it would be worse after the 35th Amendment was passed, he realized. The wiretap, the bug, the electronic eavesdroppers would have public approval.

"Hi, Grandma," he heard Rick say.

Immediately, Collins was on his feet, wheeling about in time to greet Hannah Baxter. When she came to him, he embraced her and kissed her affectionately on the cheek. She was a small, plump woman, aging now but with a shiny, warm face, all the features generous.

"I'm sorry," Collins said to her, "I'm really sorry."

"Thanks, Christopher. I'm just glad it's over with. I couldn't

stand his suffering or seeing him lying there like a vegetable—
not any longer—a man of his vitality. I miss him. You don't
know how much I miss Noah. But that's life. We all have to face
it." She half-turned. "Rick, you go inside and leave us. And no
television shows or recording them until tonight. You open your
schoolbooks. I don't want you falling behind or your father will
be upset with me."

After the boy left, Hannah Baxter sat down at the ceramic-
topped table, and Collins took his place again.

Hannah spoke nostalgically about Noah Baxter a little
longer, about when he had been well and about their good times
together, but at last her voice trailed off. She sighed. "Don't let
me go on," she said. "How are you doing with your work?"

"Not easy. I can appreciate what Noah went through."

"He used to say it was like having an office in quicksand. No
matter what you did, you sank down further. Still, if anyone can
handle it, you can, Christopher. I know that Noah always had
great faith in you."

"Is that why he sent for me the last night, Hannah?"

"Of course."

"What did he say to you?"

"I was at his side when he came out of the coma. He was desperately weak, and not too articulate. He recognized me, whispered something endearing, then he asked me to do him a favor.
'Bring Chris Collins here,' he said. 'Must see him. Urgent matter. Important. Must talk to him.' It wasn't as clear as that, but it
was what he was trying to say. So I sent for you. I'm sorry you
couldn't get there in time."

"Hannah, why didn't he tell you what he wanted to tell me?"

The thought had never occurred to her. "Why, he wouldn't do
that. It was business, I'm sure. He rarely discussed business
with me. He always saw the person his business was intended
for. In this case, he had something to tell you. It's too bad he
didn't get the chance."

Collins wanted to say that the Colonel had got the chance,
via Father Dubinski, but since she did not know this, Collins in-
stinctively decided not to involve her.

"I wish I could have talked to him," Collins said. "He could have straightened me out about a lot of things. About the job, I mean. For instance, there are some files I can't find. We've looked through the ones in the office. My secretary says one file cabinet, Noah's personal one, was sent to the house here after he became ill."

"That's right. I kept it in his study."

"Could I spend a few minutes going through it, Hannah?"

"I don't have it. That file cabinet isn't here now. It was moved out the day after Noah died. Vernon Tynan called me. He asked if he could borrow it for a month or two. He said he wanted to check through it to be sure there was no top-security material in it. I was relieved to let him have it. All that security material Noah was always handling made me nervous. So if there's anything you need, you'll have to go to Vernon for it. He'll be cooperative, I'm sure."

Odd, Collins thought. What did Vernon T. Tynan want with Colonel Baxter's private papers? But there was no time to examine that now.

"Actually, Hannah, what I'm looking for is a Justice Department paper connected with the 35th Amendment. It has a name. It's called The R Document—The R Document. Did you ever come across it in the file?"

"I never went through the file. There was no reason to."

"Well, do you remember if Noah ever spoke to you about something called The R Document?"

She shook her head. "No, not that I can recall. As I told you, he rarely confided in me about business matters."

Disappointed, Collins continued. "Can you think of anyone—any friends—he might have spoken to about it?"

She pointed to the open cigarette pack on the table. "May I have one, Christopher?" Hastily, he pulled a cigarette out of the pack, handed it to her, and lighted it for her. "I started smoking again the day after the funeral." She puffed thoughtfully for a moment. "Noah didn't have many close friends. He was a very private person, as you probably know. There were some people he spent time with in the office, like Vernon Tynan and Adcock, but what they had was more of a work relationship. On the personal side . . . a personal friend?" She broke off, lost in thought. "Well, I guess the only one who qualifies would be Donald—Donald Radenbaugh. He and Noah were the closest of friends, until the time of poor Donald's trouble."

Momentarily the name eluded Collins, and then it fixed in his mind and he remembered the headlines.

"After Donald was tried, sentenced, and confined in Lewisburg Federal Penitentiary," Hannah Baxter went on, "well, Noah couldn't see him anymore, of course. I mean, considering Noah's position, it would have been awkward. It was like the time when Robert Kennedy was Attorney General, and his friend James Landis was involved in a tax-delinquency case. Kennedy disqualified himself. He couldn't interfere. Well, neither could Noah in Donald Radenbaugh's case. But all along, Noah believed in Donald's innocence, and he felt the whole case was a miscarriage of justice. Anyway, Donald had been one of Noah's best friends."

"Donald Radenbaugh," said Collins. "I do remember his name. It got a lot of publicity at the time—two or three years ago—a money scandal of some kind. I don't recall the details."

"It was a messy case. I don't recall the details exactly, either. Donald was a lawyer practicing here in Washington when he became a Presidential adviser in the previous Administration. He was indicted for conspiracy to defraud or extort—I forget which—a million dollars from big corporations with Government contracts. Actually, the money came from illegal campaign contributions. When the FBI zeroed in on a man named Hyland, this Hyland turned state's evidence to get a lighter sentence, and he laid all the blame on Donald Radenbaugh. He claimed that Donald was en route to Miami Beach to deliver the money to a third conspirator. When the FBI picked up Donald in Miami, he did not have the money. He insisted he'd never had it. Nevertheless, based largely on Hyland's testimony, Donald was tried and found guilty."

"Yes, it's all coming back to me now," said Collins. "I think he got a heavy sentence, didn't he?"

"Fifteen years," said Hannah. "Noah was very upset about it. He always said Donald was used as the—the fall guy—by the aides to the last President, to keep that Administration looking clean. Noah could not intercede in the trial. He did try to get the sentence lightened, but with no luck. I know he hoped to get Donald a parole after he'd served five years, but now Noah isn't here to help him. Anyway, Donald Radenbaugh is the only person I can think of who might help you—besides Vernon Tynan."

"Are you suggesting Radenbaugh might know something about The R Document?"

"I can't say, Christopher. I simply don't know. But if this document was a paper or a project Noah was concerned with, he very well might have discussed it with Donald Radenbaugh. He often asked Donald's advice on difficult matters." She ground out the stub of her cigarette. "You might visit Lewisburg in your official capacity, arrange to see Donald, say you want to help him the way Noah intended to. He might be cooperative, might give you the information you need. I could write him and tell him he can trust you, that you were a protégé and friend of Noah's."

"Would you do that?" Collins asked eagerly. "Of course I'd try to help him."

"I certainly would and shall. I intended to write Donald a few words anyway, about what happened. I don't think he gets much mail anymore except from his daughter. He has a lovely daughter named Susie, who lives in Philadelphia now. I'll tell him you'll be visiting him. Do you know when?"

Collins turned a calendar page in his mind. "I have to be in California the end of the week to deliver a speech. I should be heading back a few days after that. Okay, you can tell Mr. Radenbaugh I'll be seeing him in a week or so. Definitely, no later. It's a good lead, Hannah, and I appreciate it." He rose, went to her, kissed her cheek. "Thanks for everything. You stay well, and keep busy. If there's anything Karen or I can do for you, please call."

Leaving, heading for the car, he felt much better. Radenbaugh was a real possibility. But then his mood dampened. First he would have to confront Vernon T. Tynan with the mystery of The R Document. He was uncertain how to do it, but it would have to be done sooner or later. By the time he had got into the limousine, he had decided. The sooner the better.

* * *

THE FOLLOWING MORNING AT ten-thirty, Chris Collins met with Vernon T. Tynan in the Director's seventh-floor conference room adjacent to his office in the J. Edgar Hoover Building.

Collins had hoped that the meeting would take place in Tynan's office. Collins had wanted to see if Noah Baxter's private file cabinet was in that office. But Tynan had been waiting for him in the hall when he reached the seventh floor and led him into the conference room. There, Tynan had insisted that Collins take the chair at the head of the table, while he sat in a chair to the Attorney General's right.

As Collins drew the manila folder out of his saddle-leather briefcase that contained the latest crime statistics from California, he watched and listened to the Director joke with his secretary, who was serving tea and coffee. Since meeting with Father Dubinski in the rectory of Holy Trinity Church, Collins had entertained a growing suspicion about his FBI Director. But now, as he observed Tynan's light-heartedness with his secretary, the suspicion seemed unreal and was gradually dispelled. Tynan's pugnacious face was wreathed in a smile. There was an openness and directness about him that was disarming. How could one be suspicious of the leading lawman in the land? Perhaps the priest had misunderstood or exaggerated the threat from Tynan's emissary.

"Don't forget, Beth," the Director called after his secretary as she was leaving, "no interruptions." The door closed, and Tynan devoted himself to his visitor. "Okay, Chris, what can I do for you?"

"I just need a few minutes," said Collins, sorting his papers. "I'm reworking my speech for Los Angeles. I'm including the latest FBI reports on crime in California—"

"Yes, we broke them down just for California. That's where the action is for us. You got them? I sent them over yesterday."

"I have them here," said Collins. "I want to be sure I have the very latest figures. If anything new has come in—"

"You're right up-to-date," said Tynan. "The worst yet.

They'll be effective in your speech. Make them realize out there that they, more than the citizens of any other state, need Constitutional help."

Collins studied the topmost sheet in his hand. "I must say, these California crime statistics are unusually high compared with the other large states." He looked up. "And they are absolutely accurate?"

"As accurate as the police chiefs in California want them to be," said Tynan. "You'll be quoting their own numbers back to them."

"Just want to be sure I'm on solid ground."

"You're on solid ground, all right. With those figures, you'll be laying perfect groundwork for going into the 35th Amendment."

Collins took a sip of the lukewarm tea. "I'll be going into the 35th, of course. Although I'm being careful not to overdo it. I'd hate to enter into a real debate with anyone on it. I don't look forward to that session on TV. Frankly, I haven't had time to study the bill closely, all its ramifications, since becoming Attorney General."

"I'm not worried about how you'll handle yourself," said Tynan airily. "You did well enough on the 35th during your Congressional hearings. You know as much as you need to know."

"But maybe—" Collins hesitated. "—maybe I don't know *everything*."

Tynan displayed a flicker of fretfulness. "What else is there to know?"

The moment had come. Collins shut his mind's eye and plunged. "There's something—some kind of supplement—called The R Document. What about that? How much does it have to do with the 35th Amendment?"

Collins wore an ingenuous expression on his narrow features. All innocent curiosity. He focused closely on Tynan to see if his reaction betrayed anything.

Tynan's hooded eyelids had lifted. His small dark eyes had widened. But they were blank. Either he was a consummate actor or the reference to The R Document meant absolutely nothing to him.

Collins broke the silence by prodding him. "What should I know about The R Document?"

"The what?" asked Tynan.

"The R Document. I thought you could brief me on it, so that I'm prepared for anything."

"Chris, I have no idea what you're talking about. Wherever did you come up with that? What is it?"

"I don't know. I was cleaning out some of Noah Baxter's old papers. I happened to see the title on one of Noah's memo notes concerning the 35th. Something about checking it out in relation to the Amendment. That's all there was on the memo."

"Do you have the memo? I'd like to see it. Might refresh my memory."

"No, dammit, I don't have it anymore. It went into the shredder with a lot of Noah's dated papers. But it stuck in my mind, so I thought I'd mention it. I thought if you'd heard of the document, it might help me." He shrugged. "But if you haven't—"

"I repeat," said Tynan firmly. "I haven't the slightest idea what you are referring to. It was probably Noah's synonym—or whatever you'd call it—for the 35th Amendment. I can't imagine anything else. Anyway, I don't know a thing about it. You can be confident you have all the information you require to do a bang-up job in California. You do your job, we'll do ours, and you can be certain California will ratify. It's all our chips on one bet in another month—and Chris, I don't intend to see us lose the pot."

"Nor do I," said Collins, packing his papers. "Well, I guess I'm in pretty good shape."

Once in the hall, and alone, Collins walked thoughtfully down to the sixth floor, reviewing the meeting. There had been no crack in Tynan's armor. There had not been anything in his response, in his behavior, to indicate that he had knowledge of a paper—a dangerous paper, Baxter had called it on his deathbed—known as The R Document.

Still . . .

As he walked to the elevator, his eyes fell on the huge open well in the center of the sixth floor. He veered toward it and looked up. There was no roof above it. He peered down far below at the open pedestrian plaza on the ground floor. On his first tour of the new FBI building, he had asked his guide, a Special Agent, why there was this big opening in the center of the building and why it was uncovered on top. The guide had replied, "To make our FBI headquarters seem less secret, less closed in, less ominous and forbidding. We've made it appear wide open so that we will appear wide open to the public."

Appear wide open, Collins thought.

Perhaps the Director had taken on the look of his building, a deception of openness to camouflage the truth.

Collins continued slowly toward the elevator where his daytime bodyguard, Oakes, was waiting.

Well, he decided, there was still California, where he might learn more about Tynan and his operation. And after that, there was still Lewisburg, where he might learn even more about Tynan and The R Document.

Noah Baxter, in his dying breath, had urged him to expose a trick called The R Document at all costs at once.

Had Noah realized, Collins wondered, that he was sending him into a maze with only blank walls? At the same time, Noah would not have directed him on this blind odyssey unless there were a door somewhere.

Entering the elevator, he vowed to find it fast.

BACK IN HIS OWN office once more, Director Tynan stood grimly in the center of the room, awaiting Harry Adcock.

When Adcock entered, shutting the door softly behind him, Tynan was staring absently at the carpet. Without raising his head, he said, "He just left."

"What did he want?" asked Adcock, coming to the center of the room.

"He tried to play games with me. He said he was here to get some help on the speech he's delivering in Los Angeles." Tynan snorted. "Bullshit."

"What did he really want, chief?"

"He wanted to know if I'd ever heard about something called The R Document."

"Had you?"

Tynan raised his head. "I didn't even know what he was talking about."

"Where did he hear of such a thing?"

"I don't know. He talked about seeing it on one of Noah's memos." Tynan snorted again. "He was lying." He met Adcock's eyes. "He's a pretty nosy fellow, our Mr. Collins, pretty nosy. He seems to be looking for ways to make trouble."

Adcock nodded.

"Sit down, Harry."

Tynan moved around his desk and settled into his swivel chair, as Adcock lowered himself into the seat across from him.

Tynan lay back in his swivel chair, arms crossed on his barrel chest, eyes set on the ceiling.

After a while, he spoke. "I thought he was a nice kid, one of those lightweight intellectuals, still wet behind the ears. I also thought, considering that Noah brought him in, he was a team player. I'm not so sure of that anymore. I think he's a smart-ass and I think he's definitely looking for trouble."

"Like what, chief?"

"Like thinking he can outsmart Vernon T. Tynan." The swivel chair groaned as he sat straight up in it. "You know, Harry, this building is J. Edgar Hoover's monument. I know what I want my own monument to be. I want it to be the 35th Amendment ratified as part of the Constitution. I don't care if I'm not remembered for anything else, as long as I'm remembered for that."

"You will be, chief," said Adcock fervently.

"Yeah? Well, I want to be sure our Mr. Collins understands that, too. I think we better start keeping an eye on him. Not only here—but in California." His pause was almost a threat. "Especially in California. Yeah. Let's talk awhile about that, Harry— about Mr. Collins and about California. I've got a few ideas. Let's try them on for size."

IV

D ESPITE THE SPEECH HE was scheduled to deliver, and the damn television show, Chris Collins had looked forward to the California trip. He had purposely kept his plans light. He would arrive in San Francisco on Thursday afternoon, check into his favorite suite at the St. Francis Hotel, and meet, over drinks, with two of the United States Attorneys from California's four judicial districts. After that, he would wait for his nineteen-year-old son, Josh, to come over from Berkeley. Following their reunion—he had not seen the boy in eight months—they would go out to Ernie's and enjoy a long and leisurely catch-up dinner.

It hadn't worked out that way at all.

Two days before his departure from Washington, Collins had telephoned Josh to set their date.

There had been the obligatory questions and the abbreviated answers.

"How've you been, Josh?"

"Busy as hell. Too much homework. Lots of outside activities."

"Well, how is school?"

"You know. The usual."

"Still as excited about Political Science?"

"Sure, if they didn't make it so boring."

"Have you seen your mother lately?"

"Not since her birthday. I went to Santa Barbara for two days. Helen's okay. Only she can't get off my back."

"How's her husband?"

"I guess they get along. Me, I can't stand him. What's there to talk about to an over-the-hill tennis pro with arthritis? And worse, he insists on calling me 'son.'"

Collins could not resist laughing, and finally Josh had laughed, too. Actually, he was not a humorless boy; indeed, he was very sharp when it was worth his trying, and extremely intense about the world around him. Physically, he was very much like his father. He was tall—over six feet; wiry, with a gaunt face.

Collins had asked him if he still had his beard. He replied that he had only half as much as before. Mary had insisted that he trim it. Yes, he was still living with Mary in unwedded bliss, and she'd recently redone their apartment on Stuart Street, had repainted the interior herself. He was thoughtful enough to inquire about Karen, whom he'd met only twice. Collins had weighed telling him about her pregnancy, and finally had told him he would have a brother or sister in five months. To Collins' relief, Josh was delighted and full of congratulations.

"When are we going to see you both?" Josh had inquired.

"That's why I'm calling," Collins had replied. "You'll be seeing me this week if you're free. I'm flying to San Francisco Thursday."

He went on to explain the purpose of his visit to California.

There was a brief silence, and then Josh had asked, "Are you going to be plugging the 35th Amendment in that speech, Dad?"

Collins had hesitated, sensing storm warnings. "Yes, I am."

"Why?"

"Why? Because it's my job. I'm part of the Administration."

"I don't think that's a very good reason, Dad."

"Well, there are other reasons. There are some good things to be said for the 35th."

"I can't think of one," Josh had retorted. "I'll be honest with you. I told you I was busy with outside activities. Well, I'm busy, every spare moment I have, fighting the passage of that Amendment. I might as well tell you—I joined Tony Pierce's group; I'm an investigator for Defenders of the Bill of Rights. We're going to make a fight of it in California."

"I wish you luck. I'm afraid you're going to lose. The President is putting everything he has behind the bill."

"The President," Josh had said with contempt. "His head is as empty as a volleyball. He'd push the whole country under the rug if he could. Tynan's the one we're all worried about. He's a Xerox of Hitler—"

"I wouldn't be that hard on him, Josh. He's a policeman, with a tough job to do. He's anything but a Hitler."

"I can prove you're wrong," Josh had burst out.

"What do you mean?"

"The advocates of the 35th are always arguing it'll never be invoked except in a serious emergency, like an attempt to overthrow the Government."

"That's absolutely correct."

"Dad, I think the people behind the bill—I'm not saying you, I mean Tynan and his gang—they intend to do much more with it, once they have the Amendment."

"Do much more with it? Like what?"

"I don't want to discuss this on the phone. But I can prove it."

"Prove what?" Collins had demanded, trying to contain himself.

"I'll show you. I'll take you there. We've all investigated it, and it'll open your eyes. You've got to see for yourself to believe it. We—meaning some of us in Pierce's DBR—were saving this as one of the big things we want to expose a few days before the legislature votes on the 35th. But my friends aren't going to object if I show it to you, considering who you are. Maybe this'll change your mind."

"I'm open to anything reasonable. If you won't tell me what it is on the phone, perhaps you can tell me where it is. You understand, my time is very limited."

"It'll be worth your time. I'll take you there. Do me a favor, Dad. Do me just this one favor."

Collins had faltered. Never in recent memory had his son asked a favor of him.

"Well, maybe I can make the time. What do we do?"

"We meet in Sacramento at noon Thursday."

"Sacramento?"

"From there we drive to a place called Newell . . ."

And that was how, because he was a father as well as the Attorney General and because he loved his son, he had flown into Sacramento, California, instead of San Francisco, after having transferred his meeting with the United States Attorneys to Los Angeles.

He had arrived in Sacramento just before noon. Josh—clean, sunburned, beard neatly trimmed—had been waiting, clearly filled with an inner excitement. After embracing, they had gone straight to a rented Mercury. They had been followed by Special Agent Hogan, who would accompany them, while the relief agent, Oakes, awaited their return that evening, when Collins was scheduled to fly directly to Los Angeles.

Now, after what had seemed hours on the road, Josh assured him that they were nearing their destination. He had not, and would not, divulge their actual destination. "You've got to see it for yourself," he had repeated several times.

As their driver had headed north on U.S. Highway 5 to Weed, and then veered northeast on U.S. 97 to Klamath Falls, Oregon, and then had backtracked into California again, Collins had the growing feeling that he had too easily succumbed to what would prove to be a wild-goose chase, a teenager's paranoidal trip. Nevertheless, he tried to remain good-natured about it, smoking, attempting to divert with small talk, meanwhile feeling pleasure in the presence of his gangling son.

Josh, for his part, while adamantly secretive about what he intended to show his father, was anything but silent about the way he and his group felt about the 35th Amendment.

He was arguing against it again. "One of the few things great about this country is the Bill of Rights," he was saying. "The 1st through the 10th Amendments guarantee the freedom of religion, press, speech, assembly, petition, and they give us freedom from search, give protection to those accused of crimes, promise trial by jury, do not permit excessive fines or cruel punishment—"

Collins wriggled restlessly in his seat. Why do sons assume their fathers know nothing? Or have forgotten everything?

"—and now along comes the 35th Amendment to suspend all these freedoms and rights."

"All bills of rights regard liberties as relative, not absolute," Collins suggested quietly. "As Emerson said, constitutions are merely the lengthened shadows of men. They are invented by men to protect themselves from one another. When they fail to do that, when the fate of human society is at stake, more drastic measures must be taken by men for society's own sake."

Josh refused to accept that. "No way," he said. "There's only one test. Look around the world. Every truly free government has a bill of rights that can't be tampered with by the government. Only dictatorships, tyrannies, unfree governments have no bills of rights or have bills of rights that are qualified and can be revoked by the parties in power in peacetime. England had the Magna Charta in 1215 and the Bill of Rights of 1689, and these and other bills gave the English freedom from arbitrary arrest, the guarantee of trial by jury, freedom of speech and petition, habeas corpus, protection of life, liberty, property. France has a Bill of Rights based on the Rights of Man and Citizen, enacted in 1789, six weeks after the fall of the Bastille. Here again the rights—of equality for all citizens, of care for women and children and for the aged and infirm, of work without discrimination, of social security and education, and so forth—are not qualified by any trick 35th Amendment. The same holds true in West Germany and Italy. Why, in West Germany their Bill of Rights cannot be amended, the way we're trying to amend ours. But you go to other countries that have bills of rights, mainly Communist or dictatorship countries, and you always find a joker in the deck. Take Cuba. Freedom of expression guaranteed, sure, except that your private property can be confiscated 'as the government deems necessary to counteract acts of sabotage, terrorism, or any other counterrevolutionary activities.' Take Russia. Equal rights for all, no matter what nationality or sex, except for the 'foes of socialism.' Or take

Yugoslavia. Their constitution provides for freedom of speech, press, and so on, and then comes the joker. 'These freedoms and rights shall not be used by anyone to overthrow the foundations of the socialist democratic order . . . to endanger the peace . . . to disseminate national, racial, or religious hatred or intolerance, or to incite to crime, or in any manner offend public decency.' Who decides that? Now your President and FBI Director are trying to stick a joker in our deck of liberties. Believe me, if California says Yes to the 35th, that's the end of freedom and justice for all of us. Hell, I'd wind up in the slammer just for talking to you this way."

Exhausted from listening, Collins said wearily, "Josh, the horrors you predict will never happen. The 35th will be used to protect you—and in fact, it may never have to be invoked at all."

"Never be invoked at all? Wait'll you see what I'm going to show you in a few minutes."

"We're almost there?"

Josh peered through the windshield, over the shoulders of the driver and Hogan in the front seat. "Yes."

Collins looked out the side window into the glare of the sun. America was many countries with dramatically different landscapes, and this was America at its most desolate. In the past hour he had seen little except dry lakes, alkali beds, abandoned farms overgrown by scrub, an occasional gasoline station posing as a town. Now they were passing through a hard and forbidding terrain, mostly old lava flows and volcanic pumice and no signs of life.

Suddenly, there was life, a few people chatting in front of a store, a few others gathered near a gas pump, some shanties, and a weatherbeaten sign reading NEWELL.

Josh gave the driver directions, and after a brief interval told him to stop.

Collins was bewildered. "Where are we?"

"Tule Lake," Josh announced triumphantly.

Collins' brow furrowed. Tule Lake. It had the sound of an old and familiar place.

"Created in 1942, eight weeks after Pearl Harbor, by President Roosevelt's Executive Order 9066," said Josh. "Japanese Americans were considered security risks. So 110,000 of them were rounded up—even though two-thirds were United States citizens—and they were imprisoned in ten camps or relocation centers. Tule Lake was one of them, one of the worst of the American concentration camps, and 18,000 Japanese Americans were interned here."

"I don't like that blot on our history any more than you do," said Collins. "But what's it got to do with today—with the 35th Amendment?"

"You can see for yourself." Josh opened the back door of the Mercury and stepped outside. Collins followed his son, standing in the dry hot wind trying to get his bearings. He realized, then, that they were near what appeared to be a huge modern farm or manufacturing plant of some kind—a series of brick buildings and corrugated huts in the distance set behind a new chain-link fence.

Collins pointed off. "Is that Tule Lake?"

"It *was*," said Josh with emphasis, "but it's not anymore. It was our toughest concentration camp, built on a 26,000-acre dry lake bed. Now it's something else, and that's why I brought you here."

"Get to the point, Josh."

"All right. But before doing so, let me show you something that will make it clear." He'd been holding a large manila envelope, and now he opened it and extracted a half dozen photographs and handed them to his father. "First, look at these. We got them from the Japanese American Citizens League. These photographs of the old camp were taken from this spot just one year ago. What do you see?"

Collins studied the photographs. What he saw was sections of a broken-down chain-link fence, with rusted strands of barbed wire on top, set in chipped concrete foundations. Behind the fence, he saw some decaying remnants of barracks, scattered shells of buildings, and a crumbling watchtower.

"What about this?" Collins asked, returning the pictures to his son. "There's nothing to see in those photos."

"Exactly," said Josh. "That's the whole point. They were taken a year ago and there was nothing to see then. Just ruins." He gestured toward the scene in front of them. "Now look at Tule Lake today and what do you see?" Puzzled, Collins squinted off, as his son went on. "A brand-new security fence with electrified wire on top, and set in reinforced-concrete foundations. And out there, look at the buildings. A spanking-new brick watchtower with searchlights. Three absolutely new cement-block buildings, with four more going up. What does that tell you?"

"That there's construction work going on. That's all."

"But what kind of construction work? I'll tell you what kind. It's a secret Government project taking place in this remote area. It's a new Tule Lake being repaired and rebuilt. It's a future concentration camp being prepared for the victims of mass arrests when the 35th Amendment goes into effect."

Collins was taken aback and irritated. He had wasted a day, endured unnecessary discomfort, to be shown what was only a product of his son's immature and paranoidal imagination. "Come on, Josh, you don't expect me to buy that. Wherever did you dream this up?"

Josh's mouth tightened. "We have our sources. It *is* a Government project. It's new. It's plainly some kind of internment camp or prison. If it isn't, why the renovated watchtower?"

"A hundred Government projects might have that for security purposes."

"Not this heavy, not like this."

"Well, dammit, it's not a concentration camp or whatever you want to call it. We don't have those in this country now, and we never will again. My God, Josh, this is the same kind of nonsense, the same kind of loose rumor, that was going on back in 1971 when a few underground papers accused President Nixon and Attorney General Mitchell of reviving the Japanese relocation centers as detention camps for dissenters and demonstrators. Nobody ever proved that."

"Nobody ever disproved it, either."

Out of the corner of his eye, Collins saw that behind the

fence two men were walking toward the entry gate. "Well, I'll disprove your notion about this project," he said determinedly. "You wait here."

As Collins strode toward the gate, he saw the two men—one in military uniform, the other in T-shirt and jeans—shake hands and part company. While the uniformed man remained at the gate, the other started to return to the construction site in the distance.

Collins quickened his stride as he neared the uniformed man, who had been watching his approach with a speculative eye.

"Are you a guard here?" Collins asked.

"That's right."

"Is this private property or Federal?"

"It's Federal. Anything I can do for you, sir?"

"I'm with the Government. I'd like to have a look at your facility."

The guard appraised Collins briefly. "I dunno. Of course, if you're Government . . ." He wheeled about, cupped his hand around his mouth, and shouted, "Hey, Tim!" The retreating figure stopped, turned back. "This fellow says he's Government. You'd better talk to him."

The other figure, a burly man with a reddish face, was returning.

Collins waited. When the burly man in T-shirt and jeans reached the gate, the guard stepped aside.

"I'm Nordquist, the construction foreman," the burly man said. "What can I do for you?"

"I—I was hoping to tour this facility." He was tempted to display his credentials, identify himself as the Attorney General of the United States, but he thought better of it. Word might get out that he had taken part in this wild-goose chase, this nonsense, and he'd look like a fool. "I'm with the—the Government—Justice Department—Washington."

"You'd have to have clearance to enter. Unless you have an okay from the Pentagon or the Navy—"

"I don't," said Collins lamely.

"I'm sorry, but I can't let you in without special permission," said Nordquist. "This is definitely a restricted area."

"The Navy, you said."

"That's no secret," the construction foreman said. "This is an arm of Project Sanguine. Called ELF. You know about that?"

"I—I'm not quite sure."

"ELF—Extremely Low Frequency. A facility of the United States Navy—the communication system to contact submerged submarines. If you read the newspapers, you should know about it."

"I've missed some of the news reports during my inspection tour. At any rate, I seem to have been directed to the wrong place this time."

"Looks that way, sir. But come back with proper clearance and we'll be glad to show you around."

"Well, thanks anyway."

He watched the man leave. Then, feeling very foolish and manipulated, he trudged slowly back to where Josh was waiting in front of the car.

He tried not to be resentful of his son. He tried to be restrained. He explained the situation to Josh, repeating exactly what Nordquist had told him. "So much for that," he concluded. "Now you can tell Pierce and all your friends they're a million miles off base. It's a U.S. Navy facility and nothing more."

Josh would not have it. "Je-sus, Dad, you don't expect them to *call* it a detention camp, do you?" Stubbornly, he persisted. "Why all those barracks, or jailhouses?"

"Nobody but you says they're jailhouses."

"Navy personnel doesn't need that kind of setup. I still say why the watchtower? Why the electrified fence? Why the secrecy?"

"He said it was no secret. You can read about it."

"I'll bet. Listen, Dad, we have good sources. You just won't face up to what the President and the FBI are planning to do. They're duping you all the way."

Collins started for the car. "Maybe you're the one who is being duped," he called back over his shoulder. "Come on, let's return to civilization."

The long ride back was a silent one.

Only when they had reached the Sacramento Metropolitan

Airport and were about to say good-bye—he to proceed to Los Angeles, his son to return to Berkeley via Oakland—did Collins offer up a smile.

He placed his arm around Josh's shoulder. "Look, I don't object to your being an activist. I'm proud to have you that involved. But you've got to be very careful about making accusations. You've got to be positive about your facts before going public."

"I'm positive about this one," said Josh.

The boy's obstinance was maddening. With an effort, Collins maintained his good humor. "Okay, okay. What if I can prove to you that what we saw was a legitimate Navy project? If I can prove it, will that convince you?"

For the first time, Josh smiled. "Fair enough. You prove that, Dad, and I'll admit I was wrong. But you've got to prove it."

"You have my word that I will. Now I'd better catch that plane. I've got to meet with a state legislator who's on your side. But he's going to have to prove a few things, too."

ONCE HE HAD REACHED the Beverly Hills Hotel from the Los Angeles International Airport and announced his arrival, he had barely time enough to see his bags to his private three-room bungalow in the rear, hastily clean up and change his shirt, and hurry back to the car entrance. His appointment with State Assemblyman Olin Keefe was for ten o'clock at the Beverly Wilshire Hotel, and it was now five after ten.

His bodyguard, Oakes, who was spelling Hogan, picked him up outside his bungalow door, and quickly they traversed the winding paths leading into the hotel, crossed the lobby, and went out to his waiting Lincoln Continental. Soon they had crossed Sunset Boulevard and were driving toward Wilshire Boulevard, and in five minutes they pulled up before the Beverly Wilshire Hotel.

Inside, after learning the number of the fourth-floor suite from the operator, he called upstairs and in a moment had Keefe on the line.

"Have you eaten yet?" Keefe inquired.

"Hardly a bite all day. And there was no real food on the plane coming down here. Are you offering me something?"

"I am. I'll order right away."

"Just make it a ham and cheese on rye and some hot tea, no lemon. Be right up."

"We're waiting for you."

Collins did not miss the plural. He had been led to expect that he would be meeting with Keefe alone. Now there was someone else with Keefe, but possibly he had meant his wife.

When Collins entered Keefe's small living room, he found not one but two strangers rising to greet him, and neither was the State Assemblyman's wife.

The affable Keefe, a friendly smile on his cherubic countenance, was attired in a checked sports jacket and gabardine slacks. He pumped Collins' hand enthusiastically and immediately led him to his companions.

"I hope you don't mind, Mr. Collins, but I took the liberty of inviting two of my colleagues from the State Assembly. Since we're lucky enough to have you here, I thought the more input the better—for you and all of us."

"I'm delighted," said Collins, somewhat disconcerted.

"This is Assemblyman Yurkovich." Yurkovich proved to be a serious young man with a pinched brow, a nervous tic in his eye, a flowing rust moustache. Collins shook his hand.

"And this is Assemblyman Tobias, a veteran of the Assembly." Tobias was short, with bulging brown eyes and a bulging waistline.

"Here, why don't you take the armchair," said Keefe. "You'll want something comfortable, I'm afraid."

To Collins, that sounded ominous. He settled into the armchair, agreed that a Scotch on the rocks would be perfect, and lighted a cigarette as his host poured the drink.

"Your sandwich should be up in a minute," said Keefe. "You must be tired as the devil—all that flying today, and the time change—so we'll try not to keep you too long. In fact, we'll start right in."

"Please do," said Collins, accepting the Scotch and taking a drink.

The others were seated on the sofa, and Keefe hauled a nearby chair to the coffee table across from Collins.

"This is important to all of us in this room, yourself included," said Keefe. "This may be an eye-opener for you—although I understand our mutual friend, Senator Paul Hilliard, filled you in a little last week."

"Yes, he did," said Collins, trying to remember. So much had happened since the dinner with Hilliard. Also, he was tired. It was after one o'clock in the morning in his head, still on Washington time. He took another big swallow of the Scotch, hoping it would revive him. "Uh, yes, he wanted me to see you about some—some discrepancy in California's crime rate—the statistics. Do I have it right?"

"You have it right," said Keefe. "I hope you won't object to a free and open discussion on this and other matters of concern to you."

"Of course not. Be as free and open as you wish."

Suddenly, Keefe was less affable, even faintly troubled. "I prefaced with that because if you'll really allow for a frank discussion, well, Mr. Collins, it might not be a pleasant evening for you."

This was unexpected. "What are you leading up to?" Collins asked, more alert now. "Speak your mind."

"Very well. I'm trying to say that the three of us—as well as many more in the California State Legislature who are afraid to speak out—are gravely distressed by the tactics you and your Department of Justice are employing to win this state in the 35th Amendment vote."

Collins finished his drink and stubbed out his cigarette. "What tactics?" he demanded. "I've employed no tactics whatsoever to influence the vote here. You have my word for that. I've done nothing in this matter."

"Then someone else has," interjected Tobias from the sofa. "Someone in your Department is trying to scare the legislators of this state into ratifying the 35th."

Collins scowled. "If that is happening, I for one, don't know a damn thing about it. You're making vague allegations. Do you want to be more specific?"

"Let me take it from here," said Keefe to his colleagues. He swung around toward Collins. "Very well, we'll be specific. We're talking about your crime statistics reports, which get such wide publicity here. Those statistics of violent crimes and conspiracies have been deliberately inflated by the FBI to scare the people and legislators of this state into supporting the 35th Amendment. Since the time Senator Hilliard discussed this matter with you, I've personally interviewed a dozen—actually, fourteen—community police chiefs about this. More than half agreed that the figures they are sending to the FBI are not the figures being released by the Department of justice. Somewhere along the way the real statistics have been doctored, exaggerated, even falsified."

Shaken by the intensity of the speaker, Collins said, "That's a grave charge. Have you got written statements from these police chiefs to back it up?"

"No, I do not," said Keefe. "These complaining police chiefs won't go that far. They're too dependent on the goodwill and cooperation of the FBI to antagonize the Bureau. Basically, too, they are sympathetic toward the FBI. They're in the same business, and their business is bad these days. I think the police chiefs spoke of the matter to me only because they resent being made to look incompetent. No, Mr. Collins, we have not an iota of proof in writing. You have asked us to take your word that you are not involved in this. You in turn will have to take our word about the tactics being used by the FBI."

"I might be prepared to do so," said Collins, "but I'm afraid Director Tynan would take a dimmer view of hearsay evidence. Certainly you can see my position. I can't go in to Director Tynan, challenge his integrity, that of the entire Bureau, without written evidence corroborating what you've been charging. Now, if you could actually get those police chiefs to put something in writing—"

"I can't," said Keefe, helplessly. "I've tried, but it's no use."

"Maybe I could try. They might be willing to file a complaint with me, as Attorney General, where they would refuse to do so with you. Do you have the names of the police chiefs you interviewed?"

"Right here." Keefe had started for his brown briefcase, lying open on a tabletop, when the doorbell sounded. He detoured to the door, let the Room Service waiter in, and directed the sandwich tray to Collins. After signing the bill, he waited for the waiter to leave, then went to his briefcase.

Collins had lost his appetite, but he knew he would be hungry later if he did not eat. He opened his ham-and-cheese sandwich, spread some mustard inside, and forced himself to take a bite. He was drinking his tea when Keefe returned with a notebook.

Keefe tore out three pages and handed them to Collins. "The police chiefs who wouldn't talk, they're crossed out. The other eight talked. You'll find their addresses and phone numbers there. I hope you have some luck. I doubt that you will, but I'll hope for the best."

"I'll try," said Collins, folding the pages and putting them in his jacket pocket.

"The problem is," said Keefe, seated again, "that some faceless person or persons in your Department—they're mounting a deliberate campaign of fear in California. They seem determined to shove the 35th down our throats at any cost—at the cost of honesty, at the cost of decency."

"If you mean tampering with statistics—"

"I mean much more," said Keefe.

"Tell him," insisted Yurkovich from the sofa. "Tell him the whole truth."

"I'm going to," Keefe assured him. He waited for Collins to swallow his mouthful and put down what was left of his sandwich, and then he resumed. "It's not pretty, what we're going to tell you. Tampering with statistics, Mr. Collins, is the least of it. Someone in Washington is tampering with our very lives."

Collins uncrossed his legs and sat up. "What do you mean?"

"I mean there's been a concerted campaign by the Federal Bureau of Investigation to intimidate certain members of the legislature, to frighten us by using blackmail—"

The word *blackmail* sent Collins' memory back to the meeting with Father Dubinski in Holy Trinity Church. The priest had spoken of blackmail then. Now this California legislator was doing the same. Collins listened for what was next.

"—subtle blackmail," Keefe went on, "but still blackmail, the vilest kind possible. This has been directed primarily at state legislators who have been wavering, who have not made up their minds about the 35th. The attack has been aimed at legislators who—well, who are vulnerable."

"Vulnerable?"

"Whose private lives have not been an open book. Legislators who might have something in their pasts that they don't want made public. Most have been afraid to object or protest. But Assemblyman Yurkovich and Assemblyman Tobias—while they thought it unwise to denounce the FBI—"

"Because the blackmail was too low-key," Yurkovich interrupted. "It wasn't obvious. Our complaints could be turned aside, even refuted."

Keefe agreed. "Yes. Anyway, my two colleagues, since they couldn't effectively protest publicly, were prepared to come here and protest to you personally. At first they worried that you might be part of the plot. But Senator Hilliard convinced me—even before you did—and I convinced them, that you were honest and trustworthy and perhaps too new to your job to know what's going on behind your back." Keefe paused. "I hope this estimate of you is correct."

Collins found a cigarette and brought it to his lips. He was not surprised to find that his hand was trembling. "Honest and trustworthy, yes. But what's going on behind my back? Go on, tell me more."

Yurkovich spoke up. "Let me tell what happened to me. Mr. Collins, I was once an alcoholic. Until eight years ago. I finally had myself confined in a sanitarium for treatment. I licked it. I've been straight ever since. It's been known to no one except my immediate family. A week ago, two FBI agents—one named Parkhill, the other Naughton—visited me in my office in Sacramento. They said that they needed my help on an investigation they were conducting. It was a difficult investigation. Such inquiries into the breaking of Federal laws would be made easier once the 35th was passed. But for now they had to do it the slow way. They required information on a certain sanitarium, a drunk tank, where, they had learned, a California legislator had once been confined for five months. Perhaps I could tell them more about the proprietors of this sanitarium."

Yurkovich ceased his recital briefly, wagging his head in renewed disbelief. "It was diabolical the way they let me know. My absolute secret was in their hands. I was sickened."

For the moment, Collins was sickened, too. "What did you say to them?"

"What could I say? I acknowledged I'd been a patient in the sanitarium. I went along with their pretense that they were investigating the owners of a national chain of sanitariums who were also involved in illegal drugs. I told them what I had heard and seen while I'd been confined. When it was over, they thanked me. I asked them if all their information would remain secret. One said, 'You may be called upon to give public courtroom testimony.' I told them I couldn't do that. The agent said, 'Well, that's not in our hands. You might speak to the Director, if you wish. He might come to some understanding with you.' Then they went away. And I had the message. The 35th is good for the country. Vote for the 35th and the Director won't let your hospitalization be made public. Fail to cooperate and it will be made public."

"What are you going to do?" asked Collins.

"I struggled to get where I am," said Yurkovich simply. "I like where I am. I come from a conservative district. I was elected by a constituency that trusts only sober officials. I have no choice. I'll have to vote for the 35th."

"You're sure their investigation wasn't legitimate?" said Collins. "Isn't it possible you may have misconstrued their remarks?"

"Unlikely, but possible. You judge for yourself. As for me, I'm taking no chances."

The rotund man seated beside Yurkovich on the sofa lifted an arm. "Neither am I," said Assemblyman Tobias.

"You mean the same thing happened to you?" asked Collins.

"Almost the same," said Tobias. "It was a day later. Only the FBI didn't come to me. They went to— Well, I have a lady friend, and they called on her." He sighed. "I'm a solid married man with kids. That's the way it looks on the surface. Actually, my wife and I were through long ago. But for the kids' sake we stayed married, and after the kids were gone we continued to maintain a front. It gave her a social life. It kept me in my Government life. For most of those years, I've had a woman on the side, a separate residence. No one on earth knew about it except the three of us. Then, last week, the FBI called on my woman friend. One agent's name was Lindenmeyer, I remember. They were very gentlemanly with her, once they realized how frightened she was. They tried to get her to relax. For a while they talked about other things, not personal things. They even talked about the 35th Amendment—oh, very casually. Finally, they got down to business. I was on a committee concerned with Government contracts. They were investigating someone on the committee who was under suspicion. Routinely, they were checking other members of the committee. They wanted to know if I ever discussed Government contracts with her. She tried to say she didn't know me very well. They merely ignored her protests. They had the facts. They knew how many days a week I spent with her for how many years. When they left, they said if it came to it—yes, they emphasized 'if it came to it'— they might have to subpoena her."

Collins let out his breath slowly. "I can't believe it."

"I believe it," said Tobias. "I can't prove this was done with design, to make me change my vote. But I've got to protect my wife and the woman. And myself too, I guess. So I'm changing my vote. I despise the 35th. But I'm going to declare Aye loud and clear when it's my turn to vote. There, now you know it all, Mr. Collins."

Collins let it sink in. He felt even more sickened. "Has this happened to any other legislators?"

"I don't know," said Tobias. "It's certainly nothing we want to talk to each other about. We each have our private lives, and we want to keep them private."

Collins regarded his host. "What about you, Mr. Keefe?"

"Nobody's visited me, because they know where I stand, and they know I'd kick them out. I have a private life, too, and I suppose they could dredge up something. But I wouldn't give a damn. I don't have as much at stake as my friends, I'd rather be exposed in any way than give in to those bastards, whoever they are."

"Who do you think they are?" asked Collins.

"I don't know."

"I don't know either," said Collins. "It's not my office, you can be sure. If this is a deliberate campaign, it could have been ordered by anyone from the President to the FBI Director to someone under them."

"Can you do anything about it?" Keefe wanted to know.

Collins stood up. "I'm not sure. Again, we have no hard evidence that these visits were intended as intimidation. They may have been actual inquiries with a sound basis for investigation. Or—they may have been a form of blackmail."

"How are you going to find out which?" Keefe asked.

"By investigating the investigators," Collins said.

BACK IN THE BEVERLY Hills Hotel, at the reception desk, Chris Collins picked up a telephone message along with his bungalow key from the clerk.

He unfolded the message. The call had come an hour ago. It read:

> *The supervisor at Tule Lake told you the facility was no secret, that it had been written about in print. We all spent hours researching it this evening. Project Sanguine has been mentioned in print. But the Navy's supposed facility at Tule Lake has never once been mentioned in print. Not one word has ever been published about it. Thought you would want to know. Josh Collins.*

He had almost forgotten. There was his promise to his son that he would prove the Tule Lake facility was not a future internment camp. There was that to be done. There was also the manipulation of California crime statistics to look into. There was the whole coincidental business of FBI agents' probing California state legislators. Above all, overriding all the others, there was The R Document.

First things first.

He walked around the reception desk, recalling that the pay phone booths were near the entrance to the Polo Lounge. He found them, and they were vacant.

Closing himself in the nearest booth, he dialed directly long distance to the Deputy Attorney General, Ed Schrader, at home. He knew that he would awaken him—it was almost three in the morning in Virginia—but he wanted to know the facts as soon as possible. Tomorrow, he would be too busy.

A sleepy voice answered the phone. "Hello? Don't say it's the wrong number—"

"It's the right number, Ed. This is Chris. Listen, there's something I want you to find out for me the earliest tomorrow morning, or this morning. Got a pencil?"

He explained that the United States Navy had a land-based submarine communication system called ELF or Project Sanguine. One of its major facilities was currently under construction, nearing completion in Northern California.

"Find out what you can about it. I'm not leaving for the television show until about twelve fifteen, so I should be in my suite holding meetings until then. Ring me up as soon as you have some information. Now turn over and go back to sleep."

Leaving the phone booth, he met his bodyguard in the lobby, led him along the twisting walks bordered with foliage to his bungalow, bade him goodnight, and went inside.

He was tired to the marrow of his bones.

Briefly, he rattled around the bungalow living room, removing his suit coat and tie, trying to get some perspective on the events of the day—especially the meeting with Keefe, Yurkovich, and Tobias. Their charges against some party, unknown, in the FBI, or someone higher up, had been grave. He tried to assess the veracity of the three legislators. He could discover no motive for any one of them to lie to him. What purpose would there be in their inventing these stories? To what end? He could find no answer. Therefore, they must be telling the truth. Yet he knew that he could not act on what they had told him, could not report this to the President or to Tynan or Adcock, without personal verification. He wasn't sure where to begin. He would wait until morning, when his mind was clearer.

Taking off his shirt, he walked into the darkened bedroom and went on into the bathroom, turning on the light. He undressed, washed, brushed his teeth, studied the dark circles under his eyes, then reached for his pajamas. His pajamas weren't hanging on the back of the door, and he realized the hotel maid had probably laid them out on the pillow of his double bed.

Turning off the bathroom light, he groped his way naked toward the bed, where a strip of illumination from a crack in the living-room door fell on his pajamas. Eager to pull them on, and to drop into bed and into sleep, he had reached down—when suddenly something warm and fleshy touched his right thigh.

He emitted a startled gasp, his hand darting down to find another hand moving up his thigh.

His heart was pounding crazily.

"What in the hell—" he blurted.

"Come to bed, darling," he heard a feminine voice purr.

He was too busy fumbling for the lamp, desperately trying to find the switch, to remove the woman's hand that had curled around his penis.

In a moment, the dim light threw a half circle of yellow on the bed, and there she was wriggling closer to his side of the bed, smiling up at him, her outstretched hand between his legs, fondling him. He was petrified, too incredulous to speak or act. She was young, perhaps in her early twenties, with flowing auburn hair, pouty red lips, large shimmering breasts, a flat belly, and a long triangle of pubic hair.

"Hello," she said in a low small-girl's voice. "I'm Kitty. I thought you'd never get back."

"Who in the hell are you?" he burst out. His hand darted down and grabbed hers, forcing it to release his penis. "You've made a mistake. You're in the wrong—"

"This is the bungalow number I was given. I was told to wait for Mr. Collins."

Then it wasn't a mistake. What juvenile old acquaintance would pull a crackpot gag like this on him?

"Who told you to come here?" he demanded.

"I'm a present from a friend of yours."

"What friend?"

"He never gave his name. They never do. But he paid in cash. Two hundred dollars. I'm expensive." She smiled for the first time. "He said this was to be a surprise, that you'd like it. I promise you that you will, Mr. Collins. Now, come here like a good boy—"

"How—how did you get in?"

"A few of the employees know me. I tip well." She studied him. "Aren't you cute? I like tall men. But you talk too much. Now come on to bed with Kitty. I promise you a good time. I'm staying all night."

"The hell you are!" he almost shouted, grabbing her wrist as she began to reach between his legs again. He wrenched her arm away from him. "Now get out, right now—get out. I don't want you or anybody else. Someone was just trying a practical joke, a childish joke—"

"I was paid—"

"Get out!" He had her by both arms and yanked her to a sitting position. "Get dressed and leave here immediately."

"Nobody's ever treated me like this."

"Well, I am." He snatched up his pajamas. "By the time I'm out of the bathroom, I expect you to be dressed and gone."

He went into the bathroom and angrily yanked on his pajama trousers and buttoned the pajama top.

When he emerged, she had just finished fastening her blouse, and now she stepped into her navy blue skirt.

"Hurry up," he said.

She zipped the skirt. "Your friend said you might act like this at first, but not to take it seriously." She cocked her head at him, smiled again, and started toward him. "You are kidding, aren't you?"

He took her arm roughly and spun her toward the door. "Get moving."

"Let go, you're hurting me."

He eased his hold on her, but pushed her into the living room and propelled her hastily to the front door.

At the door, breathing heavily, he relented slightly. "I'm sorry somebody used you this way," he said. "It was wrong, and I'm sorry. Good night."

She tried to pull herself together and leave with some dignity. "No loss," she said. "You probably couldn't get it up anyway."

He yanked open the door, and as she passed in front of him to go, he saw a shadowy figure pop up from behind the hedge below the bungalow. It was a man lifting a camera.

Acting on instinct, Collins ducked behind the door just as the strobe flash went off. He fell against the door, slamming it shut; lay against it, panting, knowing the photographer had caught Kitty but missed him.

After a while, he turned the lock on the door. Shaken, he stumbled toward the console to mix a drink.

Uncertain as he was about everything that had happened this day, he was positive about what had happened this night. This had not been a stupid practical joke perpetrated by some old college or social friend. It had been far more diabolical. Somebody had tried to set him up, compromise him.

But who? And why? Proponents of the 35th Amendment? Unbelievable, since so far he had been publicly on their side. Unless they wanted to be sure he remained on their side. Enemies of the 35th? Equally unbelievable to think that men like Keefe or Pierce would go to this length to try to force him to switch.

Crazy, he thought. Then, still shaken, he made another drink, to bring daylight closer, when all things made more sense.

DAYLIGHT HAD, INDEED, BROUGHT definition to the murky things that had filled his mind during his restless sleep.

The morning had brought some illumination.

The late and long breakfast with the two United States Attorneys had dispatched a variety of routine Justice Department matters. A meeting with a delegation of three lawyers from the American Bar Association had been mostly social. An interview with a young lady reporter from the *Los Angeles Times* had been largely an exercise in trying to avoid too strong a commitment to the 35th Amendment, speaking about long-range reforms that were necessary in America's justice system, and probing to learn a journalist's views on the escalation of crime in Southern California.

Finally, Collins had been alone with the telephone.

He had intended to call the eight police chiefs who had complained to Assemblyman Keefe that the FBI had been doctoring crime statistics upward in California. He had spoken to only three, and then called no more. Once convinced they were talking to the Attorney General, all three had become guarded in answering his questions. While one admitted "a slight discrepancy" between the figures he had reported to the FBI and those that had been released, he blamed it on "probable computer error," and all three had refused to acknowledge that they had complained to Keefe about exaggerations in the FBI statistics. Each had said, in a different way, that Assemblyman Keefe had misunderstood him.

Either the police chiefs had protested to Keefe but had had second thoughts about going on record against the FBI with the Attorney General, or Keefe *had* misunderstood them. In any case, this telephone inquiry had been inconclusive.

Then Collins had been struck by another approach. Last night, with the legislators, he had jotted down the names of the FBI Special Agents who had interviewed Yurkovich and Tobias. He sought and found the slip with the agents' names: Parkhill, Naughton, Lindenmeyer.

Collins had wondered if he should try to trace them through the Bureau's field offices in California or by calling Adcock or Tynan directly. He decided to be more circumspect. After a while, he put in a direct call to Marion, his secretary.

"Marion, I want a query made of the FBI. It's not to come from me. Just a run-of-the-mill check from anyone in the Office of Legal Counsel. To someone on a lower level in the Bureau. Got your pencil? Okay. Have them ask if two of the FBI's Special Agents in California, one named Parkhill, the other Naughton, interviewed State Assemblyman Yurkovich last week." He spelled out the last name for her. "Then have them ask if a Special Agent Lindenmeyer interviewed—" He realized he did not have the name of Assemblyman Tobias' lady friend. "—uh, interviewed anyone in Sacramento during an investigation of a State Assembly committee on which State Assemblyman Tobias sits. I'm in the hotel. Get right back to me."

Waiting, he had puttered around the bungalow living room, then had taken out a copy of his speech and polished up a few phrases. In fifteen minutes, the phone had rung and it was Marion.

"This is weird, Mr. Collins," she said. "The FBI says it has no Special Agents named Parkhill or Naughton or Lindenmeyer in California. In fact, it has none by those names in the entire country."

Like so much else, this had proved mind-boggling. No agents named Parkhill or Naughton or Lindenmeyer. Yet, Assemblyman Yurkovich had been interviewed by Parkhill and Naughton, and Tobias' lady friend had been interviewed by Lindenmeyer. It could mean that both Yurkovich and Tobias had got the names wrong. Impossible. Or that they had both lied to Collins. Pointless.

Or it could mean one more thing—as improbable, but far more sinister.

It could mean that the FBI had a special corps of agents—a secret corps, names unlisted—deployed to intimidate the lawmakers of California.

Collins entertained that possibility. Normally, Collins was a factual and realistic person, rarely given to flights of fancy or contemplations of melodrama. Normally, he would have dismissed this possibility of a secret corps as too sinister to treat seriously—except for one fact.

His predecessor in office had saved his dying words to warn him of a terrible danger—a danger called The R Document. If one could accept as fact the existence of a piece of paper menacing the—the what?—the security of the country?—one could also accept the possibility of unknown FBI agents' threatening California Assemblymen, as a known one had threatened Father Dubinski.

Collins didn't like it. As he went into the bedroom to change into a suit, before leaving to tape the television show with

Pierce and to deliver his speech to the ABA, he didn't like the idea that he had been elevated to a position where he was supposed to know everything about crime in this country. Yet activities were taking place around him, activities that resembled criminal acts and about which he knew next to nothing. All of this, one way or another, had been engendered by the atmosphere created by the 35th Amendment. God, he thought, what would it be like if the 35th actually became the law of the land?

He had just finished changing when the telephone in the living room began to ring. He hastened into the room and picked up the receiver on the fifth ring.

He heard the voice of Ed Schrader in Washington.

"Chris, about the assignment you gave me last night."

He had quite forgotten his call to Schrader last night. It had been about the facility at Tule Lake that his son had showed him, the construction of a new branch of the Navy's Project Sanguine. He had wanted Schrader to confirm this Navy installation's existence only to prove that his son, Josh, was wrong in his internment-camp paranoia and to bring the boy to his senses.

"Yes, Ed. What did you find out?"

"I have this from authoritative sources at the Pentagon. The Navy's Sanguine Project—or ELF, as they call it—was completed three years ago. There are no new installations under construction or any even being repaired. None of their facilities is anywhere near Tule Lake."

He couldn't believe his ears. "Are you telling me the Navy has no project based at Tule Lake?"

"None whatsoever."

"But the construction foreman there told me— No, never mind. But goddammit, something is being built up there. It's a Government project. They're building something."

"Well, it's certainly not what you heard."

"No—no, I guess it's not," he had said slowly. "Thanks, Ed."

For the first time, he had admitted to himself the possibility that his son, Josh, might be right.

And that Keefe, Yurkovich, and Tobias might be right, too.

All during the twenty-minute drive to the network studios, he had reviewed the mounting evidence of the sinister. The R Document, which was a danger to be exposed. Doctored crime statistics in California. A secret internment camp at Tule Lake.

But finally, it had been the smallest event of all that had unsettled him the most.

His mind went to the photographer planted outside his bungalow last night, trying to catch him with the hooker who had been planted inside. That had not been hearsay. That had been experienced firsthand.

He was filled with suspicion and distrust toward those around him, the advocates of the 35th Amendment, as well as toward the Amendment itself. Above all, he was in no mood to defend the Amendment on national television. He was sickened by the role he had to play. He wanted to turn around and run.

But it was too late. They had reached Beverly Boulevard, and he could see the network studios up ahead.

Collins sat in the chair of the dressing room, a bib protecting his shirt, watching the reflections in the mirror as the makeup man applied a light brown pancake powder to his haggard features.

He could also see, in the mirror, the producer of *Search for Truth*, a tailored young woman named Monica Evans, when she reappeared in the doorway behind him.

"How's it going, Mr. Attorney General?" she asked.

"I guess I'm almost ready," Collins said.

"A few more minutes, Monica, and he's all yours," the makeup man promised.

"I hope you're running on schedule," Collins added. "Right after this, I'm due at the Century Plaza for a speech to the Bar Association. It's going to be close."

"You'll be out of here in plenty of time," Monica Evans assured him. "Tony Pierce is already on the stage with our moderator, Brant Vanbrugh. They've been made up. They're prepared to go as soon as you are."

For Collins, this was a small relief. He had dreaded the idea of being cooped up in this makeup room with Tony Pierce before the show and being forced to talk to him. A formal discussion with Pierce on camera was bad enough. But a private conversation would have been unendurable.

"I'll be waiting in the hall to take you to the studio," Monica Evans said, and then she disappeared.

Collins continued to observe himself in the mirror, and he was not happy with what he saw. Despite the cosmetics, the creams and powders that filled in every crease and crevice of his features, he appeared in his own eyes like a cadaver the mortician was trying to make presentable.

Why, he wondered, was he here to defend a bomb that would blow the Bill of Rights out of the Constitution? What, he wondered, had brought him to side with anti-libertarians like President Wadsworth and Vernon T. Tynan? How, he wondered, had he become a champion of the horrendous 35th Amendment?

In the stark lighting of the theatrically arranged bulbs surrounding the mirror, there was sudden clarity. Until now, he had rationalized his position glibly and persistently. As a good among the bads, he could modify their course. Yet he had failed to do so, had not even really tried. As a Cabinet member, he had chosen to stay on because he had unfinished business, meaning his own solution to crime, which was a more human and decent one. Yet he had not acted upon this business. As Attorney General, he could get other things done that were of more importance than the 35th Amendment. But he knew that his other work was meaningless compared with the overriding importance of the new amendment.

In short, all his rationalizing had been pure bullshit.

He knew why he was here. He knew what had brought him here. He knew how it had come about.

It was naked now, seen in the clarity of the mirror, and he could identify it.

It was ambition. Yes, ambition was the motor that drove him in the wrong lane.

Ambition to get someplace, to show his father. To get somewhere on his own. Grammar-school Freud, but as simple as that. To be what he wasn't, in order to make it. To show his father. To be somebody at any price. But it was ridiculous, this moment. There was nothing to show his father. His father was dead. There was only he himself. And now there was little of himself left.

"All right, Mr. Collins," the makeup man said, removing the bib, "you're ready to go."

Go where? He got out of the chair. "Thanks," he said.

In the hall, he found Monica Evans, and he followed her quickly into the vast television studio.

They emerged from behind a row of scenic flats into a bright square of lights. There were three bulky cameras, two of them being moved. Technicians were bustling about. Attention was focused on a small platform that had been dressed as a private-library set, with three swivel chairs grouped around a massive table. Two men were conversing on the platform.

"Let me introduce you to Brant Vanbrugh, the moderator, and Tony Pierce," said the producer.

Although Collins had never met Pierce face-to-face before, he recognized him at once from his newspaper pictures and previous television appearances. Seeing Pierce in person was a disappointment. Collins wanted a villain, and what he saw instead was a disarming and winning human being. Pierce had sandy hair and a freckled, open young-middle-aged face, one alive with enthusiasm. He was trim, springy, five feet ten, in a custom-tailored single-breasted suit.

Collins' heart sank. He had hoped not only for a villain but for an enemy, and now the only enemy he could find was no one other than himself.

Monica Evans brought him forward and effected the introductions.

"I'm glad to meet you at last, Mr. Collins," Pierce said. "The little I know about you is from what I've read and from your son, Josh. He's quite a boy."

"He speaks highly of you," said Collins, miserably certain that Pierce was eyeing him to discover how such a father could have produced such a son.

"Gentlemen," the moderator interrupted, "I'm afraid we don't have much time." He was a brisk young man, deceptively resembling a juvenile lead, but with the mind (Collins had seen the show before) of a steel trap. Ambitious, Collins thought. Then he thought, Look who's talking.

Vanbrugh led them to their respective chairs on either side of him. As someone fastened the small microphone around Collins' neck, he heard Vanbrugh addressing them again.

"We'll be taping in two minutes. This edition of *Search for Truth* will air coast-to-coast on prime time tonight. What you do here goes on as is. No editing. There'll be two commercial breaks. Here's the format. I'll open with the proposition to be discussed: 'Should California ratify the 35th Amendment?' I'll do the introductory material on the 35th. I'll tell what it is, and where it stands today. The camera will be tight on me. Then the camera will pull back to reveal you, Mr. Collins. I'll introduce you to the audience as the United States Attorney General and give some of your credentials. Then the camera will cut to Mr. Pierce and me, and I'll introduce you, Mr. Pierce, as a former FBI Special Agent, a practicing attorney, and head of the lobby opposing the 35th Amendment and backing the Bill of Rights. Then I'll call on you, Mr. Collins. You'll have about two minutes to make an opening statement. I'd suggest you concentrate on why you are supporting the 35th Amendment. I imagine you'll want to paint a strong picture of the criminal landscape in America today, and argue that drastic measures are required to preserve our society. Next, your turn, Mr. Pierce. You can have your two-minute opener. Don't debate Mr. Collins yet. Just state your views on why you oppose the Amendment. After that we'll play it by ear. You can start your debate. Interruptions are okay, but don't step on each other's lines." He looked off. "We're about to start. When the red light goes on above the middle camera, we're taping. Good luck, gentlemen, and let's keep it lively."

The red light above the middle camera began to shine.

Feeling ill and fuzzy-headed, Collins only half-listened to Vanbrugh's opening remarks.

He heard his name and knew he was being introduced. He summoned up a sickly smile for the camera.

Next, he heard Tony Pierce's name. He glanced past the moderator. Pierce's open, freckled face was grave.

He heard his own name again, and the question.

From a distance, he heard himself speaking.

"At no time since the Civil War have our democratic institutions been so seriously threatened as they are today. Violence has become commonplace. Back in 1975, ten out of every 100,000 Americans died by murder. Today, twenty-two out of every 100,000 Americans die by murder. Some years ago, three mathematicians at the Massachusetts Institute of Technology, after making a study of the increasing crime rate, concluded, 'An urban American boy born in 1974 is more likely to die by murder than an American soldier in World War II was to die in combat.' Today, this cruel possibility has doubled. It was out of a need to stop this upward spiral of violence, including murder, that the concept of the 35th Amendment was born."

Laboriously, he continued until he saw the fifteen-second card, and with relief he concluded his opening statement.

Now he heard Tony Pierce speaking, every sentence a blow, and he winced inside and tried not to listen.

Two minutes more, and he knew the debate had begun.

He heard Pierce speaking once more. "Human beings have struggled for freedom—for freedom from tyranny—for at least 2,500 years. Now, overnight, if the 35th Amendment is passed, that struggle will end in America. Overnight, at the whim of the Director of the FBI and his Committee on National Safety, the Bill of Rights could be suspended indefinitely—"

"Not indefinitely," Collins interrupted. "Only in an emergency, and only for a short time, perhaps a few months."

"That's what they said in India in 1962," said Pierce. "They had an emergency and they suspended their Bill of Rights. It remained suspended for six years. Then they suspended it again in 1975. Who can guarantee that won't happen here? And if it does happen, it means the end of our free way of life. We have proof of that. Such a thing has happened before in the United States, and it has always meant disaster."

"What are you saying, Mr. Pierce?" Vanbrugh interjected. "Are you saying the Bill of Rights has been suspended before in our history?"

"Unofficially it has, yes. Our Bill of Rights has been unofficially suspended, or overlooked, or ignored, numerous times in our past, and when this has happened, we have suffered deeply."

"Can you cite any specific examples?" asked the moderator.

"Certainly," said Pierce. "In 1798, after the French Revolution, the United States feared the infiltration of radical French conspirators who might want to overthrow our Government. In an atmosphere of hysteria, Congress ignored the Bill of Rights and passed the Alien and Sedition Laws. Hundreds of people were arrested. Editors who wrote against these laws were clapped into jail. Ordinary citizens who spoke out against President John Adams were also thrown into jail. Because Thomas Jefferson campaigned against this madness, this suspension of the Bill of Rights, people were brought to their senses and Jefferson was elected President.

"Other examples abound. During the Civil War, writs of habeas corpus were ignored, and civil trials gave way to military trials. After World War I, Attorney General A. Mitchell Palmer invoked the Red Menace and went on a witch-hunt that led to the arrest, without the use of warrants, of 3,500 people and the deportation of 700 aliens. Chief Justice Charles Evans Hughes characterized these arrests as one of 'the worst practices of tyranny.' With the beginning of World War II, American citizens who happened to be of Japanese descent were deprived of their property and confined to detention camps. Not long after, in 1954 to be exact, Senator Joseph R. McCarthy rashly accused 205 persons employed in the U.S. State Department of being members of the Communist party, thus instigating his own Red Scare. McCarthy, a reckless, publicity-hungry demagogue and hopeless drunkard, smeared and destroyed countless innocent Americans by labeling dissent and nonconformity as treason. In the end, through his excesses, he destroyed himself before the nation during the thirty-six days of the Army-McCarthy hearings.

"More recently, the Organized Crime Control Act of 1969, the dream child of President Richard M. Nixon and Attorney General John N. Mitchell, effectively suspended the Bill of Rights by providing for preventive detention of accused criminals, no-knock entry of private homes, limits on the rights of the accused to see evidence illegally obtained against them, and electronic eavesdropping for forty-eight hours without warrants and for a longer period with warrants. Commenting on this Organized Crime Control Act, Senator Sam J. Ervin of North Carolina called it 'a garbage pail of some of the most repressive, nearsighted, intolerant, unfair, and vindictive legislation that the Senate has ever been presented. . . . This bill might better be entitled "a bill to repeal the 4th, 5th, 6th and 8th Amendments to the Consitution." ' "

"Yet democracy survived," said Collins.

"Barely, barely, Mr. Collins. And one day it may not survive such assaults on our liberty. As Charles Péguy once observed, tyranny is always better organized than freedom. If all those horrors I've mentioned were committed with a Bill of Rights in effect, imagine what will happen without a Bill of Rights, after the 35th Amendment is ratified. Mr. Collins, our Constitution, with its Bill of Rights, has survived longer than any other written Constitution on earth. Let's not destroy it with our own hands."

"Mr. Pierce," said Collins, "you speak of our Constitution as if it had been chiseled in stone or handed down from heaven—as something inflexible, not subject to change. As a matter of fact, our Constitution today is merely a product of compromise. Before it was signed, there were many versions of it, it was many things, and it can still be many things—"

"That's not the point, Mr. Collins," Pierce interrupted. "The point—"

Vanbrugh quickly came between them. "One second, gentlemen. I'd like Attorney General Collins to expand on what he was starting to say. You were saying, Mr. Collins, there were many versions of the Constitution—"

"And the Bill of Rights, also," added Collins.

"—before a final version was signed. I find that interesting. Many members of our audience may not realize that. Do you want to explain?"

"I'd be glad to. I'm only trying to prove that we aren't tampering with the Constitution when we try to change it. I'm only saying it was many things when it began, and it can still be many things. That's why we have amendments. The word *amendment* derives from the Latin word *emendare*—meaning to correct a defect or modify something for the better."

"But those different versions of the Constitution and Bill of Rights?" Vanbrugh prompted again.

"Yes. Well, as you may know, a group of fifty-five men from twelve states met from May until September of 1787 in the Pennsylvania State House—which is called Independence Hall today—to draw up a Constitution that would bind thirteen individual states into a nation. The average age of these men was forty-three. Perhaps patriotism and survival were not the only incentives for these delegates. Half of them owned public securities. If they could write a Constitution that would form a new government, their securities would rise in value. At any rate, if you think the Presidency, as we have it in the Constitution today, is sacred, consider the fact that Alexander Hamilton wanted a President appointed for life. Edmund Randolph and George Mason wanted three men to serve as President at the same time, while Benjamin Franklin suggested that a council rule the United States. The Convention voted five times in favor of having the President appointed by Congress. It was the delegation from Virginia that first suggested a single 'national executive.' They did not even call him President. It was Randolph who opposed this kind of one-man office, describing it as 'the fetus of monarchy.'" Collins glanced at the moderator. "Do I have time for more?"

"Please go on," Vanbrugh urged him.

"Perhaps many people think that the creation of the Senate, as outlined in the Constitution, is also sacred. Not so in the beginning. Some members of the Convention wanted the various state legislatures to appoint Senators. Hamilton wanted the Senators appointed for life. James Madison suggested Senators serve nine-year terms. When it was agreed Senators should be elected by the people, some delegates meant elected by people who were property holders and therefore stable. It was John Jay who said, 'The people who own the country ought to govern it.' In the end, a compromise was reached. The state legislatures could vote for Senators, and the Senators would serve six-year terms. Not until 1913 did the 17th Amendment change this, giving all citizens the right to select Senators. As for the Bill of Rights, there was no Bill of Rights—none at all—when the Constitution was signed. Most of the Founding Fathers felt the Constitution itself was a Bill of Rights, and no amendments had to be added. I repeat, the wisest men in America felt no Bill of Rights was necessary at the time. In the light of our past, I don't see what injury we can do our Constitution in the present century by appending to it a 35th Amendment which would merely temporarily suspend the Bill of Rights if necessary to preserve our country."

"Mr. Vanbrugh?" It was Tony Pierce trying to be heard. "May I respond to the Attorney General's version of American history?"

"Your turn, Mr. Pierce," said the moderator.

"Mr. Collins," said Pierce, "despite everything you've said, we *do* have a Bill of Rights today. How did we get it? You omitted mentioning that. We got it because the people wanted it, because the people felt the Constitutional Convention had been wrong in leaving it out. The various states wanted people's rights and states' rights spelled out, they wanted this before they would ratify the Constitution. Patrick Henry of Virginia suggested twenty amendments, among them the first ten later adopted. Massachusetts wanted the ten amendments. Other states did. When the First Congress met in 1791, Madison proposed twelve amendments. Congress agreed on ten, and sent them to the thirteen states for ratification. They were ratified and the Bill of Rights became effective in December of 1791."

"You're implying all the states wanted a Bill of Rights," said Collins, "and that's simply not true. Three of the original thirteen states refused to ratify the Bill of Rights. In fact, they didn't do so until 1939, a century and a half later."

"I'm afraid you're quibbling, Mr. Collins," Pierce shot back. "What is meaningful is that from the beginning we had a Bill of Rights that guaranteed all our people three main rights—freedom of religion, freedom of speech, freedom of trial. It was Thomas Jefferson who insisted, 'A Bill of Rights is what the people are entitled to against any government on earth, general or particular, and what no just government should refuse or rest on inference.' Our Bill of Rights was important, and remains important. Surely Jefferson would have opposed your 35th Amendment as vehemently as I am opposing it now. What you are arguing for is an amendment to void the Bill of Rights, and I am saying to do so is to void democracy itself."

Collins felt cornered and helpless, and because he felt cornered and helpless, he compensated with anger. "Mr. Pierce, it is to *preserve* democracy that I am supporting the 35th," he said heatedly. "What will void democracy is permitting our present plague of lawlessness and anarchy to escalate totally out of control, to let the murderers, kidnappings, bombings, assassinations, conspiracies, revolutions—to let all these overwhelm us. In a few years there won't be a democracy. There won't even be a country. Who are you going to give rights to if there is no country?"

"I'd rather have no country than a country without freedom," retorted Pierce. "But there will be a country as long as there are people—free people and not slaves. There are better ways to control crime than by offering dictatorship. We might begin by offering people food, jobs, housing, justice, compassion, equality."

"I believe in all those things, too, Mr. Pierce. But we must stop the killing first. The 35th Amendment may stop the killing. After that, with order restored, we can start attending to our other priorities."

Pierce shook his head. "We'll be able to attend to nothing once our human rights are lost. And make no mistake about it, under your 35th our rights *will* be lost. I was just rereading a book last night—" He plucked a paperback off the table and opened it. "—a book called *Your Freedoms: The Bill of Rights* by Frank K. Kelly, Vice-President of the Fund for the Republic. Listen to what he has to say: 'If we lost our Bill of Rights, what would happen to our way of life? Here are some of the things that could happen: The Government could keep young men in the military services for indefinite periods, without giving any explanation or justification for this policy. Young men and women leaving school could be assigned to jobs in industries where the Government asserted the workers were needed. Young people could be forced to take these jobs. Students protesting against Government policies . . . could be thrown into Federal prisons by order of the President. Americans, young and old, could be required to give up their property for public use without compensation . . . The names of persons writing critical letters to their congressmen might be turned over to the police, and such persons could be arrested and imprisoned . . . Editors who printed articles in their newspapers criticizing the Government would be subject to arrest at any time, night or day . . . ' "

Pierce was going on and on, and Collins unconsciously began shrinking back into his chair. The fight he had tried to fake had gone out of him. He didn't belong here, not on the side where he sat, and he was filled with loathing for the other man inside him, the ambitious monster who had put him here.

He waited. He listened. He attempted a few more feeble, halfhearted defenses. He did his duty. The minutes passed, the endless thirty minutes, and finally the torture was over.

He fumbled to remove his microphone as Vanbrugh and Pierce stood up, both amiable, both ready to chat.

Collins ignored them. "Excuse me," he said to Vanbrugh, "but where's the men's room?"

"Across the hall to the left."

Collins spun around, went hastily across the television stage, out the door into the hallway, and swung left.

He found the bathroom and rushed inside. Luckily, no one else was there. He made it to the toilet basin just in time.

He hung over it a moment, ashen.

Then he threw up.

After a while, he washed his face and hands, and tried to regain his composure. He stared at himself in the mirror.

If he had wondered where he finally stood on the 35th Amendment, he knew now. And strangely, his conscience hadn't told him where to stand. It was his stomach that had.

* * *

IT WAS AN HOUR later, and he had made up his mind as to what he must do. It wasn't what he wanted completely, but it was a start—a good start.

As he left the elevator that had brought him two floors below the main lobby of the Century Plaza Hotel, he knew that he had definitely decided upon his next act. While his bodyguards and the local police officers helped him push through the mob of press photographers and spectators, Collins crossed the vast lower lobby and entered the Los Angeles Room of the hotel.

Escorted along the fringe of the upper tier of tables, he was not ready for the impact of so many bodies jammed together in this cavern of a hall lit only by a mammoth central chandelier and one set of four chandeliers on the far side of it. Clutching the leather folder that held his speech in his left hand, striding awkwardly, he came onto the bright stage and the dais, where officers of the American Bar Association rose to welcome him. His public recognition was not yet high, but a scattering of applause from below followed him to his seat.

Small talk, small talk, the amenities, as he was directed to his place beside Chief Justice John G. Maynard.

Shaking hands with the Chief Justice, Collins was once again impressed by the idol of his youth. Maynard was one of the few public figures in America who seemed to have been type-cast for their roles. His mass of white hair, deep-set probing eyes beneath thick brows, hooked nose, and square jaw gave him the appearance of an honest Caesar. His bearing, his carriage ramrod-straight, gave him an air of vigor and youth remarkable for a man in his mid-seventies.

For Collins, the next move was difficult. He barely knew Chief Justice Maynard. He had met him no more than three times, briefly, during Government receptions, and had never spoken to him at length. Actually, there had been a fourth time very recently—the occasion when Chief Justice Maynard had sworn him in as Attorney General in the White House.

Aware that the president of the American Bar Association

had gone to the podium, that the proceedings were about to begin, Collins was pressed by the necessity to act now. He sought Maynard's attention, saw that he was occupied by the lady to his left, and bided his time. In a few moments, Maynard had turned away from the woman to devote himself to the introductory remarks.

Collins touched his sleeve and leaned toward him. "Mr. Chief Justice—"

Maynard bent toward Collins. "Yes?"

"—I wonder if I could have five minutes alone with you in private after we leave here?"

"Why, certainly, Mr. Collins. We have rooms upstairs, on the third floor. We won't be going back to Washington until this evening. Mrs. Maynard is out shopping, so we can be quite alone."

Pleased, Collins sat back again, feeling better. But as he listened to the windy introduction of himself as the first speaker, his mind fixed on the 35th Amendment, and the feeling of oppression returned.

On his lap rested his speech recounting the acceleration of crime in the United States and the ways in which the law and judiciary had developed and changed to meet it. At the beginning of his speech and at the end were pleas for the necessity of Constitutional revision, when required, with particular emphasis on the importance and value of the 35th Amendment. Skimming the statements he would shortly be making, Collins was uncomfortable.

Finding his pen, he quickly reread three quotations in the opening pages.

He examined the first:

As President George Washington stated in his Farewell Address to the nation in September, 1796: "The basis of our political systems is the right of the people to make and to alter their constitutions of government."

Collins crossed out the paragraph.
He examined the next paragraph.

And as Alexander Hamilton said a dozen years later, in an address to the United States Senate, "Constitutions should consist only of general provisions; the reason is that they must necessarily be permanent, and that they cannot calculate for the possible change of things." It is the general nature of the articles that allows for amendments to meet the emergencies of history. It is the general nature of our Bill of Rights that can allow it to incorporate the 35th Amendment, to solve the problems of this generation, without altering the integrity of the document as a whole.

Swiftly, Collins ran his pen through this paragraph, deleting it also.

He went to the third page.

In 1816, Thomas Jefferson wrote a friend the following: "Some men look at constitutions with sanctimonious reverence, and deem them like the Ark of the Covenant, too sacred to be touched. They ascribe to the men of the preceding age a wisdom more than human, and suppose what they did to be beyond amendment." Jefferson believed our own Constitution not above revision . . .

In firm strokes, Collins cut that paragraph as well.

With these excisions, what remained was still an argument for flexibility, for consideration of new laws to handle new problems, but now the argument was milder, watered down—more a suggestion offered for debate.

He heard Chief Justice Maynard whisper to him, "That's what I call writing up to a deadline."

He glanced at Maynard. "Second thoughts," he said.

Then he heard the president of the American Bar Association from the podium. "Ladies and gentlemen, it is my pleasure to present to you the Attorney General of the United States—Christopher Collins!"

As the applause rose, he came to his feet to speak.

* * *

TWO HOURS LATER, WITH his own turgid speech behind him, with the Chief Justice's brilliant speech still ringing in his ears, Collins sat on the edge of the straight-backed chair in the quiet of Maynard's suite trying to form into words what had been on his mind throughout the afternoon.

"Mr. Chief Justice," Collins began, "I'll tell you why I wanted to see you alone. I'll come directly to the point. I'd like to know your views on the 35th Amendment. How do you feel about it?"

The Chief Justice, relaxed on the couch, filling his pipe with tobacco from a leather pouch, raised his head with a frown. "Your question—is it inspired by the Executive Branch, or is it your own?"

"It is inspired by no one. It is my own, growing out of my personal concern."

"I see."

"I have great respect for your opinion," continued Collins. "I'm eager to know your thoughts on what might be the most controversial and decisive bill ever put before the American people."

"The 35th," murmured Maynard, lighting his pipe. He puffed a few seconds, then studied Collins. "As you might guess, I'm against it. I'm very much against such drastic legislation. Improperly applied, it can suffocate the Bill of Rights, turn our democracy into a totalitarian state. Certainly we have a serious problem in this country. Crime and lawlessness are rampant as never before in our history. But curtailment of freedoms provides no permanent solution. It may bring peace, but it is the peace brought on by death. Poverty, we know, is the mother of crime. End poverty, and you are nearer to ending crime. There is no other way. I hold with Ben Franklin—give up liberty to buy safety and you deserve neither liberty nor safety. The 35th Amendment may buy safety. But it will be at the cost of human liberty. It's a bad bargain. I strongly oppose it."

"Why don't you come out and publicly say so?" asked Collins.

Chief Justice Maynard sat back, puffing at his pipe, and eyed

Collins shrewdly. "Why don't you?" he countered. "You are the Attorney General. Why don't you speak out against it?"

"Because I'd no longer be the Attorney General."

"Is that so important?"

"Yes—because I think I can do more good where I am. Besides, my voice wouldn't be listened to as yours would. Except for my official position, I'm relatively unknown. I don't have your credibility. Surely you saw the recent California statewide poll on the most admired Americans. You polled 87 percent. People will listen to you here, and so will the state legislators."

"Wait a moment, Mr. Collins," said Maynard, setting down his pipe in an ashtray. "I'm afraid you've thoroughly confused me. When you asked me why I am not speaking out against the bill, I responded by asking you the same question. I think I expected you to say you aren't speaking out against it because you are all for it. Instead, you indicate you're on my side. Yet you want me to be the one to denounce it publicly. I simply don't understand. I thought you, as well as the President, the Congressional leaders, the FBI Director, were all supporters of the 35th. Even in your speech today you seemed to indicate the 35th should be given careful consideration. That's confusing."

Collins nodded. "Perhaps because I've been confused myself. The speech was written before today, and delivered at the instigation of President Wadsworth. Since yesterday I've become increasingly suspicious of the Amendment, and fearful of how it might be misused. I think I now agree totally with you about it. I think I would resign rather than defend it again. But for now, I'd prefer to stay in office. I'm faced with some unfinished business. I want to finish it before taking a real stand. Meanwhile, time is running out here in California. Someone the people and legislators will listen to should be heard. That's why I urge you to speak out. You, alone, could kill it."

"It may be killed without my help."

"I doubt it. Not according to the President's private polls."

"All right, I'll tell you why I can't speak out against it," said Maynard. "I don't know whether you're aware of it, but a year and a half ago the justices of the high court came to an ethical agreement. None would partisanly discuss, in speech or writing, any legal matter that might one day come before the court. It would be impossible for me to discuss in public an amendment I may later be required to interpret or rule upon while I am in office."

"Yes, I see," said Collins in despair. "I guess there's just no way for you to tell the public what you really think of the 35th."

"No way that I can see," said Maynard slowly. "At least, no way, as long as I'm on the Bench." He was thoughtful a moment. "Of course, there would be one way. I could always get off the Bench. I could resign. Then I'd be free to speak out." He shook his head. "But present circumstances don't seem to warrant such a drastic step."

"Present circumstances," repeated Collins. "But can you envision any future circumstances that might make you want to resign and speak out against the 35th?"

Maynard considered the question. "Well, yes, I suppose there might be several possibilities that could move me to act. Certainly if I were convinced that the men and the motives behind the 35th were evil, if I were certain that in their hands the 35th would present a true and immediate danger to the country, I would resign from the Bench and speak to the people. At present, I am not so convinced. But if I were to be, I would step down and raise my voice immediately. In short, if there were more to it than meets the eye—"

That instant, Collins thought of The R Document, of the danger that did not meet the eye but was real in Noah Baxter's deathbed warning. "Chief Justice Maynard," Collins interrupted, "have you ever heard of something called The R Document?"

"The R Document? No, I think not. What is it?"

"I'm not sure. Let me explain." Slowly, he related to Maynard the circumstances of Colonel Baxter's death and his portentous last words. "As far as I can deduce, it seems to be a paper or plan that exists which is supposed to—to supplement the 35th Amendment in some way. As you heard, it is something Baxter considered dangerous. It may be the something, involved in the 35th, that does not meet the eye."

"It may be," said Maynard. "It certainly sounds ominous."

"If I uncovered it, and it proved to be a danger, could that make you act?"

"It might," said Maynard cautiously. "It would depend on its contents. Let me see it, or anything like it, first—and then I'll give you my answer."

"Fair enough." Collins stood up. "I'm resuming my search. If and when I find The R Document—you'll be the first to hear from me."

Chief Justice Maynard rose. "I'll be waiting to hear from you. Once I've heard from you, I'll be ready to make a decision."

As Collins left Maynard's suite, his mind felt clearer. He knew where he stood on the 35th, at last. He knew there was an ally to help him stop it, if he came up with the elusive missing evidence against it.

And he knew one source who might give him a clue to the missing link.

He must return to Washington. But after that, sometime next week, he must go calling on someone at Lewisburg Federal Penitentiary in Pennsylvania.

THE FOLLOWING MORNING, BEHIND the locked doors of the office of the Director of the FBI in the J. Edgar Hoover Building in Washington, D.C., two immobilized figures sat listening to a tape spinning slowly on the large silver recorder set on the coffee table between them.

Vernon T. Tynan and Harry Adcock had been listening, wordlessly, for nearly a quarter of an hour. The last of the tape was playing.

Faithful to life the voices came out of the speaker.

"As you heard, it is something Baxter considered dangerous. It may be the something, involved in the 35th, that does not meet the eye."

"It may be. It certainly sounds ominous."

"If I uncovered it, and it proved to be a danger, could that make you act?"

"It might. It would depend on its contents. Let me see it, or anything like it, first—and then I'll give you my answer."

"Fair enough. I'm resuming my search. If and when I find The R Document—you'll be the first to hear from me."

"I'll be waiting to hear from you. Once I've heard from you, I'll be ready to make a decision."

Silence, except for the rubbing of the remainder of the blank tape.

"Sonofabitch!" Tynan exclaimed, his face livid, as he jumped to his feet. "That fucking Benedict Arnold, turning against us like this! Shut that goddam tape off, Harry."

Quickly Adcock stopped the tape, then pivoted to watch as his superior paced the office.

Tynan hammered one big fist into the palm of his other hand. "That dirty, rotten bastard Collins. I'm going to have his neck for this. He won't get anywhere, trying to subvert us, but we're going to put him out of the way fast. Maynard's the one that bothers me more. That puking Red-loving liberal—he's the one who can be real trouble if he ever goes back into California to bad-mouth us and the 35th."

"He can't, chief, without any evidence. He said he wouldn't without evidence."

"I don't trust him. He just might make up his mind to do us in. I'm not taking any chances—not any more, not with either of them. We're going to beat Maynard and Collins to the punch."

"Collins should be easy to defuse," said Adcock. "You only have to take this tape over to the President—he'll fire his Attorney General in one minute flat."

Tynan held up his hand. "No, Harry. You and your boys did a great job in Los Angeles. The tapes are precious, every one, but I don't think it would be wise to let the President in on our procedures. He can be pretty square. Besides, he's leaving everything to us. He doesn't want to be involved. No, I think it would be better to handle Mr. Attorney General Collins and Mr. Chief Justice Maynard in our own way."

Adcock watched him walk thoughtfully behind the swivel

chair at his desk. Adcock waited, then asked, "Any ideas, chief?"

The Director nodded. "A few. I don't know if both of them will go further. Collins has indicated he will, but I don't think he has anywhere to go. At any rate, they're both potentially dangerous to the country—and to us. We've been forewarned. Now we have to be forearmed. We have to be ready for any eventuality. Once we have the ammunition, we can hold on to it, use it only if we are forced to."

"I couldn't agree with you more, chief."

"I think we can start with our Attorney General Collins. I want the Bureau to run a quiet check on him."

"But he was checked out thoroughly before Congress confirmed him as Attorney General," Adcock protested.

Tynan waved his hand, as if dusting their first effort aside. "Routine, that first investigation was routine. I want an elite force, a small strike force composed of our best agents, assigned to the investigation today. Handpick them, Harry. The ones who know how to handle a low-key high-priority job. The ones who can be trusted completely, who have absolute loyalty to their Director. I want Collins checked ten times more thoroughly than the first time."

"How far do we go?"

"All the way. Go after everyone ever connected with him at any time in his life. Go after his first wife, Helen Collins—or whatever her name is now. Go after their son. Go after his second wife, Karen Collins, and their housekeeper. Run down any relatives he's been close to. Don't overlook his friends like Senator Hilliard. Don't overlook anyone."

Adcock was standing at something like attention now. "Will do. It's as good as done, chief."

"One week. I want the investigation completed in one week."

"One week," Adcock promised.

"Okay. Next, John G. Maynard. I think our illustrious Chief Justice can also stand a minute examination. I know this was done before he was confirmed. But that was—was—"

"Fifteen years ago."

"Have our task force investigate him as if it had never been done before. Have them bear down hard on his friends, enemies, associates, family, and his contacts with them in the last seven years. I want every step Maynard has made, every statement, letter, investment, activity, gone over with a magnifying glass. If Collins went public against us, he might hurt us a little in California, but not fatally. If Maynard decided to turn against us, he could destroy us. I want to be prepared. That's all, Harry—just to be prepared."

Adcock came forward to the desk. "Chief, if you'd like my opinion, even if we found something on Maynard, it would never be enough to stop him once he made up his mind to oppose the 35th."

"It could discredit him."

"Maybe. But you saw the polls on how he's admired."

"I know. Well, let's try to get the goods on him anyway, and hope what we find is strong enough." Tynan reflected on the matter. "You're right, Harry. Collins would be easy to wipe. Maynard is something else. It might take more." He seemed to be talking to himself. "If he resigned to come out against us, nothing would stop him. He'd go all the way." Tynan's countenance darkened. "Then we'd have to go all the way, too. It would be him or us. There's one thing . . ."

He had drifted off into deeper deliberation.

"Yes, chief?" Adcock prompted.

Tynan shook his hand above the chair. "It needs more thought." Then he added, "It also needs money—lots of it."

"The President has a fund—"

"No," Tynan interrupted. "Too public. Besides, like I said, I don't want the President involved. We should do our own job, and he can reap the benefits. We need a war chest from a source that—that can't be traced." Suddenly he hit the palm of his hand with his fist. "By God, Harry, I've got it!"

Galvanized by his idea, Tynan came around his chair, sat in it, and dialed his secretary on the intercom.

"Beth? Pick up the phone. . . . Okay, get me the file on Donald Radenbaugh. Get it in here on my desk fast."

He hung up and lay back, beaming at his assistant.

Adcock was plainly puzzled. "Radenbaugh is locked up in Lewisburg."

"I know."

"I thought you were looking for a lot of money?"

Tynan grinned. "I am. And I know who's got it, and who won't talk. Just wait, Harry, have patience, and trust old Vernon T. Tynan."

In minutes, Beth appeared with the file. "This is just an abstract of the case. We have some complete files—"

"This'll do, Beth. Thanks."

When he and Adcock were alone, Tynan opened the file and began skimming the typed sheets of paper inside. As he leafed through the pages, he paused here and there, mouthing aloud some fact as he read. "Radenbaugh, Radenbaugh . . . Extortion . . . To deliver money in Miami Beach, according to . . . No money . . . Then the trial . . . Guilty. Fifteen years . . . Umm, two years and eight months served . . . Yes."

He closed the file folder. He looked up at his assistant with a smack of satisfaction. "Perfect," he said. "I must say, if this works, I'm a genius. If our Chief Justice interferes, we'll be ready for him."

"I don't understand, chief."

"You will, soon enough. Right now, just follow orders. You can get onto the Collins investigation after this. First do this." He paused, turning it over in his mind. "Do this. Shut yourself in your office and call Warden Bruce Jenkins at Lewisburg Federal Penitentiary. Confidential call. Tell Jenkins it's all just between us, in absolute confidence. He can be trusted. The warden owes me plenty. Okay. Tell him I want to see one of his inmates, Donald Radenbaugh, outside the prison walls tonight—after midnight—say, two o'clock in the morning. Find out a place to meet where nobody'll know—where I can have a nice private talk with Mr. Donald Radenbaugh. A lot's at stake, Harry, everything's at stake, so get it right."

V

It was a quarter to two in the morning, and except for the moon it was very dark, and Harry Adcock drove slowly in the darkness.

For the third time in an hour, Vernon T. Tynan, in the front seat beside him, asked, "You're positive no one knows we're out of town?"

"No one, I'm positive," Adcock reassured him. "I even got up a phony schedule of your activities in Washington for the evening, and left it lying around."

"Good, Harry, very good." Tynan squinted ahead through the windshield at the heavy foliage and trees guarding this little-used side road. "I can't see a damn thing. You're sure you know where we are?"

"I'm following the warden's instructions to the letter," said Adcock. "Jenkins spelled it all out."

"How much longer before we get there?"

"Any minute, chief."

They had flown in a small private jet plane from Washington, D.C., to Harrisburg, Pennsylvania. By arrangement, they had been the only passengers in the jet. In Harrisburg, a rented Pontiac sedan had been waiting for them at the airport. Adcock had taken the wheel from the start, with Tynan beside him and a

red-marked topographic map of the Lewisburg quadrangle between them. They had driven out of Harrisburg, crossed the
bridge over the Susquehanna River, and proceeded due north
on U.S. Highway 15 running along the west bank of the river. It
had taken an hour and a half, covering approximately fifty
miles, to reach their first landmark, Bucknell University, off to
their right. They had continued on into the city of Lewisburg, a
ghost town that slept in these hours after midnight.

Passing the city's high school, Adcock had slowed to a crawl
while he consulted the map.

He had put the map down and searched the thoroughfare
ahead of him. They had reached the far side of the city.

Adcock had pointed to his left. "You turn here to come to
the entrance of the Penitentiary. Jenkins said we should ignore
that, go straight on northeast on Highway 15, then turn left at
the Evangelical Hospital, and go north past the side of the
Penitentiary—"

"Will anybody be able to see us from there?" Tynan had
asked worriedly.

"Naw, chief. We'll be out of sight. Besides, look what time it
is. Anyway, we go along, then make another turn when we
reach the side road through the forest. We go on through the
woods to the southern edge and then we see the walls and water
tower of the Penitentiary, and that's where we wait."

Now they were moving at a snail's pace through the forest.

Adcock bent over the wheel, and Tynan leaned forward at the
same time, peering through the windshield at what seemed to
be the end of the road and the fringe of the wooded area.

"I think we're there," Adcock muttered. "He said there would
be a clearing between some trees to the right. Yup, right on the
nose. Here it is."

He swung off the road to the right, then veered sharply to the
left and parked. Some distance ahead they could make out the
silhouette of the front section of the concrete wall surrounding
the prison, the tops of several larger buildings in the jailyard,
and two water towers, one to the right and the other behind
Lewisburg Federal Penitentiary.

Adcock reached to the dashboard and cut off the headlights.

He indicated the silhouettes beyond. "There are some tough cookies in that maximum-security hole," he said.

"Some," said Tynan. "Donald Radenbaugh isn't one of them. He's one of the softies, one of the political prisoners."

"I didn't know he was a political prisoner."

"He isn't, technically. Yet he is. He knew too much about what went on up there. That can be an offense, too."

Tynan fidgeted in the darkness of the front seat, looking through the windshield and waiting.

Several minutes had passed when Adcock tugged at Tynan's sleeve. "Chief, I think I see them coming."

Tynan peered through the windshield intently, narrowing his eyes, and finally he made out two specks of light approaching head on. "Must be Jenkins," he said. "He's using only his parking lights."

He fell silent, continuing to follow the progress of the other car as it drew closer.

"All right," Tynan said suddenly, "here's how we'll do it. I'm getting into the back seat. I'll be in the back to meet him. You stay right where you are, behind the wheel. You can listen. Don't speak. I'll do all the talking. You just listen. We're both in on this."

Tynan opened the front door of the Pontiac, stepped out, closed it, opened the rear door, got inside, and slumped in the far corner of the back seat.

The other car had entered the clearing and drawn up ten yards behind them. The engine choked to a halt. The parking lights went out. A door opened and closed.

There was the crunch of footsteps.

The wizened face of Warden Bruce Jenkins came down to appear in the window next to Adcock, who jerked his thumb over his shoulder. Jenkins bobbed his head and moved back, and now his face was at the rear side window. Tynan rolled the window halfway down.

"Hi, Jenkins. How've you been?"

"Good to see you, Director. Fine, fine. I got who you want with me."

"Any problem?"

"Not really. He wasn't too anxious to see you—"

"He doesn't like me," said Tynan.

"—but he came. He's curious."

"You bet," said Tynan. "We better not waste any time. It's late enough. You better bring him here. Let him in through the other side, so he can sit next to me."

"Very well."

"After we're through, and he gets out, and you secure him, you come back here. I may want to talk to you. I may want you to do a little more."

"Sure."

"One more thing, Jenkins. This meeting never took place."

The warden's face cracked into a smile. "What meeting?" he said.

Tynan waited. In less than a minute, the opposite back door of the car opened.

Jenkins poked his head in. "He's here."

Donald Radenbaugh was standing stiffly just beyond the warden. Tynan couldn't see his face, only that his wrists were together.

"Is he handcuffed?" Tynan asked.

"Yes, sir."

"Take those damn cuffs off, will you? This isn't that kind of meeting."

Tynan heard the jangle of keys, and saw the warden unlocking the handcuffs and removing them. He watched the prisoner massaging his freed wrists. He heard the warden say, "You can get into the back seat."

Donald Radenbaugh stooped to enter the car. His head and face were visible now. He hadn't changed much in his nearly three years of incarceration. Thinner, perhaps, slightly, in his oversized dull gray prison garb. He had a dry bald head, a blond fringe of hair and sideburns, eyes made smaller by the bags under them behind steel-rimmed glasses, a thin sallow face and thin pointed nose, with an untidy, diminutive blond moustache beneath it, and a weak chin. He was pale and sullen. Probably five feet ten, Tynan guessed, and maybe 170 pounds.

He had climbed into the car and sunk into the back seat, as far away from Tynan as possible.

Tynan made no effort to shake his hand. "Hello, Don," he said.

"Hello."

"It's been a long time."

"I suppose it has."

"Would you like a cigarette? Harry, give him a cigarette, and your lighter."

Radenbaugh held out his hand to accept the cigarette and the lighter. After he lit the cigarette, he returned the lighter. He drew heavily on the cigarette twice, exhaled a cloud of smoke, and seemed more relaxed.

"Well, Don," Tynan resumed, "how've you been?"

Radenbaugh grunted. "That's a helluva question."

"Is it that bad?" asked Tynan solicitously. "I thought they had you in the prison library."

"I'm in jail," said Radenbaugh bitterly. "I'm in jail, cooped up like an animal, and I'm innocent."

"Yeah, I know," said Tynan. "I guess it's never good."

"It's rotten," said Radenbaugh. "There's everything to protect you from us—sliding steel doors, triple locks, sensors on the concrete wall. But there's nothing to protect us on the inside—beatings, knifings, rapings, dope peddling. The cage and key men, the hacks—prisonese for guards—I guess I'm beginning to talk like the rest of them—each one trying to act tougher than the other. Lousy food, no exercise, and a cell six feet by eleven. How would you like to spend your best years on a planet six feet by eleven? The big event is getting a haircut. Or maybe a letter from your daughter. It stinks. Especially when you're innocent. There's just no hope."

He lapsed into angry silence, inhaling and exhaling the cigarette smoke.

Tynan studied him in the gloom. "Yeah, the lack of hope—I guess that's the worst of it," he said sympathetically. "Too bad about Noah Baxter. I guess he was your second-to-last chance to get out of here earlier. Too bad."

Radenbaugh glanced up sharply. "My second-to-last chance?" he repeated.

"Yeah. I'm your last chance, Don."

Radenbaugh's gaze held on him. "You?"

"Me." Tynan nodded. "Yes, me. I came here to offer you a deal, Don. Strictly business, and between us. I can give you something you want. Freedom. You can give me something I want. Money. Are you ready to listen?"

Radenbaugh did not speak. But he was listening.

"Okay," continued Tynan, "let me give it to you all at once, short and sweet. You've got a million dollars in cash stashed away somewhere in Florida. Let's not argue if you've got it or not. I've read the record over carefully. A reliable witness swore you left Washington with the money. You were to deliver it in Miami. You never delivered it. You knew you were fingered, so you never delivered it. When you were picked up, you didn't have it."

"Maybe I never had the money," said Radenbaugh calmly. "Maybe I was telling the truth."

"Maybe," said Tynan agreeably. "Again, maybe not. Maybe you buried it. For a rainy day. Let's just go on that assumption. That you buried it. If I'm right, then there's a nice cool million in cash somewhere down there in Florida. It's not earning you a dime interest. It should. It should be worth something to you— not in twelve years from now, but right this minute, today. What can money like that buy? Well, what do you want more than anything in the world? Freedom? You said it yourself, prison is rotten, stinking. You want out. I can't make you innocent when the court said you were guilty. But I can make you a free man. Do you want to hear more?"

Radenbaugh reached toward the door, rolled down the window a few inches, and threw away the butt of his cigarette. Reclining again, he turned his head toward Tynan. "Go on," he said.

"That million dollars," said Tynan. "I need part of it. I'm no hog. I could ask for it all, and maybe get it. I'm not asking for it all. I want only part of it—let's say for an investment. In return,

I'll cut your fifteen-year sentence down to what you've served, as of tonight, or a few nights from tonight. It's not easy, but I can arrange it. For your part, you'd then go down to Miami, dig up your money, deliver part of it to an intermediary. You'd deliver $750,000 to the intermediary, and you'd keep the remaining $250,000 to get a fresh start. And our deal would be satisfactorily concluded. How does that grab you?"

He eyed Radenbaugh, but Radenbaugh gave no response. He sat staring straight ahead, lips compressed, face tight.

"Okay, I guess you want to know a few details," Tynan went on. "There's one catch. You'll have to go along with it, or the whole deal's off. I told you this wasn't easy. It isn't. I'm not empowered to parole you or free you. No one is, except members of the parole board—and I happen to know they won't let you out—not until the next twelve years are served. I can't get Donald Radenbaugh out of Lewisburg Federal Penitentiary. But I can get *you* out."

Radenbaugh looked at the Director now.

"It's tricky, but I can manage it," continued Tynan. "To protect both of us, you'd have to take on a new identity the day you were released. It's not simple, but it can be done. It's been done successfully before. Since 1970, at least 500 informers, Government witnesses, persons who turned state's evidence have been given new identities by the Chief of Criminal Intelligence in the Department of Justice, and they've been secretly relocated. It's worked every time, and it can work again. Only this time I couldn't do it through the Department of Justice. I'd have to handle it myself."

Tynan sought some reaction from Radenbaugh. There was none. Tynan continued.

"First, we'd get rid of Donald Radenbaugh. That's a must, to make it all come off. Warden Jenkins would put out a story that you were dead—that you had died of a heart attack or were stabbed to death. Probably that you died of natural causes. Less fuss. Next, we'd release you. We'd get rid of your fingerprints, alter your appearance, give you a completely new identity, new name, and papers with everything from a birth certificate to a Social Security card to an auto rental credit card and driver's license to back up that new name. You'd be on your own from next week on—totally free, fully alive, and with a fat bankroll. But remember, there'd be no more Radenbaugh. I know you have a daughter, some other relatives, friends, but they'd be in mourning. They could never know the truth. I realize that might be rough on you, but it's part of the price you pay for the deal— that and the $750,000."

Tynan halted, and looked absently out the car window before finally shifting around to Radenbaugh.

"There you have it," Tynan said. He tried to make out the hands on his wristwatch. "We've just about run out of time, Don. You've heard my first and last offer. You've got to decide Yes or No. If you choose to say No, and prefer to rot in prison for another twelve years, and are lucky enough to avoid being stabbed to death, and at last get out when you're an old man— well, you can keep all the money and keep your old name— that's your choice. If you choose to say Yes, then there's no more prison, you're free, and you still keep a sizable share of the money, and you've got a new life you can enjoy as another person. That's also your choice."

Tynan paused to let it sink in.

After a few moments, Tynan resumed with emphasis. "It has to be one or the other tonight. In the next five minutes, in fact. If it's No, then you can open that door and get out, and Jenkins will be waiting with the handcuffs to take you back to your cell. If it's Yes—just say the word—then I'll instruct you and the warden, you'll do as you are told, and in a week you'll have a quarter of a million dollars and a free life. When you leave prison, you'll only have to follow the simple instructions that'll be in the pocket of your new suit along with an air ticket to Miami and a hotel reservation."

Tynan paused.

"Okay, Don," he said softly, "it's up to you. What's your decision?"

IT WAS NOT UNTIL five days later that Chris Collins got to Lewisburg Federal Penitentiary.

After his flight back to Washington from Los Angeles, Collins had reported to President Wadsworth on his visit to California. The report had been brief, because Collins had omitted much of his actual activity. He had made up his mind, at least for now, not to reveal to the President the visit to Tule Lake; the conference with State Assemblymen Keefe, Yurkovich, and Tobias; the private meeting with Chief Justice Maynard. He could not speak of these matters because he was, as yet, uncertain of the President's own role in the suspicious happenings in California. Instead, he had discussed his television debate with Tony Pierce. Then he had spoken at length of his speech to the American Bar Association. He had tried to make it sound like a triumph, but the President had been well informed and had bluntly voiced his disappointment. "You underplayed and understated our case for the 35th Amendment," he had told Collins. "I really intended to have you come on stronger. Nevertheless, things are looking up. We had some good news today."

The good news had proved to be Ronald Steedman's latest poll of the California Legislature. In the State Assembly, among the members prepared to take a position, those favoring the Amendment led those opposing it 65 percent to 35 percent. In the State Senate the findings had been closer, with 55 percent for and 45 percent against. With difficulty, Collins had masked his dismay.

By then, Collins had been obsessed by his desire to visit Lewisburg, to get to his one remaining possible source on the secret of The R Document, and he had hoped to make the trip his second or third day back in Washington. But demands on his time by the President and by his own Criminal Division and Civil Rights Division had made an immediate trip impossible.

At last, through his subordinates in the Bureau of Prisons, he had arranged the trip.

Knowing that he could not explain or justify the real purpose of the visit, he had invented a phony one. He was working on recommendations for a revised Prisoner Rehabilitation Act, and to do so he must make a tour of Lewisburg Federal Penitentiary.

And so, in step with Warden Bruce Jenkins, he was making a

hasty inspection of the prison. He had endured the clothing and sheet-metal factories; had visited the classrooms, the hospital, the library; had suffered closely supervised interviews with inmates in their cells.

Now the last of the inspection tour was over, and for Collins the most important part of it was to begin.

He had begged off having lunch, claiming an important appointment in New York.

"Is there anything else I can do for you?" Warden Jenkins inquired.

"You've done quite enough," said Collins graciously. "I have everything I need. I'd better . . ." He hesitated, effectively. "As a matter of fact, there is one more thing. We have a tax case going, and the name of one of your inmates has come up constantly. I wonder if I could see him in private for five or ten minutes?"

"Absolutely," said Warden Jenkins. "Just tell me who it is, and I'll have him brought in and you can talk to him alone."

"His name is Radenbaugh. Donald Radenbaugh. I'd like to see him."

Warden Jenkins did not hide his surprise. "You mean you didn't see this morning's paper? Or watch TV?"

"I'm afraid not."

"Donald Radenbaugh is dead. I'm sorry. He died three days ago. Dropped dead of a heart attack. We withheld the story until his next of kin could be located. We released it last night. It was announced early today."

"Dead," said Collins hollowly. He felt ill. Then his one high hope of learning about The R Document was dead also.

"Your timing was off by three days," said Jenkins. "Bad luck."

In despair, Collins was preparing to make his immediate departure, when suddenly a thought struck him. "Did you say you withheld the news three days because you had to locate Radenbaugh's next of kin?"

"Yes. He had a daughter in Philadelphia. She happened to be out of the city. We finally found her—not only to notify her of the death but to determine disposition of the body. With her consent, we buried him locally at Government expense."

"How did she take the news?"

"Naturally, she was pretty broken up by it."

"Are you saying Radenbaugh was close to his daughter?"

"Except for former Attorney General Baxter—who'd been a friend—Susie was the only one who stayed in touch with him regularly."

"Do you have her address?"

"Not actually . . ."

"How did you notify her?"

"She has a post-office box at the main post office in Philadelphia. We wired her, and when she got it, she phoned us."

"Can I have her post-office-box number, Warden?"

"Why, yes." He went to his desk, peeled through a series of folders, and opened one. "It's P.O. Box 153, William Penn Annex post-office station, Philadelphia 19105."

"Thanks," said Collins. "And you say she was in touch with her father regularly?"

"Yes."

"Maybe she knew some of his business. Maybe she could help me."

"Maybe. But I doubt it."

"I doubt it too," said Collins, discouraged. "We'll see."

It had been an incredibly streamlined operation. So far it had gone without a hitch.

Seated in the rocking cabin of the sleek motorboat as it zoomed across the artificial channel that separated the southern tip of Miami Beach from Fisher's Island, he tried to review the events of the past week.

Six nights ago, in a wooded area outside Lewisburg Federal Penitentiary, he had parted from FBI Director Vernon T. Tynan, agreeing to make the bizarre deal offered to Donald Radenbaugh, convict.

Two nights ago, crouched in the rear of the warden's car, he had been driven out of the sleep-stilled prison as Herbert Miller, citizen and free man.

Since his meeting with Tynan, there had been only one visitor he knew by name, and that had been Tynan's assistant, Harry Adcock. There had been three others also, but they had been nameless. Radenbaugh recalled that he had been placed in solitary confinement, to isolate him from the other inmates. In solitary, he had hosted an elderly man with a limp who had applied acid to change—painfully—his fingerprints. Next there had been an optician to take away his steel-rimmed spectacles and fit him with contact lenses. Then there had been a barber, who had shaved off his moustache and sideburns, dyed his fringe of blond hair a deep black, and fitted him with a black hairpiece. Finally, there had been Adcock, with papers (a birth certificate, an honorable discharge from the U.S. Army) and cards (a driver's license, a car-rental credit card, a Social Security card) to replace the credentials in his old wallet and to transform him officially into the respectable Herbert Miller, aged fifty-nine. There had been a dark brown suit of the latest cut to replace the one he had worn to prison, which was no longer in style and thus might be conspicuous.

There had been Adcock's oral instructions. Immediately after his release, he was to proceed to Miami on a red-eye flight. In Miami, a room had been reserved for Herbert Miller in the Bayamo Hotel, located on West Flagler Street. The following day or evening, he would be free to dig up his hidden one million dollars. He would not be followed. Late morning of the next day, he would meet with a realtor named Mrs. Remos in the suburban community of Coconut Grove and from her get the name of a safe plastic surgeon in the area who would perform cosmetic surgery around his eyes before he left Miami. That night, he would go to a waiting motorboat at the Municipal Pier in Miami Beach and be taken to Fisher's Island. There, at the first oil-storage tank, he would be hailed as Miller. He would give the password twice, the password being "Linda." He would drop the package containing three-quarters of a million dollars and return to his boat. Back in Miami Beach, he could proceed with his surgery. After that, he would be totally free to go where he wished, do what he liked.

"You'll get your new suit just before you leave prison," Adcock had said. "In the right-hand side pocket there will be an envelope. In it will be your air ticket to Miami, the location of your rendezvous with the motorboat, a map of Fisher's Island showing you where the drop is to be made, and enough money to carry you until you get your hands on your quarter share of the loot. Just do what you've been told. Don't get any tricky ideas. They'll only endanger your health. Got it?"

He had got it all.

He had taken the red-eye special and arrived at Miami International Airport on schedule.

He had checked into the dilapidated Bayamo Hotel on schedule.

He had rented a car, constantly making certain he was not being watched or followed, and had driven into the Everglades west of Miami. There he made his way on foot to the bank of the mangrove swamp where he had secreted the million dollars in a metal box over three years ago. He had emptied the contents of the box into some grocery bags he had acquired, placed the bags in a suitcase he had purchased, and retraced his steps to his car.

The rest had gone easily. In his hotel room, he had removed a quarter of a million from the suitcase and placed it in a second suitcase that he had had ready. At night, he had taken the second suitcase, with his share of the money, to Miami International Airport and shoved it inside a locker. Leaving the airport, he had picked up a copy of the next morning's Miami *Herald*. Scanning it, he speculated about whether the demise of the late Donald Radenbaugh had been announced yet. On the sixth page he had found an unflattering three-year-old picture of the bald, bespectacled Radenbaugh, and his obituary. It had felt strange to read of his own death, to learn how little he had achieved and how overshadowed it had been by the summary of his felony trial and conviction. It was unfair. It had not said that he was innocent. And finally, he had grieved for his beloved Susie, left with such a legacy. He wondered if he would ever dare contact her and reveal the truth. He knew he dared not. People who could invent a new human being were people not to be crossed.

The next day, according to his instructions, he had had only one appointment before the critical evening's mission. Late in the morning, he had driven out to Coconut Grove and in a real-tor's bungalow had had a brief and satisfactory meeting with Mrs. Remos, an elderly mulatto who had expected him "You are fortunate, Mr. Miller, indeed fortunate," Mrs. Remos had said. "We recently lost the dependable plastic surgeon we have always used, but just two days ago we found a replacement. He is Dr. García, most competent, and because of his temporary situation he can be counted as safe. He was smuggled in recently from Cuba, and until we get his papers he is an illegal alien. We must proceed with caution. You will be free tonight? Ah, after ten o'clock. Very well. Dr. García will be waiting for you in your hotel room at ten fifteen. We would rather he not ask for you at the desk. We would prefer to have him in your room, waiting. You have your door keys? Ah, good, let me have it. Your hotel will have an extra one for you in your mailbox, I'm sure. Dr. García will examine you, inform you what can be done, and arrange the time and place for the surgery. Ten fifteen, then? It is agreed."

Radenbaugh had used up some of the afternoon sightseeing and shopping, and then returned to his hotel room to wait for evening. When night had fallen, he had taken his heavy suitcase downstairs, gone outside, and proceeded by taxi across the MacArthur Causeway to Miami Beach and the Municipal Pier. By eight o'clock he had found his contact, handed the suitcase to the phlegmatic Cuban proprietor of the motorboat, and then boarded it himself.

Now, as planned, he was en route. It was less than half a mile to Fisher's Island for the final payoff and the climax of his deal.

Once more, he tugged the hand-drawn map out of his coat pocket and committed it to memory.

Fisher's Island was an abandoned 213-acre piece of land, totally unoccupied, bearing thickets of wild Australian pine trees, a rotting ghost of a mansion on a private estate once owned by the founder of Miami, and two oil-storage tanks.

Tonight, Radenbaugh reflected, it would be populated by at least two persons, Radenbaugh himself and someone unknown.

The motorboat was slowing and sputtering to a stop.

Radenbaugh leaned forward and saw the pilot signaling to

him. Nervously he gripped the suitcase and, bending low, made his way out of the cabin and stepped up onto the wooden dock. The pilot called out to him, and then he remembered, and reached back to accept the powerful flashlight.

Setting foot on the island, he began to ascend the trail. The landmarks he had memorized were clear. The only difficulties were the darkness, despite his flashlight, and the burden of the suitcase with three-quarters of a million dollars in cash inside.

After a while—he had lost all track of time—he made out the first of the oil-storage tanks, caught the area of the drop in the beam of his flashlight, and started toward it.

He was a dozen yards from the tank, wheezing as he hiked in the stillness, when he heard a rustle. He halted. He heard a voice.

"You are Mr. Miller?"

The voice was high-pitched and with a definite Spanish accent.

"I am."

"Put out the flashlight."

Quickly he snapped off the flashlight.

The accented voice came out of the darkness again. It was near. "What is your word?"

He'd almost forgotten. He remembered. "Linda," he called out. "Linda," he repeated.

There was a grunt. "Leave right where you are what you have. Go back the way you came, go back to the boat."

He lowered his suitcase to the ground beside him. "All right," he said. "I am going."

He turned away quickly, and tried to make haste as he sought the road. In the dark, without the flashlight on, he was confused, and he stubbed his toe and fell. Rising, he went more slowly.

After a few minutes, he stopped to catch his breath. Then he caught something else. The drift of voices, two voices, chattering cheerfully behind a clump of trees.

He had not thought of the money much since recovering it from the edge of the mangrove swamp. Now, almost for the first time as a free man, he allowed himself to think about it. He wondered why Tynan wanted so great a sum, without strings. Maybe personal financial troubles. He wondered why it had been entrusted to what sounded like two persons, at least one of whom was of Spanish origin. He wondered who they were. Possibly FBI agents. He was tempted to have a look. Donald Radenbaugh would not have given in to such temptation. Herbert Miller would and did.

Instead of returning to the road, he cut diagonally through a scattering of pine trees. He moved carefully, so that he would not stumble and fall again, and in five minutes he saw a light.

He crept closer, slipping from behind one tree to the next, until he was no more than thirty feet away. He stopped and watched, and listened, holding his breath.

There were two of them, all right.

One, plainly illuminated by his partner's lantern, was kneeling beside the open suitcase, either counting or examining the money. His partner, standing over him holding the lantern, was indistinct.

The taller man with the lantern asked, "It is all there?" He spoke an unaccented English.

The one kneeling, busy, said, "It is here."

The man with the lantern said, "Ah, you will be very rich— the rich Señor Ramon Escobar."

"Holy Jesus, will you shut up, Fernandez?" barked the one who was kneeling, and then he looked up fully into the direct light of the lantern and sputtered something in Spanish. Radenbaugh could see him now: short, curly jet black hair, long sideburns, ugly face with deeply sunken cheeks and a livid scar along his jawbone.

As the person addressed as Escobar once more devoted himself to the contents of the suitcase, the two men continued conversing, but now only in Spanish.

Watching them further was pointless, and Radenbaugh backed away and gingerly started toward the road. His curiosity had not been satisfied. He could not believe this pair, Escobar and Fernandez, were FBI agents. Who were they, then? What did they have to do with Director Tynan?

When he found the road, and resumed walking to the landing, he ceased to speculate about what he had seen. He was more occupied with himself, and his own future.

The passage back to Miami seemed faster and was infinitely more relaxed.

Ashore on the mainland again, and unencumbered, he knew that he was free and on his own completely, at last.

And then he knew that he was not.

There remained one final piece of unfinished business. This morning he had made arrangements—courtesy of Vernon T. Tynan, via the realtor named Mrs. Remos—to meet in his hotel room with an illegal alien and plastic surgeon named Dr. García.

Going to a taxi stand, Radenbaugh remembered the appointment was for ten fifteen. He also remembered that he had not eaten for hours, and he was now ravenously hungry and in a celebratory mood. The choice was between returning to his depressing hotel room, still starved, to wait for Dr. García and finding a place to satisfy his hunger, which would make him a little late for his appointment. He did not want to miss Dr. García. The plastic surgery was vital, and Radenbaugh was eager to know what the surgeon could do with the shape of his eyes as well as the bags under them. He also wanted to know how long he'd have to wait to have the job done, and how long it would take for his scars to heal. Still, he was sure Dr. García would not mind his being a little late, would wait, having a key to his room and being able to make himself comfortable there. Yes, Dr. García would wait. He wasn't in a position to get jobs like this every day.

By the time he reached the taxi stand, Radenbaugh's mind was made up.

He got into the back of the lead cab. "There's a restaurant on Collins Avenue, a mile or so past the Fontainbleau Hotel—I don't know the name, but I'll point it out to you," he told the driver.

He calculated that he could have a leisurely dinner with a carafe of wine and still be no more than a half hour late for his meeting with Dr. García. The important thing was that this evening he had fulfilled his part of the deal, and Tynan had ful-

filled his, and their business was over. It was a time to celebrate.

An hour and fifteen minutes later, a full meal under his belt,
Radenbaugh felt better and was ready to meet with Dr. García
and collaborate in the final transformation of Radenbaugh to
Miller. Aware that he would be three-quarters of an hour late,
Radenbaugh hastened to catch another taxi, directed it to the
Bayamo Hotel, crossed the Biscayne Bay bridge, and was soon
back in Miami proper.

As his cab swung into West Flagler Street and headed toward
the Bayamo Hotel, he saw a crowd up ahead—people in the
streets, a fire truck backing away, two police squad cars. The
commotion was in the vicinity of his hotel.

"You can let me out here on the corner," he told the cabbie.

He made his way rapidly up the block toward a scene of frenzied activity. When he arrived at the fringes of the crowd, he
saw that all the attention was centered on the Bayamo Hotel.
Helmeted firemen were dragging their hoses out of the lobby.
Smoke was still curling out of shattered third-floor windows.
Radenbaugh realized with a start that his own room was on the
third floor.

He turned to the spectator nearest him, a bearded young man
wearing a University of Miami sweat shirt.

"Hey, what's happened here?" Radenbaugh asked.

"There was an explosion and fire on the third floor about an
hour ago. Destroyed four or five rooms. I think I heard them say
someone was killed and a couple of people were injured."

Radenbaugh searched ahead and saw three or four men and
women—one with a microphone, obviously reporters—
interviewing a fireman, probably the fire chief. Hurriedly,
Radenbaugh elbowed and shoved his way through the mass of
people, muttering that he was press, until he reached the front
line of spectators. He was directly behind the spokesman for
the fire department.

He strained to hear what was being said.

"You say one fatality?" a reporter was asking.

"Yes—as far as we know, only one so far. The occupant of
the room where the blast occurred. He must have been killed

instantly. The room was gutted by fire and he was incinerated. His name—let me see—yes, here, we found some shreds of paper—presumably his name was—he was a Mr. Herbert Miller. No further identification."

Radenbaugh had to cover his mouth to prevent his gasp from being audible.

Another reporter asked, "Have you determined the cause of the explosion? Was it a gas leak or a bomb?"

"Can't say yet. Too early to tell. We'll have more for you by tomorrow."

Trembling, Radenbaugh turned away and pushed back through the crowd to the sidewalk.

Dazed, he tried to think about what had happened. Rarely did a man live to be a witness to one, let alone two, of his obituaries.

Tynan had killed Radenbaugh to resurrect him as Miller. Once Tynan had his three-quarters of a million, he had set out to kill Miller. In fact, officially now, he *had* killed him.

The dirty, dirty double-crossing swine.

But there was nothing he could do about it, now or ever, Radenbaugh knew. He was extinct, a nobody, a nonperson. Then he realized there was real safety in this, as long as he was never recognized again, as Radenbaugh or Miller.

He would require a plastic surgeon after all—poor Dr. García—and he would require one as soon as possible. For that, he needed a place to hide, and he needed someone in whom he could place his trust. There was no one—and then he remembered there was someone.

He started away, to find another taxi, one that would take him to Miami International Airport.

THE NEXT MORNING, CHRIS Collins, at his desk in the Department of Justice in Washington, D.C., eagerly took the call from the Deputy Attorney General.

"Well, Ed, what did you find out?"

"Yes, post-office box 153 in the Philadelphia William Penn Annex post office was and still is rented to a Miss Susan Radenbaugh."

"Her address? Did the postal people have one?"

"You're in luck. It's 419½ South Jessup Street. Hey, Chris, what's this all about?"

"I'll let you know when I find out. Thanks, Ed."

Collins hung up, jotting the street address on his pad. Briefly, he contemplated the address. Well, he thought, maybe Lewisburg hadn't been a total waste. He had missed his big chance because Radenbaugh had died three days too soon. But there was one thin strand left that might lead to The R Document. The next of kin. Susan Radenbaugh, the bereaved daughter. She had been close to her father. She had remained in contact with him. If he had known about The R Document, she might have heard of it too.

A very long shot, but the only shot, Collins reflected.

He got up, traversed the large office, and put his head into his secretary's alcove office.

"Marion, how's my schedule for the rest of the day?"

"Booked pretty solid for a Saturday."

"Anything we can cancel or postpone?"

"I'm afraid not, Mr. Collins."

"What about tomorrow?"

"We-ll, let me see. . . . You're sort of light in the morning—"

"Good. Change any appointments I have. And get right on the phone and book me on the earliest Metroliner to Philadelphia in the morning. It's important. At least, I hope it is."

VI

I T WAS A SMALL, nondescript wood-frame house behind a larger residence on South Jessup Street in Philadelphia. It had probably been a guesthouse once, but was now a rental, perfect for a single person who wanted privacy.

Before leaving Washington, D.C., Chris Collins had learned what he could about Susan Radenbaugh. There was little to know. She was Donald Radenbaugh's only child. She was twenty-six years old. She had graduated from the University of Pittsburgh. She was employed by the Philadelphia *Inquirer* as a feature writer.

When Collins personally had telephoned the newspaper to make an appointment with her, he had been informed that she was home ill. Collins could understand this. She had lost her remaining parent. She would need a little time to pull herself together. Collins had not bothered to call her at home. He was certain she would be there.

Once he had arrived in Philadelphia, he had directed the chauffeur of his rented car to take him straight to the address on South Jessup Street. He had left his car, driver, and bodyguard a half block from his destination and returned to the address on foot.

Now, from the sidewalk, he looked up the driveway toward

the porch of the rear house, and finally he started toward it. He tried to think how he would approach Susan Radenbaugh. Actually there was nothing to plan. Either her father had told her something about The R Document or he had not. It was his last faint hope. After Susan, dead end.

He covered the small plot of backyard, reached the front door of the rear house, and rang the bell.

He waited. No answer.

He rang the bell again without getting any response, and had just about decided that she had gone to the store or was off to her doctor when the door opened partially. A young woman peered out at him from the crack of doorway. She was attractive, with blond hair down to her shoulders and a scrubbed face that seemed unnaturally pale and set.

"Miss Susan Radenbaugh?" he asked.

She gave him a tentative, worried nod.

"I called your newspaper this morning to make an appointment. The city desk said you were home ill. I came in from Washington to see you."

"What do you want?" she asked.

"I want to talk to you briefly about your father. I'm sorry that—"

"I can't see anyone now," she said abruptly. She was plainly distraught.

"Let me explain—"

"Who are you?"

"I am Christopher Collins. I'm the United States Attorney General. I—"

"Christopher Collins?" She recognized the name. "What are you—"

"I must talk to you. Colonel Noah Baxter was a close friend of mine, and—"

"You knew Noah Baxter?"

"Yes. Please let me in. I'll just be a few minutes."

She hesitated, and then pulled back the door. "All right. But only for a few minutes."

He went past her into the cramped, tasteful living room, heavily decorated with colorful cushions. There was a door to the left that probably led to a bedroom, and an archway to the right revealed a small dining table and an entrance to the kitchen.

"You can sit down," she said.

He sat down on the edge of the nearest object, an ottoman. She did not sit. She stood across from him, nervously brushing her hair back.

"I'm very sorry about your father," he said. "If there's anything I can do—"

"It's all right. Are you actually the Attorney General?"

"Yes."

"The FBI didn't send you?"

He smiled. "I send them. They don't send me. No, I'm here of my own accord. On a personal matter."

"You said you were a friend of Colonel Baxter's?"

"I was. I believe your father was also."

"They were very close."

"That's why I'm here," said Collins. "Because your father and Colonel Baxter were friends. The night Colonel Baxter died, he left a message for me in what turned out to be his dying words. It was about a matter I've been pursuing ever since. I couldn't get the information from Colonel Baxter, but it occurred to me that your father might have heard something about it from the Colonel. I know the Colonel often confided in your father."

"It's true," said Susan Radenbaugh. "How did you know that?"

"From Mrs. Baxter—Hannah Baxter—who suggested I visit your father in Lewisburg. She felt he might know something about the matter. I did go to Lewisburg two days ago, only to learn of your father's death. Then I heard you were the one person your father had stayed in touch with. It occurred to me that your father might have spoken to you about the matter I've been investigating. I decided to track you down and see you."

"What do you want to know?"

He took a deep breath, and he posed the question. "I wonder if your father ever spoke to you about something called The R Document?"

She looked blank. "What's that?"

Collins' heart sank. "I don't know. I had hoped you would."

"No," she said firmly, "I've never heard a word about it."

"Dammit," he muttered under his breath. "Forgive me. I guess I'm disappointed. You and your father were my last bets. Well, I tried and that's that." He came wearily off the ottoman. "I won't bother you anymore." He hesitated. "Let me say just this. Colonel Baxter believed in your father. In fact, before his stroke he was working on getting your father a parole. Since then I've reviewed his case, and I agree with Colonel Baxter. Your father was a fall guy. I too planned to work on his parole. I promised Mrs. Baxter I'd discuss the parole with your father when I went to see him about The R Document. Hannah Baxter told me she would write your father to expect me, to cooperate with me." He shrugged his shoulders. "Well, I guess I'm always too late."

He saw the girl's eyes widen and her hands go to her mouth, as she looked past him, and suddenly there was a third voice in the room.

"You're not too late this time," someone said from behind Collins.

He whirled around and found himself confronted by a stranger standing under the archway leading from the living room to the dining room.

The older man seemed vaguely familiar, yet was unknown to him.

The man walked toward him and stopped. "I'm Donald Radenbaugh," he said quietly. "You wanted to know about The R Document? What do you want to know?"

IT WAS MORE THAN a half hour before The R Document was mentioned meaningfully again.

First, there had been Collins' incredulity to deal with. Radenbaugh dealt with it briefly. "Radenbaugh risen from the dead," he had said. "I am dead, but in name only. Otherwise, I'm very much alive. We'll get into me when I know more about you, and how you got to me."

Then, there had been Susan's incredulity to deal with. Her father dealt with it early. "You can't understand how I took the chance of revealing myself, Susie? Especially to someone from the Department of Justice? It's because I need someone, besides you, whom I can trust. I think I can trust Mr. Collins. He sounded sympathetic even when he didn't know I was here. I need help, Susie. Maybe if I do something for him, he'll do something for me."

Finally, there had been Radenbaugh's own incredulity to deal with. He had dealt with it by demanding to know how Collins could possibly know about The R Document or suspect that Radenbaugh knew anything about it. "You may have explained to my daughter. I couldn't hear anything you were telling her at first. I was hiding in the kitchen. Later I came closer, to listen. Before we can go any further, you had better tell me how you got here."

They had settled down facing each other on the daybed, backed by the cushions piled against the wall of Susan's living room.

Collins had spoken carefully, slowly, frankly, in full detail, of the events that had occurred since the night of Colonel Baxter's death. Finally, he had talked about seeing Hannah Baxter. While she had disclaimed any knowledge of The R Document, she had thought that if Noah had confided its contents to anyone it might have been to Donald Radenbaugh.

"Yes, she wrote me to expect a visit from you," Radenbaugh had said.

"And I went to visit you," Collins had said. "The warden told me you were dead. But here you are."

"Now I know how you got here," Radenbaugh had said. "Now let me tell you how *I* got here. And how lucky I am to be here. It's quite a story. You'll have to suspend disbelief completely."

Collins had listened, mouth agape, often unable to suspend disbelief. Vernon T. Tynan's secret nocturnal meeting with Radenbaugh, and his offer of freedom in exchange for three-quarters of a million dollars, had been a stunner. It had also raised the question of why Tynan required a large sum of money so badly that he would take such a risk, but Collins had not interrupted with the question. He had continued to listen, as Radenbaugh had related his story to the moment of the destruction of his hotel room where his alter ego, Herbert Miller, had been neatly obliterated.

At the end of Radenbaugh's recital, Collins had had no more doubts about what had been happening in California.

"Tynan," he had said aloud.

"He's behind everything," Radenbaugh had agreed. "It's simple to see why. I read the 35th Amendment. It'll make him the most powerful man in America. More powerful than the President. Yet I'd bet there's not one bit of concrete evidence against him."

Collins had thought about it. "Not so far as I know. Unless—unless he's involved with The R Document. Can we talk about that now?"

"We can. But before we do, I want three things from you."

"Name them."

"First, I want the plastic surgery completed on my face. The eyes, at least. That would probably be enough. I don't think I'd be recognized today, but if I were, I'd be dead for sure. Tynan would see to that."

"No problem. We have a surgeon in Carson City, Nevada, that the FBI doesn't know about. Both the Cosa Nostra and the CIA use him, if that amuses you. When would you want it done?"

"Immediately. Like tomorrow."

"Done."

"Second, I need a new identity. Donald Radenbaugh died in Lewisburg. Herbert Miller died in Miami." He had pulled out his wallet, removed three cards, and handed them to Collins. "A driver's license, a car-rental credit card, and a Social Security card—all that's left of Herbert Miller. No good now. I need new papers. I've got to be *somebody*."

"They have to be prepared in Denver," Collins had said. "You'll have them in five days. What else? There was one more thing."

"Yes. A solemn promise from you."

"Go ahead."

"That if it is ever possible, one day, to tell the truth about what Tynan did, about my supposed death, you'll do so—and after I've returned my share of the money, you'll help restore to me my own name and get me my parole or pardon."

"I don't know if that will ever be possible."

"But if it is?"

Collins had considered his dilemma briefly. Could he, as the nation's number one law officer, deal with a convicted felon? Collins had known that his legal duty was clear—to make no promises to Radenbaugh, to take him into custody. But he had also known, considering the uniqueness of the circumstances, that he had a higher duty, a duty to his country. That came first. That transcended all narrow legalisms.

He had had his answer. "Someday, if it is possible, I'll do it," Collins had said. "Yes, I'll help you. I swear to that."

"Now I can tell you about The R Document."

All that had transpired in the first half hour or more, and now they had reached what for Collins was the moment of truth.

Radenbaugh took a cigarette from his daughter, smiled at her as he lit up, and swung around to face Collins on the daybed.

"I don't know all about it," he said slowly, "but I do know something. It may be of help to you. The 35th Amendment— The R Document was an unwritten part of it—I mean, it was a part not made public—came into being before I went to jail. It troubled Noah Baxter very much. True, he was a conservative, and hard-nosed about many things, but he was a decent man and a strict Constitutionalist. He did not like to misinterpret the Constitution and he did not like to tamper with it. But as crime got worse and worse in this country, and the pressure was on, he was backed into a corner. He had a job to do, and he saw it couldn't be done, and order in the country couldn't be restored, unless the laws were changed. He thought the 35th Amendment was too stringent. He had grave misgivings about it. But he went along. I always felt he regretted it. In the end, I suspect, he was in too deep to get out."

"I think you're right," said Collins. "As I told you, in his last breath, he said, 'I must speak—they cannot control me now—I am free, I no longer have to be afraid anymore.' Free of whom? Afraid of whom or what?"

Radenbaugh shook his head. "I don't know. I only know he got into it deeper than he wanted to, and he was much troubled, and had no one to confide in except me. So he would tell me what he wanted to, when he was in the mood. It was under those circumstances that he first mentioned The R Document. He brought it up several times after that. He wished Tynan hadn't got him involved with the 35th or The R Document."

"Tynan?" said Collins with surprise. "I thought President Wadsworth instigated the 35th Amendment and everything connected with it?"

"No, it was all Tynan. He was the author and creator of the 35th and The R Document. He sold the bill of goods to the President, and the Congress. At least, he sold them the 35th. I don't know if anyone besides Tynan and Baxter—and me, of course—ever heard of The R Document."

"Mr. Radenbaugh, tell me what it is."

"The R stands for Reconstruction—The Reconstruction Document."

"Reconstruction of what? The United States?"

"Yes, exactly. The R Document was a secretly conceived plan to supplement and implement the 35th Amendment. It was a blueprint for reconstructing the United States, turning it into a crimeless country under the 35th. The document fell into two parts. Baxter knew of only one part. The second, he told me, was then still being worked out by Tynan. The first part was the pilot program."

Puzzled, Collins said, "The pilot program? What's that?"

"I was just getting to it. I told you Tynan conceived the 35th Amendment. Here is how he conceived it. In trying to develop new laws to recommend to the President and Congress, new laws that might reverse the rapidly escalating crime rate in the nation, Tynan hit upon the idea of making a study of crimeless or near-crimeless communities in the United States. If cities could be found that had remarkably low crime rates, then what were the elements in the structure of those communities that made this possible?"

"So far, sensible," admitted Collins.

"So far," said Radenbaugh. "Well, Tynan's aides fed the computers, and they whirred, and they came up with a handful of almost crime-free communities. In every case, each of those communities was a company town."

"A company town?"

"The United States is full of them. Usually it's a community built and operated solely to support a single company. Typically, let us say, Morenci, Arizona, where Phelps Dodge has its open-pit copper mines. Every home, store, business building is owned by Phelps Dodge. Public utilities are provided by Phelps Dodge. The life of the community is controlled by the company. Now, not all company towns are crimeless. I don't know if Morenci is. But in certain other selected towns, crime was almost nonexistent. These were usually small, remote communities, where a single company or person dominated the life of the town."

"A dictatorship."

"In a sense. At least, a place where there were powerful and tight economic and social controls. Among these communities that Tynan found to be near-crimeless, there was one that fascinated him. It had the best longtime record. It suffered virtually no crime or disorder. It was called Argo City, and it was owned entirely by the Argo Smelting and Refining Company of Arizona. Tynan made a thorough investigation of that community. He found the secret to Argo City's record. He found that in this community the Bill of Rights, most of the freedoms under the Bill of Rights, had been suspended. The inhabitants did not seem to object. They were satisfied so long as they were economically and physically secure. Using the legal structures of this town, Tynan developed his idea for the 35th Amendment. He decided that what could work in Argo City, Arizona, could work throughout the United States of America."

"Fascinating," said Collins. "And diabolical."

"Even more diabolical was what Tynan did to this town. He had to be positive that every aspect of the 35th Amendment would work in real life. So he used the people of Argo City as his guinea pigs. How was he able to move in his agents and do this? He investigated the company that had been running the town, and he found that Argo Smelting and Refining had been getting away with tax fraud for years. Tynan put pressure on the board of directors, and they were quick to make a deal. If Tynan would not report his findings to the Justice Department, they would give him and his aides a free hand in running the community. So Tynan, as he might run the Committee on National Safety under the 35th Amendment, ran a prototype safety committee in Argo City. It was his proving ground to see how the 35th would work in action."

"My God, incredible," said Collins. "You mean that city, without a Bill of Rights, exists today."

"As far as I know, it does."

"But that can't be done in a democracy. It's illegal."

"It'll be legal once the 35th passes in California," said Radenbaugh. "Anyway, the results of that experiment represent the first half of The R Document."

"And the second half of The R Document?"

Radenbaugh threw up his hands. "I don't know."

Collins pondered what he had heard. "I can't believe this has been going on. What about the results? Did it work in Argo City?"

Radenbaugh stared at Collins. "You'd have to see for your-self." He paused. "Would you like to?"

"You're damn right I would. I want to get to the bottom of Tynan's plot. There's a lot at stake. Is it safe?"

"There aren't many visitors to that town. At least, there weren't, the last I heard. But just the two of us won't be conspicuous."

"There might be three of us."

"Three?" said Radenbaugh. "That could be dangerous."

"It would be worth the risk," said Collins.

THE MOMENT THAT CHRIS Collins had returned to Washington, D.C., he had instigated a crash research project to investigate company towns in the United States—company towns in general and Argo City, Arizona, in particular.

The research had gone forward silently and swiftly, and now, four days later, he had the manila folders containing the basic facts fanned out on the blotter of his huge desk in the Department of Justice.

He began to review the facts. He saw at once that the American company town was a natural and innocent phenomenon connected with the nation's growth. If a company opened a mine in a remote area, it required men to work the mine. To lure employees to some out-of-the-way section of the country, these companies had to provide a city for families to live in. To make a city, the company had to build houses, establish businesses, provide recreational facilities and medical care. The company also had to provide local government and police protection. In the end, the company did everything for the people, and in return the people submitted to control by the company and belonged to it.

Collins read the record. There had been Pullman, Illinois—ten miles outside Chicago—built by George M. Pullman, the millionaire who had held a monopoly on railroad sleeping cars. Pullman housed his 12,000 employees in his own city. According to a photocopy of a turn-of-the-century clipping taken from *Harper's New Monthly Magazine:* "The Pullman companies retain everything. No private individual owns today a square rod of ground or a single structure in the entire town. No organization, not even a church, can occupy any other than rented quarters. Certain unpleasant features of social life are soon noticed . . . bad administration . . . favoritism and nepotism . . . the all-pervading feeling of insecurity. Nobody regards Pullman as a real home. The power of Bismarck in Germany is utterly insignificant when compared with the power of the ruling authority at the Pullman Palace Car Company in Pullman. Every man, woman, and child in the town is completely at its mercy. Here is a population where not one single resident dares speak out openly his opinion about the town in which he lives."

Because George M. Pullman gouged his dependents by levying higher utility charges and rents than neighboring communities, his inhabitants revolted. They sued and eventually they broke his hold on the privately owned community.

But Pullman, Illinois, had been an exception. Most modern

company towns seemed decent enough. There was Scotia, California, owned by the Pacific Lumber Company. There was Anaconda, Montana, owned by Anaconda Copper. There was Louviers, Colorado, owned by E. I. du Pont de Nemours and Company. There was Sunnyside, Utah, owned by the Utah Fuel Company. There was Trona, California, owned by the American Potash and Chemical Corporation.

And then, in the final folder, there was Argo City, Arizona, owned by the Argo Smelting and Refining Company—and Vernon T. Tynan and the Federal Bureau of Investigation.

The material available on Argo City was skimpy—suspiciously skimpy. The research made instantly clear the difference between Argo City and the average company town elsewhere. In the average company town, not everything was possessed by the company and not all the people were dominated by the company. Sometimes people could buy and own their homes. Sometimes outsiders could open businesses. Usually, persons not working for the company could live in the community. Not so with Argo City. Apparently, everything—every home, every commercial enterprise, every public and Government facility—was owned and regulated by the company. There was not a shred of evidence that any outsider—a person not working for the company—had ever been able to acquire a house or open a shop in the city's history.

And there had been no serious crime or disorder in Argo City—none whatsoever—for over five years.

It was too good—or too horrible—to be true.

Collins closed the folder.

There was only one way to know the truth. To see for himself. If what he saw was a preview of America under the 35th Amendment, then there was someone else, besides Radenbaugh and himself, who must see it, someone who could stop the 35th Amendment, if necessary.

His decision was made.

He picked up the telephone and got his secretary. "Marion, these telephones, were they debugged today?"

"No longer necessary, Mr. Collins. The scrambler equipment you ordered was installed this morning."

This eased his concern. His phone had a scrambler at last, which meant all his outgoing phone calls would be rendered unintelligible until they reached the destination of his call, where they would be unscrambled and rendered into intelligible conversation.

Feeling reassured by this precaution, with the telephone in his hand, he was ready for the next step. "Put through this call," he said. "Get me Chief Justice Maynard immediately. If he's not in, locate him. I must speak to him at once."

ON A HOT, DRY late Friday morning in early June, they had converged on Phoenix, Arizona, by air, from three different places.

Chris Collins, his plane reservation made in the name of C. Cutshaw, had arrived from Baltimore's Friendship Airport—via Chicago—at the Sky Harbor Airport in Phoenix on a 727 jetliner at eleven seventeen. He was the first.

Shortly after, Donald Radenbaugh, traveling under his new name of Dorian Schiller, had arrived from Carson City, via Reno and Las Vegas, on a DC-9. He was to have been the first, arriving at ten twelve, but his flight had been delayed an hour and fifteen minutes.

Finally, Chief Justice John G. Maynard, answering to the name Joseph Lengel, had been scheduled to arrive from New York City on a 707 at eleven forty-six.

It had been agreed in advance that Collins and Radenbaugh would not wait for Maynard, that it would be unwise for the three of them to enter Argo City together and register at the Constellation Hotel together. It had been agreed that Collins and Radenbaugh would proceed to Argo City at once, to be followed by Maynard after his later arrival.

Collins had waited impatiently in the air terminal until the announcement that Radenbaugh's delayed flight had landed. He had not recognized Radenbaugh until the other had been almost fully upon him. The plastic surgeon in Nevada had done his work well. Something had happened to Radenbaugh's nose, which was still slightly swollen. When Radenbaugh had removed his oversized sunglasses, it could be seen that the bags had been removed from beneath his eyes, replaced by bruises that were fading, and the eyes themselves were smaller and almost Oriental. His entire appearance had been altered considerably.

"Mr. Cutshaw?" he said with amusement.

"Mr. Dorian Schiller," said Collins, handing Radenbaugh a manila envelope. "Your official baptism is in there. The people in Denver were very efficient. Anything you'd ever want to know about Dorian Schiller is in that envelope."

"I can't tell you how much I appreciate it."

"Not half as much as I appreciate where you're taking us today. I hope it proves to be what you heard it was. Then it'll be completely up to John Maynard." He had glanced at the terminal's wall clock. "He'll be here in about twenty minutes. He'll be taking a taxi to Argo City." Collins gestured toward the exit. "I have a rented Ford outside."

They had driven southwest, through the broad green fields with their glistening rows of irrigation ditches, before reaching the expanse of desert. They had driven steadily in the direction of the Mexican border.

Presently they had come upon the yellow road sign with the black lettering:

ARGO CITY

POPULATION 14,000

HOME OF ARGO SMELTING AND REFINING CO.

Radenbaugh, at the wheel, had pointed across Collins' chest.

"There it is—the copper-mine pit. A mile and a half wide and about 600 feet deep. That's where most of the male population works."

In short minutes they were in the center of Argo City—a single broad paved main street, with four or five intersections. Collins had been able to identify a number of the clean, well-maintained buildings. There had been a vast, sprawling, glass-fronted general store. The U.S. Post Office. The Argo City

Theatre. Something called the City Maintenance Shop. A small park, neat, with walks leading to the Argo City Public Library. A steepled Episcopal church. A two-story brick edifice identified as the home of the Argo City *Bugle*, presumably the town newspaper.

The tallest building was the Constellation Hotel—four stories, in good repair, and despite its name, of Spanish-style design.

They had parked in the strip of a lot next door, sauntered past an Indian shop featuring Navajo dolls, baskets, leather goods, silverwork, and pottery, and entered the tiled lobby of the hotel, which ran around an open central patio.

"Looks like a miniature of the J. Edgar Hoover Building," Collins had whispered. "Tynan probably built it."

Radenbaugh brought a finger to his lips. "Enough of that, Mr. Cutshaw," he had murmured out of the corner of his mouth.

At the desk they had registered as Cutshaw and Schiller, from Bisbee, Arizona. They required their adjoining single rooms only until late afternoon, when they would be checking out.

A bellhop had taken Radenbaugh's briefcase and Collins' overnighter, accompanied them up in the elevator to the third floor, led them to their rooms down the cool hall, obligingly opened the door between the rooms, examined the air conditioning, waited for his tip, and departed.

Now they were alone in Collins' room.

It had been agreed they would wait for Chief Justice Maynard before going out into the city.

"Once he gets here, he'll dismiss his taxi," Collins said. "We'll leave for Phoenix together. By then it won't matter." He scratched his head. "To me, the town seems ordinary enough. Everything appeared perfectly normal, as far as I could see."

"Wait'll you see more," Radenbaugh told him. He opened his briefcase. "I made a list last night of everything I could remember Noah Baxter telling me about the place, when he was discussing The R Document."

"And I have a list of things to visit or look into, made up from the research my staff prepared," said Collins. "Let's put the two lists together. Then, when Maynard gets here, we can decide which seem most promising, and dole out the assignments."

They worked for fifteen minutes preparing a master list of what Argo City offered, and when they were through they were satisfied.

"I only hope we can find what we want in four hours," said Collins.

"All we can do is try," said Radenbaugh. "Everything will depend on how people we see and talk to buy our cover story. Do you have the letter?"

Collins patted the breast of his coat. "Right here. No trouble. Someone in Justice got stationery with the Phillips Industries letterhead overnight. I don't know how it's done, but they did it. Then I dictated the letter of introduction."

They reviewed and rehearsed their cover story, and tried out suspicious, difficult questions on each other. Their cover story had them in Argo City as representatives of Phillips Industries, which had secured permission from the Argo Smelting and Refining Company for an inspection of certain civic improvements in Argo City. These improvements would be considered by Phillips Industries in some remodeling and city planning soon to be done in Bisbee, Arizona.

"What's Maynard going to use for a cover?" Radenbaugh wanted to know.

"His story is altogether different. We registered for the afternoon. He's registering overnight, even though he'll leave with us. Essentially, he's a tourist. A retired lawyer and senior citizen from Los Angeles. He's traveling from L.A. to Tucson to visit with his son and daughter-in-law, see a newly arrived grandchild. He's stopping in Argo City overnight not only to get some rest after a long trip, but to look into the possibility of buying a home here. He's been through here once before and was attracted by the community. Now he's considering settling down here."

Radenbaugh wrinkled his swollen nose. "I'm not sure of that one."

"It should do for four hours. Trying to become a resident of Argo City? That should turn up plenty."

"Maybe."

Collins had one more thing on his mind. "Do you think anyone here—the city manager, newspaper publisher, police chief—anyone—has ever heard of The R Document?"

"No one. Not even the board of directors of Argo Smelting. No one knows they're guinea pigs for Tynan's master plan for the United States next year and in the years to come. The R Document can be known only to Vernon Tynan, and maybe his sidekick—I forget his name—"

"Harry Adcock."

"Yes, Adcock—and, of course, the late Noah Baxter. Then there's me, there's my daughter, there's the priest who first told you about it, and there's you. I doubt if anyone else has even heard the name."

"Argo City is only part of The R Document, you said. I want to know the rest of it. I've been hoping we might turn up some clue here."

"You might. But I wouldn't count on it."

"Well, I guess all that matters is what we find out here today," said Collins.

"You mean to kill the 35th in California?"

"Yes. If we don't find anything here—"

"Or if we get caught and exposed."

"—I'm afraid I'll have to throw in the towel. This is it, Donald. It's going to be a tense afternoon."

"I know."

Collins held up his watch. "John Maynard should be here by now."

Ten minutes later, Maynard rapped on the door and was admitted to Collins' room. He resembled anything but the dignified, imposing Chief Justice of the United States. In his broad-brimmed brown hat, sunglasses, open shirt, rumpled khakis and ankle-high boots, he resembled an old prospector who had just wandered into town after two weeks in the blazing desert.

"Here we are," he said, "all together in this godforsaken place. It was a rough ride, that taxi ride from Phoenix. I sent the cab back. That was right, wasn't it?"

"Yes," said Collins. "We'll leave here together."

Maynard tossed his hat on the bed and sat down. "But now

we have to start. We have little enough time." He looked at Radenbaugh. "You, I gather, are Donald Radenbaugh."

"Forgive me," said Collins hastily, and he formally introduced them.

Maynard held his gaze on Radenbaugh. "I hope you're not wasting our time. Your report on Argo City was shocking, to say the least. I hope it was accurate."

"I reported only what I had heard from Colonel Baxter," said Radenbaugh defensively. "The Reconstruction Document was based on Director Tynan's study of Argo City."

"Umm. So we're to see the future United States in microcosm, our country as it will appear after the 35th Amendment is passed and invoked. Well, Mr. Radenbaugh, I tell you honestly, I find it hard to believe that the conditions Colonel Baxter told you prevail here actually do exist. I don't think any community in the United States could get away with that for long."

"Many have, at least to a degree," said Collins. "I made my own study of company towns. While there were none as totalitarian as this one is supposed to be, there have been some awful practices and restraints."

"Umm. I suppose anything is possible. If it were actually true here . . ." He lapsed into thought. "Well, that would certainly put a new light on everything. We'll have to find out first-hand, and quickly, what's really going on. Mr. Collins, where do we begin?"

Collins was ready. He took up his notes. "I'd like to suggest, Mr. Chief Justice, that you start by visiting the Argo City Realty Company. After all, you are supposed to be considering living here. Then, playing the role of a retired attorney, you might drop in on the local judge, possibly through him get to the sheriff. Also, pay a visit to one of the general stores, maybe the supermarket, and get into conversation with some of the customers."

"Not so fast," said Maynard, who had a scrap of paper on his knee and was scribbling down his assignments.

Collins waited and then continued. "If you have time, look in on the Argo City *Bugle*. Go through some of the back copies. You won't have much time for that, but it might give you an opportunity to chat with a reporter or the editor."

"It's going to take some ingenuity," said Maynard.

"We'll be in and out of here before anyone becomes suspicious," said Collins. "As for Donald and me, we'll work the library, post office, try to see the city manager. We'll go as far as we can go. We should all talk to as many ordinary citizens as we can. For example, at lunch question a waitress or two. Or stop some people in the street to get directions, and try to engage them in conversation. Let me see . . ." He caught the time on his wristwatch. "It's now one fourteen. We should all meet back here in my room at five o'clock. We can compare our findings, and possibly by then we will know the truth. Shall we go? You leave first, Mr. Chief Justice."

Maynard stood up, set his hat on his head, and went out the door. Five minutes later, Collins signaled Radenbaugh, and together they left the room for the elevator, to descend upon Argo City.

THE CITY MANAGER PUSHED his gold-rimmed spectacles higher on his nose, and his round, pink face above the bow tie beamed out at them across his empty desk top.

"I'm afraid that's about all the time I can give you, gentlemen." He indicated the electric clock on his desk. "Four fifteen. I have another appointment waiting."

He pushed out from behind his desk, and circled it to lead Collins and Radenbaugh to the door.

"Glad you could come by, gentlemen," the city manager said. "Hope I was of some help. Remember this, an attractive community leads to attractive people, and promotes peace. As I told you, and the sheriff will confirm this, we have a handful of misdemeanors in Argo City annually, but no felonies. We've had no public disorders in five years, since we instigated the local law against public gatherings. Our civil servants are all content and productive. There's an occasional rotten apple, like that history teacher I mentioned, but we're getting rid of her quickly, and no harm done." He opened the door to let them out. "Well, good luck with your remodeling and rebuilding job in Bisbee. If you do half as well as we've done, you'll be proud of the result.

When you see Mr. Pitman at Phillips Industries, give him my personal regards."

He watched Collins and Radenbaugh depart. When he turned back into his office, he found that his secretary had followed him.

Noticing her perplexed expression, the city manager asked, "What is it, Miss Hazeltine?"

"The two gentlemen who just left . . . Did I hear you say they were here to get information to help them remodel and rebuild Bisbee?"

"That's right."

"But it must be wrong, sir. The city of Bisbee was thoroughly overhauled, replanned, and rebuilt just a few years ago. I have a file on it from the Bisbee Chamber of Commerce."

Now it was the city manager who appeared thoroughly perplexed. "That can't be."

"I'll show you."

Minutes later, the city manager had gone through the file of clippings, photographs, and maps of Bisbee, Arizona, all extolling the work just completed in rebuilding portions of the city.

He looked stricken. Immediately, he put through a person-to-person call to Mr. Pitman of Phillips Industries in Bisbee.

After that, he phoned the sheriff.

"Mac, two outsiders were just here posing as personnel from Phillips Industries—the Bisbee branch—asking all kinds of nosy questions. They had a letter from Pitman of Phillips Industries. He never heard of them. I don't like this, Mac. Should we arrest them?"

"No. Not until we find out who they are. You know our orders."

"But, Mac—"

"You leave it to me. I'll get right in touch with Kiley. He'll know what to do."

ON THE SECOND FLOOR of Argo City High School, Miss Watkins, a prim, severe-looking middle-aged woman, had left her class to join Collins and Radenbaugh in the hallway.

"The principal phoned. He said you were waiting to see me. What can I do for you?"

"We heard you were fired, Miss Watkins," Collins began. "We wanted to ask you some questions."

"Who are you?"

"We're from the school board in Bisbee. We are here making a survey of the school system in Argo City. We were chatting with the city manager, when he mentioned your case. He said you got out of line—"

"Out of line?" she repeated, puzzled. "I was doing my job. I was teaching American history."

"Anyway, they gave you notice."

"Yes, today's my last day."

"Can you tell us what happened?" asked Radenbaugh.

"I'm almost ashamed to repeat it," she said. "It's too ridiculous. My class was about to embark on a study of the Founding Fathers. To enliven the study, I remembered an old clipping I'd saved from a newspaper in Wyoming before I came here." She fished into her purse, drew out a yellowing clipping, and handed it to Collins. "I read it to my tenth-grade history class . . ."

Collins and Radenbaugh read the lead of the Associated Press story: "Only one person out of 50 approached on Miami streets by a reporter agreed to sign a typed copy of the Declaration of Independence. Two called it 'Commie junk,' one threatened to call the police . . ."

Miss Watkins pointed to the last part of the story. "Other people who bothered to read the first three paragraphs of the Declaration of Independence had similar comments. One said, 'This is the work of a raver.' Another said, 'Somebody ought to tell the FBI about this sort of rubbish.' Still another called the author of the Declaration 'A red-neck revolutionist.' And you can see there, the reporter circulated a questionnaire containing an excerpt from the Declaration of Independence among 300 members of a young religious group, and 28 percent answered that they thought the excerpt had been written by Lenin."

She took the clipping back. "After I read it to my students, I told them I wasn't going to let them go through my course without reading the Declaration of Independence and the Constitution properly, or without understanding those classic documents."

"Did you mention the Bill of Rights?" asked Collins.

"Well, of course. It's part of the Constitution, isn't it? In fact, I got into quite a discussion with my class about the basic freedoms and civil rights. My students seemed highly stimulated. However, several of them went home and told their parents about it, and it got all exaggerated and distorted, and before I knew it the head of the Argo City Board of Education came down on me as a troublemaker. A troublemaker? What trouble? I said I was only teaching history. He insisted I was fomenting dissent, and he said he would have to terminate me. Truly, I still don't understand what happened."

"Aren't you going to protest your dismissal?" Radenbaugh wanted to know.

Miss Watkins seemed genuinely surprised at the suggestion. "Protest? To whom?"

"Surely there must be someone."

"There isn't. Even if there were, I wouldn't think of doing so."

"Why not?" persisted Radenbaugh.

"Because I don't want to get involved in such things. I just want to be let alone. I believe in live and let live."

Collins entered the discussion again. "But they won't let you live, Miss Watkins. At least, not your way."

She seemed momentarily confused. "I don't know. I guess there are rules here, like everywhere. I must have accidentally broken one. But it's nothing I'd make a—a public fuss over. No, I wouldn't think of doing that."

"What happened the last time you taught the Constitution?" Collins wondered.

"I had never taught it before. I used to teach European history. The city manager's wife taught American history, but she retired last semester and I was moved over to replace her."

"What are you going to do now, Miss Watkins? Stay in Argo City?"

"Oh, no, they wouldn't let me. Unless you work for the company or city, you can't stay. They wouldn't give me another job. I suppose I'll go back to Wyoming. I don't know. It's very upsetting. I just don't know what I did wrong."

"Do you want to tell us more?" Collins asked.

"About what?"

"About what goes on here?"

"Nothing goes on here, really nothing," she said too emphatically. "I think I'd better get back to my class. If you'll excuse me now . . ."

She disappeared inside the room.

Radenbaugh looked at Collins. "Who said it, Chris? If fascism ever comes to the United States, it'll be because the people voted it in."

"Amen," said Collins. He took Radenbaugh by the arm. "We'd better get back to the hotel. There's a lot to decide."

BY FIVE MINUTES AFTER five o'clock the three of them had assembled in Chris Collins' room in the Constellation Hotel.

Collins was the first to speak, addressing himself to Chief Justice Maynard, who had just sat down on the hard bed, had removed his hat, and was now mopping his wet brow.

"Well, Mr. Chief Justice, what did you find out?"

Maynard seemed dazed. "In a word, it's—it's—shocking."

"Unbelievable," agreed Collins.

"Who could even imagine this going on in the United States?"

"It's going on, all right," said Collins grimly. "The people here are so indoctrinated with it, they don't know what's happened."

Maynard nodded heavily. "Yes, that was my impression."

"It's late," said Collins, "and I think the sooner we get out of here and head back for Phoenix, the better. We can discuss it in detail in the car. But right now, let me sum up what Donald and I found out. Between us, we covered a lot of ground, spoke to a lot of people."

"So did I," said Maynard. "I even saw the sheriff and the newspaper editor. They talk and they don't realize what they're saying. It's become a way of life. Never in my experience, here or abroad, at least since the Second World War, have I seen a population living such a robotlike existence. Or dwelling under such an insidious oppression."

Collins rose, and moved restlessly around the room. "Let me tell you, in a nutshell, what Donald and I found out. The Argo Smelting and Refining Company owns the only basic food and clothing stores in town. The mining employees are paid salaries, but they are also given coupon books, with scrip, which is good only in the company stores. When they run out of money, they can use the scrip to buy on credit. Thus, most of them wind up in hock to the company."

"A subtle form of slavery or economic bondage," added Radenbaugh.

"But there is much that is less subtle. The company owns every acre of land, owns or controls the city hall, sheriff's office, schools, hospital, theater, post office, church, repair shops, city newspaper, this very hotel. The company librarian bans books—not so much sex books as political books and history books. The post office screens—a euphemism for opens—all incoming and outgoing mail. The school board determines what the teachers should teach. The sheriff sees that peddlers and salesmen are not given permits. The hotel allows no one to stay more than two days. Strangers are picked up for vagrancy after three days. The company censors the minister's sermons. Unmarried men and women are segregated by sex into four company boardinghouses, which are filled with informers. As to general housing—"

"I looked into that," said Maynard. "I pretended I was considering buying a house and settling down here. It was fruitless. Only employees of Argo City Smelting are eligible to buy homes. The company holds the mortgage on every house that is bought. Mortgage payments are deducted from salary. If the owner decides to leave town, he must sell his house back to the company. On rented homes, the rents are also deducted from paychecks."

"More bondage," said Radenbaugh.

Collins moved toward Maynard. "What else did you find out?"

Maynard's gray head wagged from side to side. "Enough to sicken me. I have never encountered such blatant disregard for the Bill of Rights. I stopped once to have a salad in a company cafeteria. While at my table, out of curiosity, I jotted down on a napkin—two napkins, actually—the basic rights offered in the first ten amendments to the Constitution—the Bill of Rights adopted in December, 1791. Next to each amendment, I wrote down how the amendment is observed in Argo City. Listen to this—"

He tugged the two napkins out of the pocket of his khaki jacket and exchanged his sunglasses for a pair of square-lensed reading glasses.

"—just listen to this," Maynard resumed. "The 1st Amendment guarantees freedom of religion, press, speech, and the rights of assembly and petition. Here in Argo City you attend one church or none at all. You read one newspaper, the *Bugle*. All outside newspapers and most magazines are banned. Did you know that? Television consists of one local UHF station—company-controlled, of course. National programs are video-taped, and only certain ones are shown. The same for radio. Taped shows are played. All radios are sold by the company, ones with special band filters so they can't pick up Phoenix or other cities. Free speech is crippled all the way. Speak out of turn, and an informer reports you. You are out of a job and out of your home. No public gatherings and demonstrations permitted. The last one occurred four years ago. It was broken up, and the workers protesting lack of safety regulations were arrested. The jail was too small to hold them, but unbeknownst to anyone, there is an internment camp outside of town, in the desert—"

"An internment camp?" Collins blinked, remembering his son, Josh, and the trip to Tule Lake.

"Yes. Four weeks' confinement in that camp ended the protest. There has never been another since." Maynard tried to make out his writings on the first napkin. "The 2nd Amendment gives the citizen the right to keep and bear arms, meaning it gives each state a right to have a militia. But not in Argo City. Only an elite group of company employees—higher-placed, dependable ones—can and do own weapons. The 3rd Amendment says no soldier can be quartered in a private residence without consent of the owner. Five years ago, a ruling was made here that permits the police, in time of emergency, to move in and live under anyone's roof. The 4th Amendment gives people the right to be secure against unreasonable search. An Argo City ordinance allows the sheriff's men to enter any home without a warrant. The 5th Amendment protects the accused in a capital crime—only a grand jury can indict a civilian, by the way—and it guarantees due process, and says no one need be a witness against himself. Well, there's no grand jury in Argo City. A judge decides whether the evidence makes a trial necessary. The judges, of course, are appointed by the company. The 6th Amendment guarantees that the criminally accused shall have a speedy trial, impartial jury, be confronted by the witnesses against him, have the assistance of counsel for defense. In Argo City you can languish in jail indefinitely before being tried. No juries here. One of the judges sits as both judge and jury, like it or not. Witnesses against the accused need not appear in person. Counsel for the defense is supplied by the company." Maynard uttered a sigh. "As Stanislaw Lec once said, 'The dispensing of injustice is always in the right hands.'"

"Cripes," muttered Radenbaugh. "Wrong as they were, at least I had twelve jurors and I chose my own defense attorney."

Maynard picked up his second napkin and read from it. "The 7th Amendment. Well, this also guarantees the right to a trial by jury—that is, in suits of common law. This has been entirely ignored in Argo City. The 8th Amendment promises no exceseive bail, protects the citizen against excessive fines or cruel and unusual punishment. Well, here, for as little as a misdemeanor, the bail is set so high that the accused rots in prison until he is tried. I wasn't able to learn the amounts of fines. But apparently cruel and unusual punishment is the norm. Guilty people lose their homes. Protests or felonies send you to a barbed-wire internment camp in the hot desert. God knows what else they have in their books. The 9th Amendment safeguards other rights not specified in the Constitution. I didn't find out much tying into that, except that Argo City citizens apparently have no clear rights other than the right to eat and sleep, under certain conditions. The 10th Amendment reserves all powers not delegated to the Federal Government by the Constitution to the states and the people. Here, obviously, all powers delegated by the Constitution to the Federal Government, the states, or the people are totally controlled by the company."

"Or by Vernon T. Tynan," said Collins.

"Or by Tynan, yes," Maynard agreed. He stuffed the napkins back in his pocket. "Gentlemen, how in the devil could this have happened? I can see the Federal Government's not being aware of what's going on here. But the state of Arizona—one would think the state would be aware and act upon it."

"No, I can see how the situation would be allowed to exist," Radenbaugh said. "Ten to one the Arizona Corporation Commission, which is supposed to control corporations, is itself controlled by the Argo Smelting and Refining Company. Then Tynan had something on Argo Smelting, and he moved in on them for his grand experiment."

Maynard was more agitated than ever. "This is absolutely the most appalling situation I've ever encountered."

"We can't sit by and let it go on," Collins said. "As Attorney General, I've got to act. I can send a team of investigators in here—"

Maynard raised a hand. "No, that's not of immediate concern. Argo City and its 14,000 people are not the issue. They are merely part of the larger issue. You said it yourself, Mr. Collins. There's more at stake—far more."

"You mean the 35th Amendment."

"We know that crime-free Argo City inspired Director Tynan to develop the 35th Amendment. We know he tested aspects of the 35th, and refined them, using Argo City as a laboratory for suppression and repression in the last four years. We know we have today seen a preview of the entire United States a year from now, and in the years to come, if California ratifies the 35th and makes it part of the Constitution."

The Chief Justice stood up and aimlessly crossed the room, immersed in some inner conflict, but when he returned to

Collins and Radenbaugh, his creased countenance had opened up at some private resolution.

"Gentlemen," he said, "I've made my decision. If it is up to me, California cannot and shall not pass the 35th Amendment."

Collins could not hide his elation. "Are you— What are you going to do, Mr. Chief Justice?"

"I'm going to do what I promised you I'd do if you uncovered evidence that this democracy is in real danger," Maynard said. "You've shown me one part of The R Document, apparently Director Tynan's master plan. I have seen fascism accepted as the price for security. Now I can see this fascism brought to the entire nation, all under the guise of law. I can't and won't let it happen." His eyes held on Collins. "I'm going to speak to the President first. I'm going to try to persuade him to reverse his position. If I fail, then I'll come forward and be heard. If my influence, Mr. Collins, is what you believe it to be, there will be no 35th Amendment, no more Argo Cities in America, and our time of agony will be ended."

Collins grabbed Maynard's hand and pumped it warmly. Radenbaugh nodded approval. "We'd better get moving," Maynard said gruffly. "I'll go to my room to get my things. I'll meet you in the hall in two minutes flat."

Maynard hastened out the door.

Jubilantly, Collins and Radenbaugh took up their effects and started to leave. At the door, Collins halted Radenbaugh.

"Where are you going from Phoenix, Donald?"

"Back to Philadelphia, I guess."

"Come to Washington. I can't put you on the Federal payroll. But I can put you on my private one. I need you. Our work is not done. Once Maynard kills the 35th Amendment, we'll need a new and decent program to substitute for it; one that will bring about a reduction in crime without sacrificing our civil rights."

Radenbaugh looked moved. "You really can use me? I'd be glad to, but—"

"Come on. Let's not waste time."

In the hall, they met Maynard emerging from his room. They descended in the elevator together. Collins checked them out at the desk, and then the three crossed the lobby and exited into the warm late afternoon.

As Collins and Radenbaugh proceeded to the parking lot, Maynard halted to buy the latest edition of the Argo City *Bugle* from a bearded blind vendor seated on a box next to the hotel entrance. As the vendor heard the clink of the coins, the eyes behind his dark glasses remained vacant, but his mouth curled in a smile of thanks.

Maynard hurried to catch up with his companions. Minutes later, Radenbaugh drove the Ford out of the parking lot, heading back through Argo City toward Phoenix and free air.

IN FRONT OF THE Constellation Hotel, the blind vendor pocketed his money, came to his feet, and placed what was left of his stack of newspapers on top of the box.

Tapping his white cane, he hobbled past the hotel, continued on past the parking lot, then turned toward the filling station on the corner. Following his cane, he made his way unerringly to the nearer of the two telephone booths in the rear.

He entered one booth, closed the glass door, and propped his white cane in a corner. Finally, glancing behind him, he removed his dark glasses, pocketed them, took the receiver in his hand, dropped a coin into the slot, and absently studied the numbers on the dial as he waited.

The operator came on. He gave her the number. After a few moments, he deposited the quarters.

He waited. The telephone was ringing. A voice came on at the other end.

The vendor cupped the mouthpiece of the phone.

"Please put me through to Director Vernon T. Tynan," he said urgently. "Tell him it is Special Agent Kiley reporting from Field Office R."

He waited again. Only seconds.

Tynan's voice came on loud and clear, and with equal urgency. "What is it?"

"Director Tynan. Kiley here at R. There were three of them. I recognized only two. One was Attorney General Collins. The other was Chief Justice Maynard. . . . Absolutely no question. Collins and Maynard . . ."

VII

IT WAS MIDMORNING OF the following day, and President Wadsworth had telephoned twice within the past fifteen minutes.

For the first time in memory, Director Vernon T. Tynan had avoided taking a call from the President of the United States. With Harry Adcock, behind closed doors, he had been deeply occupied listening to a tape that Adcock had delivered. It was the tape taken an hour before of a private telephone conversation between Chief Justice Maynard and President Wadsworth. The Chief Justice had initiated the call, and his curt conversation with the President had lasted no more than five minutes.

The President's first call to Tynan had come as Adcock arrived with the critical tape. "Tell him I'm not in my office yet," Tynan had instructed his secretary. "Tell him you'll try to locate me." The President's second call had come as Tynan was still listening to the tape. "Just say I'm still not in," he had ordered his secretary, "but that you expect me any minute."

He had heard the tape to its end.

Adcock shut off the machine. "Do you want to hear it again, chief?"

"No, once was enough." Tynan leaned back in his swivel

chair. "I must say I'm not surprised. After Kiley reported from Argo City last night, I suspected this would happen. Now it's happened. Well, I'd better call the President back and hear his replay of it."

Seconds later, Tynan was connected with the Oval Office of the White House.

"Sorry to have missed you," Tynan said breathlessly. "Just walked in. I had two appointments on the outside, and neglected to let Beth know. Is it something urgent?"

"Vernon, we're cooked. The 35th is as good as dead."

Tynan simulated astonishment. "What are you saying, Mr. President?"

"Just before I phoned you, I had a call from Chief Justice Maynard."

"Oh?"

"He wanted to know if I'd ever heard of a place known as Argo City, Arizona. It rang a bell immediately. The place you discussed with me last night when you were briefing me on the latest Bureau activities. I told Maynard Yes, I knew about it, that it was a community the Bureau had been investigating for several years. I told him you personally had been leading the investigation of Federal crimes in that city, and would soon be submitting your findings to Attorney General Collins."

"Correct."

"Well, Maynard took another view of your activities in Argo City."

Tynan acted utterly bewildered. "I don't understand. What other view could he take?"

"He had the notion that you had been using Argo City as a test site for the 35th Amendment. And the results, while they may have pleased you, were horrifying to him."

"That's absurd."

"I told him it was absurd—exactly that. But the old coot would not be swayed."

"He's off his rocker," said Tynan.

"Whatever he is, he's against us. He said he'd never publicly expressed himself on the 35th, but he was now prepared to do so. Then he tried to strong-arm me."

"Strong-arm you, Mr. President? In what way?"

"He said if I publicly withdrew my support of the 35th, he would gladly remain silent. But if I refused to do so, if I refused to change my position, then he would speak out."

"Who the hell does he think he is, threatening the President?" said Tynan indignantly. "How did you answer him?"

"I told him I had consistently stood behind the 35th, and I would continue to stand behind it. I told him I believed in it and wanted it ratified as part of the Constitution."

"How did he take that?" asked Tynan with pretended anxiety.

"He said, 'Then you're forcing me to act, Mr. President. I'm stepping down from the Bench and into the political arena, so I can speak out while there is still time.' He said he was flying to Los Angeles this afternoon. He'll spend all of tomorrow at his Palm Springs home. The day after, he's going to drive back to Los Angeles. He said, 'I'm holding a news conference at the Ambassador Hotel to announce my resignation from the Supreme Court, and I'm going to announce my willingness to appear as a witness before the Judiciary Committees of the California State Assembly and the California State Senate to speak against passage of the 35th Amendment.'"

"He's actually ready to do that?"

"No question, Vernon. I tried to argue some sense into him, but to no avail. He's off to California in a few hours. And we're in the soup. The minute he comes out against the 35th, we're finished. He'll turn the whole legislature around. Who could have imagined this would happen? All our efforts, our hopes, destroyed by the interference of one man. What can we do, Vernon?"

"We can fight him."

"How?"

"I'm not sure. I'll try to think of something."

"Think of something—anything."

"I will, Mr. President."

Tynan hung up, smiled at the telephone, raised his head, and smiled at Adcock.

He winked. "We certainly will think of something, won't we, Harry?"

* * *

CHRIS COLLINS WAS IN high spirits that evening. For the first time he was relieved of the strain of the last weeks and ready to relax.

Returning from work, and just as he had stepped into the house, there had been the awaited telephone call from Maynard. The Chief Justice had arrived minutes ago at Los Angeles International Airport, and before he and his wife got into their car to drive to Palm Springs, he wanted to inform Collins of what had transpired that morning. He had indeed spoken to the President on the phone. He had asked the President to reverse his position on the 35th Amendment. The President had refused to do so. Maynard had then advised the President that he was leaving for Los Angeles, where he would announce his resignation from the Supreme Court and say that he intended to speak out, in Sacramento, against passage of the 35th Amendment. He would spend a day in his Palm Springs study writing his resignation speech and his strongly worded statement to the state legislative committees.

"I hope this does it," he had said.

"It will, it will," Collins had promised, bursting with excitement. "Thank you, Mr. Chief Justice."

"Thank *you*, Mr. Collins."

Karen had been hovering nearby, wondering, and the moment that he'd hung up, Collins had leaped to his feet, grabbed up his wife, started to lift her from the floor, remembered her pregnancy, and merely hugged and kissed her.

Quickly, he had explained to Karen—without going into detail, without mentioning Argo City—the Chief Justice's decision to come out publicly against the 35th.

Karen had been genuinely thrilled. "How wonderful, darling. Good news at last."

"Let's celebrate," Collins had said. He had felt light of head and body, as if he had shed pounds of pressure. "Let's go out on the town. You name it."

"The Jockey Club," Karen had sung out, "and Tournedos Rossini."

"You get dressed. I'll make the reservation. Just the two of us. No business, just pleasure, I promise you."

A half hour later, after showering together, they were in the bedroom, almost dressed.

Collins was pulling on the trousers of his best navy blue suit, stuffing his shirttails inside, when the telephone rang.

"You get it," Karen called out from the dressing table. "My nail polish isn't dry."

Collins went to the dressing table and prayed it wasn't business. Only a few of the people who had his home number were not connected with the Department of Justice.

He picked up the receiver. "Hello?"

"Mr. Collins?"

"Yes?"

"This is Ishmael Young. I don't know if you remember . . . ?"

Collins smiled. As if anyone would be likely to forget that name. "Of course I remember. You're Director Tynan's ghost."

Ishmael Young said seriously, "I hope I'm not really remembered that way. But that's right. I'm doing Tynan's autobiography, and you were kind enough to see me last month." He hesitated, fumbled for the right words, then, with a new immediacy in his voice, blurted out, "I know how busy you are, Mr. Collins, but if it's humanly possible I must see you tonight. I won't take much time—"

Glancing at his wife, Collins interrupted. "I'm afraid I am tied up for the evening, Mr. Young. Perhaps you can call me at the office on Monday, and we can make a—"

"Mr. Collins, believe me, I wouldn't bother you if it wasn't important. To you, as well as to me."

"We-ll, I don't know—"

"Please."

The tone of Ishmael Young's voice made Collins capitulate. "All right. Actually, my wife and I were going to have dinner together at The Jockey Club."

"I'm sorry. But—"

"Never mind. We'll be there at eight thirty. You can join us."

After he hung up, he saw Karen looking at him inquiringly.

Collins shrugged. "He's ghostwriting an autobiography for Vernon Tynan. He has to see me tonight. I guess I'm curious enough to want to know why. At least he's a nice guy. I hope you don't mind, honey."

"Silly, I never expected it to be two." She pointed to the telephone. "Better call The Jockey Club back and make it three. Besides, I'm as curious as you."

THE JOCKEY CLUB, LOCATED in the Fairfax Hotel on Massachusetts Avenue, was crowded to overflowing by nine o'clock that evening. Nevertheless, the best table in the restaurant had been reserved and held for Chris Collins and his party.

"You see," Collins had whispered to his wife, "there are some advantages to being Attorney General."

"Or to being a big tipper," Karen had replied.

Ishmael Young, who had been awaiting them outside on the corner, had been unusually anxious and constantly apologetic ever since their arrival.

Now, again, as their drinks arrived, and Young absently fingered his Jack Daniels and soda, he was apologizing. "I hate intruding on your private evening like this."

"We're delighted to have you," said Collins expansively. He was feeling wonderful, and he held up his Scotch and water in a mock toast. "Here's to the defeat of the 35th Amendment." He waited for Karen to take up her vodka and tonic, and for the writer to join in the toast, and then he drank. Setting down his glass, he said to Young, "You didn't know, did you, that I'm not supporting the 35th anymore?"

"But I do know," said Young.

Collins did not hide his surprise. "How could you? It's a personal decision. It's nothing I've made public. And nothing I will make public as long as I'm a member of the Administration." He cocked his head at Young. "How did you find out?"

"You forget," said Young. "I'm working with Director Tynan. The Director knows everything. And I'm his ghost."

Collins' mood had sobered. "I see. So he knows, also?"

"Yes."

"I should have guessed." He took a big swallow of his drink. "I tend to underrate him. I should remember he is formidable."

They fell into brief silence. Ishmael Young fiddled with his drink, apparently trying to formulate something he wanted to say. At last, he spoke. "I wanted to see you tonight for—for two reasons. One has to do with you. The other with me. First, you."

But he didn't go on immediately, and Collins said, "Well, what is it?"

"I want to discuss Tynan."

Collins was momentarily exasperated. "If you mean you want to ask more questions about what I think of Tynan for your book, let me tell you right off, I have nothing more to say."

"No, it's not that," said Young quickly. "It's not about the book. I didn't barge in on your dinner to *ask* you about Tynan. I really came because I wanted to *tell* you about Tynan. I wanted—"

"To tell me what?" Collins interrupted impatiently. "What do you want to tell me?"

Karen reached out to touch Collins' arm. "Please, Chris. Let him speak."

Ishmael Young gave Karen a grateful nod, nervously pushed up the knot of his tie, and patted at the strands of hair combed to cover his bald pate.

Although still irritated by the writer's fidgeting and his reluctance to come to the point, Collins obeyed his wife and waited.

"He doesn't like you, you know," said Young.

"Who? Tynan?"

"He doesn't like you at all," Young repeated.

"I'm not surprised," said Collins, "but how did you find out?"

"I'm there, with him, every week. I'm there, but lately he doesn't seem to realize it half the time. He talks on and on. He answers the phone. He makes calls. He leaves notes and memos lying around. Mostly, by now, he's not aware of me. It is as if I'm not a person. He may be right. I'm a blotter."

"So he doesn't like me," said Collins.

"I decided if he doesn't like you, then I should. Anything or anyone Tynan is against, well, it has to be good. As you know, when we first met, I told you he's not my kind of guy. I made up my mind he's not your kind either. I realized, whether you'd admit it or not, we're on the same side. That's why I wanted to see you at once, to warn you about something."

Karen looked troubled, but Collins remained impassive. "Go on."

"All right." He lowered his voice. "Tynan and the FBI have been investigating you."

"Oh, Chris," Karen gasped.

Collins waved her silent. He held on the writer. "So what else is new? If that's all—"

"But I thought—"

"Naturally I was investigated by the FBI. It's their job. They had to investigate me the minute the President nominated me for Attorney General. It was routine."

"No, you misunderstand, Mr. Collins. I know they investigated you weeks ago. I know that was routine. I'm trying to tell you that Tynan instigated a new and secret investigation of you the other day. It's in progress right now."

Collins blinked at Young—letting it settle in, finally comprehending. He exhaled, and said, "Well, now . . ." Then he said, "Are you sure?"

"Positive. Not the first time Tynan's checked on you, either. Once, last month, I overheard him speak on the phone about Baxter and the Holy Trinity Church and make a reference to the Collins thing—"

Collins interrupted. "I know about that. This is more important right now. You say you're positive? You heard that Tynan was investigating me again?"

"Absolutely. I was with him a long time yesterday. He got this call. When I'm there and we're working, he usually takes calls only from the President and Adcock. The call wasn't from the President. While he was on the phone, I went into the bathroom, but I left the door partly open. I could hear his side of it. Your name was never mentioned. But there was some reference—I don't remember exactly what—that made it clear they were talking about you. It had to do with an investigation now going on. Tynan finally said to Adcock, 'Well, keep trying. And keep after the others.' "

Karen had picked up the last. "The others? What did he mean by that?"

"I have no idea," said Ishmael Young. He turned back to Collins. "But there was no question the discussion was about you. Does it make sense? Would there be any reason for him to investigate you now?"

"There might be, yes, there could be," said Collins slowly.

"Well, I thought I shouldn't waste any time in warning you," said Ishmael Young, "so that you can have your guard up."

"I appreciate it," said Collins sincerely. "Thank you— Ishmael." He glanced distractedly around him, found their waiter, and beckoned him. "I think this calls for another round of drinks."

After Collins had ordered, Karen drew closer to her husband. She tried to repress her agitation. "What does all this mean, Chris?"

"I'm not sure, darling. Probably nothing." He tried to comfort her. "Not all investigations are sinister. Sometimes they're done to check on someone I'm associated with, in order to protect me."

"That could be true," Young said hastily to Karen, also eager to reassure her.

"But at least he ought to tell you," said Karen to her husband, "not do this sort of thing behind your back. I mean, you're his boss. Really, he's a horrible man."

The second round of drinks had appeared, and Young lifted his glass. "That's something I'll drink to, Mrs. Collins." His eyes roved the vicinity to see if anyone was listening. "He— meaning you-know-who—is the worst bastard—forgive me— the worst egomaniac and the most unprincipled bastard I've ever met."

They drank, and before the conversation could resume, the maître d' had appeared to take their order.

They all agreed on Onion Soup Gratinée for starters, then Collins ordered Tournedos Rossini for Karen, waited while

Young examined the menu again and finally asked for Beef
Stroganoff, and for himself ordered Coq au Vin.

Ishmael Young had returned to his Jack Daniels. "In fact,
speaking of Tynan," said Young, addressing Karen, "I can find
no one who loves him except—and I'm only guessing here—
except his mother and Adcock. Everyone else either respects
him or fears him or plain hates him."

Collins became interested. "Except his mother and Adcock,
you said. Was that just a crack about his mother? Or were you
being literal? Does he have a mother around?"

"You wouldn't believe it, would you? That Vernon T. Tynan
could have a mother. Well, he has. Just a stone's throw away
from here. Rose Tynan. Eighty-four years old. She's in the
Golden Years Senior Citizens Village in Alexandria. Nobody
knows this except Adcock and myself, but Tynan goes to see
her every Saturday. Yes, the monster has a certified mother."

"Have you seen her?" asked Collins.

"Oh, no. Verboten. Once, when I was interviewing him about
his younger days, he couldn't remember something, but he said
his mother would know and he'd find out from her. I told him I
didn't know his mother was alive. He said, 'Oh yes, but I don't
talk about it for security reasons, for her safety.' He wanted to be
sure I didn't put it in the book, that she was alive, but he said I
could refer to her and he wanted some nice things in it about her.
And he told me a little of her background. That's how I know."

"Interesting," said Collins.

"I can't imagine Tynan's having a mother," said Karen. "It
makes him sound almost human."

"Don't be fooled," said Ishmael Young. "Caligula also had a
mother. So did Jack the Ripper."

Collins was amused, but Karen was serious about pursuing
Tynan further with Ishmael Young. "Mr. Young, if you dislike
Director Tynan so much—"

"I never said I disliked him. I hate him."

"Very well. If you hate him, why are you working with him
on his autobiography?"

"Why? I'll tell you why. . . ."

But he didn't right away, because the waiter had rolled up a cart with the onion soup and was ladling it into bowls and serving them.

No sooner was the waiter gone than Young picked up where he had left off.

"When I met your husband, I told him I was pressured into writing this book. Now I'd like to explain that, if I may." He turned toward Collins. "Actually, it is the other reason I wanted to meet with you tonight. I said the first reason had to do with you, and the second with me. I hope you don't mind my bothering you with a problem I have. It has to do with Tynan, and why I'm writing his *Mein Kampf*."

"Please go ahead," said Collins.

"I was bullied into writing his damn book," said Young. "I didn't want to, but Tynan made me do it. What happened was— I'd been living in Paris for some time, researching a book I intended to write not as a ghost but on my own—a book on the Paris Commune. Among the people I interviewed two years ago were an exiled British professor and his wife. Professor Henderson—he was an expert on the Commune—had been deported from the United States long ago for involvement in anarchist activities. The Hendersons had a daughter, Emmy, with whom I fell deeply in love. The first and only time in my life. And she fell in love with me. We agreed to get married. The only trouble was—I *was* married. Separated for some time, but married. The plan was that I'd return home to New York, get a divorce, then send for Emmy and marry her. Well, that divorce took some doing—"

"I know about those things," said Collins, taking Karen's hand.

"Finally, I lucked out. Had a moderate best seller—a political biography. By turning all the earnings over to my wife, I got my divorce. I prepared to send for Emmy. Meanwhile, Vernon T. Tynan had discovered me and decided I was the only person to write his autobiography. I refused. Tynan doesn't like being turned down. He investigated me. He learned about Emmy and her parents. He learned that Emmy, like her parents, had been a confirmed anarchist. Unlike her parents, she had been a passive one, an intellectual one. She's a gentle, sweet person and a political theorist, no more. Well, there Tynan had the goods. He confronted me with it. If I refused to cooperate with him on his book, he'd block Emmy's entrance into the United States on the ground that she was an undesirable alien. On the other hand, if I collaborated with him on the book, he'd forget it and allow her to enter the United States the moment the book was done. That was the carrot he dangled in front of me. What could I do? I had to bite. That's why I agreed to write his book."

"Awful, making you do it that way," said Karen.

"Then what's your problem?" Collins wanted to know.

"My problem is—Tynan double-crossed me. Two weeks ago, I got my hands on a whole new cache of material, of additional research for the book—papers, tapes, whatnot. Tynan gave it to me to copy. Lots of it was from the late Attorney General's papers, lots was new material of Tynan's. I've been copying this research so I can return the originals to Tynan. Well, yesterday, going through some of these papers, I came across a memorandum Tynan had written to Baxter—apparently he'd forgotten he'd sent it—advising him that Emmy Henderson, among others, was to be banned from entry into the United States since she was an undesirable alien. The memorandum had been written *after* his promise to me that she would be admitted. He still intends to punish me for turning him down in the beginning. You can imagine how I felt. I wanted to confront him with this blatant double cross, but I was afraid to. I didn't know what to do. Then I realized that a carbon of the memorandum was surely in the files of the Immigration and Naturalization Service as well, and that the Service falls under your control. So that's the other reason why I wanted to see you tonight. To ask if you could help me."

Collins did not hesitate. "Yes, Immigration is one of my departments. I can rule on the admissibility of aliens. I'll be only too glad to look up your Emmy's file. For your part, you send me what papers you have on her application. I'll review the case. If she is what you say she is—"

"I guarantee she's clean."

"—then I'll overrule Tynan's recommendation and see that she's admitted."

"Mr. Collins, I can't tell you how happy you've just made me. You don't know how I appreciate this, what it means. You don't know what I owe you."

Collins smiled. "I know what *I* owe *you*. But that's not the consideration. It's a matter of justice."

Karen was the only one at the table who was still disturbed. "I want you to do this, Chris. But I'm worried about Tynan. He won't like it. He could be vindictive."

"Just don't worry," Collins told his wife. "I know how to handle the matter." He looked at Young. "You go right on doing his book as if you don't know a thing. I'll take care of this quietly. He'll never know it happened."

Karen seemed relieved, yet still concerned about Tynan. "Does he do this sort of thing often? Director Tynan, I mean. Interfering in people's lives? Behaving this way? It's incredible."

Ishmael Young shook his head, before returning to his food. "There's nobody like him. With his investigative apparatus, he's Big Brother incarnate. Hell, I'm sure there is nothing in your life, Mrs. Collins, or your life, Mr. Collins, or my own life that Vernon T. Tynan doesn't know about. I've come to the conclusion that he's the most powerful man in the country. If he isn't, he will be, once the 35th Amendment is passed."

"It won't be passed," said Collins quietly. "The day after tomorrow it'll be dead, and we'll all be alive again. So don't worry about Tynan. Just eat up, finish your drinks, and be merry. Tonight we celebrate."

When Karen Collins, wearing her sheer pale blue nightgown, emerged from the dressing room into their bedroom, the lights were out except for the lamp beside her bed. The electric clock beneath the lamp told her it was ten minutes before one o'clock in the morning. On the far side of the bed, already tucked in, her husband lay with his head deep in the pillow, his back to her.

She lifted the blanket and slid into her side of the king-size bed. Lifting herself, she leaned over him. His eyes were closed.

"Thanks for a lovely evening, darling," she whispered.

"Uh-huh," he murmured wearily.

She lowered her head and put her lips to his cheek. "Good night, dearest. You're so tired. Sleep well."

She thought she heard him say good night.

She looked down at him for a brief interval, finally lifted herself again, shifted over to her side of the bed, and settled on her back, not having turned off the lamp as yet. She stared thoughtfully up at the ceiling.

Her mind went back to the evening, to The Jockey Club, to that pudgy little writer named Ishmael Young.

He had said early on: "The Director knows everything."

He had said later on: "Hell, I'm sure there is nothing in your life, Mrs. Collins, or your life, Mr. Collins, or my own life that Vernon T. Tynan doesn't know about."

She thought about it, as she stared up at the ceiling, and she thought about the time in Fort Worth, Texas.

She could feel agitation grow within her, and she was suddenly scared.

Turning her head toward him on the pillow, she fixed on the back of his head, and licked her dry lips. There was still time to talk. Maybe not pillow talk, maybe not a good thing to do at a time when he was so tired—but it was time to talk.

"Chris," she called out. "Chris, darling, there's something I've got to tell you—something I've never had a chance to tell you before. I feel I have to now. I should have before, but anyway, it's something you have to know. It has to do with not long before we met. Just listen, darling. Just let me talk. Will you, darling?"

She waited for his response, and then she heard it.

He was snoring softly.

Too late.

With a troubled sigh, she turned away, raised her hand to turn off the lamp, then fell back deeper into the pillow, eyes open in the darkness.

She shivered—remembering the past, wondering about the future.

She closed her eyes, living behind them a while, until sleep began to draw darkness inside her.

Maybe, she thought—her last comforting thought—I'm being childish and silly and scared by the night. There are no monsters out there. Only people. People like thee and me. Good night, Chris. Together we're safe, aren't we?

With that, she felt herself sink down, down, down to the place where dreams begin.

IN THE J. EDGAR Hoover Building, Harry Adcock, having finished his light lunch, left his seventh-floor office and made his way to the elevator. His destination on this Sunday afternoon, as it had been every day since the chief had given him the high-priority assignment, was the FBI's computer complex in the rear of the first floor.

Descending in the elevator, Adcock recalled the exact wording of Tynan's assignment.

Start with our Attorney General Collins. I want the Bureau to run a quiet check on him . . . I want Collins checked ten times more thoroughly than the first time. . . . Go after everyone ever connected with him at any time in his life.

Adcock had wasted no time in assembling two top-notch Strike Forces. The larger one, carefully handpicked from over 10,000 Special Agents on the outside, was to work in the field. These agents had been selected not only for their experience and skill, but for their personal loyalty to the chief. The smaller Force had been gathered from the most trustworthy, tight-lipped personnel inside the headquarters here, and they were to concentrate on the so-called paperwork.

The two Forces had plunged into the Collins investigation immediately. They had gone about their business silently and unobtrusively—insofar as this was possible—and in the work-filled days since they had begun, they had produced reams of material. Collins' life had been turned inside out, as had been the lives of his relatives, associates, friends.

To date, at least as of yesterday, the results had been miserably disappointing to Adcock. Everything found out about Collins and those close to him had been legitimate, lawful, upright, honest, decent, confirming the Bureau's original investigation. Almost every closet door had been opened. Not one had contained a skeleton. It was sickeningly unnatural, and Adcock did not believe it. He had been around too long, seen too much of the worst in human beings, to believe in purity. If you dug deep enough, long enough, hard enough, you would hit pay dirt—sooner or later, dirty pay dirt.

Of course, he had kept Tynan apprised in a general way about the progress of the investigation. Since Tynan was never interested in details, only in end results, Adcock had not told the chief of the daily failures to unearth anything of practical value. He had told him only that things were moving along; clues and leads were being followed up from Albany to Oakland.

Hopefully, today would be a better day, and there would be something satisfying and useful to report to the chief.

Reaching the first floor, Adcock emerged from the elevator and proceeded past the ornamental fountain to the FBI's computer complex.

Inside, he glanced at the wall sign that read FBI NATIONAL CRIME INFORMATION CENTER. At once, he felt reassured. Then his eyes passed over the electronic gimmickry in the vast room—the control typewriter, the control console, the magnetic tape units, the 1,100-lines-per-minute printer—and he felt even more reassured. No human impurity could escape detection by these machines, just as no human frailty could avoid detection by the persistent bloodhounds in the field.

Wandering through the complex, Adcock searched for Mary Lampert. She was a senior communications officer, and his major contact down here. Unable to spot her, he stopped to ask an operator where she was. He learned that she had just stepped out and would be back in a few minutes.

Adcock found a chair and sat down to wait.

Surveying the computer network again, remembering the Identification Division upstairs, thinking of the agents in the field, Adcock knew that he would have good news for the chief sooner or later. It was merely a matter of time.

The language in Adcock's head was the language of relentless statistics. To make himself feel better, he reviewed them.

Computer network. From 40,000 Federal, state, community

agencies in fifty states, data came in to feed the system. Data were collected and stored not only on people with arrest records, not only on potential criminals or troublemakers, but on dissenters in general, on Congressmen, on Government officials, on critics of the United States—hell, on practically everyone over ten years old. Take the arrest records alone. About 49 percent of the population would be arrested once in their lifetimes, counting certain traffic violations. During their lifetimes, 90 percent of black urban males would be arrested at least once, and 60 percent of white urban males would be arrested at least once. All of these arrests were in the data banks. With the crime rate the way it was, even skipping traffic violations, about 9 million people would be arrested this year. About half would not be prosecuted, or would have the charges against them dropped, or would be tried and acquitted, but all of them would also land in the data banks. Besides data from 275 million police records, there were also data stored from 350 million medical case histories, from 290 million psychiatric accounts, from 125 million business credit files.

Identification Division. Every day, every single day, 34,000 new sets of fingerprints came into the FBI—about 15,000 of these from police agencies, and about 19,000 from Government agencies, banks, insurance companies, license bureaus, and other sources. Every damn day, mind you. Back in 1975, the FBI had 200 million sets of fingerprints on file. Today, maybe 250 million. One-third of the cards were in the criminal files, and two-thirds in civil files.

FBI agents in the field. There were over 10,000 out there, including the Strike Force working on this investigation. The Strike Force had been interviewing the subject's relatives, friends, acquaintances, business associates, as well as visiting schools, clubs, shopkeepers, bankers, doctors, lawyers. They were out there, yeah, wiretapping and bugging, shadowing and tailing, planting informers, taking photographs. They were out there entering unoccupied apartments and houses, examining the contents of garbage cans, opening and inspecting and resealing mail.

Marvelous. Who could escape Tynan's army? If there were impurities, they would be found, they certainly would be found.

Harry Adcock was glad he had taken his mental inventory. He was feeling better and better.

His reverie was interrupted by a feminine face bent close to his own. He could smell the perfume, and he heard her whisper, "Hello, Harry."

He raised his head. Mary Lampert had returned.

"Did I keep you waiting long?" she asked.

"No, no. What do we have today?"

"Come into the office."

In her austere cubbyhole, he settled down across from her desk. He watched her go to the fireproof file cabinet and unlock it. He liked to watch her, and again admired the chief's taste. She didn't look like a senior communications officer, but she didn't have to because that was only one of her jobs, Adcock reminded himself. He continued to observe her as she opened the file drawer. Mary Lampert was thirty-two years old and five feet seven. She wore a fluffy hairdo, had cool green eyes, a broad-bridged short nose, moist and sensuous full lips. Her dress was molded to her breasts, which were high and firm, and to her generous thighs, revealing the line of her panties.

Adcock's acned face relaxed in pleasure.

She was coming toward him. "Here it is," she said, handing him the manila folder. "There's the latest data covering the last twenty hours."

He opened the folder and scanned and thumbed the pages. When he finished, pleasure had left his countenance to be replaced by disgust. "God damn," he said. "Nothing."

Mary nodded. "That's what I thought, too. Looks like a surveillance report on the Cub Scouts and Brownies of America."

"We've got to keep trying, Mary. The chief expects—"

The telephone jangled, and he broke off his speech while Mary answered the phone.

"Oh, really?" she said into the phone. "I'll be right up."

Adcock looked at her questioningly.

"Identification Division," she said. "You wait here. I'll be back in a jiffy. It has to do with our case. I don't know what."

She started for the door. Again he watched her as she left, the pantie line across the buttocks beneath her dress. He must remember to tell her to wear that dress the next time she saw the chief.

This brought his mind entirely to Vernon T. Tynan—to his responsibility to Tynan, how he had always done everything possible to please Tynan and make him happy, how he could not let him down in their pursuit of that traitorous Collins.

He had never let the chief down before, and he did not intend to do so now, especially not now, when there was so much at stake. Tynan had always taken care of him, and hell, he'd give up his life for Tynan, if necessary.

He knew, all right, about how people in this crappy town talked about their relationship, meaning himself and Tynan. He'd always suspected the talk, but he knew for sure that night they'd bugged a high-level Washington society party—Congressional types, State Department people, the like—and he'd made out on the tape a group gossiping and laughing. He'd heard them gossiping and laughing about Vernon T. Tynan and Harry Adcock, those two aging homosexuals. He'd always known that the talk went on, but here it was: Tynan and himself as fags.

He'd never been more furious.

Not that it mattered, but it was just so smart-ass wrong and unjust.

True, Adcock loved Tynan, but as a man can love a man without being a homosexual. Hell, he loved Tynan and worshipped him. As for the rest, Adcock had had a real woman once—too long ago to define her features now—but she had died before he could marry her, in a time before he'd joined the FBI. Tynan was not a substitute for her, but rather for the father he had never known, having known only an orphanage in his youth. In fact, there had been a few other women during his early years in the FBI, just bed partners, but once he really rose in the FBI, once Tynan took over, there were no others. He had dedicated himself to the Bureau—to Tynan and the Bureau—and to no one and nothing else. He had taken an unsworn pledge of celibacy, with the FBI as his lifetime religious order.

As for Vernon T. Tynan, my God. Those smart-asses out there didn't realize Tynan was normal about women, only careful and discreet, considering his critical position. Once a week, as long as Adcock could remember, Tynan had been visited by some young woman sent to him by a grateful madam in Baltimore. Because Tynan did not like to get too involved, dared not, he kept these women at arm's length. He permitted them to go down on him, and no more.

Then three years ago, when the madam had died or retired, Tynan had sought a new outlet for his sexual needs. He had to be cautious, but fortunately he had hit upon a brilliant solution. The FBI was beginning to take on more female personnel, not only as secretaries and clerks but as Special Agents and computer operators. When an opening came about for a communications officer in the computer complex, Tynan had suggested that his old side-kick, Adcock, personally screen the female applicants, and run a check on the best of them as to their computer experience—and sexual compliance—and then hire the most talented.

Mary Lampert got the job. Her job ordinarily consisted of five days a week at FBI headquarters and one night a week at Vernon T. Tynan's suburban home. One evening out of every seven—each Friday night—Mary Lampert, camouflaged by files under her arm, went to Tynan's heavily secured Georgian house near Rock Creek Park. She joined the chief in three or four drinks. She undressed him. She undressed herself. They played around on the bed. Then she moved her head down between his legs. Like clockwork, once a week, every week, for three years. Who in the hell were those smart-asses to say Vernon T. Tynan wasn't normal?

Boy, Adcock thought, it would sure shake up those smart-asses in the capital city to know how normal the Director and the Associate Director were—probably the only normal human beings (except for the President) in this depraved community. And it was just as normal, Adcock thought, for him to sublimate himself to Tynan, for him to be the loyal and devoted servant of the truly greatest man in the United States of America.

That was why he couldn't disappoint Tynan now in this all-important matter of the Collins investigation.

Yet despite all their concentration and efforts, there had been no break in the case.

He was becoming gloomy and discouraged once more when he realized that Mary Lampert, senior communications officer, was standing before him, beaming down upon him.

With a flourish she laid a fingerprint card and a sheaf of paper-clipped sheets of paper on his lap.

"Good news, Harry," she said.

He was startled. "What is it?"

"The Collins investigation," she said. "Just came through. See for yourself."

He took up the sheaf of papers, examined the fingerprint card, puzzled, and slowly began to leaf through the papers, one by one. Quickly his puzzlement vanished.

"My God!" he said—and at last he was beaming, too.

It was ten minutes to eight in the morning, and Chris Collins stood before the bathroom mirror and finished shaving with his single-edged razor. He lathered his face once more, then ducked low over the bowl, scooped up two handfuls of warm water, and rinsed the soap off his face.

Straightening, he began to hum as he considered himself in the mirror. Lately, the mirror had reflected a long, narrow face that seemed perpetually haggard and made him seem old beyond his years. But this morning his face was—or seemed to be—as healthy and unlined as that of a young athlete.

Perhaps the transformation was due to his still exhilarated mood.

Ever since the call from Chief Justice Maynard two days ago, when the jurist confided that he was resigning from the high court and preparing to speak out against the 35th Amendment, Collins had been unremittingly cheerful. Not even the later news, the night before last at dinner—Ishmael Young's warning to him that he was being secretly investigated by the FBI—had cast a pall on Collins' good mood. Several times yesterday, reflecting on Tynan's behavior, he had weighed confronting the Director and revealing what he knew. Certainly, that would have embarrassed Tynan and put an immediate end to the investigation. But finally, Collins had decided that he didn't give a damn. He'd let Tynan play his useless game. For one thing, Tynan would learn nothing. There was nothing in Collins' past, or in his present activity, to hide. For another thing, his contest with Tynan was just about over. Collins knew that he now held the trump card.

Persuading John G. Maynard to speak out had been the ultimate victory. With this, all tactics of the opposition would be obliterated. Tynan's dream of glory, of gaining dictatorial power through the 35th, would be ended the moment Chief Justice Maynard raised his voice in Sacramento against the Amendment. Even Tynan's mysterious weapon, The R Document, whatever it really was, could be forgotten. Despite Baxter's deathbed warning that it must be exposed, The R Document would be rendered impotent and harmless by Maynard's statement today in Sacramento.

Wiping his face dry, Collins freed a fresh blue shirt from a hanger and put it on. As he buttoned it, he calculated the precise moment of victory for democracy in the United States. The clock on the tiled ledge below his bathroom mirror told him it was exactly eight o'clock here in Washington, D.C. That meant it was five in the morning in California. About now, Maynard would be rising from his bed and preparing for the two-hour drive from Palm Springs to Los Angeles. There, at nine o'clock, as Collins was breaking for lunch here, Maynard would hold his news conference, stun the nation with his resignation, stun all of California with the word that he was flying to the state capital to urge the legislature to vote down the 35th Amendment. There, at three in the afternoon, just as Collins was leaving his office for home and dinner here, Maynard would be reading his electrifying statement against the 35th first to the Judiciary Committee of the State Assembly, then to the Judiciary Committee of the State Senate.

Mere hours from now, the California Assembly would be voting on the Constitutional Amendment, with the Senate voting after that. But it would never reach the Senate. It would die forever in its first test in the Assembly. Maynard's judgment, his influence and prestige, would have carried the day.

Collins found himself whistling, "Glory, glory, hallelujah," realized that that was pretty corny, and stopped. He had pulled on his necktie and knotted it, preparing to join Karen for a hasty breakfast before hurrying to the office, when he heard a knocking on the bathroom door.

"Chris?"

"Yes?"

"There's a gentleman here to see you. A Mr. Dorian Schiller. He says he's a friend."

Collins opened the bathroom door. "Dorian Schiller."

"I didn't recognize the name. That's why I didn't let him in. I'll tell him—"

Karen had started to turn away, when Collins reached out and grabbed his wife by the shoulder. "No, wait, Karen. That's the assumed name I gave Donald Radenbaugh."

"Who?"

"Never mind. I'll explain later. He *is* a friend. Let him right in. I'll be there in a second."

While his wife went off to the front door to admit Radenbaugh, Collins found his suit coat in the dressing room. Slipping into it, he wondered what Radenbaugh wanted at this hour. Since their return from Argo City, he had met with Radenbaugh only once, although he had spoken to him daily on the phone. He had settled Radenbaugh in a two-room suite in the Madison Hotel at 15th and M Streets, and had brought him all available notes and research on an alternative plan to combat crime and disorder in the nation. It was an alternative plan to replace the 35th Amendment, one Collins wanted to introduce at the President's first Cabinet meeting following California's rejection of the 35th.

Radenbaugh's appearance here this morning was a surprise. Collins had made it clear to Radenbaugh that it would be best that he not venture far from the confines of the hotel, that he stick close to his rooms. He had been too well known in Washington. Although his person had been considerably altered, someone who had known him well might recognize him. That could lead to trouble, possibly even to his extinction. Collins wanted him in Washington only long enough to develop the newly devised crime bill, while an effort was made to find him some kind of reasonable job in a small community in a remote part of the country.

Concerned, Collins left his dressing room, passed through the bathroom and bedroom, strode up the corridor, and entered the living room. He expected Radenbaugh to be seated, but Radenbaugh was on his feet, pacing agitatedly. Karen was at the coffee table, setting down a breakfast tray.

"Donald," Collins greeted him. "I hadn't expected you. You've met my wife . . . ?"

Radenbaugh halted, as if he hadn't heard, but Karen called out that they had already introduced themselves. She added, "I brought you some juice, coffee, toast. I'll leave you two to talk."

Karen left them.

Radenbaugh stared at Collins, his face a picture of misery.

"Bad news," he said at last, "very bad news, Chris." Before Collins could react, Radenbaugh went on quickly. "It's been on television since six this morning. I always turn on the set when I get up. I tried to call you right away, but I had misplaced your unlisted number. So I came right over."

Collins did not move. He had a premonition of disaster. "What is it, Donald? You look a wreck."

"The worst news possible." He was breathing like an asthmatic. "Chris, I don't know how to tell you—"

"Dammit, what is it?"

"Chief Justice Maynard and Mrs. Maynard—they were murdered in their beds last night—killed by a common housebreaker."

Collins felt his knees go liquid. "Maynard—murdered? I—I can't believe it."

"In Palm Springs, California, around two thirty this morning. Maynard and his wife, Abigail, they were in bed asleep. As far as can be reconstructed, someone got in through the service-porch door. The person entered their bedroom. Apparently, Maynard was awakened. He tried to get out of bed or made some kind of move. The gunman shot twice with a Walther 9-millimeter P-38—got him in the chest and in the head—killed him instantly. This roused Mrs. Maynard, and the gunman fired three bullets into her—"

"Oh, Christ, I've never heard anything like this!"

"I was shocked out of my skin. I didn't know how to tell you."

Collins moved disconsolately around the room, constantly hitting a fist into the palm of his hand. "A tragedy like that. Who could have imagined? I mean—not only this senseless killing of one of the nation's greatest men—really, one of the greatest—but destruction of our last hope to put an end to the threat of a virtual dictatorship. Dammit, what in the hell is this country coming to?"

"You mean, what will it come to," Radenbaugh said. "Where's your television set?"

"In here," said Collins, starting back into the corridor.

Radenbaugh followed him. "I gather it's been on the tube direct from Palm Springs since six this morning. Let's find out what's happening."

They entered the book-lined paneled study. The television set was built flush into the wall. Radenbaugh sat forward on the couch as Collins turned the set on, waited, adjusted the picture and sound.

Collins took the arm of a captain's chair and drew it up close to the set. Dumbly, he watched what was taking place on the screen.

The camera was panning the front of the contemporary desert house where the tragedy had occurred. A cordon of police was stationed before the walk to the house. Plainclothes detectives kept going and coming through the open front door. Off to one side, dozens of neighbors, many still in nightclothes, stood stricken, observing the scene.

Now the mobile unit's camera held on the network's reporter, moved in close on him.

"This is the scene where the tragedy occurred not three hours ago," the network reporter announced. "Here, on this quiet, peaceful side street of California's most famous resort town, nearly abandoned in the heat of the summer, the Chief Justice of the United States, John G. Maynard, and his wife, Abigail Maynard, met death violently at the hands of an unknown assailant." The reporter, holding his microphone, gestured toward the house starkly illuminated by both police and television lights. "The bodies were removed a little over an hour ago. Not only the bodies of the Chief Justice and his wife, but the body of the as yet unidentified murderer, who was cut down by police bullets before he could escape." The reporter held his microphone higher as he squinted straight into the camera. "Let me recap once more what is known of what happened here in Palm Springs, California, early this morning . . ."

Collins sat mesmerized before the screen, listening.

Apparently, the intruder had been acquainted with the layout of the Maynard home. After coming through the service porch, he had headed for the bedroom, intent on getting Mrs. Maynard's valuables. His entrance into the bedroom had awakened Chief Justice Maynard. The police theorized that Maynard, realizing what was happening, had half risen from his bed, reached out, and pressed a silent-alarm button on the wall. The alarm had been installed by the local police a half dozen years before to give their eminent resident greater security. The silent alarm was connected directly to police headquarters. The police had been alerted at once.

Meanwhile, the moment the killer had seen Maynard move, he had opened fire on him. When Mrs. Maynard had sprung upright, fully awake, he had opened up on her. The two had been shot to death in a matter of seconds. Then, instead of fleeing, the killer had remained in the bedroom to complete his task. Unaware that his first victim had set off a silent alarm, the killer had ransacked the bedroom for money and jewels. Having pocketed Mrs. Maynard's necklaces and rings, and finally the Chief Justice's wallet, he had retreated from the house the same way he had entered. On the front sidewalk, he had started for his Plymouth (rented in Los Angeles earlier) parked two blocks away. Suddenly, he had been caught in the spotlight of a police squad car that was bearing down on him. He had started to run, stopped, spun about, and opened fire on the police officers as they left their car. They had answered him with a hail of bullets, and mowed him down on the sidewalk. Aside from the stolen goods in his pockets, he carried not a thing on his person. His identity remained unknown.

The network reporter had finished his recap. He said, "We now return to our newsroom in Los Angeles for the latest developments in the murder of Chief Justice and Mrs. John G. Maynard."

In his captain's chair, watching, listening, Collins felt utter despair. "What's the use," he said.

"Here, have a cigarette," said Radenbaugh, offering him his open pack.

Collins plucked a cigarette from the pack, then laid it on a table. "I'd better have some coffee first."

He pushed himself out of the chair, made his way to the living room, took up the breakfast tray Karen had left, and returned with it to the study. He poured the lukewarm coffee for Radenbaugh and himself. Drinking from his cup, Collins settled into the captain's chair once more and gave his attention to the screen.

A television newscaster, behind a half-moon desk, had picked up a sheet of paper just placed before him.

"And another late development," he announced. "Chief Justice John G. Maynard's arrival in Los Angeles the day before yesterday was unexpected. Neither members of his staff in Washington nor his colleagues on the High Bench could explain this sudden unscheduled trip. But now we do have a little clarification. Immediately after his arrival in Los Angeles, he and his wife took off for their winter residence in Palm Springs. The morning after reaching his residence, Chief Justice Maynard contacted an old friend in Sacramento, James Guffey, speaker of the State Assembly, and stated that he would like to fly up to the capital the next day—that would have been this afternoon—and appear before the Judiciary Committee of the Assembly. He said that he wanted to discuss the 35th Amendment with the members before it was put to a vote on the Assembly floor. Speaker Guffey was very pleased, and advised the Chief Justice that he would be called as the committee's last and most important witness. Guffy said this morning that he had no idea what Maynard was going to say about the Amendment, that Maynard had not mentioned if he was going to come out for it or against it. Guffey added that during the course of his telephone conversation with Maynard, he had chided the Chief Justice for going to Palm Springs out of season. 'What are you doing there?' Guffey had asked him. Maynard had replied, 'I need some place where I can have some peace and think. I had intended to write my statement here. But I've decided just to spend the day mulling it over, and tomorrow I'll speak to your committee extemporaneously. I have a good idea of what I want to say.' Now death has stilled the Chief Justice's voice, and we shall never know what he intended to say in this all-important matter of the crucial 35th Amendment vote in California. It was also learned that before proceeding to Sacramento, the Chief Justice had intended to hold a news conference at the Ambassador Hotel in Los Angeles. Had he lived, that conference would be taking place a few hours from now. I've just been alerted that the press secretary to the President of the United States is about to read a statement from President Wadsworth relating to the violent and untimely death of the Chief Justice. We now take you to our White House correspondent in Washington, D.C. . . ."

Collins turned away from the television set. He looked at Radenbaugh. "I guess it's our funeral, too, Donald."

Radenbaugh nodded tiredly.

Collins heaved a sigh. The initial shock was over, and he felt only an overwhelming depression. "You know, I can't think of anything worse that's happened in my lifetime." He gestured toward the screen. "Now it's their country."

"I'm afraid so," said Radenbaugh.

They both fell silent, concentrating on the television screen.

The White House press secretary was finishing his reading of President Wadsworth's eulogy and condolences. Collins' attention slackened.

The President's statement contained the usual lofty, banal, sometimes insincere remarks: When a great man dies, part of humanity dies with him. Make no mistake about John G. Maynard's greatness. He now joins the pantheon of immortals who sought to bring a full measure of justice to this land. There stand Marshall, Brandeis, Holmes, Warren, and beside them, as tall, stands John G. Maynard. Now, truly, he belongs to the ages.

And along with Maynard, democracy, too, will belong to the ages, thought Collins. Dead. A relic of the past. Without Maynard, the wave of the future was the 35th Amendment—and Vernon T. Tynan—and the nation would be cast in his mold.

No sooner had he thought of Tynan than he heard Tynan's name announced by the network's White House correspondent.

". . . Vernon T. Tynan. We now take you to the office of the Director of the Federal Bureau of Investigation."

Instantly, Tynan's familiar small head and broad shoulders appeared on the screen. His seamy face was properly set in a look of grief and mourning. He began to read from a sheet of paper in his hand:

"This brutal and senseless slaying of one of the nation's outstanding humanitarians has been a loss that cannot be expressed in mere words. Chief Justice Maynard was the nation's friend, my personal friend, a friend of truth and liberty. His loss has wounded America, but because of him America will become strong enough to survive and will survive all crime, all lawlessness, all violence. I am sure if Chief Justice Maynard were alive, he would want us to view this tragedy in a larger sense. This systematic decimation of our leaders and our citizenry must be brought to a stop, so that Americans can walk their streets and sleep in their beds in the full knowledge that they are safe and free."

Tynan looked up into the camera, seeming to meet Collins' eye as Collins' glare met his.

Tynan cleared his throat. He resumed speaking.

"Fortunately, Chief Justice Maynard's vicious slayer did not escape. He has met his own violent end. I have just been informed that this killer has been fully identified. His identity will be announced shortly by the Federal Bureau of Investigation. Suffice it to say, for now, the killer was a former convict, a man with a long arrest record, yet he was allowed to be free and roam our streets under the ambiguous and loose provisions of the Bill of Rights. Had the Bill of Rights been amended a month ago, this terrible murder might have been averted. While the 35th Amendment would never be put into effect except in the case of conspiracy and rebellion, its passage alone would engender a positive atmosphere that would relegate slayings like these to the past. Ladies and gentlemen, we've learned a lesson today, this day of grief. Let us work together, hand and hand, to make America secure and to keep America strong."

Tynan's face had left the screen, to be replaced by that of a reporter in the network's Washington newsroom.

Ignoring the television set, Collins yanked his chair toward Radenbaugh. He was furious. "That bastard Tynan, how dare he? Did you hear him? Making hay for his goddam amendment before Maynard's body is even cold."

"And twisting it around so that it sounds as if Maynard would actually have welcomed the 35th," said Radenbaugh. He pointed to the screen. "Look, I think they're going to identify the killer."

"What difference now?" said Collins. Nevertheless, he returned his attention to the television screen.

"Yes, we have it," the newsman was saying, "the identity of the person who murdered Chief Justice Maynard. It has just been confirmed and released. The killer has been definitely identified as one Ramon Escobar, thirty-two years old, an American citizen of Cuban extraction, a resident of Miami, Florida. Here are photographs of him from the files of the FBI. . . ."

Immediately, both a full-face and a profile shot of Ramon Escobar were flashed on the screen. The pictures revealed a swarthy, ugly young man with curly black hair, long sideburns, sunken cheeks, and the livid slash of a scar on his jawbone.

"Oh, no!" Radenbaugh gasped. "No . . . !"

Startled, Collins whirled toward him, in time to see Radenbaugh stagger to his feet. Radenbaugh's eyes were wide, his features drained of blood, as he kept poking a finger toward the screen, trying to mouth something.

Confused, Collins came quickly to his feet in an attempt to

calm his companion. The jutting finger Radenbaugh had been poking toward the screen had become part of a fist. Radenbaugh was shaking his fist at the screen.

The quavering words finally came bursting forth. "That's him, Chris!" Radenbaugh shouted. "That's him! That's the one!"

Collins grabbed Radenbaugh. "Donald, get hold of yourself—what is it?"

"Look at him there, the man who killed Maynard! He's the one I saw. Did you hear his name? Ramon Escobar. I heard it— I heard it on Fisher's Island, outside Miami, that night. The face—it's the same face, exactly, I recognize it—the man on Fisher's Island—the one Vernon Tynan had me pass the $750,000 to—the same one, the one who took the three-quarters of a million from me. Chris, for God's sake, do you know what this means?"

Ramon Escobar's face had disappeared from the screen, to be replaced once more by that of the network newsman. Hastily, Collins crossed the study and shut off the television set. He turned around, shaken, remembering Radenbaugh's story of his release from Lewisburg, of his recovering his million dollars from the Everglades, of his taking three-quarters of a million in a motorboat to Fisher's Island to deliver it to the two men Tynan had designated to receive it.

Now Maynard's murderer had proved to be one of those two.

"Believe me, it's the same man, Chris," Radenbaugh was saying. "It means Tynan wanted my money to get rid of Maynard. It means that he had me sprung from prison to get his hands on enough money to pay a professional assassin, money that couldn't be traced, foolproof. Tynan engineered the murder. He was ready to go to any length to prevent Maynard from killing the 35th, even to the length of killing Maynard himself."

"Stop it," Collins said sharply. "You can't prove it."

"My God, man, what more proof do you need? I was there with Tynan when he made me the offer. He got me out of jail, got me a new identity, sent me to Miami and to Fisher's Island, had me turn over three-quarters of a million to—to whom? To the very man who assassinated Chief Justice Maynard last night. What more proof do you need?"

Collins was trying to think, to sort it all out. "I don't need more proof, Donald," he said. "I believe you. But what would anyone else believe?"

"I can go to the police. I can tell them what happened. I can tell them I gave this killer the money on Tynan's behalf."

Collins shook his head. "It won't work."

"Why won't it work. Harry Adcock knows the truth. Warden Jenkins knows the truth—"

"They won't talk."

Radenbaugh had Collins by the lapels of his coat. "Chris, listen. The police will believe me. I'm me. I was there on the island. We can get rid of Tynan. I can tell the whole truth."

Collins removed the hands from his coat. "No," he said. "Donald Radenbaugh could tell the truth. But Donald Radenbaugh doesn't exist—the witness doesn't exist—"

"But I'm here!"

"Sorry. Dorian Schiller is here. Donald Radenbaugh is dead. There isn't a shred of evidence he's alive. He just doesn't exist."

Radenbaugh suddenly sagged. He finally understood. He looked at Collins helplessly. "I—I guess you're right."

As if transformed, infused with a new resolve, Collins came alive.

"But *I* exist," he said. "I'm going directly to the President. Hearsay or not, I believe all you've told me, all I've learned for myself, and I'm going to lay it all out for the President. There's simply too much to be ignored. He's got to hear the facts—that the real lawlessness and crimes in this country are being committed by Vernon T. Tynan. There's no way the President can avoid facing the truth. Once he knows, he'll do what Chief Justice Maynard meant to do—speak out to the public, disown Tynan, denounce the 35th Amendment—and have it voted down once and for all. Pull yourself together, Donald. Our bad dream is almost over."

VIII

THE PRESIDENT OF THE United States sat up straight in the black leather swivel chair behind the Buchanan desk in the Oval Office of the White House.

"Remove him?" he repeated with a slight rise in the inflection in his voice. "You want me to fire the Director of the FBI?"

They had been seated here in the Oval Office—President Wadsworth behind his desk, Chris Collins in the black wooden pull-up chair beside the desk—for twenty minutes, talking. Or rather, Collins had been talking, and the President had been listening.

When Collins had applied for the appointment this morning, the President's calendar had been full. Collins had invoked "emergency," and the President had agreed to give him a half hour after lunch, at two o'clock.

From the moment that he had entered the Oval Office, Collins had ignored the amenities, had planted himself down across from the President and then plunged into his impassioned account. "I think you should know certain things that are going on behind your back, Mr. President, horrendous things," Collins had begun, "and since no one else will speak to you of them, I think I'll have to be the one to do so. It won't be easy, but here goes."

Then, almost in a monologue, Collins had recited the incidents and occurrences that he had encountered from the time of Colonel Baxter's warning about The R Document to Donald Radenbaugh's identification of Chief Justice Maynard's slayer. He had spilled it out nonstop, with a trial lawyer's clarity, omitting no detail.

He had concluded, "There can be no justification on earth for breaking the law to preserve the law. The Director has been the main mover in this. Based on the evidence I've just presented to you, Mr. President, I think you have no choice but to remove him."

"Remove him?" the President repeated. "You want me to fire the Director of the FBI?"

"Yes, Mr. President. You've got to get rid of Vernon T. Tynan. If not to punish him for his criminal actions, then to restore your leadership and safeguard the democratic process. While it will cost you the 35th Amendment, it will preserve the Constitution. And we can work out a better plan to guarantee law and order in this country, one based not on repression and potential tyranny, but on the improvement of the social and economic structure of our society. However, nothing is possible until Tynan goes."

The President had remained remarkably unruffled throughout Collins' recital. Except for smoothing his graying hair, rubbing his aquiline nose, cupping a hand over his receding jaw, he had listened quietly and without any display of emotion.

Now his features still remained phlegmatic. His only movement was to lift an ornate letter opener, absently weigh it in one hand, then put it back down on the desk.

He spoke again. "So you really think Director Tynan deserves to be fired?"

Collins could not be sure whether the President was coming over to his side or merely trying to probe deeper.

One last try, the clincher.

"Absolutely," said Collins emphatically. "The grounds for dismissal are innumerable. Tynan should be removed for unlawful conspiracy, for misuse of his office in trying to get a bill passed that could invest him with superpower. He should be fired for blackmail and interference with due process. The only thing I'm not accusing him of is murder, because I can't prove that. The rest is obvious. With his removal—on whatever grounds you choose, based on the available evidence my office can give you overnight—the 35th will sink of its own accord. But actually, you might undo all the evil that Tynan has done to date by personally undertaking what Chief Justice Maynard had intended to do himself—by speaking out against the 35th and seeing that California votes it down. I don't think that'll be necessary after you're rid of Tynan, but it would be a judicious act and gain you added respect."

The President sat silently for a brief interval, seeming to contemplate all that he had heard. Quite unexpectedly, he lifted himself from his black leather chair, turned his back on Collins, carried his slight, erect frame to the left-hand window framed by green draperies, and stood there gazing out at the White House lawn and at the Rose Garden.

Collins sat taut, waiting. Mentally, he crossed his fingers. The jury on the Tynan case was out. Soon the verdict would be in. The right verdict would solve everything. Collins sat rigid and hoped.

After what seemed an interminable interval, the President stepped away from the window and started back toward his chair. He stopped behind his chair, set his arms lightly on top of it, laced his fingers together, and rested his eyes on Collins.

"Well, now . . ." he said. Then he continued, "I've been considering everything you've told me. I've been examining it closely. Let me tell you how it strikes me. Let me be as frank with you as you've been with me."

Collins gave a short nod, and waited.

"Your grounds for firing Director Tynan," the President said. "Chris, let's try to be as objective as we can. You know the law better than any man. You're the country's first lawyer. You know a person is innocent until *proved* guilty. Theory, rumor, innuendo, suspicion, hearsay, deduction are not factual evidence or irrefutable proof. Your evidence is a tissue of talk, not facts."

Collins came forward in his chair to interrupt, but the President held up the palms of both hands.

"Wait, Chris," he said. "Let me go on. Let me say what I want to say. What are the direct charges you raise against Director Tynan? Let's look at them. You have Tynan tampering with crime statistics in California. Can you prove it, really prove it? You have Tynan building internment camps across the nation. Can you prove it? Can you find me the agency constructing those camps? Can you show me evidence that the structures are meant for dissidents? You have Tynan making a deal with Radenbaugh, freeing this prisoner from Lewisburg, giving him another identity. Can you prove it? Can you prove the deal was made, that Tynan made it, that Radenbaugh is not dead as the prison announced? You have Tynan ordering laundered money to be passed on to Maynard's murderer. Can you prove it? As you have admitted, you can't prove it, can you? You have Tynan using the people of some company town in Arizona as guinea pigs for the 35th Amendment. Can you prove it? We know Tynan has been investigating that town, but can you prove that he was using it instead for some nefarious purpose? You have Tynan as the Professor Moriarty of some sinister plot embodied in something, in some plan, called The R Document. Can you prove it? Can you say you heard this from Colonel Baxter personally? Can you prove this document exists? Or if it exists, that it is dangerous? Can you tell me what it is and where it is?"

President Wadsworth caught his breath, and then went on.

"Chris, what have you got but a fabric sewn together from fanciful speculations and conjecture? Based on these charges, lacking irrefutable evidence, you want me to fire the Director of the FBI, one of the most efficient and popular men in the country? Chris, have you lost your mind? Fire Tynan? For what? Your case is impossible, Chris, impossible."

Collins had recoiled during the last and sat defeated, deflated. He had expected some doubts from the President, some discussion, but not an outright attack on his case.

Desperately, he tried to rally. "Mr. President, proof comes in many forms. I know I could come up with proof that would satisfy you, given time. But we have no time. Get Tynan out of the way first. He's dangerous. We can back up criminal charges against him later. I tell you, from what I've heard and witnessed, Tynan will do anything, absolutely anything, to get rid of the Bill of Rights, to get the 35th passed into law, to destroy this democracy . . ."

The President's face had gone frosty. "I also want the 35th passed," he said. "Does that say I want to destroy this democracy?"

"No, of course not, Mr. President," Collins conceded hastily. "I'm not implying that everyone who supports the 35th is against a democratic government. The fact is, I supported it for a while, went along, publicly. As far as the people out there are concerned, I still support it. I've never denounced it publicly, and don't intend to, as long as I'm part of this Administration."

The President softened slightly. "I'm glad to hear that, Chris. I'm glad you have some sense of loyalty."

"I certainly have," said Collins. "The question is—does Tynan have the same loyalty? It goes beyond that. It goes to a sense of what democracy stands for. You and I know. Does Tynan? In our hands, the 35th would never be misused. But in his hands . . . ?"

"There is not one bit of evidence that he would interpret the law any differently than you and I."

"In the light of all that I've told you, you can say that? Even if I can't prove everything, you've certainly got to admit—"

"It's no use, Chris," the President broke in. He came around his chair and settled into it with an air of finality. "Chris, I'm sorry. I respect facts. I listen to facts. Based on what you've told me, I don't find the facts favoring your side. I don't see sufficient grounds for dismissing Tynan. Make an effort to see it from my point of view. Tynan's reputation as a patriot is impeccable. Removing him on such flimsy evidence would be like arresting George Washington for creating disorder or tossing Barbara Fritchie in jail for subversion. Firing him would be a disservice to the country, and be political suicide for me as well. The public trusts Tynan. People believe in him—"

"Do *you?*" Collins demanded to know. "Do *you* believe in him?"

"Why not?" countered the President. "I've never found him

less than cooperative. He's been one of our best public servants. Occasionally, he's inclined to be overzealous, to cut corners in his eagerness to get things accomplished. But when all is said and done—"

"You intend to keep him and his 35th Amendment," said Collins. "Nothing I can say will dissuade you. You're determined to stand with him."

"Yes," said the President, flatly. "I have no other course, Chris."

"Then I have no other course either, Mr. President," said Collins, rising slowly to his feet. "If you are going to keep Tynan, then you can't keep me. I have no choice but to resign as Attorney General. I'll go back to my office now and write a formal letter of resignation—and spend every hour of the next twenty-four fighting that amendment in the California Assembly, and if I fail there, I'll spend every hour I have left fighting it in the California Senate, if it comes to that."

He gave the President a curt nod, and had started for the nearest door when he heard the President call out his name. He halted at the door and looked over his shoulder.

President Wadsworth was plainly distressed.

"Chris," he said, "before you do anything you'll regret later, think twice about it." He shifted uneasily in his executive chair. "This is a critical period—for us, for the country. This is no time to rock the boat."

"I'm getting off the boat, Mr. President. I'll sink or swim on my own. Good day."

With that, he left the Oval Office.

PRESIDENT WADSWORTH STARED AT the door a long time after Collins had departed. Finally, he reached for his telephone. He buzzed for his personal secretary.

"Miss Ledger? Call Director Tynan at the FBI. Tell him I want to see him alone, as soon as possible."

CHRIS COLLINS' FIRST TASK, upon returning to his office, was to telephone his wife.

Until this morning, he had not kept Karen abreast of all the events that had been taking place in his life during recent weeks. Now and then, since the night he had learned of The R Document, he had told her some of the happenings. But this morning, after viewing the television news reports on the Maynards' murder, and after Donald Radenbaugh had finally returned to his hotel, Collins had gone through the kitchen and sat with Karen in the small dinette and filled her in on everything.

Karen had been aghast. "What are you going to do, Chris?"

"I'm going to see the President as soon as I can. I'm going to lay it all out before him. I'm going to ask him to fire Tynan."

Karen had immediately been apprehensive. "Don't you think that's dangerous?"

"Not if the President agrees with me."

He had been confident, even as he left Karen for the office, that President Wadsworth would agree with him.

Now, four hours later, he knew that he had never been more wrong in his judgment.

Karen answered the phone. Her voice was edgy. "What happened, Chris?"

"The President did not agree with me."

He heard her groan of disbelief. "But how couldn't he?"

"He said I had no proof of anything. He made me sound like a paranoidal idiot. He sided with Tynan right down the line."

"That's terrible. What are you going to do?"

"I'm going to resign, and I told him so. I thought I'd better tell you."

"Thank God." He had never heard her sound more relieved.

"I'll wind up my work here shortly, write my letter of resignation and send it over, then clean out my desk. I'll be a little late for dinner."

"You don't sound happy, Chris."

"I'm not. Tynan goes scot-free. The 35th passes into law. There remains the unfinished business of The R Document. And me, I'm impotent and unemployed."

"You'll get over it, Chris," she assured him. "There's so

much else to do. We'll put the house up for sale. We'll move back to California—maybe next month—"

"Tonight, Karen. We're heading back to California tonight. We're catching the late plane. I want to be in Sacramento in the morning. I want to do some lobbying. The 35th goes to the Assembly floor in the afternoon. If I fail, at least I'll go down fighting."

"Whatever you say, darling."

"I'll see you later. I've got a lot to do."

After hanging up on his wife, Collins considered the work load on his desk. Before he attacked it, there was something else that had to be done. He summoned his secretary.

"Marion, on my appointment schedule—cancel everyone I'm supposed to see today, the rest of the week, and the weeks after."

He saw her raised eyebrows.

"I'll explain to you later. I'll explain before we both go home tonight. Just tell everyone I'll be out of the city. We'll get back to them. Another thing, Marion, book me—and Mrs. Collins—on the latest flight to California tonight—to Sacramento. I'll take care of the hotel."

"But, Mr. Collins, you were going to Chicago tonight."

"Chicago?" he repeated, bewildered.

"Have you forgotten? You're scheduled to address the Society of Former Special Agents of the FBI tomorrow at their convention. You're the main luncheon speaker. Following the speech, you have a meeting set up with Tony Pierce."

He had forgotten completely. During his first week in office he had agreed to address the conclave of the Society of Former Special Agents of the FBI. Along the way, after his private resolution to oppose the 35th, he had also decided to meet with Pierce, his onetime antagonist on television and the head lobbyist of the Defenders of the Bill of Rights. Through his son, Josh, Collins had located Pierce, who had agreed to meet with Collins at the Chicago convention of ex-FBI agents.

"I'm afraid I'll have to cancel that appearance in Chicago, Marion. I've got to go to Sacramento."

"They won't like it, Mr. Collins. You're giving them no time to find a substitute speaker."

"There's always someone," he said brusquely. "I'll tell you what—I'd better talk to them myself. I'll call them after I get some of this work out of the way. As for Tony Pierce, you can handle him. Call his DBR headquarters in Sacramento, locate him, tell him I'm canceling Chicago and ask him to stay put in Sacramento. Tell him I'll see him in Sacramento tomorrow morning. I'll call him first thing in the morning to arrange our meeting. Got it?"

She bobbed her head. "I'll take care of Mr. Pierce." She hesitated. "You really want me to cancel all your other appointments?"

"Everything. No more questions. I've got tons of work."

After Marion had left him, Collins settled down to dispose of all the immediate work—reports and briefs to be read, papers to be signed—on his desk. One of the memorandums, he was pleased to see, was addressed to the Immigration and Naturalization Service: his personal clearance for Ishmael Young's bride-to-be, Emmy, to enter the United States from France. He signed it and took it to Marion, ordering her to dispatch it at once, with a copy to be sent to Ishmael Young.

Returning to his office, he paused before the fireplace to review what was left of his last afternoon as Attorney General of the United States. Next, he would write his letter of resignation. After that, he would clean out his personal effects from his desk drawers and gather up what was his own in the small sitting room beyond Marion's cubicle. Finally, he would call Chicago and get out of the speech he was scheduled to make tomorrow.

First, his letter of resignation.

He walked over to the silver carafe next to the telephone console beside his desk, poured a glass of water, and drank it. He looked at the glass-fronted bookshelves of legal tomes on the wall facing him. He roamed about the huge office, trying to compose his letter. Simple or majestic? Neither. Aggressive or defensive? Neither. At last, he struck the right note. He was tendering his resignation from the post of Attorney General for a compelling reason of conscience. After much soul-searching, he had decided that he could no longer go along with the Administration's stand on the 35th Amendment. He felt that he could better serve his conscience, and his country, by resigning to devote his efforts, unhampered, to opposing passage of the 35th Amendment. The right note.

He hurried back to his desk, pulled out a sheet of his official stationery, and quickly committed to paper what he had composed in his head.

Then he decided that instead of sending the handwritten letter over to the White House, he would have it typed up and would sign it. Photocopies of a typescript letter would be easier for the news media to handle than copies of a handwritten one. Yes, he would have Marion type it, he would sign it, he would have photocopies made.

He reread his letter of resignation, then stood up, seeking means of improving it. He wandered about his office once more, and finally he wandered into the vast conference room next door. Moving across the patterned red carpet, he paused before a painting of Alphonso Taft, Attorney General under President Ulysses S. Grant. He wondered why in the devil that was here, reminded himself to have it removed tomorrow, then remembered that he himself would be removed tomorrow. He continued around the room, past the long conference table surrounded by its sixteen red leather chairs. Before the middle of the opposite wall, he halted, facing the white marble bust of Oliver Wendell Holmes.

It was at the marble bust that his secretary, Marion, caught up with him.

"Mr. Collins," she said breathlessly, "Director Tynan is here to see you."

"Tynan?" he said. "Here?"

"He's in the reception room right now."

Collins was confounded. This was utterly unexpected. Not once during Collins' short tenure of office had Tynan personally come calling at the Department of Justice.

"Well, tell them to send him in."

He speculated on what this was all about. One thing for sure: Tynan was the last person he wanted to see today. He awaited the Director's presence with distaste.

Presently, he saw Vernon T. Tynan's great bulk loom in the doorway to the conference room. Tynan, muscular beneath his tight double-breasted navy suit, came striding toward him. The crabbed features of his face held their permanent scowl, revealing nothing of his mission.

When he reached Collins, he said, "Sorry to break in on you like this, but I'm afraid it's important." He patted the briefcase under his arm. "Something I have to discuss with you now."

"All right," said Collins. "Let's go into my office."

Tynan did not budge. "I think not," he said evenly. He glanced about the conference room. "I think it might be better here." Then he added, "I wouldn't want anyone to overhear what we've got to discuss. I don't think you would, either."

Collins understood. "Vernon, I don't have my office hooked up. I don't believe in taping my visitors."

Tynan merely grunted. "You miss a lot, then." He threw his briefcase on the conference table before the chair next to the head of the table. "Let's sit down. What I have to say won't take long."

Annoyed, Collins took the red leather chair at the head of the table and sat a few feet from the FBI Director. Waiting, Collins found his package of cigarettes, offered Tynan one, was refused, took one for himself, and put his lighter to it. After a puff or two, he drew a glass ashtray closer and said, "Well, to what do I owe the honor of this visit?"

Tynan placed his hands flat on the table. "Let's get right down to it," he said. "I heard from the President a little while ago. I heard you'd just been in to see him. I heard that you intended to resign from office—and I heard the reasons why."

"If you know the reasons why, I guess I don't have to go into them again."

Tynan arched back in his chair, looked Collins up and down, then shook his head. "That was dumb of you," he said with a crooked smile. "Trying to get Vernon T. Tynan fired was a very dumb thing to do. I figured you for being smarter than that."

Collins tried to control himself. "I did what I had to do."

"Did you, now? Well. So did I."

With maddening deliberation, Tynan began to unlock and open his briefcase.

"Yes, so did I," he repeated mockingly. "And since you've been looking into my affairs—and you have—"

"I certainly have."

"—I thought it only fair to take the time to look into your affairs."

"I'm perfectly aware of your recent activities," said Collins. "I knew you were investigating me again."

Tynan glanced at him. "No kidding? You knew and didn't do anything about it?"

"There was no reason to do anything. I have nothing to hide."

"You're sure of that?" Tynan had been going through the contents of his briefcase, and now he removed a manila folder. "Well, anyway, I thought you'd be flattered to know we've looked into you with great care—with tender, loving care."

"I appreciate your interest," said Collins. "Now surprise me. What did you find?"

Tynan's scowl deepened. "I'll tell you what I found. I found something you've deliberately hidden from the public—or, possibly, something that's been hidden from you." He opened the folder, briefly studied what was inside, then met Collins' eyes. "You're setting out to obstruct the one piece of legislation that can save this country from ruin. You've been poking into a lot of people's lives, including my own. You haven't bothered to see if your own house is in order. Well, before you present yourself to the public as Mr. Clean, you'd better be sure your life—and the lives of those around you—is simon-pure."

"Meaning what?"

"Meaning you happen to be married to a woman with a very suspect recent past. I think it might serve us well to discuss your wife's past."

Collins felt a flare of anger at this man who took it upon himself to pry into the personal lives of others. His anger overcame his immediate curiosity about what Tynan had up his sleeve. "Vernon," he said, "I don't know what the hell you are implying, but I'm telling you right now I don't intend to discuss my wife or any other member of my family with you. The Senate held hearings on me. My life is a matter of public record. The Senate confirmed me. There is nothing else to discuss."

Tynan would not be put off. "I'm afraid there is something more to discuss. I think you'll want to talk about it. A little matter that was overlooked in our first investigation of you, a matter you'll very much want to know about."

"I won't have my wife dragged into our differences."

Tynan heaved his shoulders. "Up to you, Chris. Either you listen to me and tell me what to do. Or your wife will have to tell it to a judge and jury again." He paused. "Now, can I go on?"

Collins could feel his heart thump. This time, he remained silent.

Tynan glanced at his papers once more and resumed speaking. "Your wife was a widow when you met her. That was a little more than a year ago. Her name was Karen Grant. Her husband's name was Thomas Grant. Is that right?"

"That's right. You know it's right, so why—"

"It's wrong, and I know it's wrong. Her maiden name was Karen Grant. Her husband's name was Thomas Rowley. Her married name was Karen Rowley."

Collins had not known that, but he was quick to defend her. "So what? There's nothing unusual about a widow's using her maiden name."

"Maybe not," said Tynan. "Or maybe there is. Let me see . . . you met her in Los Angeles, where she was working as a model. Before that, she lived with her husband in—in—"

"Madison, Wisconsin."

"She told you that? She misinformed you. She lived with her husband in Fort Worth, Texas. Her husband died in Fort Worth."

Collins pushed back his chair as if to rise and terminate this inquisition. "Vernon, I don't give a damn."

"You'd better," said Tynan coldly. "Do you know how your wife became a widow?"

"For God's sake, her husband was killed in an accident."

"An accident? Really? What kind of accident?"

"I've never questioned her about it. The subject isn't exactly a pleasant one to revive." Then he added, "I believe he was hit by a car. Does that satisfy you, Vernon?"

"No, it does not satisfy me. According to the FBI records from Fort Worth, he was not hit by a car. He was hit by a bullet—at close range. He was murdered."

Prepared as Collins was for some disturbing information, this was an unexpected blow. His poise dissolved.

Tynan continued relentlessly. "All evidence pointed to your wife as the murderer. She was arrested and tried. After four days of deliberation, she got a hung jury. Possibly because of her father's influence—he was a political bigwig in the area—he's dead now—the authorities decided not to initiate a second trial. She was released."

"I don't believe it," Collins protested. Tynan and the conference room came into and out of focus, and Collins tried to regain his composure.

"If you have any doubts," said Tynan coolly, "this will resolve them." He lifted some papers from his manila file folder and placed them neatly in front of Collins. "A summary of the case, condensed from court records, identified with the appropriate case number. And photostats of three newspaper clippings. You will recognize Karen Rowley in them. Now we get to the crux of the matter. . . ."

Collins ignored the papers in front of him, and held on his adversary and the crux of the matter.

Tynan went on. "The jury did not find your wife guilty. On the other hand, they did not find her innocent. They did not acquit. They disagreed for four days, could not resolve their differences and reach a verdict. They reported a hung jury. As you know better than I, that leaves the case wide open and casts a shadow of doubt on your wife's behavior. This is the part that interested me. I suggested to our agents that they pursue their investigations further. They did. They reconstructed the murder, interrogated the witnesses again, and in the course of their inquiries came up with a new lead. It has proved to be quite valuable. How the local authorities could have overlooked it, I can't imagine. But sometimes they can be slipshod. As you know, the FBI is never slipshod."

Collins did not respond. He waited.

"We have a new witness, one previously overlooked, a woman who claims to have seen Karen Rowley—or Karen Grant or Karen Collins, whichever you prefer—an eyewitness who claims to have heard an altercation, heard Karen tell Rowley she'd like to kill him. The witness decided to leave the Rowleys' house, and as she did so, she had a glimpse of Karen with the weapon in her hand, standing over her husband's body," Tynan paused. "Actually, there's more." His voice dropped. "I hate to get into it. But of necessity, it would come out if the witness took the stand. It's pretty dirty stuff. . . ."

Collins felt the constriction in his chest. He continued to remain silent.

Tynan resumed, picking his words slowly. "Many weekends, your wife used to go visit her father alone. Or say she did. Rowley, her husband, finally became suspicious. He had her followed. He learned—well, how should I put it?—he learned Karen was an active participant in a sex group in Houston. They got together, undressed, indulged in nude sex orgies. And she took part—sometimes with assorted men, sometimes with women, straight sex, perversions . . . I won't go into details, but—"

"That's a filthy lie, and you know it!" shouted Collins, half out of his chair.

Tynan sat unruffled. "I wish it was, but it isn't. Our witness overheard Rowley accuse Karen of all that." His hand moved to the folder. "Would you like to see the testimony that the witness gave us in private?"

"No, thanks."

"Anyway, after that scene, the witness heard the gunshot, and had the glimpse of Karen standing over Rowley's body." Tynan studied Collins briefly, then spoke again. "Now, this witness won't come forward of her own free will. She doesn't want to be involved in such a messy affair. But if forced to testify under oath, she will do so. It would mean a second trial. This time it is unlikely there would be a hung jury. However, it will please you to know, I did not permit my people to submit their new evidence to the District Attorney in Fort Worth. I thought that would be improper without consulting you first. Furthermore, despite her—her own weaknesses—God knows what led her to behave as she did—I have a certain amount of sympathy for Mrs. Collins. In a different way, her husband was an even more unsavory character. He was after her money—her father's money—and he used her. He probably threatened to expose her sexual misconduct to get more money out of her. Some might say she had considerable provocation to act as she did. Certainly that was a consideration in my mind when I ordered the evidence withheld. Finally, perhaps most important, I would prefer not to embarrass a member of the Administration, of the President's team, at a crucial time like this. I think you can understand that. I think everyone connected with the case has suffered enough, and there is no need to make it a public matter again. Under the proper circumstances, it could all be easily forgotten."

Collins was sickened—not only by the information about Karen and the threat to her, but by Tynan's undisguised blackmail. The revulsion he felt toward the man burned inside him. Until now, he had never felt capable of killing another human being. This moment, he wanted to get his hands around Tynan's neck. But he held on to his sanity.

He sat very still, trembling only inside.

At last, he was able to speak. "You're willing to forget it, you say, under the proper circumstances?"

"That's right."

"What are the proper circumstances? What do you want from me?"

"Only your cooperation, Chris," said Tynan blandly. "Very little, actually. Oh, let's say what I'd want from you is your pledge that you'll stay on the team with the President and myself and support the 35th Amendment to the very end. What I would not want from you is any disruptive performance like a resignation at this time or any public statement denouncing the Amendment. That's the price. Very reasonable, I think."

"I see." Collins watched as Tynan closed his folder and carefully returned it to his briefcase. "Aren't you going to let me see the rest of the evidence?"

"I'd better hold on to it for safekeeping. You have enough to go by. You also have your wife. She'll fill you in on anything you haven't heard."

"No, I mean the name of the new witness you found. I'd like to have that, at least."

Tynan smiled. "I think not, Chris. If you want to see the witness, you'll have to see her in court." He locked the briefcase. "I guess I've said about all there is to say. You definitely have enough to go by. What happens next is up to you."

"Vernon, you're the worst slimy bastard that ever lived."

Tynan's smile held. "I don't think my parents would have found that credible." He became serious. "If I have a fault, it is that I love my country too much. If you have a fault, it is that you love your country less. It's because of my country that I want your decision now."

Collins stared at him with loathing. Finally he let go, gave up, and slumped back in his chair.

"Okay," he said wearily, "you win. Tell me again—exactly what do you want me to do?"

IT WAS THE FIRST time in his marriage that he had hated to return home to his wife.

He'd had no stomach for work after Tynan had left him, but he had deliberately stayed on late in the Justice Department, wanting to be alone, wanting to think. He had been torn by conflicting emotions. There was shock at what he had learned of Karen's background. There was disappointment in her for having withheld the events of her recent past from him. There was confusion about her guilt or innocence in her husband's death (a jury had deliberated four full days and still had not been able to clear her). There was fear that harm would befall her now that Tynan was ready to have the case reopened.

Overriding all that was the picture Tynan had painted of Karen's secret sex life on the outside. The naked orgies. The promiscuity. The chain of perversions.

Collins didn't believe it. Not a word of it. Still, the images remained, would not go away.

He had no idea how to feel about her, what stance to take toward her, how to handle her. These attitudes were unresolved in his office, and they remained unresolved now as he inserted the key in his front door, unlocked it, and entered his home.

He wanted to put off the confrontation, avoid her, but he knew it would be impossible.

Apparently she had heard him enter.

"Chris?" she called out from the dining room.

"I'm here," he called back, and headed into the corridor to the bedroom.

He had pulled off his necktie, was divesting himself of his suit coat, when she appeared.

"I've been on tenterhooks all day," Karen said, "ever since you called, just waiting to hear what happened. I started to pack. We are going to California, aren't we?"

"No," he said dully.

She had been walking toward him, to kiss him. She stopped in her tracks. "No?" Her brow creased. She searched his face. "You did resign, didn't you?"

"No, I didn't."

"I—I don't understand, Chris."

"I wrote the letter of resignation. Later I tore it up. After Vernon Tynan came to see me. After he left, I tore it up. I had to."

"You—had to," she repeated. "You tore it up because of—" She looked stricken. "—because of me?"

"How did you know?" he asked with astonishment.

"Because I knew it might happen. I knew he'd do anything to stop you from opposing him. The other night at dinner, when that writer, Ishmael Young—when he said Tynan investigates everyone around him, knows everything about everyone who counts in a person's life—I knew. I knew he might go after you—and find me. I was very scared, Chris. That night, when we were going to sleep, I decided for the hundredth time to tell you. I really meant to tell you. I started to, but you'd already fallen asleep. Then in the morning everything else happened, got in the way. I should have told you. Oh, heaven help me, what a fool I've been. Such a poor secret. One you should have heard from me."

"I should have known, Karen, if only to be able to protect you."

"Yes, you're right. But not to protect me. To protect yourself. Now that Tynan's told you . . . I don't know what Tynan's told you—but you'd better hear the story from me."

"I don't want to hear it now, Karen. I've got to go out of town to deliver a speech. When I get back from Chicago—"

"No, listen." She had come up close to him. "Tynan told you—what? That my husband was killed by a gunshot wound in Fort Worth, in our bedroom? That I'd been overheard more than once saying I wished he was dead? The truth is, we'd had another terrible fight. One of a million fights. I ran out, went to my father's. Then I decided to return home. Try one last time. There was Tom on the floor. Dead. I had no idea who had killed him. I still don't know. But several people had heard us fight, had heard me say I wished he was dead. It's true. I had said it a number of times. Naturally, I was accused. The evidence was flimsy, circumstantial, but we had a new D.A. trying to make a name for himself. I was indicted, tried. It was the worst kind of torment. Is that what Tynan told you? Did he tell you all that?"

"Most of it. He said you got a hung jury."

"That hung jury," she said contemptuously. "Eleven of them were for my acquittal from the first minute. One man, the twelfth, held out for guilty for four days before the jury gave up. That one holdout was finding my father guilty, not me. He'd once been fired by my father, I learned afterward. The D.A.'s office didn't want to try me again because the evidence and jury had been so overwhelmingly in my favor. They knew it was useless. They freed me, and dropped it. To escape the notoriety, I stopped using my married name and left town. I went to work in Los Angeles, where I met you a year or so later. That's all of it, Chris. I never told you because it was past, it was behind me—I knew I was innocent and after I fell in love with you, I didn't want anything to spoil our relationship or put doubts in your mind. I didn't want the sordid affair to soil what was so fresh and lovely between us. I wanted a new start. I should have told you. I should have, but I didn't, and that was a mistake."

She caught her breath. "I'm glad it's out at last. Now you know the whole story."

"Not quite the whole story, according to Tynan," he said. "Tynan's found a new witness, a woman who says she saw you standing over Rowley with the gun. The witness saw you or heard you do it."

"That's a lie! I didn't do it. It's an absolute lie. I came in and found Tom dead. Tom had already been murdered."

Listening to her, watching her closely and uneasily, he listened and watched for truth, and felt he had it, yet the images of her persisted. Karen stripped naked, Karen sick-crazy in a roomful of equally naked strange men and women. Karen locked in perversions with males, with females.

"There's still more, Karen," he found himself saying. He had not meant to speak of the orgies, to give credence to them, but he felt compelled to have it all out. "I don't believe any of it, but I must tell you. The witness told Tynan . . ."

He spilled it out.

As he spoke, her horror mounted. When he was done, she was near collapse. "Oh, no," she whimpered. "No, no—such terrible lies—every word made up, untrue. Absolute fantasies. Me? Behave like that? You know me, Chris, you know me in bed. I'm shy, I— Oh, Chris, you can't believe it—"

"I don't, I told you."

"I swear on the life of the child we're going to have—"

"I know it's not true, darling. But there's a witness who will swear under oath that it is true, that and the murder—"

She seemed to rally her strength. "Who is this witness?"

"I don't know. Tynan wouldn't tell me. But that's what he's holding over our heads. He threatened to open up the case again unless I played ball. So I decided to remain on the team."

"Oh, Chris, no." She went into his arms, fiercely holding on to him. "What have I done to you?"

He tried to soothe her. "It's not important, Karen, darling. All that's important is you. I believe you, and we'll never speak of it again. Let's forget Tynan—"

"No, Chris, you've got to fight him. You can't let him do this.

We've nothing to be afraid of. I'm innocent. Let him reopen the case. In the long run, it won't hurt us. The main thing is, you can't let him blackmail you into silence. You've got to fight back, for my sake."

He disengaged himself from her. "I'm not fighting back, for your sake. I'd never subject you to another ordeal like that. We're just going to forget it and go about our lives as before."

He started to move away, but she followed him across the bedroom. "But it'll never be like it was before. Chris, if you're afraid to fight him over this, you must believe his version of the story, not mine—"

"That's not true! I just won't let you suffer that hell again."

"You're going to give in, keep silent, while the California Assembly passes the 35th tomorrow and the California Senate ratifies it three days later? Oh, Chris, please don't let it happen."

Collins held up his wristwatch. "Karen, look, I've got twenty minutes to change, eat, finish packing, and call Tony Pierce in Sacramento before the driver comes by to take me to the airport. I'm addressing a convention of ex-FBI agents in Chicago tomorrow. I have to be there. I've got to hurry." He took her in his arms and kissed her. "I love you. If there's more to talk about, we'll talk about it tomorrow night."

"Yes," she said almost to herself. "If there is a tomorrow night."

IX

STANDING AT THE PODIUM, before the six hundred assembled guests crowded into the pale gold Guildhall ballroom of Chicago's Ambassador East Hotel, Chris Collins turned another page of the speech he had been reading to the annual gathering of the Society of Former Special Agents of the FBI. He saw that only one more page of his speech remained to be read, and he was grateful.

His delivery of the speech had been lifeless, and the reception until now lukewarm.

Collins was not surprised. There were too many factors that had inhibited both the content of his address and its delivery. There had been lack of concentration. There had been discouragement. There had been caution.

He had been unable to concentrate because his mind had been elsewhere. Back in the conference room of his office suite in the Department of Justice, where Vernon T. Tynan had bested him, blackmailed him into silence about how he really felt. Back in the bedroom of his house, where he and Karen had suffered the revelation of the murder and trial in her past. Back in his native California, where it was early afternoon in Sacramento and where in less than an hour the State Assembly would

convene to become the first of the two state houses to vote on
the 35th Amendment.

He had been deeply discouraged during his flight to Chicago
last night, throughout this morning, and during the meal with
his hosts. His mood of defeat and depression had pervaded his
entire speech. Each succeeding hope to defeat the 35th Amendment in California, in either the Assembly or the Senate, had
been cut down. The death of Chief Justice Maynard had been
the cruelest blow. Maynard, alone, could have turned the tide,
and he had been ruthlessly eliminated at the eleventh hour.
Then, the refusal of the President to dismiss Tynan, which
might have brought Tynan's activities into the open and dam-
aged the Amendment, had been another blighted hope. His own
determination to fight the Amendment alone in these fading
days had been a cause for some small optimism, but Tynan had
effectively suffocated it. There was left only The R Document,
and so far it had eluded him, constantly hidden from sight and
out of reach.

Above all, to the detriment of his speech, he had been shackled by caution. Or maybe fear was the better word—shackled
by fear. The members of the Society of Former Special Agents
of the FBI whom he had come to address were preponderantly
Tynan men. Under J. Edgar Hoover, the society of FBI alumni
had numbered 10,000 former agents. Many of them, after leaving the FBI, had gone on to have successful careers in law, in-
dustry, banking, thanks to Hoover's patronage and support.
Now, in Vernon T. Tynan's tenure, the society of FBI alumni
had a membership of 14,000 men and women—although only a
few were women—and the great majority were still subject to
the FBI discipline ingrained in them and grateful for Tynan's
seal of approval that had helped catapult them upward in their
new careers. For Collins, this was a hostile audience. Not that
they knew he differed from them. Only he knew. But it was
enough to disturb him.

The speech that he and Radenbaugh had prepared had been
carefully honed to suit this audience. Since he knew that he
could not attack the 35th Amendment, Collins had decided to
avoid voicing any opinion on the resolution. He had proceeded

on the assumption that the resolution would be made into law, and had dwelt on the point that more was needed to contain crime and lawlessness in America. He had expounded, in broadest terms, upon the other reforms needed in the country. He had dealt with crime and its causes. He had dealt with the social roots of crime.

He had known, from the start, that this would not excite his pro-Tynan audience. These ex-FBI agents wanted a ringing affirmation of their Director's 35th Amendment. They wanted rockets and fireworks proclaiming the death of the obstructionist Bill of Rights and the birth of the new Committee on National Safety headed by Tynan. Instead, they had got the wet blanket of social reform. They had been let down and bored.

Also, Collins had been conscious of the fact that the audience was infiltrated by Tynan's spies and informers, ready to report to the master any deviation Collins made from the text ordained by the Director. Anticipating this, after his confrontation and deal with Tynan yesterday, Collins had reworked his speech several times on the flight to Chicago and in his hotel suite this morning, watering it down constantly until it was a puddle. Any slip into dissent, he was aware, spelled a special kind of doom for Karen.

He knew, of course, that there was also a small coterie of listeners in the audience who were anti-Tynan and anti-35th. He did not know who they were, but he did know that Anthony Pierce was their leader. Collins had even been cautious about contacting Pierce late last night and again this morning. It would be dangerous for Karen if Tynan learned that he had sent for Pierce and was meeting with him privately after the speech. This morning Collins had gone to an obscure telephone booth outside the hotel to call Pierce. He had arranged to meet with Pierce not in his own suite but in an unoccupied single room of the Ambassador Hotel—reserved under another name—after he had finished speaking and had left the ballroom. They had agreed to watch the live television report on the California Assembly vote in this room, and if necessary, he would risk revealing to Pierce his defection from the Administration's stand on the 35th and help the lobbyist in any strategy possible to defeat it in the State Senate three days from now.

All of this had been on Chris Collins' mind as he had tried to read meaning into his address.

He had reached the last page of his speech. He tried to devote himself to it, to infuse it with feeling.

"And so, friends, we have arrived at the crossroads," Collins continued. "We are on the threshold of dramatically changing the Constitution of the land in our pursuit of law and order. But to maintain a peaceful society of human beings, more, much more, is needed. I have outlined some of these needs here today. Allow me to summarize them in the words of a former Attorney General of the United States."

Collins paused, scanned the rows and rows of faces before him, and then undertook to quote the words of this former Attorney General.

"He reminded us firmly to remember the following: 'If we are to deal meaningfully with crime, what must be seen is the dehumanizing effect on the individual of slums, racism, ignorance, and violence, of corruption and impotence to fulfill rights, of poverty and unemployment and idleness, of generations of malnutrition, of congenital brain damage and prenatal neglect, of sickness and disease, of pollution, of decrepit, dirty, ugly, unsafe, overcrowded housing, of alcoholism and narcotics addiction, of avarice, anxiety, fear, hatred, hopelessness and injustice. These are the fountainheads of crime. They can be controlled.' We must act now. Thank you for your kind attention."

He had not told them the name of the former Attorney General he had quoted. He had not told them the words had originated with Ramsey Clark.

The applause was light, and his agony was over.

He returned to his seat, relieved, shook a few limp hands, and prepared to wait out the last speakers and final business of the formal convention.

Half an hour later, he was free. He left the Guildhall ballroom and was joined by Hogan, his bodyguard, who saw him up in the elevator to his corner suite, 1700–01 on the seventeenth floor. At the door, he told Hogan that he would be in his suite the rest of the afternoon. He suggested this was a good time for Hogan to go down to The Greenery, the hotel's café, and grab a bite to eat. The bodyguard was quick to assent.

Once inside his suite, Collins waited a brief interval, then opened his door and glanced into the corridor. It was empty. Hastily, he slipped out of his rooms, found the stairs, descended to the fifteenth floor, and located the unoccupied single room with the number 1531 on its door. Making certain he had not been followed, he entered it, leaving the door ajar.

He took inventory of the room. A double bed. An armchair. Two straight chairs. A dresser. A television set. Unprepossessing for a member of the President's Cabinet, but it would do the job.

He was tempted to telephone Karen in Washington, if only to reassure her again. He considered the wisdom of using the telephone, but before he could decide, he heard a short knock on the door. He spun about prepared to greet Tony Pierce alone, but to his surprise not only Pierce entered the room but two other men as well.

Collins had not seen Pierce since they had been adversaries on the television show *Search for Truth*. He cringed inside at the remembrance of his role and performance on that show, and he wondered what Pierce must be thinking of him at this moment.

On the surface, Pierce seemed to display no resentment and no reluctance about their second meeting. The freckled, frank face beneath the head of sandy hair was as good-natured and enthusiastic as ever.

"We meet again," he said, shaking hands with Collins.

"I'm glad you could come," said Collins. "I wasn't sure you would."

"I welcomed the chance," said Pierce. "I also wanted you to meet two of my colleagues. This is Mr. Van Allen. And this is Mr. Ingstrup. We were all together in the FBI, and we resigned within a year of one another."

Collins shook hands with each of them. Van Allen was a blond with a prominent jaw and restless eyes. Ingstrup had a shock of chestnut hair and a weather-beaten visage that sported an untidy brown moustache.

"Do sit down," Collins said. As the others took their places on the bed and the two chairs, Collins remained on his feet. "You must wonder why I asked you to meet with me here," Collins said to Pierce. "You must wonder what we have in common to talk about. In your eyes, I'm FBI Director Tynan's superior, and a Cabinet member in President Wadsworth's Administration, a cabal that is advocating passage of the 35th. In my eyes, you are the hard-core opposition to the 35th. Don't you find it surprising that I wanted to see you?"

"Not at all," said Pierce, fishing for his pipe and finding it. "We've been keeping an eye on you, even up to early yesterday afternoon when you were planning to go to California to testify against the 35th Amendment. We know where you're at today."

Collins was genuinely startled. "How could you possibly know that?"

"Since we can trust you now, we can tell you," said Pierce cheerfully, enjoying this. As he tamped tobacco into the bowl of his pipe, he went on. "After the three of us left the FBI, we went our own ways. I formed a law firm. Van Allen here has a private detective agency. Ingstrup is a writer, with two exposés of the FBI under his belt. We all shared a single belief. That Vernon T. Tynan, for whom we'd worked so long a time, was a dangerous man, dangerous for the country. We saw him becoming more threatening every year. We found other former FBI agents around the United States who felt precisely as we felt. All of us still possessed the discipline, know-how, skills we had learned and practiced in the FBI. We asked ourselves, Why not put all this knowledge into practice? Why not work to protect each other, to save the FBI from that megalomaniac, and to defend democracy itself? So, at my suggestion, we set up a loosely knit, unpublicized organization of ex-FBI agents who would be fact finders and investigators—to counter Big Brother, who was watching our every move. We don't have an official name, but we like to call ourselves the IFBI—the Investigators of the Federal Bureau of Investigation. We have sympathetic informers everywhere. We have six in your Department of Justice, including two in Tynan's J. Edgar Hoover Building. We gradually learned of your defection to our side. Yesterday we learned you were planning to fly to Sacramento. From our previous dossier on you, we deduced that you were making the trip to break from the President and Tynan and to denounce the 35th publicly."

"That's correct," admitted Collins.

"Yet you are not in Sacramento this minute," said Pierce. "You are here in Chicago. In fact, I was surprised when I found the message from you last night. I worried that your change of travel plans might mean your political plans had changed again also. But then I decided that this could not be, or you would not have wanted to see me."

"Once more, correct," said Collins. "My politics remain the same. I'm wholeheartedly against the 35th. I wanted to go to Sacramento to fight it. At the last minute, something came up—"

"Tynan came up," said Pierce simply.

Collins wrinkled his forehead. "How did you know?"

"I didn't," said Pierce, "but I was sure."

Van Allen spoke for the first time. "Tynan is everywhere. Never underestimate him. He's all-knowing and he's vindictive. He picked up where J. Edgar Hoover left off. Remember Hoover's OC—Official and Confidential—files? Hoover had his gumshoes getting information on Dr. Martin Luther King's sex life. He had personal information on Muhammad Ali, Jane Fonda, Dr. Benjamin Spock, and at least seventeen high Government officials, Congressmen, newspapermen. Well, that was amateursville compared with what Vernon T. Tynan has done. He has tripled Hoover's OC files. He has used them consistently for blackmail. For the good of the country, he would tell you—"

"Patriotism," interrupted Ingstrup, "is the last refuge of a scoundrel, to quote Dr. Samuel Johnson."

"Absolutely," Van Allen went on. "When Tynan assigned me to investigate the personal lives of the Senate and House majority leaders—that was some time before the 35th was presented to Congress—I guess he wanted to be sure it passed—I went to him and objected. I told him I'd prefer another assignment. 'I'll be happy to arrange that, Van Allen,' he said to me. The next thing I knew, I had been reassigned—away from the Washing-

ton office. I was notified of my transfer to the FBI field office
in Butte, Montana. That's Tynan's Siberia. I got the message. I
resigned."

"That's right," said Pierce. "When I mentioned the fact that
all three of us had resigned from the FBI, I didn't mean we did
so amicably. Van was to be sent into exile, as he's told you, and
he quit. Ingstrup was the main speaker at his daughter's high
school graduation. He spoke of the role of the FBI in our
democracy, and made the mildest suggestions for a reform or
two in the Bureau. It got back to Tynan overnight. Immediately,
Ingstrup was demoted, his job downgraded, and he resigned.
Still Tynan was not satisfied. When Ingstrup tried to get another
job in law enforcement, Tynan's long arm followed him. Tynan
informed one and all that Ingstrup had a dishonorable record
with the FBI. When Ingstrup turned to free-lance writing, his
first book was a critical assessment of the FBI's operation. Tynan set out to block the publication of the manuscript. He was
successful enough so that Ingstrup had to settle for a vanity
publisher. Fortunately, the book became a big seller."

"And what about you?" Collins inquired.

"Me?" said Pierce. "I protested Ingstrup's demotion. I defended him. Tynan's only response was a curt memo notifying
me of my transfer to Cincinnati, Tynan's second Siberia. I knew
the FBI held no future for me after that. So I quit. No, Chris—
if I may call you Chris—nobody tangles with Tynan and wins."

"You're tangling with Tynan now over the 35th."

"And I don't expect to win," said Pierce. "But I'll give it the
old college try. Anyway, when you said you had planned to oppose Tynan but something had come up to change your plans, I
knew the something was someone named Tynan. I assume
you're not going to come out in the open on our side."

"I can't," said Collins helplessly. He studied the three in the
room with him, these veterans of Tynan, these men who had
gone out on a limb to oppose the Director of the FBI and his
mammoth apparatus, and he suddenly felt close to them. They
had gained his confidence completely. He decided to tell them
how Tynan had, at the last minute, rendered him impotent. "All

right, I guess there's nothing to hide. I'll tell you why I can't side with you in public."

Pierce offered him a half smile. "You can trust us, Chris."

Collins pondered how much to tell them, even where to begin. "I went to see President Wadsworth yesterday. I told him that I had information that Tynan had been responsible for the murder of Chief Justice Maynard—"

"Wow!" Pierce exclaimed. "We hadn't heard that. Do you know it to be a fact?"

"I believe it to be a fact. I have it from a person who was involved. But I can't prove it. I couldn't prove that, or a number of other things, to the President. Nevertheless, I laid out a good case against Tynan. I demanded that the President fire Tynan. He refused. I told him that I had no choice, then, but to resign and go to California and take a public stand against the 35th Amendment. I was prepared to do so, as you have learned."

"But then you ran into Tynan," said Pierce.

"Exactly. The next thing I knew, there he was in my office in person."

"To blackmail you into silence," said Ingstrup.

"Yes, he was ready to blackmail me," said Collins.

Pierce was refilling and lighting his pipe. "Tell us what happened."

Haltingly, Collins complied. He related every detail of the evidence Tynan had collected against his wife, and of the new eyewitness being held in the wings.

"There was nothing subtle about it," Collins concluded. "He offered me the terms of surrender. I could not resign. I could not go to California. I could not voice my opposition to the 35th. If I accepted these terms, Karen was safe. Her case in Fort Worth would not be reopened. If I defied him, went ahead, then Karen would have to stand trial again. I had no place to go. I surrendered on his terms."

"But she told you she was innocent," said Van Allen.

"Of course she did. She *is* innocent. I believe her. Still, I couldn't let her be put on the rack again. I had to give in." He threw up his hands. "And here I am—Samson with a crew cut."

He saw Pierce glance at Van Allen, who gave an almost imperceptible nod, then saw Pierce look at Ingstrup, who also nodded. Pierce's gaze rested on Collins once more. "Maybe we can help you, Chris," he said.

"How?"

"By getting into this ourselves, with our little counterforce, our IFBI. We have one of our best men in Texas—a rancher, Jim Shack. He was an FBI agent for ten years, but he became fed up after Tynan became Director. We have two others down there, still members of the FBI, who hate Tynan. They might be able to do a lot for you—maybe even give Samson a hairpiece."

"I don't know what they could do."

"For one thing, they might check out your wife's old case, find out what it was really all about. Then, they might poke around, try to find out if Tynan actually has a new witness, as he claims—or if he's faking, rigging a blackmail scheme on evidence that doesn't exist."

"I hadn't thought of that."

"You'd better. It's barely possible."

Collins frowned. "I don't know. I don't like to take the risk. If Tynan found out—"

"Jim Shack and the other men are very discreet. They're better than the best Tynan has today."

Collins was still worried. "Let me think about it."

"There isn't much time," Pierce reminded him. "The California Assembly votes today—"

"Hey!" exclaimed Van Allen, jumping out of his chair. "It's on television. We almost forgot."

He hastened to the television set on the dresser.

"Yes," said Pierce. "Let's see if all our lobbying with the Assemblymen did any good. If they should vote against it, it's all over for Tynan, and our work is done. But if they pass it—"

"What are the odds?" asked Collins, finding a seat in the armchair.

"At last count, the Assembly was leaning toward passage. It's the State Senate that's a flip of the coin. Yet you never can tell. Let's see."

The television set was on. All four in the room gave it their undivided attention.

The camera was focused on the gold-lettered motto over the framed portrait of Abraham Lincoln above the elevated speaker's rostrum. The motto read, LEGISLATORUM EST JUSTAS LEGES CONDERE.

"What does it mean?" Van Allen asked.

"It means, 'It is the duty of legislators to make just laws,'" explained Collins.

"Ha," said Pierce.

The camera was slowly pulling back to show the desks below the speaker's rostrum where bills and resolutions were processed. Now the camera revealed the eighty Assemblymen at their individual desks in the chamber and the standing microphones in the five aisles.

The third and last reading of the resolution, the 35th Amendment, was taking place.

"Section 1. Number 1. No right or liberty guaranteed by the Constitution shall be construed as license to endanger the national security. Number 2. In the event of clear and present danger, a Committee on National Safety, appointed by the President, shall meet in joint session with the National Security Council. Number 3. Upon determination that national security is at issue, the Committee on National Safety shall declare a state of emergency and assume plenipotentiary power, supplanting Constitutional authority until the established danger has been brought under control and/or eliminated. Number 4. The chairman of the Committee shall be the Director of the Federal Bureau of Investigation."

"Tynan, the Tynan clause," Pierce said to no one in particular.

The reading on the television set continued.

"Number 5. The proclamation shall exist only during such time as the emergency is declared to be in effect, and shall be automatically terminated by formal declaration upon the emergency's resolution. Section 2. Number 1. During the suspensory period, the remainder of all rights and privileges guaranteed by the Constitution shall be held inviolable. Number 2. All Committee action shall be taken by unanimous vote."

The hushed voice of the network newsman came on.

"The critical vote is about to begin. Each Assemblyman votes by moving a toggle switch at his desk. If he votes 'Yes,' a green bulb lights up alongside his name on the scoreboard in the front of the chamber. If he moves his toggle switch to 'No,' a red bulb lights up alongside his name. Keep your eye on the electric scoreboard, where the votes are automatically totaled. A mere majority will pass this Constitutional Amendment. That means, if the total vote in favor reaches forty-one, the 35th Amendment is passed in this chamber. A vote of forty-one opposed means it has been voted down. If it is voted down, that would spell the end, the death of the much-debated 35th Amendment. If it is passed, that would put the final decision as to its ratification or rejection into the State Senate of forty members three days from now." He paused. "The vote is beginning."

Collins sat glued to his chair, watching.

The bulbs were lighting on the screen, as the minutes ticked by.

Collins watched the electric scoreboard and the tallies. The green bulbs dominated the screen. The count moved to thirty-six, then to thirty-seven, then thirty-eight, thirty-nine, forty, forty-one.

A roar of delight could be heard from the visitors' gallery, intermingled with groans, and now this was interrupted by the voice of the newsman.

"It's over in the California State Assembly. The 35th Amendment has gained its majority vote, forty-one votes out of eighty. It has been passed in the first of the two houses. Now its fate is entirely in the hands of the California State Senate less than seventy-two hours from now."

Pierce left the bed and turned off the set. "I was afraid of that." He studied the others. "Looks like our work is cut out for us." He stepped toward Collins, who was sitting stiffly in the armchair. "Chris, we need all the help we can get from you. Let us try to help you, so that you can be free to help us."

"You mean Karen?"

"Your wife. Tynan's blackmail. Let me get Jim Shack and the other two into Fort Worth."

The discouraging event on the television screen had already made up Collins' mind for him. "Okay," he said, "go ahead. I appreciate your offer." He had decided that his last hope lay with these three men. "As a matter of fact, there's something else you might help me with, if you can. It's something which, if exposed, could defeat the 35th in the Senate."

"Anything that can do that gets my help," said Pierce, returning to his place on the edge of the bed.

Collins had come to his feet. "Have any of you ever heard about a paper, possibly a memorandum, called The R Document?"

"The R Document?" repeated Pierce. He shook his head. "It doesn't ring a bell. No, I haven't heard of it."

Van Allen and Ingstrup also signified they had not heard of it.

"Let me tell you about it, then," said Collins. "It all began the night Colonel Noah Baxter died. I first learned of it a few days later . . ."

Omitting no detail, Collins revived the familiar cast of characters and recapped the events of recent weeks, as the other three listened enrapt. For an hour, Collins talked—about Colonel Baxter, the Colonel's widow, The R Document ("danger—dangerous—must be exposed . . . I saw—trick—go see"), Josh's Tule Lake internment camp (Pierce had nodded knowingly), Assemblymen Keefe and Tobias and Yurkovich and the doctored crime statistics, Warden Jenkins and Lewisburg Penitentiary and Susie Radenbaugh and Donald Radenbaugh himself, Radenbaugh and Fisher's Island, Chief Justice Maynard and Argo City, Radenbaugh and Ramon Escobar.

Everything was laid out before them, except the most important evidence of all. The R Document. That remained missing.

When he was done, his voice hoarse, Collins expected to find incredulity in their faces. Instead, they seemed unmoved, as they considered what they had heard.

"You're not shocked?" Collins said.

"No," replied Pierce. "It's because we've seen too much, heard too much, know too much about Tynan."

"You believe me, don't you?"

"Every word," said Pierce, rising to his feet. "We know Tynan is capable of—and has the capability to do—anything to satisfy his own ends. He's utterly ruthless, and he's going to win, unless we take advantage of our own capability. If you give us your full cooperation, Chris, we'll set our entire counterforce of ex-FBI agents and informers into motion within hours. I want you to stay here tonight, Chris. You can go back to Washington in the morning. I'll send Van out for some food and drinks. Let's hole up here until midnight and work out our plan. Then the three of us will separate, hit the pay phones, get the lines buzzing to our counterforce members. By morning they should all be on their assignments. How does that sound to you?"

"I'm ready," said Collins.

"Great. The most important contacts we'll reserve for ourselves. Fast as possible, we'll have to go over the ground you've already covered. I know you did a thorough job, but investigation is our life. We might be able to elicit information you couldn't. Further, people you've already seen may remember some detail during a second telling that they'd previously overlooked. I'll interrogate Radenbaugh again myself. Van Allen will go to Argo City to case the town once more. Ingstrup will sit down with Father Dubinski. And you, I think you should see Hannah Baxter again, Chris. I think you could do better with her than any of us. Is that okay?"

"I'll see her again," promised Collins. "What about Ishmael Young?"

Pierce considered this, then shook his head. "No. I'm sure he's on our side, but he's too close to Tynan. He might let something slip accidentally. If that happened, all our heads would roll." He paused. "Now, is there anyone else?"

Collins had a thought. "Ishmael Young mentioned, the last time I saw him, that Vernon Tynan has a mother. She's in the Washington area. Tynan sees her once a week."

"No kidding? Tynan with a mother. I can't believe it."

"It's true."

"Well, obviously, we wouldn't dare interview her. But still—who can tell? Let me sleep on it. Any other ideas, Chris?"

"No."

"Well, we have more than enough to go on—certainly enough to keep us occupied in the seventy hours we have left. Now let's take off our coats and ties, get Van to bring up some drinks, and settle down to some real planning."

"What's left to plan?" asked Collins.

"Our field force, remember? I'll contact Jim Shack to get into Fort Worth tomorrow to tackle your wife's case. But we have more than fifty other men and women almost Shack's equal. They're going to be looking at every rock Tynan ever lived under. No stone will be unturned."

"Do you think we have a chance?"

"If we have good luck, Chris."

"What if Tynan finds out?"

"That would be bad luck," said Pierce.

IT WAS NINE EIGHTEEN in the morning when Chris Collins returned to Washington. His limousine was waiting outside National Airport. He ordered Pagano to take him directly to his house.

Opening his front door, he let himself in quietly, assuming that Karen might still be asleep.

He went through the house and entered the bedroom, intent on changing his clothes and getting back to the office as soon as possible. He saw at once that the bed was made. Wondering where Karen was, he backtracked through the house, calling her name, expecting to find her in the kitchen. She was not in the kitchen.

Collins returned to the bedroom. The house was unnaturally still. He entered the bathroom and immediately saw the note scotch-taped to the mirror. He pulled it free, recognizing Karen's handwriting, and from the time scrawled on it he realized that it had been written the night before. With some apprehension, he began to read it.

> *My darling,*
>
> *I hope this doesn't upset you. I'm really doing this for our sake. I'm leaving for Texas on a late plane.*
>
> *I feel miserable about what I've done to you. I should never have withheld anything at all about myself from you. I should have known that as a public figure you were vulnerable, and I should have known that someone like Tynan would ferret out the information about me and misuse it. I swear to you that I am innocent.*
>
> *I'm afraid, however, I have not fully convinced you. The fact that you would not allow this to come out into the open, were afraid of a second trial (for my sake, I know), tells me you don't know how that trial might end. I have no fear of that, but I know you have.*
>
> *Anyway, since you would not defy Tynan (because of me), I've decided to defy him myself. I've decided to go to Texas, find his so-called new witness, and wring the truth out of her. I did not want to wait till you came home. I did not want you to talk me out of this. I want to prove my absolute innocence—to you, to Tynan, to everyone—no matter how long it takes, and I felt that only I myself could do this.*
>
> *Don't try to find me. I'll be in Fort Worth staying with friends. I won't be in touch with you until I've solved our problem. Don't worry. Let me do this my way. The important thing is—I love you. I want you to love me—and trust me.*
>
> *Karen*

Collins dropped the note on the sink, and rocked back on his heels, dazed. Her act was the last thing on earth he had expected. She had hoped this would not upset him, she had written. She had hoped right. He wasn't upset. He was stricken. The thought of his pregnant wife alone somewhere in Texas, somewhere in Fort Worth, out of reach and deeply troubled, was almost more than he could handle. He was tempted to take the first flight to Fort Worth and try to find her. But that would be a needle-in-the-haystack undertaking. Yet something must be done.

Before he could put his mind to it, he heard the telephone ringing in the bedroom.

With a silent prayer that it might be Karen, he hurried to the phone and picked up the receiver.

It wasn't Karen. He recognized the male voice. It was Tony Pierce.

"Good morning, Chris. I came in on American right after you. I'm in Washington now."

"Oh, hi . . ." He almost addressed Pierce by his first name, but caught himself in time, remembering the ground rules worked out in Chicago last night. No mention of Pierce and his friends on the telephone.

"One thing to report," said Pierce. "We just got information that Vernon Tynan is flying to New York on business tomorrow night, and then going on to Sacramento. He's scheduled to make a personal appearance Friday before the State Senate Judiciary Committee. He's going to give the 35th a strong pitch. He'll be the last witness before the bill goes to the Senate floor."

Collins was still too distraught about his wife to react to the news about Tynan or consider its implications. "I'm sorry," he said, "but I'm afraid I won't make much sense right now. I just came home and found a note from my wife. She's—"

"Hold on," Pierce interrupted. "I can guess. But don't discuss it on your phone. Are there any public phone booths in your neighborhood?"

"Several. The nearest—"

"Don't tell me. Just go there. Call me. I'll be waiting. I gave you my number last night. Do you have it?"

"Yes. Okay, get right back to you."

Collins snatched up Karen's note and hastened out of the house. The official limousine was waiting, and Collins signaled his driver to stand by, then called out to Pagano that he'd be right back.

A few minutes later, he had walked two short blocks and

turned into the filling station. He made his way to the telephone booth, closed himself inside, deposited his coins, and dialed Tony Pierce.

Pierce answered immediately. "You can talk now," he said. "It's safe. Did your wife run off?"

"To Texas. She wants to vindicate herself."

"I'm not surprised."

"Well, I am. I can't understand her doing it. I realize she wants to clear herself for me, but that means defying Tynan. It's foolhardy. She should know better. She should know that nobody can beat Tynan at his own game. Trying to snatch one of Tynan's witnesses from under his nose and wring the truth out of her. Karen doesn't realize how dangerous that can be."

"You mentioned she'd left you a note," said Pierce calmly. "Do you mind reading it to me?"

Collins pulled Karen's note out of his pocket and read it to Pierce.

When he finished, he said, "I've got a good mind to go to Fort Worth today and try to find her."

"No," said Pierce firmly. "You stay put. We'll find her for you. I'll notify our man down there—Jim Shack, remember?— and get him on her trail. It would save time if we had some leads. Her note says she's staying with friends in Fort Worth. Do you have her address book at home?"

"We keep a joint address book. But I think she has an old one of her own around somewhere."

"Good. The minute you get back to the house, dig up that old address book, if she left it behind. Then— No, better not read those addresses from your phone—use another pay phone on the way to the office—then read me the names and addresses of all of Karen's friends in the Fort Worth–Dallas area. I'll pass them on to Jim Shack."

"Very well."

"I'll also have Jim Shack find Tynan's star witness. Your wife would be too emotional to handle her. But Shack can tackle the job."

"Thanks, Tony. Only—how are you going to find Tynan's witness? He wouldn't let me see his file."

"No problem. I told you we have two informers in the FBI building. One is a night man. He'll get a chance to peek at the dossier on Karen after Tynan and Adcock have gone home. He'll relay the name of the witness to me and I'll pass it on to Shack. Trust us to handle this. Your wife—and her case—are in good hands."

"I can't tell you how grateful I am, Tony."

"Never mind," said Pierce, "we're all in this together. I'd like to spring you in time to get to California and counteract Tynan's testimony. If he's the only Government witness, he'll stampede the Senators into passing the Amendment. My other hope is that we can nail down The R Document by tomorrow. We're seeing Father Dubinski and Donald Radenbaugh for follow-up interviews in the next few hours. What about you? Are you going back to see Hannah Baxter today?"

"She couldn't make it today. I phoned her from Chicago—from the airport—this morning. Woke her up, but she was nice about it. She agreed to see me tomorrow morning. We have an appointment at her place at ten."

"Okay. If there's anything new, I'll call you at your office. Is your phone clean for incoming calls?"

"It will be by the time you call. I'm having it debugged every morning now."

"Good. I'll be in touch."

FOR THE FIRST TIME in many years, Vernon T. Tynan was on his way to see his mother on a day that was not Saturday.

Besides the fact that it was Wednesday, there were other unusual aspects to Tynan's visit to Alexandria. For one thing, he had not bothered to bring his OC file on celebrities. For another, he was not going to have lunch with his mother. For yet another, it was not a quarter to one but three fifteen in the afternoon.

What had inspired this precedent-shattering trip was a telephone conversation Tynan had had with his mother no more than ten minutes ago. She did not call him regularly, but occasionally she did call, and this had been one of the times.

"Am I disturbing your work, then, Vern?" she had asked.

"No. Not a bit. How are you? Is everything all right?"

"Never better. I was just wanting to thank you."

"Thank me?"

"For being such a thoughtful son. The television set works perfectly now."

He had not known what the devil she was talking about. "What do you mean?" he had asked.

"I want to thank you for having the television set fixed. The repairman came late this morning. He said you'd sent him. It is very nice of you, Vern, to think of your mother and her problems when you are so busy."

He had been silent as he tried to assemble his thoughts.

"Vern? Are you there, Vern?"

"I'm here, Mom. Uh—I may see you in a little while. I have some business in Alexandria. I'll put my head in for a minute."

"That's an unexpected treat. Again, thanks for sending the repairman."

After he had hung up, Tynan had tilted back in his chair, still trying to sort it out.

It could have been a mistake, the wrong address. Or it could have been something else. In any case, one thing for sure: He had not sent any television repairman to fix his mother's set.

Immediately, he had heaved himself out of his chair to find his driver and car and get himself over to Alexandria as fast as possible.

Now, having arrived before his mother's apartment in the Golden Years Senior Citizens Village, he left the back seat and entered the building. He tested her alarm button, uttered an expletive because it was not on, then let himself into the apartment.

Rose Tynan was in her contour chair before the television set. She was watching an afternoon variety show. Tynan absently brushed her cheek with a kiss.

"You're here," she said. "I'm so glad you could come. Can I get you a bite?"

"Never mind, Mom. I stopped by for only a minute." He indicated the set. "So it's better now. I can't remember—what was wrong?"

"What?" she asked over the din of the television program. With a wheeze, she leaned forward and lowered the volume.

"I was trying to remember what was wrong with the set."

"Sometimes the picture jumped around."

"So the repairman came this morning? At what time?"

"Maybe eleven or a little after."

"Was he wearing a uniform?"

"Of course."

"Do you remember what he looked like, Mom?"

"What a silly question," said Rose Tynan. "He looked like a repairman. Why?"

"I wanted to be sure they sent out their best man. How long was he here?"

"A half an hour, maybe."

He wanted to pursue this without worrying her. "By the way, Mom," he said casually, "did you watch him fix it, to see he was doing his job? Were you in the room with him all the time?"

"We talked a little while. But he was very busy. Finally I went to do the dishes."

"Okay." Tynan walked over to the sofa and looked at the black telephone on the stand beside it. "Mom, where can I find a screwdriver?"

With an effort, she struggled out of the contour chair. "I'll get it. What do you need with a screwdriver?"

"I thought I'd check your telephone while I'm here. I couldn't hear you very well when you called. Maybe I can adjust it."

The moment that his mother returned with the screwdriver, Tynan disconnected the base of the telephone. Next, he removed the casing. The inner mechanism lay bare. He began to examine it minutely.

After an interval, he exhaled softly, murmuring, "Ahh."

He had located the monitor—a transmitting bug smaller than a thimble encased in adhesive and resin—the electronic eavesdropper that picked up both sides of a conversation on an FM receiver hidden somewhere else in the city where the conversation could be taped. The device was the very one the FBI had been using.

Tynan extracted the monitor from the telephone, pocketed it, and restored the casing and base to the telephone.

"Was something wrong, then?" Rose Tynan asked.

"Yes, Mom. It's okay now." The important thing was what they—whoever they were, exactly—had picked up on the telephone since this morning. He tried to remember if he had told his mother anything of importance, in the last several Saturdays, that she might have repeated today to a friend on the phone.

"Mom, have you used the telephone today? Not early this morning, but since around eleven o'clock?"

"I'm trying to remember."

"Try hard. Anybody call you? Or did you call anyone?"

"Only one call to me. Mrs. Grossman."

"What did you discuss?"

"It was for a few seconds. About a new recipe she found. Also, I talked to you."

"That's all?"

"Yes, that's all. Except—wait—was it today?—it was today—I had a long talk with Hannah Baxter."

"Can you remember what you two talked about?"

Rose Tynan began to recite the matters she and Hannah Baxter had discussed. It was all trivial, inconsequential. "She tries to keep busy," Rose Tynan was concluding. "She misses her husband so much. Having her grandson, Rick, in the house means she's not alone, but it's not like having your close one, especially when he was the Attorney General. Of course, she will have the Attorney General there tomorrow—"

Tynan had been only half-listening, but now he perked up. "What do you mean, having the Attorney General there tomorrow? Maybe you're confused. Noah was Attorney General, but he's dead."

"She meant the new Attorney General—what's his name?"

"Christopher Collins?"

"That's the one. He's coming to see her tomorrow morning."

"Why? Did she say why?"

"I don't know. She didn't say."

"Collins going to see Mrs. Baxter," he said more to himself

than to his mother. "Well, now. What time did you talk to Hannah Baxter on the phone?"

"On the phone? I didn't say I talked to Hannah on the phone. I talked with her in person. She dropped by to have coffee with me this morning."

"In person," Tynan said, with relief. "Good. Well, I've got to run, Mom. Got a lot to do before going to California tomorrow. And one thing. Don't let in any more repairmen without checking with me first. Just call me first."

"If that is what the Director wants."

"That's what I want." He kissed his mother on the forehead. "And thanks for all the news."

"What news?" she asked.

"I'll tell you someday." With that, he departed in haste.

IT RAINED THE NEXT morning, and the sky over Washington was dark and heavy as Chris Collins rode from the Department of Justice to the Baxter residence in Georgetown.

Throughout the drive, Collins' mood had matched the weather. He had rarely been gloomier. Since yesterday, there had been no calls whatsoever from Tony Pierce or Van Allen or Ingstrup. Apparently their interrogations and investigations in the capital, and those by their colleagues around the country, had produced no clues that might lead to discovery of The R Document. Worse, there had been no word from Jim Shack in Fort Worth about Karen. Tomorrow afternoon, at the far end of the country, in the California State Capitol, the 35th Amendment would be put to its final vote before the forty members of the Senate. A majority vote was needed to ratify. That was twenty-one members. According to an exclusive story in *The Washington Post* this morning, a source close to President Wadsworth had disclosed that Presidential pollster Ronald Steedman had informed the President that the latest and closing confidential count of the California Senators had revealed that thirty were going to vote to ratify the new amendment. By tomorrow night the 35th Amendment would be a part of the Constitution of the United States. The future had never looked so bleak to Collins.

He realized that his Government limousine had pulled up before the old white brick three-story house in Georgetown. It was exactly ten o'clock in the morning. He was right on time for his appointment with Hannah Baxter.

As Special Agent Hogan opened the rear door for him, Collins instructed his driver, Pagano, "You can wait right here." Stepping out of the car, he added to Hogan, "I shouldn't be long. Just stand by."

Going up the stairway guarded by the iron grille, Collins was too disheartened to have any expectations about this visit. He had seen Hannah Baxter once, at the outset of his hunt for The R Document, and she had been able to offer him very little. True, she had led him to Donald Radenbaugh, which had been something, but not quite enough. He doubted if she would have more to offer the second time around. This was an exercise in futility, he was certain, but he had promised Tony Pierce he would try again, and so he was trying.

He had rung the doorbell. Instead of the maid, it was Hannah Baxter herself who opened the door.

Her plump countenance was as hospitable as ever. "Christopher, how good to see you again." Once inside, she accepted his kiss, then held him off. "Well, let me see. You're looking splendid—well, maybe a bit tired. You mustn't overwork. It's what I always told Noah. I was right, you know."

"You're looking better than last time, Hannah. How are you getting along?"

"Managing, Christopher, just managing. Thank heavens I have little Rick around. When he goes to school in the afternoons, I'm absolutely lost. His parents are coming back from Africa next week. I think they'll let him stay with me until the semester's done. Maybe all summer, too. How's Karen?"

Collins wanted to tell her, but it would be too complicated, would involve Tynan, and he thought better of it. "Oh, she's fine, never better. She sends her love."

They had reached the living room.

Hannah pointed ahead to the sliding glass doors visible through the partially drawn heavy maroon draperies. "Look at the rain. Too bad I couldn't arrange sunny weather for you. We could have sat in the patio. No matter, let's make ourselves comfortable here."

Collins waited for Hannah to settle on the sofa, and then he sat down in the high-backed armchair in front of the draperies across from her.

"Is there anything I can get for you, Christopher?" she asked. "Coffee or tea?"

"Not a thing, Hannah. I'm perfectly content. I want to talk a little business. It won't take long."

"Go right ahead."

"As a matter of fact, it has to do with the same business I came to see you about last time, shortly after Noah's death. Do you remember?"

Her brow furrowed. "Not exactly. So much has happened . . . I think it was about some papers of Noah's you were trying to find, wasn't it?"

"Yes. Let me refresh your memory. It was about one missing paper I was trying to find, one connected with the 35th Amendment, a supplementary paper. Noah had wanted me to dig it out and review it. He said it was called The R Document. But I've never been able to find it. Yet I must. The last time, I asked you if you ever heard Noah mention it. You said he hadn't. I was hoping, if we tried again, you might remember some occasion when he—"

"No, Christopher. If I'd heard him mention it, I'd remember. But I never heard of anything called The R Document. Noah rarely discussed his work with me."

Collins decided to attempt another approach. "Did you ever hear Noah mention a place called Argo City? It's a town in Arizona that the Justice Department has been interested in." He repeated the name slowly. "Argo City."

"No, never."

Disappointed, he determined to go back over some old ground once more. "Last time I was here, I asked you if Noah had any old friends or business associates he might have confided in, someone who might help me find The R Document. You suggested I see Donald Radenbaugh in Lewisburg Penitentiary, which I appreciated."

"Did you see Donald Radenbaugh?" Hannah wondered.

"No. I tried to, but he had died before I could meet with him."

"Poor man. That was a tragedy. What about Vernon Tynan? Did you ask him about The R Document?"

"Right after I saw you. But he was of no help."

Hannah Baxter shrugged. "Then I'm afraid you're out of luck with that R Document, Christopher. If Vernon Tynan couldn't help you, I'm sure there is no one else who can. As you know, Vernon and Noah were very close—that is to say, they worked closely together on the 35th Amendment. In fact, on Noah's last night—Vernon and Harry Adcock were right here in this room conferring with Noah, working with him, when he had his stroke. It happened in the middle of their conversation that night. Noah suddenly had a seizure, pitched over, and fell to the floor. It was terrible."

Collins had not heard this before. "You mean, Noah was with Tynan and Adcock the night he was stricken? I never knew that. Are you sure?"

"I'm not apt to forget," Hannah said sorrowfully. "It was an unusual meeting. Noah made it a point—for my sake, I think—rarely to work at night. Oh, he worked by himself often. But I mean, to meet with other people. I remember Vernon was insistent upon seeing him that night, and he came right after dinner."

"And Harry Adcock was with him?"

She hesitated. "I'm almost certain. I'm sure about Vernon, of course. But—it was a confusing evening—I could be mixed up. Do you want to know if Harry was here also?"

"Well, it's probably not important—"

"No, I don't mind checking it for you," she said, rising. "Noah's appointment book might tell us. It's somewhere in his study. I'll find it."

She left the room. Collins sank back in the armchair, realizing he had learned nothing useful from Hannah Baxter. He sat there, plunged deeper in discouragement than ever, with nowhere else to turn, utterly lost.

He thought he heard a sound beside his chair, below it and behind it—a kind of rubbing or shuffling. He snapped his head to the left in time to see the maroon drapery mysteriously sway-ing. He looked down, and the bottom of the drapery was rising, and from beneath it crawled a boy. It was Rick Baxter, Han-nah's grandson, coming forward on his knees, his ever-present portable tape recorder in his left hand.

"Hey, Rick," Collins called to him, "what were you doing there behind the drape—eavesdropping on us?"

"The best hideout in the place," said Rick, flashing a grin that revealed the braces on his teeth.

"How's your tape recorder been working?" Collins asked.

The boy stood up, pushing his shaggy brown hair away from his eyes. He patted the leather case that enclosed the recording machine. "It's been working perfectly since you fixed it, Mr. Collins. Want to hear it?"

Without waiting for an answer, Rick pressed the rewind but-ton, hypnotically watched the tape reverse, stopped the ma-chine, then pressed down the forward button.

Rick thrust the machine out, closer to Collins' ear. "Here, lis-ten. I just recorded you and Grandma."

With a shake of his head, Collins bent nearer the tape recorder and listened.

There was Hannah's unmistakable voice, and the fidelity of the taping, even done from behind the drapery, was remarkable.

"What about Vernon Tynan? Did you ask him about The R Document?"

Then his own voice. "Right after I saw you. But he was of no help."

Then Hannah's voice again. "Then I'm afraid you're out of luck with that R Document, Christopher. If Vernon Tynan couldn't help you, I'm sure there is no one else who can. As you know, Vernon and Noah were very close—that is to say, they worked closely together on the 35th Amendment. In fact, on Noah's last night—Vernon and Harry Adcock were right here in this room conferring with Noah, working with him, when he had his stroke. It happened in the middle of their conversation that night. . . ."

"Remarkable, Rick," interrupted Collins. "I've heard enough. I'm going to be careful when I come here next time."

The boy had quickly pressed the stop button on the machine. "It's all right, Mr. Collins. I'm not employed by a Government agency. It's just my hobby."

Collins still pretended to be impressed. "Well, you did that very neatly. You could get work as an FBI agent."

"Naw, I'm not old enough. But it is fun playing FBI. I'll bet you I've made a hundred recordings from behind that drape. Nobody ever knows I'm there. Except once, when Grandpa caught me doing it."

"Your grandpa caught you?" said Collins.

"He saw part of my shoe sticking out under the drape."

"Did he mind?"

"Oh, he was sore, all right. He told me never to play a trick like that again."

Unaccountably, Collins stirred in his chair. He looked down at the boy. "I'm sorry, Rick. I didn't get what you were just saying. What did your grandpa tell you when he caught you behind the drape?"

"To never do it again, that if he ever saw me play a trick like that again he'd punish me."

"I see."

That instant Collins didn't see, only felt, but the next instant he did see.

He sat stock-still.

Noah Baxter's last words, dying words, flooded back: *The R Document—it's—I saw—trick—go see.*

Rick Baxter's last words, just now: *If he ever saw me play a trick like that again he'd punish me.*

Noah Baxter: *I saw—trick.*

Rick Baxter: *Saw me play a trick.*

Had the Colonel, with his last feeble words, been trying to direct Collins to Rick—or Rick's trick? His behind-the-draperies eavesdropping?

I saw—trick—go see.

Had the Colonel in his last conversation with Tynan, minutes or seconds before his stroke, seen the flutter of the drapery, the toe of the boy's shoe protruding beneath the drapery, and known the boy had taped their secret—and remembered it after recovering briefly from his coma?

Had he tried to tell Collins: *I saw trick,* meaning *Rick?* Or meaning *I saw* Rick's *trick* and now you *go see* him?

See what? See if Rick had taped that last confidential conversation—because it held a clue to the secret of The R Document?

Could this be? Could it possibly be?

Collins blinked down at Rick, who was still seated cross-legged on the floor beside the chair.

Collins cleared his throat, then tried to keep his voice natural. "Uh, Rick, I meant to ask you . . ." He hesitated.

The boy had looked up. "Yes, Mr. Collins?"

"Just between us, of course, but despite your grandfather's warning never to try that trick again—hide behind the drape to record someone—did you ever—Well, did you ever do it again?"

"Oh, sure I kept on doing it. I did it lots of times."

"Weren't you afraid your grandfather would catch you?"

"No," said Rick with assurance. "I was careful. Besides, that made it more fun, taking the risk."

"Well, you were pretty brave," said Collins. "Did you make any tapes of your grandfather himself?"

"Of course. Mostly him. He was the one always in here talking. You should hear some of the tapes I made of him."

Collins stared at Rick. Go carefully, his inner voice told him—very carefully. Don't frighten him. "So you kept taping your grandfather. Even up to the last night when he was with Director Tynan and he suffered his stroke?"

Collins held his breath.

"Yeah," the boy said. "Though it was pretty scary hiding there after everybody started running around."

"You mean after your grandfather had his stroke?"

"Yeah." He held up his tape recorder. "But I got every word before that."

"No kidding, Rick. I can't believe it. You actually got Noah—your grandfather—his last conversation with Director Tynan—you got it all on a tape?"

"It was easy. Like I got you a few minutes ago. Director Tynan was sitting right where you're sitting now. Grandpa was sitting where Grandma just sat. Mr. Adcock was in that chair over there. They talked about The R Document the way you and Grandma were talking about it just now."

Slowly, Collins sat upright, feeling the chill beneath his skin and the goose pimples rising on his arms. Noah Baxter's last words, and his own hunch, had paid off. He fought to keep his tone calm. "You say Director Tynan and your grandfather talked about The R Document? You heard them speak of that? No mistake?"

"Grandpa didn't talk about it. Only Director Tynan did."

"When was that, again?"

"Before they took Grandpa to the hospital. The last time Director Tynan was here. He was talking to Grandpa when Grandpa suddenly got sick."

"And you heard every word Director Tynan was saying?"

"Sure," said Rick. "I was behind the drape there like I was just now. I had my recorder on. I taped them the way I taped you."

"Did the tape come out okay? I mean, could you hear their voices clearly?"

"You heard this machine, it's perfect," said Rick proudly. "I played back the tape the next morning when Grandma was at the hospital. It didn't miss a thing. It was all there."

Collins clucked his tongue. "That's quite a machine you've got. I'll have to get one just like it." He paused. "Uh, what about that tape? Did you erase it? Or do you still have it around?"

His heart stood still as he waited for the boy's reply. "Naw, I never erase tapes," Rick said.

"Then you have it here?"

"Not anymore. I didn't keep any with Grandpa on them. When Grandpa got sick, I took the last tape—I wrote on it 'AGG,' which means 'Attorney General Grandpa,' and when it was made, 'January'—I took it and all the others and I put them in the open top drawer of Grandpa's special file cabinet along with his own tapes he made, so they would be safe."

"And Grandpa's file cabinet was moved out of here, wasn't it?"

"Yeah. Just for a while."

"Rick, do you remember what was on that last tape you made of Grandpa and Director Tynan? Do you remember what was said about The R Document?"

Collins waited. He knew the old cliché was true. People did wait with bated breath.

The boy had screwed up his face. "I didn't listen very hard— I just wanted to make my tape. The next morning, when I played it over, I just wanted to see if I got it all."

"But you must remember something that you heard. You said you heard Director Tynan speak of The R Document."

"I did," Rick insisted. "He talked about it. I don't remember any more. Director Tynan kept talking. Then Grandpa got sick suddenly—and there was all kinds of running around, and Grandma crying—and I got real scared, and shut off the tape, and stayed hidden until the ambulance came. When everyone was by the door, I got out from under the drape and ran up to my bedroom."

"That's all you remember?"

"I'm sorry, Mr. Collins, but—"

He clapped the boy on the arm. "It's enough," he said gratefully.

Hannah Baxter was returning to the living room. "Is that boy being a pest again and bothering you with his tape recorder, Christopher?"

"Not at all. We've been having a good talk. Rick has been very helpful to me."

"About Harry Adcock," Hannah said. "I just checked Noah's appointment book. Yes, he had both Vernon and Harry marked down for a visit that night."

"I thought so," said Collins. He winked at Rick, then came to his feet. "I'd better get going, and I do mean going. Thank you for your time, Hannah. And you, Rick, thank you, too. If you're ever looking for a job at the Justice Department, call me."

As he went out the door, Collins was sure it could not be raining or cloudy anymore. But it was raining still and cloudy still. The sunshine was in Collins' head. There was only one dark spot.

Noah Baxter's personal file cabinet, with Rick's telltale tape, was sitting in the private office of the Director of the FBI in the J. Edgar Hoover Building.

"Pagano," Collins said as he entered his limousine, "let me off at the first pay phone you see. I've got a very important call to make."

X

IT WAS LATE AFTERNOON when the limousine deposited Chris Collins before the ornate red building that housed the Government Printing Office.

"Park anywhere between G and H," Collins instructed Pagano. "You can watch for me in about half an hour."

He went past a group of young blacks who were chatting near the entrance, continued inside, but did not bother to enter the Publications Room. After consulting his wristwatch, he retraced his steps to the front sidewalk. He glanced about cautiously to see if he was being followed. There was no one suspicious in view. He felt fairly certain that Tynan would not bother to have him shadowed—not since their showdown and his surrender. Despite this, he had earlier given a spare house key to Pierce's colleague Van Allen, so that he could conduct an electronic sweep of the house to make sure it was safe for phone calls and talk this evening.

Satisfied, Collins started walking in the direction of the City Post Office. At the corner of E Street, he turned left and headed for Union Station.

The rain had stopped, and the air was clean. Breathing deeply, Collins walked rapidly, in long strides, feeling elated, filled with excitement and anticipation. It was going to be difficult, he knew, but now there was a chance.

Approaching the classic Roman façade of Union Station, he went past the fountain and statues in the station's plaza, dodged several taxicabs filled with passengers, ignored the line of recent arrivals waiting with their bags for transportation, and went inside.

The huge grotto inside Union Station—derived from the central hall of the Baths of Diocletian, he had once read—was almost empty. He sauntered toward the book-and-magazine stand to his left, peered in as he bought a copy of the *Washington Star,* and decided that he had arrived first.

They had chosen the waiting room of Union Station as a safe rendezvous point because FBI agents never left Washington by train anymore, not even for the short run to Philadelphia. In Tynan's regime they had all become airplane or helicopter men. The appearance of an FBI agent here now would be spotted instantly, and measures could be taken to avoid him.

Collins found a seat on an unoccupied chair facing the station's entrance, opened his newspaper wide, but did not bother to read. Over the top of it, he kept his eyes fixed on the door.

He did not have to wait long. In a matter of minutes, the middle-aged man with sandy hair came jauntily through a door. He looked in Collins' direction, gave the briefest nod, and walked on toward the magazine shop. He browsed among the racks briefly, picked up a paperback, paid for it, and crossed the station toward Collins.

Tony Pierce settled down on a chair a few feet from Collins.

"I can't get over it," Pierce said in an undertone. "It's fantastic. The kid, Rick, really got it all on his Mickey Mouse recorder?"

"So he says. It's probably a very good machine. Rick left no doubt that the fidelity of the recording was perfect."

"And he heard Tynan speak of The R Document?"

"Absolutely."

"How do we recognize the tape?"

"It's a Memorex cassette, and it's labeled 'AGG,' and it's dated 'January' in Rick's hand. It would be easy to find among

Noah's tapes. Noah used miniature Norelco fifteen-minute tapes—2¼-by-1½-inch cassettes—for his home dictation."

"You've done your homework," said Pierce, pleased.

"The question is not how to identify the tape," said Collins. "The question is how to get to it. I told you. It's in the top drawer of Noah's file cabinet in Tynan's office."

"I've done my homework also," said Pierce. "Tynan will be in his office until eight forty-five tonight. He will then leave directly from his office to fly to New York, and from Kennedy he'll catch the eleven-o'clock flight to San Francisco, and then drive to Sacramento."

"So far, so good."

"His office will be empty. We'll be nearby. The moment we're notified the coast is clear, you and I will enter the Hoover Building by a 10th Street door. I told you we have two informers in the FBI building, and one is on the night shift. He'll let us in. He'll see that the door to the Director's office is unlocked."

"But Noah's file cabinet may be locked."

"Oh, it will be," Pierce promised. "It's an old-fashioned Victor Firemaster cabinet with a combination lock. I'll unlock it. I told you we've done our homework, too."

"Great," said Collins with admiration.

"Now, about your wife—"

"Yes?"

"Just to put you at your ease. Jim Shack knows where she is in Fort Worth. She's all right."

"Where is she?"

"Shack didn't say. Never mind. More important, we had a peek at Tynan's dossier on Mrs. Collins' case. We have the name and location of the witness Tynan is keeping under wraps. An Adele Zurek. She now lives in Dallas. Does Zurek ring a bell?"

"Karen never mentioned her."

"I thought not. She was a part-time housekeeper. On the days your wife's regular housekeeper was off, Mrs. Zurek filled in. Jim Shack was going to see her this afternoon. If he has anything to report, he'll call you tonight."

"But we'll be out."

"He knows. He'll call you after ten, and keep trying until he gets you."

"Thanks, Tony."

"Now, tonight. E Street and 12th. That's two blocks from the FBI building. There's a hamburger joint with a neon sign over it reading 'Fill-Up Cafe.' Be there at eight thirty sharp."

"I'll be there," Collins assured him. "I just hope we can pull this off," he added anxiously.

"Don't worry about that," said Pierce. "Just hope what's on that tape is worth all the effort."

"Noah was the one who linked The R Document to the 35th—who warned that it was dangerous, had to be exposed. We'll have to trust him."

"It better be good," said Pierce. "Because it's our last shot before tomorrow. All our chips are riding on it." As he stuffed the paperback in his pocket, he glanced around. "Okay, I'll go first. See you tonight."

"Tonight."

IT WAS EIGHT THIRTY in the evening when Chris Collins, tense with trepidation, left the taxicab at E Street and 12th. Three doors from the corner, a red-and-white neon sign read FILL-UP CAFE.

The counter was busy, but only a few of the white Formica tables were occupied, and the one farthest off in the corner was occupied by Tony Pierce.

Collins threaded his way through the restaurant and sat down beside Pierce, who was coolly finishing the last of his hamburger sandwich. "Just on time," Pierce said, between bites.

"I'm nervous as hell," Collins admitted.

"What's there to be nervous about?" asked Pierce, wiping his mouth with a napkin. "You're only going to visit the FBI Director's office. You've been there before."

"Not when he wasn't in it."

Pierce chuckled. "You've got a point. Now let's skip a beat. What are you going to do after you get your hands on the goodies?"

"Well, Rick's tape may only tell us where The R Document can be found."

"Whatever. What do you do when you have the tape?"

"If it's as strong, as damning as Noah indicated, I'll call Sacramento immediately. I'll track down the Lieutenant Governor, since he's president of the California State Senate. I'll tell him I have vital evidence that is material to the final vote on the 35th Amendment and request that he schedule me for an appearance before the Judiciary Committee in the morning, right after Tynan makes his pitch. Hopefully, that should swing it."

"Perfect," said Pierce. "Tomorrow night at this time we should be celebrating in a classier restaurant."

"It's a long way to tomorrow night," said Collins.

"Maybe. Come on and join me in a cup of coffee. We still have a few minutes."

They had been served their coffee, and were just beginning to drink it, when Pierce pointed past Collins toward the door. "Here he comes."

Collins looked off.

Van Allen was approaching between the tables and the counter. He reached their table, bent low. "All clear," he whispered. "Tynan left for the airport ten minutes ago."

Pierce set down his cup, placed a tip on the table, and pushed back his chair. "Let's move."

After Pierce had paid the check, they emerged into E Street. They walked swiftly, silently, the two blocks to their destination. No one spoke until they reached E Street and the corner of 10th, where the massive, buff-colored, colonnaded concrete FBI structure loomed up before them across the way.

"I'll part with you here," Van Allen said. "I'll station myself across from the parking ramp. Just in case something goes wrong and Tynan happens to return. If that happens, I'll get to you before he does. Good luck to both of you."

They watched him leave. Pierce took Collins by the arm. "Let's go fast now."

They crossed the street and hastened along the 10th Street side of the J. Edgar Hoover Building. Pierce went up the steep stretch of steps two at a time, with Collins trying to follow closely behind. At the locked glass doors above, there was no one in sight, but a figure abruptly materialized out of the inner shadows. He unlocked a door and held it ajar.

Pierce pushed Collins ahead of him, into the building's public walkabout, then slipped in after him. Collins had only the briefest glimpse of the agent who had left them in. A youngish man, with a thin face, wearing a dark suit. The man was whispering something to Pierce, who nodded, gave a half salute, and caught up with Collins.

"I hope you're in good shape," Pierce said under his breath. "We're to bypass the elevator, and the escalators aren't working. We're to take the fire staircase to the seventh floor."

They started toward the stairs and began to charge up them, Collins trying hard to stay close to Pierce. At the third landing, Pierce rested a moment, allowing Collins to catch his breath, and then resumed the ascent.

They attained the seventh floor without encountering a soul. Except for their footsteps, as they circled the central well, there was a tomblike silence.

They had reached a door with the legend DIRECTOR OF THE FEDERAL BUREAU OF INVESTIGATION.

Pierce beckoned Collins past it to a second, unmarked door. He put his hand on the doorknob and tried it. The door gave, opened. Pierce went in, with Collins right behind him. They had entered directly into Tynan's private office, the room dimly illuminated by the small lamp beside the sofa.

Collins stood unsteadily, taking in the office. Tynan's desk was to the left in front of the windows looking out on 9th Street toward Collins' own Department of Justice headquarters. To the right was a seating arrangement: sofa, coffee table, two armchairs.

There was no file cabinet to be seen.

"It's in his dressing room," Pierce whispered, pointing across the coffee table to the open doorway.

They went between the coffee table and chairs and through the doorway into the narrow dressing room. Pierce sought the light switch, found it, and turned on the overhead fixture. They were standing in front of Noah Baxter's green Victor Firemaster filing cabinet.

The combination lock was on the third drawer down.

Pierce tried each drawer. Each was securely shut.

Pierce rubbed the fingers of his right hand along his thigh. "Okay," he whispered, "let me work on it. Should be easy."

Deft as a safecracker, Pierce twirled the knob of the combination lock. Collins looked on, constantly aware of the passing minutes. Only three minutes had passed, but they seemed like hours, and for Collins the suspense was becoming unbearable.

He heard Pierce utter a happy sigh, saw him try the third drawer, saw it partially pull out.

Pierce straightened up, yanked open the top drawer, and stepped back.

"All yours, Chris."

Heart pounding, Collins came forward. He looked down into the front half of the top drawer, which was neatly stacked with miniature Norelco cassettes encased in small plastic boxes, and beside them were a half dozen larger cassettes of the type that Rick had been using.

He had raised his hand to reach into the drawer when suddenly another shaft of light entered the dressing room and the sound of a grating voice behind them paralyzed him.

"Good evening, Mr. Collins," the voice greeted him. "Don't bother."

Collins spun around, as Pierce beside him had already done.

The bathroom door was wide open now, and filling it was the compact form of Harry Adcock. His countenance was scarred by an ugly smile.

He held out the palm of one hamlike hand, and in his palm lay a Memorex cassette tape. The plastic casing had already been pried open.

"Is this what you're looking for, gentlemen?" he asked. "The R Document? Well, here it is. Let me give you a better look at it." With his fingers gripping the two sides of the cassette, he pulled the plastic casing apart. Then, his gaze never leaving them, he looped a finger under the tape inside, loosened it, and slowly unwound it. Tossing the plastic casing on the carpet, he dangled the thin brown tape before them.

From the corner of his eye, Collins saw Pierce's hand dip to his coat pocket, but then he saw that Harry Adcock's free hand had moved even faster to his shoulder holster and already held a snub-nosed black .357 magnum revolver, which he pointed at both of them.

"Don't try, Pierce," he said. "Here, Mr. Collins, hold this tape for me a moment." He dropped the tape in Collins' lifeless hand, moved sideways, frisked Pierce, and located and pocketed Pierce's .38 Police Special. He smiled at both of them. "A shoot-out between the Deputy Director of the FBI and the unofficial assistant to the Attorney General wouldn't read well in the press, would it?"

He then reached out and recovered the tangled strand of tape from Collins.

"That's the nearest you'll get to The R Document, Mr. Collins."

Holding the tape in one hand, the gun in his other hand still trained on them, he retreated toward the bathroom and slowly began to back up inside it.

"Have your last look," he said. "It was never a document, you know. Never on paper. It wasn't supposed to be on tape, either. The most important things on earth are usually in people's heads and no place else."

Adcock's leg had bumped up against the toilet bowl. He dangled the loose tape over the toilet.

"Wait a minute," Collins implored him. "Just listen to me—"

"First you listen to this." Adcock dropped the tape into the toilet bowl, leaned backward, pressed down on the handle, and flushed the toilet. He seemed amused by the rushing, receding sound of the water. He grinned. "Down the drain—like your hopes, Mr. Collins." He emerged from the bathroom. "Now, what did you want to say, Mr. Collins?"

Collins bit his lip and said nothing.

"Very well, gentlemen. I'll see you out." He waved his revolver toward Tynan's office.

Adcock remained at their heels until they reached the center of the office. Then he moved crabwise away from them to the Director's desk, where he put his free hand on Tynan's large, silver-colored tape recorder.

Adcock addressed himself to Collins. "I don't know what kind of Attorney General you are, Mr. Collins, but I sure as hell know you wouldn't make even a half-assed FBI agent. A good agent doesn't overlook a thing. You and your boys debugged most of the city to conceal your secret visit here tonight, but there's one thing you didn't debug."

He pressed the PLAY button on Tynan's machine.

The voices through the loudspeaker were loud and clear and identifiable.

Rick's voice: "When Grandpa got sick, I took the last tape—I wrote on it 'AGG,' which means 'Attorney General Grandpa,' and when it was made, 'January'—I took it and all the others and I put them in the open top drawer of Grandpa's special file cabinet along with his own tapes he made, so they would be safe."

Collins' voice: "And Grandpa's file cabinet was moved out of here, wasn't it?"

Rick's voice: "Yeah. Just for a while."

Adcock had been enjoying himself. But now his finger pressed down, shutting the machine off.

"The one thing you didn't debug was Vernon Tynan's mother. She heard you were going to be at Hannah Baxter's house and she repeated it. You can underestimate the FBI, Mr. Collins, but never underestimate a mother's love—at least, a mother's love of gossip with her son—and her friends."

He waved his revolver at them once more. "You can leave this office the way you came in. Two agents will be in the hall to escort you downstairs. Good night, gentlemen. You can leave the building by the front door this time."

IT WAS THE LONGEST drive Chris Collins had ever taken back to his home in McLean, Virginia.

Crushed, he slumped in the front seat of Pierce's rented car as Pierce, also a picture of dejection, drove. In the rear seat, Van Allen was equally miserable.

Hardly a word was exchanged, until they drew up in front of the Collins residence.

As the car idled, Pierce said, "Well, you can't win them all, but this wasn't the one to lose."

"I guess it's the end of the road," said Collins. "Tomorrow it'll be their country."

"I'm afraid so."

"It's just that we were so damn close," said Collins. "The R Document—I had the goddamn thing in my hand."

Pierce shook his head. "The sadistic bastard. Well, they outsmarted us. For the life of me, I don't know how. What was all that drivel about Tynan's mother?"

"She must have found out, I guess from Hannah Baxter, that I was going to be seeing Hannah. Mrs. Tynan must have mentioned it to Vernon, so they covered the Baxter house. They took no chances of missing anything. Oh, well." He opened the front door. "Gentlemen—if I may quote Harry Adcock—gentlemen, I feel suicidal enough to get really drunk tonight. I'm going to hang one on. Want to join me?"

"Why not?" said Pierce, shutting off the ignition.

They trooped up to the front door. Collins found his key, unlocked the door, and let them all in.

They had just reached the living room when the telephone started ringing.

"I'll take it," said Collins. He looked at Pierce. "Is it safe? Can I take calls on my phone?"

"The entire house has been swept," Pierce assured him.

"Okay. Liquor's in the sideboard, ice is in the kitchen." He started for the insistently ringing telephone, calling back, "And for me—make mine hemlock on the rocks."

He snatched up the receiver, almost dropping it, and at last got it to his ear.

"Hello?"

"Mr. Collins?"

"Yes?"

"I've been trying to get hold of you. This is Jim Shack in Fort Worth. Some good news for you. I won't go into detail now, but I spent the entire afternoon in Dallas with Mrs. Adele Zurek, the witness Tynan claimed had seen your wife commit murder. It was a lie, an outright lie. And so was Karen's so-called sexual misconduct. Pure fabrication."

Collins sighed with relief. "Thank God."

"I interrogated Mrs. Zurek for hours, and when I promised you'd protect her, she cracked wide open. She confessed that Tynan had blackmailed her—she has an episode in her past that makes her vulnerable, and Tynan found out and used it against her—he promised to overlook it if she played along with him. She was too scared not to agree. But when I promised her you'd see she wasn't harmed, she spilled out the truth. The truth was, she'd heard the Rowleys fight. It was nothing unusual. She'd stayed on, finished her work, and then left to go home—that was after Mrs. Collins had already gone—and she'd got across the street, out of sight, when she saw a car drive up. A man got out—she couldn't see him well—and he went to the front door, monkeyed with it, and let himself in. She was waiting around, wondering about his entry and what to do, when she heard a shot from inside the house. She was frightened, and she ran off. The next day, when she heard Thomas Rowley was dead, she was afraid to go to the authorities, because of her own past. She didn't want to get involved, but Tynan involved her recently. About the man who probably killed Rowley—there seems to be some evidence Rowley was having an affair with this man's wife, and he got found out. We could pursue it further, if you like."

"I don't give a damn about that right now," said Collins. "The important thing is that you got to the bottom of this. You don't know how grateful I am. As long as Karen is all right—"

"She's shipshape. Perfect. She's right here in the room with me now, waiting to speak to you."

"Put her on."

He waited, and then he heard her speak, and he loved her more than ever.

She was weeping, and she was happy.

With a choked voice, she began to recount what had happened all over again. He stopped her, told her it wasn't necessary. Everything had been straightened out.

"Oh, Chris," she said, trying to control herself, "it was such a nightmare."

"It's over, darling. Let's forget it."

"But the important thing, the important thing," she said, "is now you don't have to worry about me—about Tynan. You can go to California, resign and go to California and speak out while there is still time. You will, won't you?"

His exhilaration had vanished, and her question had brought him back down to where he had been before the phone call. "It's too late, darling," he said dispiritedly. "There's nothing I could say that would matter now. Tynan's won. He outwitted me completely in the end."

"What do you mean?"

"It's too much to go into now. I'll tell you when you get home."

"I want to hear it right now. What happened?"

Wearily, he told her what had happened, recounted to her the events of the long day, with its highs and final low. He told her of the morning, when he had accidentally learned that Rick Baxter had taped the contents of The R Document. He told her of the plan to retrieve the tape that the boy had put in Colonel Baxter's file cabinet. He told her of the raid on Tynan's office in the FBI, and how Tynan had bugged him earlier and anticipated the raid, and how Adcock had been waiting with the fateful tape and had destroyed it in front of him.

"And that was it, Karen," he concluded. "Now it is gone forever—the only piece of evidence that might have saved us all."

He had expected Karen to commiserate with him, but instead there was silence at the other end of the phone.

"Karen?" he said. "Karen, are you there?"

Suddenly, her voice burst upon him, alive with excitement. "Chris, Rick's tape—that wasn't the only piece of evidence! Are you listening? Listen to me. There could be a copy of that tape—"

"A copy? What are you talking about?"

"Yes, listen. Do you remember the night we dined with—oh,

what's his name?—Tynan's ghostwriter—the one you did a favor for—"

"Ishmael Young?"

"Yes—the night we had dinner with Ishmael Young at The Jockey Club, remember? He was bitter because Tynan had double-crossed him. Tynan had promised Ishmael to allow his girl friend in from Europe if Ishmael ghosted the autobiography. But then, reading over some recent material he'd copied from Colonel Baxter's file, he found out Tynan had double-crossed him, wasn't going to admit his girl friend after all. Chris, do you understand what I'm saying?"

"I'm not sure." He tried to make sense of it. "I'm afraid I'm confused."

"Ishmael Young told us that night—I can recall almost his exact words—he told us, 'I got my hands on a whole new cache of material, of research for the book. I got papers and tapes that Tynan gave me to copy. Lots of the late Attorney General's papers. I've been copying the research so I can return the originals to Tynan.' Now do you understand, Chris? He told us he'd just made copies of lots of lots of things from Colonel Baxter's private file—Tynan wanted him to have everything for the autobiography—that would have been before Tynan knew that one of the tapes was the one made by Rick. If Ishmael made a copy of that, along with everything else—then the tape you need, The R Document, still exists—and Ishmael Young has it. I don't know that he copied it, but if he did—"

"He must have!" Collins exploded. "You're a genius, Karen! I love you—I've got to run now—I'll see you here!"

ISHMAEL YOUNG WAS NOT at home.

After reporting the newborn possibility of success to his colleagues, Chris Collins had sought Ishmael Young's telephone number in his address book and been unable to find it. Then he'd realized that he had never possessed it. Praying that Ishmael Young did not have an unlisted number, Collins had tried telephone Information. Dimly remembering that Young had a place in Fredericksburg, Virginia, Collins had communicated the area to the operator. Moments later he had not only Young's phone number, but his address as well.

He had telephoned Ishmael Young, waited nervously to hear his voice, and finally had heard it. But it had been Young's voice on a message-taking machine. The voice said, "Hello. This is Ishmael Young. I am going to be out for the evening. I won't be back until one o'clock in the morning. Please leave your name and number. Do not start talking until you hear the tone."

Collins had not bothered to leave his name or any message. Hanging up, he had decided they should be on hand in Fredericksburg when Ishmael Young returned home.

They sat around Collins' living room speculating on the likelihood of Young's having made a copy of Rick's tape along with the other material in Baxter's file. They did not drink much. They were too high on their one last resurrected hope. They watched the clock, revived the same discussion, continually and nervously got up and sat down.

By eleven o'clock, Collins had run out of patience. "There's too much at stake to sit around here doing nothing. Let's go to Fredericksburg right now and wait there. He might come home earlier."

Pierce and Van Allen agreed.

They got back in Pierce's car and drove out of Washington toward Fredericksburg.

An hour and five minutes later, they pulled up before the small bungalow Ishmael Young had rented, and they parked. Collins left the front seat, went up the walk, and rang the doorbell several times. Then he peered into the house through a front window whose shade was not pulled all the way down.

He returned to the others. "Apparently he's not home yet. Except for one lamp, it's dark inside. We'll just have to wait another fifty minutes."

At five minutes to one, headlights showed themselves at the far end of the street. A red sports car was approaching. As it reached them, it swung left in front of them and bumped up into the driveway that ran along the house.

The door of the sports car opened. A short, squat figure

struggled free, came around the car, halted on the lawn to stare curiously at them, and then bolted for the front door.

Collins, who was half out of the auto, leaped to his feet. "Ishmael!" he shouted. "It's me—Chris Collins!"

Young, who had been about to duck into his house, stopped and turned around as Collins approached him, followed by the others.

"Christ," breathed Ishmael Young, almost fainting with relief. "You sure looked suspicious out there. I thought it was someone trying to hold me up or something." He took in Pierce and Van Allen. "Hey, what's going on—at this hour, yet?"

"I'll explain," said Collins. Hastily, he introduced his two friends. "We're here because maybe you can help us. I can't tell you how important this is."

"Come on in," said Young.

"Thanks," said Collins. "We can't waste a minute."

Once they had gathered in the living room, Young stripped off his corduroy jacket as he eyed them inquisitively. "It sounds urgent. I don't know what I can do for anybody."

"Plenty," said Collins. "Do you want to see the 35th Amendment killed?"

"Do I? I'd do anything in the world to kill it. But there's no chance, Mr. Collins. When they vote in California this afternoon—"

"There is a chance. It depends on you. Where do you keep your research for Tynan's book?"

"In the next room, the dining room. I converted it into a study. You want to see?"

Puzzled, he led them into a small room that resembled a makeshift office. Near a window on the driveway side of the house was an old rolltop desk, piled high with papers. Beside it, on a sturdy stand, rested an IBM electric typewriter. Against the opposite wall stood the dining-room table, also strewn with papers, folders, and supplies. A large Wollensak tape recorder was at one end. Two more tape recorders, a seven-inch Norelco and a portable Sony, sat on a chair beside the table. Two letter-size file cabinets were backed against a third wall.

"It's a mess," Ishmael Young apologized, "but it's the way I work. Sa-ay, Mr. Collins, I hope you got my note thanking you. That was super of you, clearing up that immigration matter. I can't tell you what Emmy and I owe you."

"You owe me nothing. But you can help me, and all of us, right now. You say your research is in here? Okay, there's one piece of research I want to see, if you have it."

Young patted the hair down over his balding pate worriedly. "I want to help you in any way I can, of course—but you know, lots of this stuff is confidential. I pledged on my honor to Vernon Tynan that no one would ever see—Why, if he found out I showed you anything . . ." He broke off. "To hell with him. You stuck out your neck for me. I should do the same for you. What do you want?"

"Remember when we had dinner at The Jockey Club? You mentioned in passing that Tynan had loaned you part or all of Colonel Baxter's private file to make copies—to copy Baxter's letters and tapes for your research in order to prepare the book. Did you actually make copies of everything in Baxter's file?"

Ishmael Young nodded. "Practically everything. Certainly everything that pertained to Tynan. Except for the tapes—"

Collins' heart fell.

"—everything is done," Young went on. "I duplicated the tapes, too—that's why you see two machines over there, because I had to rent an extra one—but I haven't finished actually transcribing the tapes. That's a tedious job. I have to do it all myself, because Tynan doesn't want me to have any outside secretarial help. I started typing up what's on the tapes just three days ago."

Collins' heart lifted. "But you did duplicate or copy all the tapes taken from Baxter's file?"

"Whatever Tynan gave me, and I think he gave me everything."

"How did you copy them?" Collins asked quickly.

"Well, there were two sizes, so I had to use two different machines to play them into my larger Wollensak recorder."

"That's right," said Collins, "two sizes. Norelco miniature cassettes and Memorex normal cassettes. Did you hear them when you were recording?"

"God, no—I'd lose too much time. There's a jack, and they record from one machine to another silently."

"Where are the larger Memorex cassettes?"

"I returned them to Tynan some days ago. Those were the originals. I copied—rerecorded—maybe six of the cassettes on larger reels I had."

"Do you know what's on those spools of yours?"

"Not until I transcribe them. But I identified each one and noted its place on the larger spool. Every cassette, large or small, had some kind of identification or date. I kept a sort of index." He stepped to his desk, and found several sheets of paper clipped together. "You can see."

"I'm looking for one special Memorex cassette. It—it's marked 'AGG,' and then it's marked 'January,' on the outside. Would that help you?"

"Let me find out."

Ishmael Young began to scan and flip the pages of his tape index. In a state of feverishness, Collins watched.

"Sure, it's here," Ishmael Young announced, pleased with himself. "That tape is the first recording on my second spool."

"You have it? You're sure?"

"Positive."

"Man, oh man!" Collins exclaimed jubilantly. He gave the writer a bear hug. "Ishmael, you don't know what you've done."

Ishmael Young was at a loss. "What have I done?"

"You've turned up The R Document!"

"The what?"

"Never mind," said Collins excitedly. "Play it. Find the goddam spool you copied it on—put it on your machine and play it."

The three huddled around the large Wollensak machine on the table as Ishmael Young found the reel of tape and brought it to them. Carefully, he set it on his player, threaded the thin strip of tape through the machine, and attached it to the pickup reel.

Ishmael Young raised his head and stared at Collins, Pierce, and Van Allen. He said, "I don't know what this is all about, but I'm ready if you are."

"We're ready," said Collins. Then he himself leaned over and punched the lever marked PLAY.

The spools began to turn.

A moment later, the voice of Vernon T. Tynan filled the room.

XI

SEATED RESTLESSLY IN THE back seat of the Cadillac limousine that had brought him from San Francisco to the suburbs of Sacramento, Chris Collins came forward once more to speak to his driver.

"Can't you go a little faster?" he implored his chauffeur.

"I'm doing the best I can in this traffic, sir," the driver replied.

Collins made a determined effort to contain his nervousness as he settled into his seat again. Lighting a fresh cigarette from the butt of the old one, he looked out the window and saw the distant city growing nearer and larger. They were in the western sector of Sacramento, he noted, and had entered an area of interchanges. The driver wheeled the car into the right lane, picking up State Highway 275, which would soon lead them up before the Capitol Mall.

Soon, he knew, but perhaps not soon enough.

It was ironic, he thought, that the success of his long quest might be thwarted at its climax because of a conspiracy of nature. The fog was lifting now, he could tell, but Sacramento's Metropolitan Airport was probably still socked in by it.

Originally, he had been due to arrive in Sacramento by air at twelve twenty-five California time. His date to meet Assemblyman Olin Keefe was for one o'clock in the Derby Club of

Posey's Cottage, the restaurant where legislators and lobbyists gathered daily for lunch. If everything had gone properly, Keefe would have Lieutenant Governor Edward Duffield, president of the State Senate, and Senator Abe Glass, president pro tempore of the State Senate, on hand. Collins might yet have time enough to reveal The R Document to the Senate leaders before the Senate convened to vote at precisely two o'clock.

The final vote would take place minutes after two o'clock, he had been informed. The joint resolution would be read in the chamber for the third and last time. Further debate, by legislative agreement, would be suspended. The roll-call vote would begin. Once under way, it could not be stopped. Once tabulated, it could not be reversed or voted again. In the old days, even after voting negatively, a state legislature could consider a bill again, vote it again, and change its stand. This had happened when the 1972 Equal Rights Amendment, the 27th, had gone out to the states for ratification. Two of the states, Vermont and Connecticut, had voted against it, then later had reversed their votes. But this was no longer allowed in most states, and one of them was California. The vote following two o'clock would be final. The 35th Amendment would become the law of the land. Tynan would have won, after all—and the people would have lost.

His wristwatch told him it was nineteen minutes to two.

He dragged steadily on his cigarette, reliving the events of the night, of the morning hours, of the dawn. He relived them as if they were part of the present.

Leaving Ishmael Young's with the crucial tape, they were less in a state of manic enthusiasm than in a state of high fever. They were aroused. Their mission had become a crusade. Driving from Fredericksburg to the Department of Justice at two in the morning, they had sought to define their assignments. There was much to be done, and only a short time to do it in.

Working out of Chris Collins' office, they went about their assignments. Collins took it upon himself to make the phone calls. With the authority of his position as Attorney General, it was agreed, he would get the attention needed. Pierce accepted the task of authenticating the tape through voiceprints. They all knew the tape was authentic, but others might require absolute proof. Van Allen prepared to make Collins' reservations to California. There had been a brief discussion about commandeering a military plane. Collins had finally vetoed it out of fear that his mission might become known to the wrong parties. A commercial flight, even if it slowed him down, was safer. Van Allen also set about acquiring a portable tape machine. Once the voiceprint was made, he was to take over Young's cumbersome large reel of tape and transfer the portion that carried The R Document to a cassette for Collins' trip.

All the assignments had been carried out smoothly, except the one Collins had taken for his own.

Collins' first phone call proved no problem. He woke the head of a major network in New York, invoked his authority, spoke of emergency, and persuaded the executive to arrange for the network's manager in Washington, D.C., to cooperate. This done, Pierce then roused Dr. Lenart of Georgetown University from his bed. Since Pierce was an old acquaintance, the criminologist had grouchily agreed to scan the spoken sounds in his laboratory.

Pierce hastened off to the local network offices to pick up the portion of a film and sound track of an interview Vernon T. Tynan had recently given, as well as a videotape unit on which to play it. These, along with Ishmael Young's tape, Pierce carted off to Dr. Lenart's laboratory at Georgetown University. There, the renowned consultant in voice identification, using his sound spectrograph, applied his equipment to selected words Tynan had spoken in his network interview and those same words when he had uttered them on the Ishmael Young tape. The scanner made 400 passes over the tapes every eighty seconds, visually reproducing a series of wavy lines that caught the pitch and volume of Tynan's voice. When Dr. Lenart had finished, it was clear that the voice heard on the tape of The R Document was unquestionably Tynan's own. Dr. Lenart wrote a certificate of authentication, and packed Pierce off with his proof.

Meanwhile, Van Allen, after locating a portable tape machine for Collins to take with him to California, obtained plane reservations. The earliest flight to Sacramento left Washington National Airport at eight ten in the morning. It would bring Collins into Chicago at nine eight. There would be an hour be-

tween planes, and then Collins would depart from Chicago's
O'Hare Airport at ten minutes after ten, to arrive in Sacramento
at twenty-five minutes after twelve California time. The schedule was perfect, and Collins was pleased.

It was Collins, however, who was having trouble with his
own assignment. He had decided that he must notify the officers of the California State Senate of his impending arrival, and
make an appointment to meet with them before the joint resolution came to a vote. He wanted to tell them he had evidence of
a most devastating kind that would affect the Senate's vote on
the 35th Amendment. He wanted to tell them that, and no more.
It was useless, he knew, to explain on the phone the evidence in
his possession. It had to be heard to be believed. But even if it
were believed, there was danger in phone transmission. Knowledge of it might be passed on to Tynan, who was already in
Sacramento, and Tynan would go to any lengths to recover the
material from Collins and destroy it.

No, he would tell the Senate officers only enough to get him
an immediate hearing upon his arrival.

He began by telephoning Lieutenant Governor Edward
Duffield at his home number. He called and let the phone ring
and ring, without an answer. He called several times more, and
still no answer. Finally, he decided that Duffield probably had a
cutoff on his telephone, so that he could not be disturbed at
night. He gave up on Duffield.

Next, he tried Senator Abe Glass, president pro tempore of
the Senate. His first two calls again brought no response. His
third call summoned up the sleepy voice of a woman, who
turned out to be Mrs. Glass, who said her husband was out of
the city and could not be reached until late morning, when he
would be back in his office preparing for the vote.

Frustrated, Collins tried to think of where to turn. Briefly, he
considered calling the White House, speaking to President
Wadsworth, dumping the whole matter in his lap. Surely, the
President of the United States would have no trouble getting the
message to Sacramento. One thing bothered Collins about this.
The President might not want to get the message to Sacramento. He might want the 35th Amendment to pass, despite

The R Document, thinking he would handle the rest of it later in his own way.

No, President Wadsworth was a risk. So was the Governor of California, who was the President's political friend.

Better someone else in Sacramento, Collins decided.

And then he thought of the someone else, and he put through a call to Assemblyman Olin Keefe, and he got him immediately.

"I'm going to be in Sacramento at one o'clock this afternoon," he told Keefe. "I have momentous evidence against the 35th that must be heard before the vote. Can you round up Lieutenant Governor Duffield and Senator Glass for me? I've been trying to get them all night. No luck. I must see them."

"They'll be lunching in the Derby Club—it's in the rear of Posey's Cottage—at that time. They're sure to be there until a quarter to two. I'll tell them to wait for you. In fact, I'll stay with them."

"Tell them it's positively urgent," said Collins.

"I'll do my part. Just be on time. Once they go back to the chamber floor and the vote begins, you won't be able to reach them."

"I'll be there," Collins promised.

It was settled, and he felt easier.

After that, he stretched out on his office sofa and slept fitfully for two hours, before Pierce and Van Allen awakened him to inform him it was time to head for National Airport.

Everything went on schedule, up to a point. He left Washington on time. He arrived in Chicago on time. He departed from Chicago on time. He was expected to land in Sacramento on time.

But an hour out of Sacramento, the captain of the 727 jetliner announced that an unexpected heavy fog had engulfed the Sacramento airport and their flight was being diverted to San Francisco. Sorry about the inconvenience, but they would deplane in San Francisco at twelve thirty. There would be a special bus to take them the eighty miles to Sacramento.

For the first time on the journey, Collins was worried. He had traveled from San Francisco to Sacramento often enough, in the past, to know this would add an extra hour and a half to his trip.

Even by hiring a private car, and having the driver go the limit, he would not reach Posey's Cottage much before Duffield and Glass would be leaving it.

At the San Francisco airport, while his skycap rushed off to put a hold on a private limousine for him, Collins got on the telephone to try to locate Olin Keefe. But Keefe was neither in his legislative office nor at lunch yet. Not wanting to waste another minute trying to chase him down—or trying to find Duffield or Glass—Collins left the phone booth and hurried toward his skycap, who was beckoning him.

All of that he now relived as his limousine entered the center of Sacramento, with the elegant golden dome of the State Capitol within sight.

"Where was it again, sir?" the driver asked.

"It's a restaurant a block south of the Capitol Mall. It's called Posey's Cottage or Posey's Restaurant. It's on the corner of 11th and O Streets."

"We'll be there in a minute, sir."

Off to his left, Collins could see the expanse of Capitol Park: forty acres bearing at least a thousand varieties of trees, shrubs, flowers, and then on a gently sloping terrace there rose the Capitol building, with its shining dome and four stories surrounded by Corinthian columns and pilasters.

They crawled along in the heavy one-way traffic on N Street, turned left on 11th, and at last reached 11th and O.

"Here we are," the driver said, pointing to Posey's Cottage.

"Find a place to park," said Collins hastily. "I shouldn't be long. I'll meet you in front of the restaurant."

He had the car door open, and picking up his attaché case with the portable tape recorder inside, he hopped out.

He paused only to make out the time. It was nine minutes to two. He was fifty-one minutes late. He wondered if Keefe had managed to hold Duffield and Glass for him.

Collins hurried into the restaurant, asked for the Derby Club, and was directed to a back room with a bar. When he reached the Derby Club, he was dismayed. The room was empty except for a lone melancholy figure at the bar.

From the bar, Olin Keefe saw him and slipped off his stool.

His chubby, normally affable features were knotted with concern.

"I'd just about given up on you," he said. "What happened?"

"Fog. We had to land in San Francisco instead of here. I've been driving the last hour and a half." He looked around again. "Duffield and Glass . . . ?"

"I had them here. I couldn't hold them any longer. They went back to the Senate to get ready for the vote. There's still seven minutes before the final reading and vote. I don't know—but we can try to pull them out of the chamber."

"We have to," insisted Collins in desperation.

They went swiftly out of the restaurant, then, half walking, half running, dodging pedestrians, they headed south on 11th toward the Capitol building.

Keefe said, "The Senate chamber is at the south end of the second floor. We may barely make it before they close the doors."

Reaching the Capitol, hastening up a short flight of stone steps, they crossed the Great Seal of California, an inlaid colored mosaic, at the entrance.

"The staircase over there," Keefe directed Collins. Going up the stairs, Keefe added, "You knew Director Tynan was here this morning?"

"I knew. How did he do?"

"Too well, I'm afraid. He knocked them over in the Judiciary Committee. The committee voted overwhelmingly for ratification of the 35th. It'll go that way in the Senate, unless you can do better than Tynan."

"I can do better—if I get the chance." He held up his attaché case. "In here I've got the only witness who can destroy Tynan."

"Who?"

"Tynan himself," Collins said cryptically.

They had arrived at the Senate entrance.

While most of the forty State Senators were in their massive blue swivel chairs, a few still stood in the aisles. Lieutenant Governor Duffield, in a smart pinstriped blue suit, was on his feet behind the raised desk and microphone at the head of the chamber, squinting through his rimless spectacles at the various members.

"Hell," said Keefe, "the sergeant at arms is starting to close the doors."

"Can't you get to Duffield?"

"I'll try," said Keefe.

He hurried into the chamber, explained something to an obstructing guard, continued on his way to the front, circled to the carpeted steps, and from beneath the podium called up to the president of the Senate.

Anxiously, Collins watched the dumb play across the chamber. Duffield had leaned sideways to catch what Keefe was saying. Then he threw up his hands and made a gesture toward the filled chamber. Keefe was talking again. At last, Duffield, shaking his head, stepped down to join him. Keefe kept on talking, pointing to where Collins stood. For a hanging moment in time, Duffield seemed undecided. Finally, obviously with reluctance, he followed Keefe to where Collins waited.

They met just inside the chamber entrance, and Keefe introduced the Senate president to Collins.

Duffield's flinty face was unhappy. "Out of deference to you, Mr. Attorney General, I consented to leave the podium. Congressman Keefe says you have new evidence related to our vote on the 35th Amendment—"

"Evidence that it is vital for you and the members to hear."

"That's quite impossible to arrange, Mr. Attorney General. It's simply too late. All witnesses were heard, all evidence presented to the Judiciary Committee, the last four days. The hearings wound up this morning with Director Tynan. There's no debate, so your evidence can't be offered in debate. We're about to come to order, hear a reading of the 35th Amendment, and put it to a vote. I see no way to interrupt the process."

"These is one way," said Collins. "Hear my evidence outside the chamber. Delay the session until you listen to my evidence."

"That would be without precedent. Highly unusual."

"What I have to present to you and the members is also without precedent and more than unusual. I assure you, if I'd had this evidence earlier, I would have been before you with it. I was able to obtain it just last night. I immediately flew to California with it. The evidence is of the greatest import to you, to the Senate, to the people of California, to the entire United States. You cannot vote without hearing what I have in this attaché case."

The intensity of Collins' speech had made Duffield weaken slightly. "Even if what you have is of such importance—well, I don't know how I can prevent an immediate vote."

"You can't vote if you don't have a quorum, can you?"

"You want to ask a majority of the members to absent themselves from the chamber? It wouldn't work. There'd be a motion for a call of the house. The sergeant at arms would be instructed to bring in the absentees—"

"But I'd be finished with my evidence before the sergeant at arms could do that."

Duffield remained doubtful. "I don't know. How much time would you need?"

"Ten minutes, no more. The length of time it takes you to hear what I have to offer."

"And how are the members of the Senate supposed to hear the evidence?"

"You'll summon them informally—twenty at a time, two groups of twenty—and you'll advise them to hear what you've already heard. By then, you'll *want* them to hear it. After they've heard it, they can vote."

Duffield still hesitated. "Mr. Attorney General, this is an extraordinary thing you are requesting."

"This is extraordinary evidence I have with me," Collins insisted. He was aware that in his position of Cabinet officer, he could be even more insistent than he had been. But he was also aware of how determinedly state officials defended their states' rights. So still under restraint, but conveying a sense of urgency in his voice, Collins went on. "You must find a way to hear it. Surely, there must be some means. Isn't there anything on earth that could make you defer the vote?"

"Well, certainly there would be some factors—factors like— Well, if you had evidence to prove the joint resolution about to be voted upon was fraudulent or harbored elements of conspiracy—if you could prove that—"

"I can! I have evidence of a national conspiracy. The life or death of our republic depends on your hearing this evidence, and keeping what you've heard in mind when you vote. If you fail to hear the evidence, you'll carry the burden of your mistake to the grave. Do believe me."

Impressed, the Lieutenant Governor gave Collins a long, hard look. "Very well," he said suddenly. "Let me arrange for Senator Glass to see that we have no quorum for ten minutes. You go up to the fourth floor, to the first committee room off the elevator. It's vacant. Assemblyman Keefe will show you the way. Senator Glass and I will join you shortly." He paused. "Mr. Attorney General, this better be something."

"It's something, all right," Collins said grimly.

THEY WERE IN THE modern committee room on the fourth floor, the four of them, seated about the light-colored wooden table that stood in the center of the room.

Chris Collins had just finished explaining to Duffield and Glass the circumstances under which he had learned about The R Document, a supplement to the 35th Amendment, which Colonel Noah Baxter had warned on his deathbed must be exposed.

"I won't bother you with the details of my long quest for The R Document," said Collins. "Suffice it to say, I located it this morning. It proved to be not a document but a verbalized plan, which was caught on tape accidentally by Colonel Baxter's twelve-year-old grandson. There were three persons present when the tape was made last January. One was FBI Director Vernon T. Tynan. Another was Deputy Director Harry Adcock. The third was Attorney General Noah Baxter. Only the voices of Tynan and Baxter will be heard on this tape, which the boy made as a lark, unaware of its importance. To be certain beyond question that Director Tynan's own voice had been captured on this tape, we had a voiceprint made of Tynan's speech on the tape and Tynan's speech during a recent network interview. You will see that they are one and the same."

Collins bent over, pulled the sheaf of voiceprints and Dr. Lenart's certificate of authentication from his attaché case, and handed them over to Duffield.

The Lieutenant Governor gravely examined the materials, then passed them to Senator Glass.

"Are you both satisfied you will be hearing the voice of Director Tynan?" Collins asked.

Both Senate leaders nodded.

Collins bent over again and brought his portable tape machine out of the attaché case. He adjusted the volume to High. With deliberation he set the machine down in the middle of the table.

"We can proceed, then," he said. "You will hear Tynan's voice first, then Baxter's. Listen closely. This is the secret known as The R Document. Now, listen."

Collins reached out, pressed down the PLAY button, and then, elbows on the table, chin in his hands, he fixed his eyes on the president and the president pro tempore of the California State Senate.

The cassette in the machine was rolling. The speaker came to life.

Tynan's voice: "We're alone, aren't we, Noah?"

Baxter's voice: "You wanted to see me in private, Vernon. Well, I guess my living room here is about as safe a place as there is in town."

Tynan's voice: "It should be. We've spent thousands of dollars having your house debugged. I'm sure it's safe enough for what we have to discuss."

Baxter's voice: "What do we have to discuss, Vernon? What's on your mind?"

Tynan's voice: "Okay, it's this. I think I have the last element of The R Document figured out. Harry and I think it's foolproof. Just one thing, Noah. Don't go squeamish on me at the last minute. Remember, we agreed we must sacrifice anything—and might I add, anyone—if we are to save this nation. Now, you've been with us all along, Noah. You've agreed the Amendment is the best idea yet, the only real hope, no matter what obstacles had to be overcome to get it through. Well, there's only one more step. Remember, you've been in it with us up to now. You're in too far to back out. You couldn't back out if you wanted to."

Baxter's voice: "Back out of what? What are you talking about, Vernon?"

Tynan's voice: "It simply amounts to doing something for the people that they can't do for themselves. Bringing security to their lives. The moment the 35th Amendment becomes part of the Constitution, we put The R Document into effect—the reconstruction of the country. We put into motion all our legal prerogatives under the 35th—"

Baxter's voice: "But you can't, Vernon—you can't invoke the 35th. There has to be a real, a legitimate national emergency. Under the Constitution, with the 35th, there will have to be an actual crisis—emergency—conspiracy—before we can move. If there is none, you can't—"

Tynan's voice: "But we can, Noah. Because we *will* have our emergency, our crisis. That's been arranged, Noah. I've taken care of it myself. Often one person has to be sacrificed for the survival of the rest. One of us—you or me—probably you— will invoke the emergency in a television speech. You will address the nation. That's the essence of The R Document. I've got the essentials of the speech worked out. You'll address the nation, beginning something like this: 'Fellow Americans, I have come to speak to you in this hour of mourning. We are all equally bereaved, all suffering the deepest grief together, over the shocking assassination of our beloved President Wadsworth yesterday. His terrible death by an assassin's hand—a hand directed by a conspiracy to overturn the nation—has cost us the person of our greatest leader. But perhaps his death will serve us all in life, and will serve the life of the nation. By uniting together, we must see that such violence is never repeated again inside our borders. To this end, by the order of our new President, I am taking direct steps to curb the reign of lawlessness and terror that now exists. I am now proclaiming suspension of the Bill of Rights, as provided for in the 35th Amendment, and announcing that hereafter the Committee on National Safety—' "

Baxter's voice: "My God, Vernon! Did I hear you right? President Wadsworth assassinated—by *your* orders?"

Tynan's voice: "Don't be a sentimental slob, Noah. There's no time for that. We sacrifice one two-bit politician to save an entire nation. Do you understand, Noah? We'll save—"

Baxter's voice: "Oh, God, God, God—ohhh—"

Tynan's voice: "Noah, we—Noah—Noah! What is it? What's wrong with you? What is it, Harry—is he having some kind of stroke, or what? Try to hold him up. Let me get Hannah . . ."

End of tape.

Collins studied the faces of Duffield, Glass, and Keefe. They all sat frozen in shock.

"Well, gentlemen," said Collins, "does justice have its day in court?"

Duffield came heavily to his feet.

"Justice has its day," he said quietly. "I'll go summon the Senators."

IT WAS NIGHT IN Washington, D.C., when the sleek Boeing jet dipped earthward, floating lower and lower toward the landing strip of National Airport.

From his window seat, Chris Collins watched the lights dance toward him, rise swiftly, and then the plane touched down, and he braced himself for the jolt of homecoming.

Minutes later, he followed the line of passengers out of the plane and into the air terminal.

It was Hogan he saw first, and his bodyguard was wearing an uncharacteristic broad smile. "Congratulations, Mr. Attorney General," Hogan said, taking over Collins' attaché case. "I was upset when you got away without me. But I'd say it was worth the risk."

"It was worth anything," said Collins. "I have no luggage. The attaché case was all I needed."

"Chris . . ."

He realized Tony Pierce was also on hand to greet him. A smiling Pierce pumped his hand as they moved toward the escalator, then pulled a newspaper out of his pocket and unfolded it before him. The big black headline read:

PLOT AGAINST PRESIDENT, NATION EXPOSED
TYNAN IMPLICATED
THE 35TH AMENDMENT DEFEATED

"Chris, you pulled it off," Pierce exulted. "Did you see it? The California Senate vote was on television. Forty to zero, the 35th turned down. Unanimous."

"I saw it," said Collins. "I was in the gallery."

"Then the news conference. All the major networks broke in on their programming to show it. Duffield and Glass held a joint news conference. Told how the turnabout happened. Told of your role. Told what was in The R Document."

"I didn't see that," said Collins. "The fog lifted, and I caught the first plane for home."

"Well, Chris, you really did it."

Collins shook his head. "No, Tony. We all did it—including Colonel Baxter, Father Dubinski, my son, Josh, Olin Keefe, Donald Radenbaugh, John Maynard, Rick Baxter, Ishmael Young, and you yourself. It was everyone."

They had reached the car, which was not the one Collins used, but the President's own bulletproof limousine. The President's chauffeur, at the open rear door, offered him a proud salute.

Collins looked at Pierce questioningly.

"The President wants to see you. He asked to see you the minute you came in."

"Very well."

Collins had started into the car when Pierce's hand on his shoulder restrained him.

"Chris . . ."

"Yes?"

"Do you know Vernon Tynan is dead?"

"I didn't know."

"Two hours ago. He committed suicide. He shot himself in the mouth."

Collins thought about it. "Like Hitler," he said.

"Adcock disappeared."

Collins nodded. "Like Bormann," he said.

They got into the car. As the driver settled behind the wheel, Pierce spoke to him.

"To the White House."

When they arrived at the South Portico of the White House,

McKnight, the President's chief aide, was waiting to welcome them heartily. Collins and Pierce were led through the Diplomatic Reception Room to the elevator on the ground floor. They took the elevator to the second floor, and followed McKnight to the Yellow Oval Room.

Collins had not expected a party, but one was in progress. He could make out Vice-President Loomis; Senator Hilliard and his wife; the President's secretary, Miss Ledger; and Appointments Secretary Nichols. Then, next to the Louis XVI chairs flanking the fireplace, he saw Karen chatting with President Wadsworth.

That instant, Karen became aware of him, and she broke away from the President and came running across the room. She fell into his arms, and he kissed away her tears.

"I love you, I love you," she cried. "Oh, Chris . . ."

Over her shoulder he saw that the President was coming toward him. He released Karen, and went to meet the President. There was an odd expression on the President's face. Collins decided he looked as Lazarus must have looked.

"Chris," the President said solemnly, clasping his hand with genuine warmth, "I don't have words to thank you enough—for preserving my life, and that of the country as well." The President wagged his head. "I was an awful ass. I can say it now. Forgive me. I'd lost my sense of direction. I guess when you're afraid of Little Big Horn, you grasp at any expediency. You don't know that you're already in Little Big Horn." He smiled. "But it wasn't Little Big Horn after all, because the cavalry came in time." He searched Collins' face. "You heard about Vernon Tynan?"

"I did. I'm sorry he brought himself to such a pass."

"He must have been unhinged, these past months, to have hatched anything like that. Thank God you persisted. My debt to you can never be paid. If there's anything I can do for you—"

"There are two things you can do for me," Collins said bluntly.

"Tell me."

"There's a man who, like yourself, must be resurrected from the dead. He played a major role in helping you. I want you to help him. I want you to give him a full Presidential pardon and restore his name."

"Just prepare the pardon. I'll sign it. And the other thing?"

"The worst is over," said Collins, "but we still face the problem that gave rise to this insane plot. The problem of crime. Repression won't solve it. As a wise man once remarked, burning stakes do not lighten the darkness. There has to be a better solution—"

"There will be," interrupted the President. "We're going to do it right this time. Instead of tampering with the Bill of Rights to solve our problems, we're going to use the Bill of Rights and use it properly. Tomorrow, early, I'm going to appoint a special blue-ribbon commission—you and Pierce will be on it—to investigate the FBI, clean out all Tynan influence, make recommendations toward overhauling the Bureau and setting up new guidelines for it. After that, first order of business, Chris, I want to sit down with you and discuss a new program of economic and social legislation that will bring an end to the lawlessness and crime in our cities. We're going to do something about it at last. We had a dangerous moment. But now we're going to hold on to our democracy."

Collins nodded. "Thank you, Mr. President." He hesitated. "You know, I was thinking all the way home—in Argo City, a friend of mine said that when fascism comes to the United States, it'll be because the people voted it in. Well, the people almost did this time. Now that they know what they know, maybe they'll never come that close again. And maybe we can help them remember this lesson."

"We will. That I promise. We're going to solve what it is humanly possible to solve." He took Collins by the arm. "But not tonight." He beckoned Karen to join them. "Tonight we're going to have a drink to the future. Possibly two drinks, even three. And we're going to watch the late-night movie. Let's relax an hour or so—we can afford to, at last—before we begin again."